SENSUAL GAMES

"I am tired of this game you play," Reyn s[...]

"You play the game, sir. Laying traps wit[...] false pretenses, hoping I shall reveal so[...] Jocelyn's frustration shot skyward. H[...] convince this man to leave her alone? "[...] have no memory."

"I have been patient long enough. Who are you[...] t is your real name? What are you hiding?"

"Is there any particular order in which you would like those questions answered?"

"Hell, no."

"Then, I don't know, I don't know, I don't know." By the time she finished, she realized she was shouting as loudly as he was. That would accomplish nothing.

"You run a household with quiet efficiency, understand the teachings of Plato and adore Shakespeare. You read Latin and French, speak both fluently and play the pianoforte with great skill. You facilitate changes in a thriving business, and I discover it will most likely be profitable, yet you can't remember from whence that knowledge came? By God, do not become the innocent with me. You're a liar. Your memory is as sharp as mine."

"And you are a manipulative, detestable—Jack Nasty. Let me solve my own problems." Jocelyn turned to flee.

His arm, snaking quickly about her waist, brought her flush against him, toe to toe, chest to chest, eye to eye. Hard lips fell upon hers. The kiss, sensual and demanding, allowed no escape.

Duchess For A Day

Peggy Waide

LEISURE BOOKS   NEW YORK CITY

*For my Mom and Dad, who taught me to enjoy life each
and every day. Wish you were still here, Dad.*

A LEISURE BOOK®

July 1999

Published by

Dorchester Publishing Co., Inc.
276 Fifth Avenue
New York, NY 10001

ISBN 0-8439-4554-0

Duchess For A Day

Chapter One

The agonized scream, bursting with madness, pierced Mary Jocelyn Garnett's soul. Absently, she scratched at the lice and grime on her body, ignorant of the unholy stench that was partly her, partly the other poor souls trapped with her. She scanned the crowded, filthy chamber: unclean bodies, human excrement, sickness, death. Nothing could draw her fury today. More important thoughts demanded her attention. Freedom. Then revenge.

Turning from the pitiful sight, she sighed, her white-knuckled fingers grasping the bars that covered the small opening in the heavy iron door. "There is a hell, Sister Mary Agnes. A living, breathing hell. Here. Now."

If she thought long and hard, she could almost touch the kindly old nun, smell the ocean breeze, see the gulls soar, hear her own laughter while she ran along the

7

rocky beach with her schoolmates. What a fool! That innocent girl no longer existed.

Instead, as her eyelids wavered with exhaustion, she remembered the stern lessons about death, how the penitent and holy went to heaven. Those who didn't believe descended into darkness, sentenced to brutal torture and pain. Jocelyn had always questioned the literal existence of heaven and hell. Two months of imprisonment at St. Mary's of Bethlehem Hospital had convinced her that hell truly existed on earth.

"Sweet mercy, where is he?" she asked the cold stone wall. Expecting no answer, she held her breath when the soft tread of footsteps echoed through the empty corridor.

Escape.

She strained to peer through the tiny space in the door. The dim candles offered little light, but she recognized Jocko's wiry hair, red beard and massive shoulders. "You're late," she said.

The muscled attendant shrugged his shoulders and ignored her comment. "Hurry along, lovey. Dunna want to alarm any of your barmy friends." The key turned in the iron lock. Slowly, the door to freedom opened. "Dunna be speakin' until I give you the say-so. We'll be free of here before a cat can lick his ear."

She nodded, then followed her escort down the shadowed passageway. The damp stone walls reeked of decay and moisture. As they climbed an old flight of wooden stairs, she once again considered the wisdom of her plan. Now bone-thin, her once ripe figure more ghost-like than human, she fought to maintain the last vestiges of reality. Desperation demanded she solicit Jocko's aid.

A parolee from Newgate prison, Jocko possessed the morals of crooked overseer and a temper that equaled his size. For two months he had taunted and tormented her, but no more. After today, prepared to deal with the devil himself, she would be free.

Shaken from her trance when a second door opened, Jocelyn glanced down a cleaner, better maintained hallway. For the first time in months, she breathed fresh air that drifted through the small windows near the ceiling, saw the natural light of a new day. She tapped Jocko on the shoulder. "Where are we? You said we would sneak—"

"Dunna ruffle your feathers, ducky. We're in the north corridor now." He opened the door to a tiny room.

When she scanned the new surroundings, her eyes focused on the solitary piece of furniture, a small cot by the wall covered with wrinkled and stained linens. Fear and questions darted through her mind. She shivered, then turned to see Jocko enter. He wore an expression that confirmed her suspicions. Her entire body froze.

"All right, lovey. It's the likes of you and me." He scratched the coarse red whiskers on his chin. "Now, I been bendin' me mind to this agreement and I'm a thinkin' we could have a wee bit of fun before you leave." He leaned his massive shoulders against the door and pulled his shirt from his breeches.

"Surely, you can't expect to—"

Jocko raised his eyebrows at her question.

Jocelyn spoke faster, more frantically. "You promised to take the necklace, deliver me to safety and leave well enough alone."

"Dunna cock a snook at me, missy. Could be I gots enough blunt, or maybe I know someone that will pay me a higher coin if he hears you're making noises to be free. Either way, I intend to try me a bit of fancy goods. If you behave, I won't throw you back in the colney hatch."

Although he was difficult to understand, the huge man's intent was quite clear. She trembled when his

9

leer revealed the gaps between his rotting teeth. "I will scream to the heavens."

"Screamin's nothin' new to this place, now 'tis it?" An evil glint in his eye, Jocko pushed himself from the door, forcing Jocelyn to retreat to the corner. "Mind ye, me wee crumpet, I'm bigger and stronger and meaner than you by far. Best be mindin' your manners." With the determination of a bull, he advanced.

"Hello? Dr. Edwards?" Only the eerie silence greeted Agatha Blackburn, Dowager Duchess of Wilcott. She proceeded down the corridor to stop before a series of wooden doors. She pressed her ear to each one. Listening.

"I say, hello? Anyone there?" She paused for a response, but heard only the thumping of her own heart. "Agatha, your mind is playing with your good sense. You are lost and you are hearing things. You should have turned to the left instead of the right. Drat that man," she said irritably. "It is all his fault. You'd think he could be on time for our meeting once in his sorry life."

When she pulled away from the third door, she heard a faint, muffled cry for help. "Now that was not my imagination," she said emphatically to herself. Cautiously, she opened the door, stunned by what she saw. A bear of a man held down a pitiful-looking creature, her bodice torn to the waist. The poor girl's light brown hair, matted and snarled, hung in filthy clumps about her pale face. Her dress, the color no longer recognizable, was covered with dirt and stains that Agatha dreaded even to contemplate. Stark terror filled the girl's dark eyes. The thug, apparently lost in his own perverted pleasure, did not realize he had an audience.

In a whirlwind of righteous indignation, Lady Agatha attacked. She raised her brass-handled cane high above her and let it descend to the back of the ruffian's head.

She issued a command with enough authority to cow a regiment of soldiers. "Release that girl! At once!"

Reeling from the blow, the thug staggered to his feet, his hand on the back of his head. Blood seeped through his fingers. He whirled toward the source of the injury. "Bloomin' hell!"

"You ill-mannered earthworm. I suggest you find a large hole in which to hide." Considering the threat sufficient, Agatha turned her attention to the waif who now cowered in the corner. "My dear child, you are quite safe." She pulled a dainty lace handkerchief scented with lilacs from her reticule, preparing to dab the tears that streamed down the girl's dirty face. Agatha's temper flared anew when she noticed the bright red marks on the girl's bare shoulders. Aiming her anger at the man who defiantly lingered beside the door, Agatha said, "You ought to be whipped. What is your name?"

Like a vicious dog denied his bone, the beast took a threatening step forward, his response more like a growl. "Ain't none of your business, you meddlesome ol' sow. I'm doin' me job."

Agatha brandished her cane in the air. "Do not even contemplate another step. Besides having access to the Prince Regent himself, I happen to contribute funds to this institution to help the poor souls here. By this time, the good doctor will be searching for me, and I will have your job by day's end. If you wish to save yourself from the bowels of Newgate, I suggest you slither away from here."

The ignorant man, motionless, his hands fisted in rage, seemed to consider her words. His decision did not come soon enough to suit her fancy. "Now!" Her cane struck the floor to emphasize her words. "Beetle off before I change my mind about Newgate."

"You ain't heard the last o' me, you ain't." His threat echoed off the walls as he stomped from the room.

"Dear Lord, what a repulsive cretin," Agatha muttered. "He deserves to die a slow, painful death."

Agatha reeled toward the raspy voice that spoke. "My dear, can you understand me?"

The girl nodded, then begged. "Please help me."

"Of course. Let me call another attendant."

"No. They'll lock me away again. I couldn't bear it."

"Calm yourself," Agatha said as she watched the girl back away toward the wall, her dark eyes pooled with tears, pride and panic. A nagging familiarity about the young girl disturbed Agatha. "Sit down before you fall. You look as though the slightest breeze could topple you." Agatha sat on the cot and patiently waited for the girl to make her decision. In addition to her apparent physical neglect, she was obviously terrified and reluctant to trust anyone. Agatha sighed; she had more than enough experience with abused animals. She spoke softly. "What is your name?"

"Jocelyn."

Agatha barely heard the response. "How lovely. You may call me Agatha. Come." Agatha patted the spot beside her, but the girl remained in the corner. "Jocelyn, I dislike the injustices of the world and have even less tolerance for the mistreatment of anyone. You have nothing to fear from me. I will keep you safe. I promise."

Battered and bruised, Jocelyn observed the woman who had rescued her from certain rape. Impeccably dressed in a velvet gown designed to complement her matronly figure, her liberator wore her silver hair pulled tightly into a neat chignon at the nape of her neck. The style enhanced her sparkling blue eyes, which displayed the genuine strength of character that Jocelyn had witnessed earlier. Her smile, warm and sympathetic, revealed sincerity. Jocelyn had no idea who the woman was, or why she wandered about the halls of Bedlam, but Jocelyn knew this might be her only opportunity to plead her case and, for once, be believed. She had tried to explain so many times, but the doctors and attendants claimed her ravings were those of a lunatic.

Determined to make the woman understand, Jocelyn crossed to the cot. "Madam," she said hesitantly, "You have no reason to believe a word I say, but I don't belong here." Jocelyn inhaled a deep breath as she sat. "My parents are dead, and there is no one to help me. I woke here, drugged and blindfolded. I have been used and deceived and abandoned to this place to . . . " Jocelyn shivered as the memories collided in her mind. Agatha draped her fur-lined cape across Jocelyn's bare shoulders and encouraged her to continue.

"I don't normally sound so . . . " Jocelyn faltered while she searched for words. "So melodramatic. Neither am I insane." Haltingly at first, she told her story until the words seemed to flow with a life of their own. When she had finished, she gazed at her scabbed and filthy hands. "Will you help me? Please?" Jocelyn sat perfectly still for what seemed an eternity.

Finally, Agatha said, "I think your story is plausible enough. For years it has been rumored that a lady or two has been misplaced in this institution. Some peers of the realm prefer confinement to a messy divorce. I have also witnessed abominable acts induced by man's greed. I once knew a gentleman, Lord Arlay, who spent his nights in graveyards, robbing from the newly buried. A ghastly man. But I digress. Without a doubt, you have been ill-used. Your speech and manners indicate an education. Your dress, even in its present condition, was obviously purchased from a talented modiste, and you do seem to have your wits, but . . . "

Jocelyn detected the slight hesitation. She plunged onward with greater conviction. "I swear to blessed Saint Ninian, I speak the truth. I can't stay here another day.

13

If I must, if it means my freedom, I would rather be fouled by that thug you threw out."

Gently patting Jocelyn's hand, Agatha said, "Pish posh. Everything will be resolved. Now, child, let us begin with your full name and your age."

"Lady Mary Jocelyn Garnett. I'm nineteen."

"Your parents' names. Tell me this instant."

Jocelyn flinched at the abrupt demand. "Lord James Garnett, and my mother was called Madelyn."

"Dear God in heaven!"

After Agatha's explosive reaction, the door burst open. A thin young man with gold-rimmed glasses and a whip in his hand stormed into the room. Jocelyn leapt to her feet when the ominous leather swirled toward her.

The little man wheezed. "Thank goodness I found you. Are you well, your grace? I had no idea—"

Agatha rose from the cot like a queen, placing herself between Jocelyn and the man. With one hand on her hip, the other balanced on the handle of her cane, she said, "Do be still, Dr. Edwards, and drop that nasty whip. You have a great many things to explain."

"I apologize, madam. I assume full responsibility for my tardiness. If you have been endangered in any way—"

Agatha sent him a scorching look of disapproval.

He paused to inhale a deep breath before nervously rambling on. "Let me return this patient to her quarters."

"Do not touch so much as a follicle on her head!"

Jocelyn stood in stunned silence as Agatha issued her command, a distinct bite to every word. The kind, gentle woman of moments before had vanished.

"Dr. Edwards, this young woman is to be released to my care. Immediately."

The doctor's jaw dropped. "I beg your pardon?"

"You heard me. When I leave today, she accompanies me."

"Excuse me, Lady Wilcott, that is absolutely impossible."

"Codswollop. Nothing is impossible. Not for an intelligent, compassionate man like yourself."

Drawing himself up to his full height, Edwards was barely taller than Agatha. "Your grace, there are procedures that must be followed. First, I must check her records, then a release must be issued from the physician in charge as well as the appropriate family member."

"She has no living relatives."

"My step-uncle," Jocelyn said quietly.

"Shhh," Agatha whispered.

"Aha! See there." Edwards pointed his finger to the ceiling. "She freely admits she has an uncle. He must be consulted."

A resounding "no" flew from the mouths of both women.

"She only meant to mention that her last living relative is dead. Am I not correct, Jocelyn?"

More than willing to comply if it meant her freedom, Jocelyn nodded in agreement at the falsehood.

"See?" Agatha said. "Now, about that release?"

The doctor's expression changed from disbelief to solicitude. "Please, madam. I understand your concern. Let us retire to my office so we may thoroughly discuss this situation. Together we shall find a satisfactory solution."

"Do not patronize me. I am not a patient here, nor am I a cloth-eared child. I am, as you are well aware, a benefactress of this institution and may be encouraged to increase my endowment. Given sufficient reason."

Edwards placed his hand across his heart. "Is that a bribe?"

"Dr. Edwards, cease the theatrics. You may call it whatever you wish. I only know I will remove this young woman from these vile surroundings before

15

nightfall." Agatha paused. "With or without your approval or assistance."

"I will not break the rules and risk the loss of my position. She can only be released into the custody of a relative." He crossed his arms over his chest.

The doctor meant to follow the rules. Jocelyn knew and accepted that. Yet, having come this close to escape, she wouldn't give up. Even Agatha seemed determined to find a solution.

The older woman paced the short length of the room, obviously deep in thought. Suddenly, she offered a private wink to Jocelyn, and turned frosty eyes on Edwards. "I concede, Dr. Edwards, but allow me a few temporary concessions. First, I want a clean garment brought to this room. Next, we will deliver this young woman to your office where she will wait until I return. She will be given fresh bread and warm broth. If—"

Edwards gasped. "But—"

A single wave of Agatha's hand stalled his complaint. "If these simple requests are not met, my dear doctor, you will consider a trip to the colonies of New South Wales a luxury. Do I make myself perfectly clear?"

With his face flushed a deep red, Edwards glared at Agatha, then briskly nodded. He left the room without a backward glance.

Unable to hide the unmasked hope in her voice, Jocelyn asked, "Will you really help me?"

"Absolutely."

The sincerity in Agatha's voice gave Jocelyn even greater hope.

"My dear girl, it is a blessing you survived thus far, and sheer luck that I found you today. To leave you here would be unacceptable. Unthinkable. My intentions are above reproach. Will you trust me?"

Jocelyn felt a flicker of anxiety. She had trusted someone once before with devastating results. Trusting

Agatha, a woman she knew nothing about, could mean she was trading one living hell for another. She peeked at Agatha from the corners of her eyes and dismissed any misgivings. Freedom would be hers. That was a beginning. "Yes, madam. How will I be able to leave?"

"Let me explain." Agatha tenderly clasped Jocelyn's hand in hers. "The plan may seem a bit outrageous, but it is the best I can do on short notice. I intend to have you free of this place. Tonight. I am offering you the best protection you could possibly have, a safe haven to regain your strength, anonymity and the means to pursue that scoundrel responsible. Shall I continue?"

"Please."

Agatha beamed at her. "Since Dr. Edwards insists you be released into the care of a legal relative—"

"But that is impossible."

"I am surrounded by pessimists. Nothing is impossible, my child. Challenging yes, impossible no."

"Then how?"

The question hung in the air for a moment before a beguiling smile spread across Agatha's face. "Why, you will become the Duchess of Wilcott."

Chapter Two

Though his appearance marked him as a gentleman of worth, Reynolds Blackburn, Duke of Wilcott, ignored social etiquette, as he often did, and trudged into Boodle's disheveled from his recent journey. Upon entering the posh private club, Reyn knew certain men there considered him quick to temper, arrogant and ruthless. Their wives tended to find him distant, rude, overbearing and ferociously intimidating. Their opinions suited him perfectly. They provided an excuse to ignore the endless stream of invitations to balls, receptions and teas, any soirée dedicated to the constant assault on his bachelorhood. Unfortunately, the women of the social elite had decided long ago that he was husband material of the first issue.

Briskly exorcising those loathsome thoughts from his mind, he concentrated on the matter at hand. He removed his beaver hat, shook the raindrops from his traveling coat and tossed them into the doorman's arms.

"Good evening, your grace," the servant said. "By the by, congratulations."

Reyn cast a sidelong glance at the doorman, then disregarded the comment. The soggy, five-day trip from Wilcott Keep to London had been less than pleasant. His head ached, his back felt stiff, he wanted a decent meal and a good night's rest. But first, before he sailed, last-minute business demanded his attention.

Standing a head taller than most, Reyn easily scanned the elegant room, a haven of masculine pursuits: cigars, alcohol and cards. The Honorable Walter Hathaway, a creature of habit, sat in a tall leather chair nestled in a cozy alcove, his blond curls visible. An open newspaper lay on his lap. When Reyn reached his friend's side, Reyn raised his brow. How typical, he thought. Walter was deep into the social prattle of the London *Times*.

Reyn cleared his throat and said, "I assumed you would be here. I'm glad that certain things in life remain constant. You really must find something else to monopolize your time. Gossip is a waste of a very fine mind."

Setting the paper aside, Walter stood and grinned. "You forget, my friend, I also drink, play cards and bed women at every possible opportunity. That must count for something. Besides, there is little else for the youngest son of an earl with two older, living brothers to do."

Watching the mischievous twinkle in Walter's golden eyes, Reyn snorted at that statement. His friend worked very hard to maintain various investments. Walter's portrayal of himself as the callous, self-indulgent rakehell was simply an act. Once named as the black sheep of the family by his father, Walter did everything in his power to uphold the accusation.

A hearty slap to Reyn's already weary back accompanied Walter's greeting. "Welcome back, Reyn. I'm surprised to see you here, all things considered."

"I know," Reyn said, as he brushed away bits of dust gathered on his breeches. "My plans changed unexpectedly."

Walter practically shoved Reyn into the nearby chair. "Sit down, have a drink. We must celebrate."

Puzzled over Walter's enthusiasm, Reyn sat. "Let's not rush this celebration, Walter. The night is young. Things could still go awry."

Sitting back down, Walter poured them each a brandy. "Not if our past adventures are to be believed. I should be angry, but being one of your true friends and the tolerant fellow I am, I forgive you. So, details, you scoundrel. The who, the why, the what for?"

Before Reyn answered, two acquaintances passed by offering their best wishes. If possible, his mood dipped a notch lower. He drew his hand through the hair curled at his nape. "This is absolutely unconscionable. Innes and I have done our damnedest to keep this arrangement under the covers. I'm being applauded and have yet to do a bloody thing."

Walter chuckled. "Reputation and blind faith, I suppose. I must admit I was nearly bowled over with shock."

Reyn tried to bestow a gaze on Walter capable of penetrating most men's souls. The action was lost. His friend sat and grinned like a court fool. Wasting time. Time he didn't have. Time needed to reach his home and the docks before midnight.

Reyn started to question his friend's odd behavior. Instead, he withdrew a document from his embroidered waistcoat. "Here is a revised breakdown of the costs of our venture. As I mentioned in my letter—" He paused after he looked up to find Walter staring at him with a bemused expression. "You did receive my missive?"

Walter shook his head.

"Walter, what bedevils you?"

"I simply can't believe you are sitting here discussing business. I mean, tonight of all nights."

"I don't feel tonight will be any different from many nights I have spent before."

"Reyn, I realize my experience equals yours in this matter, and although the outcome may be the same, I would think the circumstance requires a very different approach."

"I have no idea what nonsense possesses you, but I don't have time to sit here and puzzle the matter through. I must reach the docks before——"

Walter choked on his brandy, coughed, then managed to speak. "You sail? Tonight?"

"Stow it, Walter. I explained everything in the missive had you bothered to read it. If you have questions, talk to Innes. Now, sign the papers. I must go."

"But your wife?"

The trip to London must have addled his brain. Clearly, he heard Walter incorrectly. Reyn asked, "My what?"

"Your bride. Female. Beautiful. Virginal. Dressed in white. This is all assumption on my part since I didn't receive an invitation to the momentous occasion. I didn't even know you were courting anyone. But at twenty-eight years, maybe you've come to your senses and decided to conceive an heir. Or is it love?"

Reyn furrowed his brows at Walter's absurd question. Years of adventures proved Walter capable of anything, ranging from brilliant to demonic to ridiculous. Reyn believed his actions tonight fell into the latter category. Speculating on his friend's purpose, he leaned back in his soft leather chair, his fingers steepled together. "In all the years we've known one another, I never realized you capable of carrying a grudge. I can't help the fact that my horse soundly trumped yours in the last three races, but I won't fall prey to your ridiculous jest."

"It's not true?" His golden eyes a little too wide, his mouth gaping open, Walter seemed all too sincere in his innocence.

A sinking feeling began to form in the pit of Reyn's stomach. "What gave you such a ludicrous notion?"

"The word is all over London."

Reyn hadn't thought the day could turn any worse. Disbelief gave way to anger. "God's bones, Walter. Given my views on marriage, I can't imagine you believed such twaddle. I have no intention of marrying. Now or ever. Not for love. Not for Agatha. Not even for an heir." He gulped down his brandy. "Whom did I supposedly wed?"

"That's the even greater mystery. No one seems to know."

"Who told you this?"

"I dare not reveal my sources. Given the scowl on your face, you might shoot the poor fellow. Then I'd be forced to break you from Newgate."

No matter how strong his urge to strangle Walter, or to pull the blond curls from his head one by one, Reyn knew his friend was right. Given his current state of mind and the blasphemy of the rumor, he probably would shoot the poor bastard. "When I catch the fiend responsible—"

"It's only a rumor, Reyn—"

"Easy for you to say. Your name isn't being bandied about from one London salon to another. Not that I give a damn."

"But can you imagine the reactions." Walter clapped his hands together in delight. "I have an idea. Delay your departure and accompany me to the Haversham bash tonight. Your attendance without the presence of your bride would cause quite the stir."

"No, thank you. I'll gladly sail to safer territories and leave you to clarify." Reyn noticed the waddling approach of Lord Hainesley. "Damn and blast. Hurry, Walter. Perhaps I can still escape that boor."

Walter scribbled his signature, but not in enough time. The rotund newcomer chortled. "Wilcott, you devil."

Between gritting teeth, Reyn tersely responded, "Good evening, Hainesley. If you will excuse me."

"Previous plans?" The pompous man nudged Reyn in the side, a lewd smile plastered on his face. "No small wonder. As I told Smithy, only the duke has the bollocks to be here on a night such as tonight, with the celebrations and all."

Reyn lowered his chin to his chest in an attempt to gain a modicum of control. When he looked up, he kept the grim expression on his face and hissed at no one in particular, "I swear, if I discover who passed this information, I shall personally rip off his head and spit down the hole. Walter, take care of this." With nothing left to say, Reyn stormed from the club.

In a simmering state of anger, Reyn continued to brood over unanswered questions as his carriage lumbered through the crowded streets of London toward the quiet, exclusive section of Mayfair. He muttered an expletive. Walter was right. By now all of London had probably heard the news, and for lack of anything better to do, believed the nonsense. Thank heavens he was leaving the country. However, when he returned, he'd discover the culprit and there would be hell to pay.

Before the horses had completely stopped, Reyn jumped from the carriage and pushed those troubling thoughts from his mind. He yelled to his young groom, "Davey, stay here. This will be a short stop, and we sail with the black moon's tide."

Climbing the red brick steps two at a time, he grabbed the brass door handle to find Black House securely locked. "By Henry, what now?" The sound of his incessant banging of the snout of the large boar's-head knocker echoed down the street.

The butler slowly opened the door. "Your grace?"

"Yes, Briggs, it's me. What took so long? Is Black House under siege or something?"

"Sir, I daresay we did not expect you." Briggs raised his chin as well as his grey bushy eyebrows. "I expect congratulations are in order, your grace."

Experiencing enough confusion for one night, Reyn exploded. "Bloody great hell. How did you find out?"

"I cannot believe you expected it to be kept a secret."

Reyn grumbled as he stomped through the arched doorway, passed beneath the elaborately frescoed ceiling and headed up the marble stairs to the study, his butler on his heels. He marched toward the huge mahogany partner's desk and began to shuffle through his private papers. "Trust, honor and honesty, Briggs, are precious commodities, and they seem sorely displaced these days."

"My sentiments exactly, your grace." Briggs sputtered under his breath before he continued. "But I guess some people can never earn the full confidence of others."

The sarcastic inflection of his butler's voice finally snagged Reyn's full attention. Something was disturbing Briggs down to his polished brass buttons. Looking up, Reyn asked, "Is there a problem?"

"No, your grace," Briggs said, then mumbled another thought. "Not one, apparently, of any significance."

"Something is bothering you. You've called me 'your grace' at least twice and you're mumbling."

Briggs lifted his chin a notch higher. "I am not."

"Yes, you are." When Briggs began to deny the accusation, Reyn said, "Enough! If you lift your chin any higher, your skinny little neck will snap. After twenty years, I know when you're displeased. I don't have the time for guessing games. If you have something to say, then do so."

"Very peculiar, if you ask me."

"God save me. First Walter, now you." Reyn tried to conceal the exasperation in his voice as his patience dwindled. He threw his hands in the air. "The entire town is going daft."

Suddenly, a harried-looking woman dressed in dark clothing breezed into the study. "Briggs, you lazy cow's ear. We need more—Oh, dear me." The minute she saw Reyn standing behind his desk, she turned and fled the room without another word.

Clearly puzzled by the woman's presence, Reyn asked, "Briggs, why is my grandmother's housekeeper here? Short of an official order from the king of England, you and Dolly won't remain in the same house with each other."

"Well, sir," Briggs began as a thundered demand reached the room. He grimaced, then sighed deeply. "If you will excuse me, sir."

All of London had definitely lost its collective mind. In order to escape his household with his sanity intact, Reyn had decided to ignore this new mystery when his grandmother sailed into the room wearing a large cook's apron.

Agatha attacked at once. "What are you doing here?"

"Given your current state of disarray, Dolly's presence and Briggs' sour mood, I could ask you the same thing. But, to answer your question, I do believe I live here."

"Do not be impertinent. I know that." She patted a few stray hairs into place while she spoke. "You were supposed to be in France or Jamaica or some such place."

"Spain."

"Wherever," she replied. "Why are you here? You

should have already left and were to be gone for months."

Reyn couldn't believe his ears. His patience lay on his cuff, and here his grandmother admonished him in his own home. Him. The duke. It didn't bode well for the balance of the evening. With mounting frustration, he said, "Grandmother, I feel as though I'm being led blindly through one of Lord Carlton's mazes. One that I don't have the time nor the inclination to solve. I know when you are up to your garters in scheming. So, I ask you this." He enunciated each syllable slowly and succinctly. "What the devil is going on here?"

"Do not take that tone of voice with me, young man. I am still your oldest living relative. I practically raised you from a pup. If you think you can—"

"Pardon me," Briggs said from the study doorway, "but the lady needs her grace's assistance in the kitchen."

"What lady?" Reyn asked, more confused than ever.

"Of course, Briggs." Agatha kissed her grandson on his cheek. "Never mind, dear. I shall handle everything. *Au revoir*. Have a splendid trip." With complete dismissal, she marched from the room.

Disoriented, Reyn shook his head as if the slight action might erase the last hour. He felt as though he'd been kicked by a stubborn mule, then trampled by the rest of the herd. Reaching out, he placed a restraining hand on his butler's shoulder. "What lady?"

"Lady Wilcott," said Briggs matter-of-factly. "Your wife."

The evening he thought could turn no worse spiraled out of control. Everyone close to him knew his feelings toward matrimony, that he had sworn never to marry. Surely, he had heard incorrectly. However, a new mystery had emerged. One that, if ignored, would torment him for the next three months as he sailed the Atlantic. Blast it, he didn't have time for this. He had less than two hours to find his papers and reach the docks.

Bellowing furiously, for he felt it justified, he marched in search of those threatening his sanity. All the guilty parties hustled about the large kitchen, which looked as though a battle had been fought and lost in it. He stared at Dolly stirring something on the stove while another maid boiled water at the huge stone fireplace. Briggs stood outside the back door tossing wood to the cook. Rags littered the floor, and baskets and jars covered the table. Steam billowed everywhere, the smell of chamomile and rosemary heavy in the air. Finally, his eyes settled upon his grandmother huddled over a large brass tub. Agatha crooned soft words to the scrawniest, most unsightly female, with blotchy red skin and grease-covered hair, he had ever seen.

"Ahem!" At the sound of his voice, everyone turned at once with various exclamations. Reyn spoke with a deadly calm he did not feel. "Now that I have everyone's attention—what is all this cafuffle?"

As his words sliced through the air like daggers, Jocelyn sank deeper into the tub, hoping to gain a modicum of privacy while she observed her newly acquired, incredibly handsome husband for the first time. His tawny-brown hair, worn longer than custom, was tied neatly at his nape. Dark brows framed blue eyes and long lashes any female would envy. With his long legs and broad shoulders filling the doorway, he exuded raw power and confidence. It was difficult to believe that this fierce tyrant was the kind, gentle, charming man Agatha spoke of. Jocelyn looked to Agatha with a silent plea of "what now?"

The dowager sighed. "Well, my good people, thank you for your help. You may take your leave. If I require your assistance, I shall ring." With a regal tilt to her head and a stoic smile on her weathered face, Agatha directed her full attention to her grandson. "Reyn, I have a surprise for you. I would like to introduce you to Jocelyn, the new Duchess of Wilcott." She cleared her throat. "Your wife."

Reyn stared from Jocelyn to Agatha and back to Jocelyn. "You!"

Nodding a shy greeting from the tub, waiting for the bolt of lightning to strike from his piercing blue eyes, Jocelyn witnessed the inner turmoil this stranger, her husband, experienced. He didn't seem to be taking the news well at all. His rugged beauty, coupled with the obvious strength and power radiating from his every muscle and limb, did nothing to ease her worries. Especially when he ordered in a booming voice, "Out!"

At that outburst, the servants quickly fled, their footsteps the only sound in the otherwise silent room.

Once the servants were cleared, Reyn focused on the remaining pair. "Tell me."

"Dear, oh dear, let me think," Agatha said as she apparently stalled for time. "Where shall I begin?"

Reyn placed his hands on the center table and leaned toward Agatha. In a deceptively subdued manner, he said, "Far be it for me to say, but I suggest the beginning."

Chapter Three

Three months later

At sunset, the *Esmeralda* sailed up the Thames to the London docks. Reyn, anxious to bear the news of their good fortune, left his ship to find his partners. Two familiar crew members from another of his vessels stood outside the Salty Pelican, a favored tavern on the docks. They played a game of pitch-and-toss between swigs of ale with a motley group of men.

Reyn watched money exchange hands, then said, "Well, Bigby, Cutter. I see you're making the most of your time on shore."

Bigby, the ship's cook, uncurled from his bent position and grinned, revealing the gaps between his front teeth. "Aye, sir. Welcome back."

Cutter, the tall Jamaican, stood beside Bigby. "Captain, it's fine to see ya. I can tell by ya mood ya had a good trip."

"As a matter of fact, the wind blew a good sail and

the seas were calm. But it's always pleasant to return home."

While winking at Reyn, Bigby nudged Cutter in the ribs. "More so this time, I'd wager."

Reyn dismissed Bigby's exuberant reaction as his chest swelled with pride over his newest acquisition. The craftsmanship of the *Esmeralda*, designed to deliver faster and larger shipments, would create a green-eyed frenzy amongst his competitors. "I admit it's exhilarating."

Bigby chortled loudly, blowing air from his ruddy cheeks. "Exhileratin', eh? I imagine it's more than uplifting, too, if you gets my meaning. As I always say, Cutter, the Captain manages to find the choicest of choice, time after time. Ain't that what I always say, Cutter?"

"Aye, Bigby. Send him out in a nasty storm and he'll return dry-arsed every time.

"The envy of every bloke."

"Deserving of a drink or two."

"Smiling this eve to be sure."

Reyn decided the two sailors had obviously been imbibing for a while now. "That's enough, lads. Thank you. I think." He grabbed his leather satchel and headed for a nearby hack. "Well, I'm off to find Hathaway."

"Wait, Captain."

"What is it, Cutter?"

The sailor shifted his weight from foot to foot. "We been waiting a week for you to return. Ain't we, Bigby?"

"Aye, we have. We've news from her ladyship."

That certainly got his attention. Reyn remembered, all too well, Agatha's last act of interference and his parting demands to rectify the situation. He narrowed his eyes suspiciously. "What has Agatha done now?"

"I gots a note somewhere." Bigby dug into his trouser pockets. He looked to Cutter. "You must have it?"

"I don't."

Bigby continued to search his trousers and inside his shirt with no success. "If I ain't got it, I must a given it to you."

"No ya didn't, ya old fool. Ya probably lost it just like you lost that sweet little wench from—"

"I didn't lose no wench. She—"

The men stood face-to-face like two roosters. Reyn stepped between them and said, "For the love of God, simply tell me what I need to know."

"That's simple enough," said Cutter, with a grin that matched his large frame.

Glaring at Cutter, Bigby elbowed his way to the front. "I'll be telling. She said I could tell." He turned back to Reyn. "We was to wait and hand you the message personally."

Like two bloody fools, the two sailors were grinning again, but neither bothered to offer additional information. Reyn cleared his throat, trying to keep his annoyance at bay. "Well? Are you going to tell me or not?"

"Aye, Captain, your grandmother took to Blackburn Manor. A bit under the weather, she is."

"Is she all right, Bigby?"

"Don't know for sure, sir. We didn't read the note."

Reyn's previous plans vanished, overshadowed by his concern. "I'll leave straight away. Find Lord Hathaway. Tell him where I've gone."

"Aye," said Bigby as he twisted his battered felt hat in his hands. "And, Captain, be sure to tell her ladyship that Cutter and Bigby delivered the message to you. Right and proper."

Cutter beamed proudly. "She'll want to know all right."

Reyn nodded. Considering their strange behavior and even stranger request, Reyn walked a few paces, stopped and looked back at the pair. "Lads, I'd leave the ale alone for the next fortnight or you'll be no use to Captain Timms. I believe it's pickling your brains."

Reyn's black lacquered coach raced across the wooden bridge that marked the entrance to Blackburn Manor, his home of three sprawling wings of art, luxury and masculine detail. He tried his best to ignore the doubts that plagued his mind, just as he always tried to ignore the frivolous antics of the young dandies of the *ton*. Nothing worked. Like a dimwitted child, he found himself in a state of confusion. Again. And he'd just returned from Spain. No small wonder, he thought, considering the circumstances of his departure three months ago and the strange message he had received today.

Reyn dispatched the groom to the stables and nearly tripped over Rebel, his loyal mastiff, who sat on the front steps. Excitedly, Rebel's tail wagged when Reyn bent to scratch his dog behind his ears. "On guard tonight, are we? Or did Briggs kick you out?" Rebel peeked around the open door, whimpered, then settled back on his haunches. No amount of prodding moved the dog inside.

Perplexed, Reyn crossed the threshold. The small brass wall lamps cast dancing silhouettes across the foyer, highlighting the mahogany tripod table and navy blue brocade chair. A soft, burgundy Aubusson rug covered the grey Italian marble floor. He sighed. Although a bit wary as to what he might discover, he felt glad to be home.

As he approached the stairs to the upper chambers, he noticed a shaft of light coming from the study. From the doorway, his eyes settled on a wondrous creature wrapped in silk the color of pomegranates. She sat on the cushioned window seat with her attention focused on the moonlit sky outside the huge bay windows. A book balanced on her lap and a huge black cat lay beside her, his paw draped over her leg. Reyn knew when the woman sensed his presence. She lifted her gaze to stare directly at him with eyes that reminded him of dark Turkish coffee and warm Mediterranean nights. A frown marred her exquisite features.

Reyn continued to watch in silence, a hundred questions on his tongue. The image of her hair, the subtle shades of sunrise, flowing freely through his fingers, her robe clinging sensuously to her curves, and rational thought disappeared. Silently, he cursed. First things first. *Best find out who she is.*

When she began to stand, Reyn held up his hand. "Excuse me. I did not mean to startle you. Please stay. I apologize for not announcing my presence, but one hates to disrupt such quiet perfection."

The woman folded the book in her lap, her delicate hands tightly griping the leather binding. "Perfection?"

"Most definitely."

"How long have you been watching me?"

"Not long." As if nervous, she clasped her hands together, then released them and finally placed them flat on the top of the book. He must have startled her more than he thought. Crossing to a small round table near the fireplace to pour a glass of sherry, he kept his voice calm and, he hoped, soothing. "May I inquire as to who you are, and what you might be doing in my study at this time of night?"

"I meant no intrusion. No one expected you, your grace."

When she answered only a portion of his question, he pursed his lips together. The woman seemed vaguely familiar. Quickly, he scanned the mental catalogue of women from his past. Unfortunately, no name came to mind. He considered other possibilities and felt a brief moment of panic. He stared closely at her features once again. Impossible. The woman before him now bore no resemblance to the bundle of skin and bones Agatha had brought home three months before. Besides, his orders had been clear. Annul the marriage immediately. He sipped from his glass, then said, "So, you know who I am."

"Of course."

"You seem to have me at a disadvantage."

"That is certainly not my intent," Jocelyn said, suppressing the urge to run from the room while absorbing the fact that the duke, her husband, had returned. Evidently, Bigby and Cutter had found him and delivered the missive as she requested. She nearly laughed out loud when she realized he didn't have a clue as to her identity. Their last encounter had ended in disaster. She could only wonder about his reaction when he remembered who she was, and discovered he still had a wife.

"Have we met before?" he asked.

"Perhaps."

"Impossible." A subtle smile warmed his eyes. "I could never forget someone such as you. But if we met, and I so rudely forgot, I would be more than happy to see us reacquaint ourselves." He raised his crystal glass to his lips, took a sip and said, "Let me think. I see no betrothal or wedding ring displayed on your hands. Besides, you're far too lovely to be married to any of my acquaintances. I have no female cousins or nieces coming of age, so that narrows the possibilities." He grinned. "I have it. You must be Grandmother's caretaker?"

What a lark and a bit of good luck. His ignorance would postpone any unpleasantness until tomorrow, giving her time to discuss his arrival with Agatha. Carefully choosing her answer, Jocelyn said, "I gladly offer my assistance. Your grandmother is a special woman."

"She is that. The message I received explained little and I came directly. Is she all right?"

Evidently, he cared a great deal for Agatha. "She has a mild case of pneumonia. The physician says her lungs are clearing nicely. Hopefully, she can leave the confinement of her room by week's end."

"Splendid. And how long will you grace us with your presence?"

"As long as required."

"Loyalty and devotion to my grandmother." Reyn smiled seductively and added, "That will allow us plenty of time to become better acquainted."

Leaning against the mantel of the fireplace, Reyn appeared even more handsome than she remembered. He appeared relaxed, and his face glowed a golden shade. When she found herself wondering if the rest of his body shared the same glorious color, a warm, tingling sensation began to grow in the pit of her stomach, followed by a spurt of irritation. Her husband—of sorts—was attempting to seduce a stranger, who was really his wife. Her feelings seemed extremely confusing, but no less aggravating. With that convoluted thought in mind, she lifted her chin and found herself saying, "Charming words for a married man."

His sensuous expression of moments ago disappeared to be replaced with a sneer of pure contempt. "Married? Do not believe all you hear, my sweet. Obviously, my departure did nothing to squelch that ridiculous rumor. Ask Agatha. She will clarify the matter."

Yes, Jocelyn thought. Agatha could clarify the matter for him. But he would have to wait until morning.

Striding panther-like to the chair directly across from her, the duke's gaze seized hers with blatant possessiveness. The seducer was back, changing colors as quickly as a chameleon. "Besides, if I were married, which I assure you I am not, many marriages allow for, shall we say, special friendships."

"A gentleman would not speak of such things. You are too bold, your grace."

35

"So I've been told. 'Your grace' is far to formal. You may call me Reyn. What is your name?"

Petulantly, she puckered her lips when he ignored her barb and changed topics. "Should I make you guess?"

"A woman who likes games. Most interesting." Tapping his finger across his lower lip as though deep in thought, he kept his eyes on her mouth.

Jocelyn felt her face flush, her body temperature rise. Under his intense scrutiny, she fidgeted with the sleeve of her silk wrapper, trying to think of a way to direct his thoughts elsewhere. As if by silent command, Caesar, her black tomcat, stretched and jumped directly onto Reyn's lap, where he sat with aplomb. "Fickle creature," she said.

Since Reyn believed Agatha had followed his orders and annulled the marriage, she knew it would be best if she chose a topic far from wedlock and seduction. Instead, she said, "Somewhat like men. I daresay, married men."

He raised his brows. "My mysterious beauty has claws. But I wouldn't know, being the bachelor that I am. Now, who is this fine fellow?"

His long, manicured fingers purposely stroked the cat from head to tail, a slow, sensuous caress, all the time his gaze locked with hers. Briefly, to her chagrin, Jocelyn envied the cat. Drat the man, he knew exactly what he was doing.

"Caesar."

"Caesar, hmmm. I hope you fare better than your namesake." He glanced back at Jocelyn.

To her amazement, she simmered over his lack of recognition. Be glad, she thought. "And would you know of your wife's condition?"

Looking from Caesar back to her was his only response.

Whether from curiosity or a foolhardy desire to ignite a reaction in his controlled armor, Jocelyn needled, "She, too, is quite well—or so I hear."

"Enough about that ridiculous notion." Leaning forward, his gaze on the liquid in the glass he held, Reyn changed the subject yet again. "You said you like this room?"

His masculine scent assaulted her senses. She ignored the irritating sensation, scanned the study, considered his tactics and simply nodded.

"Are you prohibited access during the days so that you must invade it during the middle of the night?"

"Actually, I have been given total freedom to do as I may, but to answer your question, I have difficulty sleeping at night. Reading helps me to relax."

His lips curled into a devilish smile. "Perhaps one night we can discuss alternative solutions to your problem."

What drivel, she thought. Agatha constantly mentioned her grandson's commanding charm. He elected to use it to his advantage when he wanted something. Regardless of her innocence of men, Jocelyn suspected he wanted something tonight: her. Reyn would change his lecherous tune when he discovered her true identity. More likely, he'd want to thrash her. She decided this game of chance needed to end and stood to exit.

Caesar bounded to the floor and wrapped himself about her ankles. Reyn stood as well. "No need to hurry off."

Jocelyn exaggerated an enormous yawn while she crossed the dark oak floor, Reyn and the cat following closely on her heels. "As you can see, I am nearly asleep on my feet."

"The cat goes with you?" he asked.

"Caesar? Of course. He sleeps with me."

"Lucky fellow." Reyn gently grabbed her elbow, forcing her to look directly at him. "Since I am not to be given the same opportunity, at least grant me a boon, something to take to my lonely bed."

Through her nightdress and robe, where his hand held her prisoner, she felt her arm tingle. Glancing down, she realized he had strong hands—lightly tanned with long, slender fingers.

"A kiss perhaps?" he said.

She sent him her most dour look.

"No? Well, at least tell me your name."

Moving to the base of the stairs, she easily recognized his attempt to sound terribly forlorn and fought the mischievous urge swelling inside her. "A name is not always the most important fact to know about someone. It does not tell you whether they are kind or gentle, intelligent or foolish, sincere or mocking. One would still wonder who they really were and what they were about."

"True, but a name to go with the face that will surely monopolize my dreams this evening if not my company, that would be a prize to treasure." The innuendo hung suggestively in the air.

Jocelyn ascended halfway up the marble staircase, turned as if considering her options and looked down at Reyn, who leaned lazily on the oak banister, a triumphant smile on his face. The man was a libertine. He deserved a sleepless night.

"Dreams?" She paused for effect. "Nightmares, perhaps."

His composure slipped a notch. He resembled Vicar Burton on watch for heretics in his parish. Succinctly, she said, "My name is Jocelyn Blackburn, Duchess of Wilcott." She lifted her chin and waltzed up the stairs. Over her shoulders, she added sweetly, "Good night, husband. Pleasant dreams."

His silence indicated he was well and truly dumbfounded. She only wished she possessed the courage to stay and witness his expression. Securely locked behind her bedroom door, she realized she had learned several important facts about the Duke of Wilcott.

He was not the devil incarnate she had thought, but a man capable of charming the crown jewels right from the neck of the Queen of England. Buried beneath the charm lay a confident man who seemed to base every action, every word, on keen observation and reason. Luckily for her, he had set his mind on seduction tonight rather than puzzles, for surely he would have guessed her identity before she fled to her room. Worst of all, she liked him but was unsure of how to deal with those feelings and her future plans. A chill ran down her spine. The handsome man downstairs was capable of ruining her entire plan.

Chapter Four

How dare she. That woman would regret her little tom-foolery of last night. The conniving minx had bested him then, but he'd be damned if it happened again. With those thoughts racing through his mind, Reyn closed the open book of Shelley's sonnets for the eighteenth time, drummed his fingertips against the leather binding, and waited. He'd been waiting since early dawn. Informed by Briggs that Lady Wilcott enjoyed her morning walk, Reyn had no choice but to delay his confrontation with the source of his sleepless night.

He gazed out the large bay window and cursed. Somewhere out there, beyond the manicured lawn, was a wife. His wife. Hell! He wasn't supposed to have a wife.

After her startling declaration in the foyer, he had considered immediate retaliation. Instead, in an attempt to rectify things in his own mind, he elected to drink himself into oblivion. All things combined, Reyn was not inclined to smile that morning, nor was he in a charitable mood. He shouted from the study. "Briggs!"

Perfectly pressed, pleated and starched, fitted with the appropriate somber expression, the butler appeared in the doorway. "Yes, sir?"

"How long does that blasted chit walk?"

"Chit, sir?"

Accustomed to his butler's pompous behavior, and the obvious attempt to bait him, Reyn said, "You know precisely to whom I refer."

"Lady Wilcott will return in time to serve your grandmother breakfast."

"I want that woman in my study the minute she steps inside this house." He emphasized his words by jamming his hands into the pockets of his trousers.

"Yes, sir. I believe you have made that request a dozen or so times."

Reyn scowled. The bland remark, typical of his butler's behavior, added to his frustration. "Someday, Briggs, regardless of your loyalty, your insolence will be your downfall. And what is wrong with Rebel? He won't set one paw inside the house."

"The cat."

"Caesar?" Impossible, he thought. Surely, one oversized tomcat was no match for his prize mastiff, Rebel. The longer Reyn stared at Briggs, the more he realized the butler spoke the truth. "Are you telling me that my dog is afraid of that woman's cat?"

"Precisely, sir."

"To rob me of my bachelorhood is one thing. To allow an oversized tomcat to bully my dog—well, blast—bring more coffee."

Reyn turned back to the windows, unsure if he stood vigilant so that he could immediately chastise his ill-fated bride, or whether he wanted to catch her unawares to judge for himself if her beauty was all that he remembered.

He shook his head in dismay. How could he even consider such a thing? Certainly, this was an unexpected predicament. He had attempted to seduce his own wife—a wife he shouldn't have, hadn't recognized, didn't want and was determined to dislike. Frowning, he amended his thoughts. *You liked her well enough last night*.

Reyn's conscience immediately offered a sound rationale for the physical attraction. He'd been at sea for weeks. Of course his body reacted to the vision she presented. He simply needed to assuage his lust, a problem easily remedied with a visit to his mistress. Involuntarily, the image of Jocelyn, dressed in that delightful scrap of silk she wore the night before, floated before him. With her hair flowing about her shoulders, he imagined her hips gently swaying as she crossed the floor toward him.

"Heaven help me," he muttered.

Then and there, he made a conscious decision. No matter how alluring, how delectable or how available, he would not bed the woman. This situation teetered on the precipice of insanity at best, and needed no additional complications. Besides, if things went according to his plan, his would-be wife would be away from Blackburn Manor before nightfall.

Voices drifted from the back of the house to the foyer. Thankful for the distraction, Reyn followed the source, pleased when he trapped his prey carrying a tray laden with food. "When did you return to the house?" Dear Lord, he sounded like the village vicar. Jocelyn's cool expression probably mirrored his.

"Good morning to you, too," Jocelyn said.

He locked his arms across his broad chest as if the motion would establish his authority and control his temper. "Did anyone bother to tell you I wanted to talk to you?"

"Only a dozen or so people. You've been busy in my absence this morning. It seems the entire staff is walking on eggshells."

Ignoring her sarcastic retort, he whirled toward his study. "Follow me."

"I beg your pardon, but that is impossible right now. I must see to Agatha."

His jaw dropped like a cannonball. What little civility he possessed vanished like an exploding comet. "As far as I'm concerned, you're lower than those who work in my kitchen. However, at this particular moment, we have business to discuss. Someone else can play the servant."

"That is not the point, your grace." Jocelyn spoke pointedly. "I have breakfasted with your grandmother every morning since her illness. It is expected, as well as a pleasant diversion for both of us, for us to break our fast together."

"Then I will simply accompany you. I have a great deal to lay at her feet." In fact, his mind brimmed with a few choice epithets.

"You will not. Agatha is recuperating nicely, and I forbid you to bully her at this time."

This was an abomination, so unexpected he would have laughed had he not wanted to toss her across his knees and give her a thorough hiding. Unfortunately, the image of her lush derriere draped across his groin brought forth another reaction. Reyn cursed, then silently reminded himself that she belonged at his feet. Groveling. Begging for a by-your-leave. This woman had stolen his bachelorhood, his freedom. She'd ruined his dog. "You forbid me?"

"Yes, I do. Go do what it is dukes do. As soon as I have finished eating, I promise I will provide you with my undivided attention so that you can bellow until the geese come home."

"I do not bellow," he said, even though he knew his thunderous response echoed throughout the house.

"Oh, sweet Mother Mary. Fine. You're as quiet as a mouse trapped in a room full of cats. Now, if you will

43

excuse me, Agatha's cocoa is growing cold." With a swish of peach muslin and streaming ribbons, Jocelyn dismissed him with dignity and grace, climbing the stairs to escape to Agatha's rooms.

Belatedly, Reyn realized that he'd just behaved like a nutter in the foyer of his own home. Him! A man accustomed to calm and reason since the age of fourteen. Like any educated man, he enjoyed a lively debate, but to visibly lose one's temper, relinquish control of one's actions, was simply unacceptable.

Most people seemed to avoid direct confrontation with him anyway. On occasion someone might question his decision, but one frigid glare usually re-established his authority. Should he increase the volume of his voice, people found a quick and deliberate exit. Rarely did anyone disobey a direct order.

Reluctantly, he admitted that those few people with the temerity to stand against him held his greatest respect.

"Hell." His day was not going as planned.

Gazing heavenward, her nerves stretched to their limit, Jocelyn prayed for patience. All through the night, she had expected the duke, full of recriminations and demands, to barge into her room. Every little noise, every creak in the house, kept her awake. Finally, at dawn, she gave up all attempts to sleep and escaped to the woods. She should have known he'd be waiting this morning. Inhaling a deep breath, she grabbed the handle to Agatha's bedroom door.

The moment the door opened, the questions popped from the dowager's mouth like fleas from a wet dog. "Is it true? Has Reyn returned?"

"You know he has," said Jocelyn, teasing the woman she had come to know and love. She carried the tray to the table beside the window, the lavender brocade drapes drawn to admit golden rays of sunshine through the sheer white netting. "You probably heard every word he bellowed as well as I did. Since, according to you, your grandson hates to lose his temper, I believe there is an impostor downstairs."

"Splendid," Agatha squealed, clapping her hands together in delight as she climbed from the pink floral satin covers. "This is better than I had hoped."

"I'm not sure I agree with you."

"For years, Reyn has prided himself on his ability to maintain his composure, regardless of the circumstances. I myself test his patience. Constantly. I have seen him deal with irritating dandies, and watched him calmly and effectively reduce grown men to whimpering pups with a simple look. The fact that he lost a shred of control, if only for a moment, means we have thrown him off balance. It forces him to feel some emotion. Anger is a fine beginning."

After Agatha sat, Jocelyn placed a lace napkin in the dowager's lap and joined her at the table. "Easy enough for you to say, hidden behind closed doors, snuggled beneath your covers. Nevertheless, I did as you instructed. I behaved like a bossy, overbearing autocrat."

The older woman patted Jocelyn's hand. "He hates to lose his temper. But I promise, no matter how angry he becomes, he will not hurt you or abuse you. All will be well. Wait and see. You did superbly."

"I kept hoping to sneak by him and reach your room before I faced his inquisition. I'm amazed your grandson couldn't hear my knees knock beneath my skirts."

"Very good. You cannot allow him to see your fear." Agatha lavished her biscuits with gooseberry jam. "Reyn has no tolerance for weaklings."

Jocelyn poured cocoa into both the women's lavender demi-cups. "You sound as if being afraid were a disease like leprosy or the plague."

"It's not that, child. It's simply understanding the difference between prudent fear and self-destructive fear. Let me explain. Prudence is having the good sense to back away when being attacked by a rabid dog or a knife-wielding thief. Forfeiting one's belief due to fear of your opponent or the challenge that lies ahead is self-destructive fear. Men seem especially preoccupied with the latter. I imagine it has something to do with the male code, honor and such. Most important, I am proud of you. Reyn is not an easy man to match wills with."

When Jocelyn remembered her explosive outbursts in the foyer, she exhaled deeply. "I admit it wasn't as difficult as I thought it would be. Both my stubborn streak and my temper are known to be formidable. Friends from school repeatedly told me I would never attract a husband with my unladylike manner, and if Sister Kathleen saw me, she'd fall in a fit of apoplexy, knowing the number of hours I spent in penance on the floor of the chapel were all for nothing."

With regal authority in her voice, Agatha warned Jocelyn, "No one will ever punish you again for your delightful, impetuous behavior. That is all behind you."

"For now, at least."

"Forever, Jocelyn!"

The commanding nod of Agatha's head signaled the end of that topic. As Agatha ravished the food on her plate, Jocelyn didn't contradict the dowager, but drank her cocoa instead. She knew Agatha anticipated a lifetime companion of sorts, her wishes made quite clear on numerous occasions. She even dropped not-so-subtle hints about the possibility of Jocelyn and Reyn making the marriage permanent.

Jocelyn disliked misleading her only ally, but had no choice. Two many complications prevented her from ever becoming the true wife of Reynolds Blackburn.

First, she would never marry without love. Based on everything she had heard about the duke, he planned never to marry at all, so the chance of him succumbing to such a frivolous emotion seemed highly unlikely.

And if that weren't enough, she knew the duke, as

well as Agatha, would never honor a marriage to an accused murderess.

Jocelyn loosened her grip on the handle of the delicate china cup, looked up and found Agatha's penetrating gaze focused on her. Belatedly, she realized her dreary thoughts must have seized her full attention.

Agatha said, "You are wearing a frown much like the one Briggs wears when Lady Hilldale slurps her tea. Where were you wandering?"

"No place important."

"Hmmm. In that case, let us move forward. Anything new from that Bow Street runner on the activities of that vile relative of yours?"

Jocelyn cleared her mind to rally to the subject. "The runner has someone working in Horace's London house. Evidently, Horace is still in the Caribbean, supposedly looking for me. He is probably spending more of my fortune. He might even purchase a plantation. I swear he intends to be well provided for, in case I return from the dead."

Agatha sipped her cocoa. "That means we must proceed as if your marriage to Reyn is legally binding. Are you still determined to follow this course?"

The bitter memories surfaced. Jocelyn couldn't keep the brittle harshness from her voice. "I will see Horace sweat in hell, as I did, before I turn him over to the authorities."

"We could tell Reyn the truth," Agatha gently suggested. "My grandson is many things, Jocelyn, but he is a fair and honorable man. He might be a better ally than an adversary."

"No," Jocelyn replied.

"Perhaps, after you know my grandson better?"

"Agatha, we must follow our original plan. Horace is a dangerous man. He will do anything to control my inheritance. Even kill. Everyone must believe my memory lost, and Reyn and I truly married. The fewer people who know the truth, the easier it will be to convince my step-uncle. When Horace returns, I will be waiting, still without a past, ready to lead him to his own demise."

"So be it. I will grant you this as long as I deem the plan to be feasible and safe for everyone, yourself included. How is my grandson's mood?"

"When I left him, he looked angry enough to split fence rails with his teeth."

"Reyn is accustomed to having his way. I shall explain everything to him as we discussed."

"Not being able to tell Reyn must be difficult for you. You've been my angel of mercy. I can never thank you enough. I hope someday you will tell me why you chose to help me in the first place."

"All in good time. As for my grandson, let me worry about him. If I thought for one moment that our endeavor would harm him in any way, we would not be sitting here. Besides, you never know what the final outcome may be. Shall we review our story once more?"

Morning waned as the two women rehearsed. A hammering knock halted their conversation, and without additional warning, Reyn burst through the door. The scowl on his face indicated his annoyance.

Agatha held out her hands in greeting. "Reyn, my dear, welcome home. Do come in and join us."

His hostility toward Jocelyn and the bizarre arrangement remained. His worry about Agatha's health had diminished his annoyance, and he felt genuinely pleased to see her up and about. He placed a tender kiss on her cheek. "Agatha, I leave you for less than three months and you make yourself ill. Did you miss me so?"

"You conceited rascal, I always miss you. However, my illness had little to do with you. It was more a case of too many parties and late nights traipsing about the city. That foul yellow fog caused by those coal stoves and such has been causing pain in the lungs and uneasy trembling in the head for many people. Something should really be done about that. Perhaps I could—"

"Hold, Grandmother, you are barely well enough to take on yet another cause. Heaven knows what you would bring home if you decided to rescue the entire city of London." He uttered his last comment with a glance toward Jocelyn.

"There was no need to charge up here and instantly ignite trouble," Jocelyn said defensively, stacking her hands on her hips. "I told you I would be down shortly."

His body mirrored hers. "Shortly? Meaning two hours ago?"

"During which I'm sure you thought of all sorts of nasty ways to berate and bully me. Well, let me tell you—"

Agatha tapped her hand on the table to gain their attention. "Enough, children. Jocelyn, if you please, I wish to talk to Reyn."

"Certainly."

Reyn watched Jocelyn kiss Agatha on the cheek, then turn to him, a stoic expression on her face that actually enhanced her classic features.

"Please remember that your grandmother is still recovering. If I hear anything that remotely sounds like bellowing, I will return and personally escort you from this room."

After she left, Reyn said matter-of-factly, "She presumes too much."

"Since I found her, I believe she sees herself as my champion."

"Is she always so dramatic?"

Agatha smiled. "Part of her charm."

Waiting for the easy banter to end so he could approach the issue at hand, Reyn rigidly stood beside the fireplace. Agatha meant more to him than anyone. To upset her gave him no pleasure, but he wanted answers. He would have them by the end of their conversation.

Agatha finished her breakfast, dabbed her mouth lightly with a linen napkin and said, "Please sit down, Reyn. My neck is cramping."

He sat in the chair Jocelyn had recently vacated, placed his chin in his folded hands and rested his elbows on the table. "Grandmother, I don't understand. I thought my instructions perfectly clear upon my departure. This marriage business was to be resolved. Permanently. During my entire trip I tried to find a logical reason for your actions, but I admit, I found none."

"I imagine that Jocelyn spewing all over you did little to soothe your irritation. Considering the circumstances of your departure, and your feelings toward matrimony, it's a small wonder you returned at all."

Rising from his chair to speak, Reyn said nothing when Agatha placed her weathered hand over his.

Agatha continued. "I have loved you since the day you graced this family with your birth. When your parents died, you became my son. In all those years, have I ever done anything to hurt you?"

"No."

"Then let me explain, but I ask you to trust my judgment if there are some things that cannot be totally clarified at this time."

Abruptly, Reyn sat, a stubborn set to his jaw. He sighed, arched a brow and waited.

Chapter Five

Jocelyn considered the seventh chime of the tall pendulum hall clock the appointed hour of doom. Slowly, she descended the marble staircase, knowing that, tonight, she must personify the fabrications Agatha had already told. She would remain calm, exercise proper etiquette and answer all the questions Reyn might have. Until her step-uncle returned to England, she could only tell half-truths and rely on the duke's code of honor not to disavow this marriage.

Jocelyn knew the ice-blue evening dress Agatha had chosen exposed a generous portion of her breasts. As she moved across the floor, the silk caressed her body like the wind on a warm summer night. Agatha had said, "If Reyn's attentions are elsewhere, he might be less vigilant with his questions." Fine, thought Jocelyn. She would do what she must. She certainly didn't care whether he found her attractive.

Upon entering the drawing room, a design of black, gold and mauve elegance, she found Reyn seated comfortably beside the fire. He sat beneath an expertly crafted wall panel of armored knights engaged in battle. She wondered if the painting wasn't somewhat symbolic of the confrontation about to take place in the same room. Her eyes drifted back to Reyn. To say the man was handsome seemed inadequate. *He's also the man who holds your future in his hand,* she reminded herself. "Good evening, my lord."

"Good evening." Reyn stood, saluted with his crystal glass and quickly downed the contents. The silken creature standing before him presented a vision capable of filling any man's mind with unchivalrous thoughts. God give him strength, but he would maintain his objectivity. After all, she was simply a woman.

As he took one last peek at the porcelain skin above the bodice of her dress, he decided total detachment would be best, keeping his distance emotionally and especially physically. It might be bloody difficult, but he would do it.

"May I fetch you a drink?" he asked.

"A bit of sherry, please." Her stance remained as rigid as her voice.

As he crossed to the walnut cabinet, he sought a suitable topic to begin the evening. An innocuous topic. Something to relieve the tension. "I expected to see you earlier today. It seems you have a convenient habit of disappearing."

"I'm sorry if my absence disappointed you, your grace, but the gamekeeper's wife began birthing. I gave assistance. I'm here now if you wish to provide me with the proper set-down."

"I was not going to . . . " Reyn snapped his mouth shut, clasping his hands behind his back as if the action would subdue any further misunderstanding. "Relax, Jocelyn. We have not been in the same room for five minutes, and already we are butting heads like two angry rams. Do you think it possible for us to have one conversation without throwing down the gauntlet?"

Jocelyn settled herself on the ivory satin chair. Her shoulders sagged when she reluctantly acknowledged that, expecting the worst, she'd wrongly interpreted his words. "I apologize for my rudeness."

"Accepted. Shall we begin again? Try for a bit of innocuous conversation? How was your day, what a fine home you have, do you think it will rain, or even how handsome you look."

She didn't know whether to laugh or cry, flee or stay. This man was such an enigma. She had truly expected him to attack the minute she entered the drawing room. The fact that he seemed content to discuss the weather did nothing to settle her nervous stomach. For the eightieth time, she reminded herself to relax, then exchanged a strained smile with Reyn. "*Do* you think it will rain?"

Graciously, he answered. "Positively. But we can hope for a warmer afternoon tomorrow. How is the gamekeeper's wife and babe?"

"Both are doing well. The father is strutting like a proud peacock—so much so, one would think he'd given birth."

As if they shared a secret while standing amongst a room filled with people, he whispered, "That was well done."

Jocelyn suppressed the grin that begged for release as the tension of only moments before began to ease. "Thank you."

"Did you have a good afternoon?" he asked.

The disarming smile changed his features from merely handsome to downright devastating and threw her off balance. His long stride brought him to her side, sherry in hand, where he stopped to watch her expectantly. Her moment of admiration passed when she realized her error in proper deportment. "Yes, I did. And you, sir, how was your day?"

"Wonderful."

The one word, spoken like a soft caress as his eyes lingered on her bare shoulders, seemed to express a multitude of things. Nervously seeking a new topic, she searched the elaborately plastered ceiling, twenty feet high. "Did you—"

"I would like to—" he said simultaneously.

"You go first," said Reyn.

"I was going to say your home is magnificent. You must love it here."

"I do. I designed much of it myself, you know. With a few exceptions, of course."

Her curiosity piqued, she asked, "Such as?"

"Take my grandmother's room. Do you honestly believe I chose a pink and lavender floral brocade with disgustingly happy cherubs for the walls? And all that lace? I believe Agatha intentionally selected the decor to ensure that she would always have a place to stay. Heaven forbid any other quest should have to tolerate such excess of . . . "

"Of pink?" Jocelyn laughingly said.

"Yes, exactly. At any rate, Agatha offered her opinion, as did my decorator and architect, but I created much of the design myself."

"You must be very proud. It's lovely." She sincerely meant every word of praise. The manor was a creation of wealth without opulence, elegance with artistic taste. A place any woman, such as herself, would be proud to call home. Shocked at the direction of her thoughts, she changed the topic. "Do you spend most of your time here or in London?"

"London satisfies certain needs, but I much prefer my estates. I find the solitude refreshing, the atmosphere less restrictive, and the outdoors invigorating."

"Absolutely." She warmed to the topic. "Being outdoors is somewhat of an obsession for me. I often walk for hours, an arduous task in London. In the country, I spend so much time outside that Agatha worries about sun spots and such. Inappropriate for a lady, she claims. One of those silly restrictions, I might add, that women must contend with. Another reason why I prefer the country. A woman must follow too many ridiculous rules when in London."

Jocelyn blushed at her ramblings, lifting her head to see his eyes, the color of robin's eggs, staring at her intently. "I tend to go on sometimes."

"Quite all right."

"Agatha fears my social skills vanished along with my past, but I admit I find it difficult to maintain the art of restraint and indifference that most women of the *ton* practice."

"Yes, I can see where too much restraint could be a hardship," he said with an easy smile on his face.

Distractedly gazing into the fire, sipping her sherry, she wondered how long the pleasantries would continue. And it was quite pleasant. Astonishingly so. She imagined a great many women eagerly sought marriage to a man such as Lord Wilcott, especially if one considered his charm and devilishly good looks.

Startled from her mental wandering, she realized that Reyn was speaking. "I beg your pardon?"

"I said that my ancestral home in the north is my favorite estate, although the distance is rather inconvenient."

"Yes. With the Pennines to the west and the wild moors to the east, there is something remote and savage about the place." She added distractedly, "Wilcott Keep suits you."

His brows arched together, a look of bewilderment in his eyes. "I meant no insult," she said quickly. "I meant savage in a primitive way, like barbarian . . . no, ferocious, maybe . . . untamed . . . " Reyn scowled furiously.

"A good savage . . . " Her voice drifted into nothingness. There was no way to explain unless she revealed her most private thoughts, which was impossible.

Reyn chuckled with genuine humor as her frown intensified. "What has you so perplexed?"

"Nothing," she answered sharply. *At least nothing I can tell you,* she thought. She could never reveal her bold vision of the duke in tight-fitted breeches, the wind softly caressing his hair and molding his shirt to his muscled torso, his arms of banded iron wrapped about a fair maiden. The fact that the female closely resembled her shocked her the most. His curiosity be hanged. He would receive no explanations.

The awkward silence passed. They waited for dinner, their time spent in easy conversation until Jocelyn's fear of the pending interrogation intensified. She could no longer delay the inevitable.

"My lord, we have discussed the weather, your home, Caesar, London, horses, even roly-poly pudding. I believe we have covered a great many subjects except the one foremost on your mind. Me."

"Amazing. We managed to remain in the same room for at least an hour without ripping each other apart." He ventured on. "Dare we risk losing the moment, or shall we wait until after dinner?"

"I would rather have the business over with. I'm not sure whether my stomach can wait and endure a six-course meal."

"As you wish." He lazily stood against the mantel and observed the young woman sitting across the room. She clasped her hands tightly in her lap—a habit, he concluded, since she did it frequently. She was right. They had danced all around the moon in order to delay this discussion.

"Let me recap the situation as I understand it. Attacked on your way to London, someone betrayed you, then left you to perish at Bedlam, where my grandmother found you raped. You convinced her you were ill-accused, so Agatha rescued you by exercising my power of attorney and marrying us to one another. Am I correct so far?"

"Not raped, almost raped," she said when he stood like an impenetrable stone wall and assumed the role of accuser. "I believe the distinction is rather significant."

Grudgingly, he noted the correction. "Due to your amnesia, you do not know who betrayed you, who your attackers were or their motive although you assume, on no apparent evidence, that the desire for your inheritance bears that responsibility. You do not even know who you are, for that matter. You believe your parents are dead and the name Jocelyn seems vaguely familiar."

Jocelyn offered no comments during his brief pause.

"The story to be told is that we met while I conducted business in the north. We fell madly in love. Your past continues to elude you, so I am expected to portray the loving husband until your memory returns, at which time justice can be served. Or until some scoundrel presents himself at my doorstep claiming previous rights."

The longer the litany against her, the greater his agitation. He began to pace the length of the room.

"After all is said and done, I find myself married, a state I swore never to endure, to a woman with no past. A woman with every legal right to all that my titles allow as long as I permit the charade to continue." After circling once, he suddenly stopped in front of her to ask in a curt, biting tone, "Does that sum up the situation correctly?"

"It is only temporary," Jocelyn said in her own defense. An undignified grunt signified his response. No matter how angry he became, she would hold her ground. "I had no desire for marriage either. Your grandmother made the suggestion. Did she explain it was the only way they would release me from Bedlam?"

"Agatha offered a paltry explanation, preying upon

my honor as a gentleman to uphold the marriage. I'll tell you now, Jocelyn, I'm not always the gentleman Agatha believes me to be."

To soothe his frustration and restore her calm, she added, "I have no designs on your fortune, your title or you. I have given the circumstances a great deal of thought, and I think with a few rules we can manage to exist together until I untangle this mess. As for your money, I have kept a ledger of everything that has been spent. I intend to repay every shilling."

"If there is an inheritance."

"There is."

"Is that fact or conjecture? You have no memory, as I recall."

"You do not believe me?" Her nostrils flared as her temper began to ignite.

"My grandmother will attest to the fact that I am a world-class cynic." He left no room for comment. "Shall I be blunt?"

Her gaze focused on the far wall. "By all means."

"My grandmother has always fallen prey to the needy, animals and humans alike. Her estates are in such chaos, what with all the strays and odd staff members she has, that she escapes to my home. I normally overlook her little foibles and interference, but this time I greatly resent the fact that she rescued you and married us. Now I find myself feeling responsible for you. I will tell you this—I find the sensation as annoying as hell. Is Jocelyn your real name? Do I parade you about London like a lovesick puppy? Do I have the benefits of a husband?"

Working himself into a fine lather, he continued. "I find it remarkable that you remember what presents a sad case of betrayal to protect your future, yet you forget details that would provide a place to begin a search for your past."

"I see." She dared not say anything more or lose every ounce of her restraint.

"Why has there been no report of a missing person such as you?"

"I don't know."

"Is there no one who misses you, claiming injury or harm?"

"I can't remember."

He snorted at her response. "I believe we once had a similar conversation. Bloody convenient, is it not?"

Jocelyn burned him with a scathing look, but kept silent. Surely, she would have permanent bite marks on the inside of her mouth from holding her tongue.

The duke combed his fingers through his hair in frustration. "In total honesty, you could be a well-trained actress, a conniving little fortune hunter, a practiced thief or an unfortunate young lady who was compromised and hence disowned by her family. But if you think I believe this prattle my grandmother concocted, the answer is no."

She fumed. *A fortune hunter? A thief?* "Perhaps I am also proficient in the art of poisons," she muttered.

Reyn gaped at the dark eyes flashing at him. "I beg your pardon? Did you just threaten to poison me?"

"Never mind, my lord. You are quite safe." She stood to speak, forcing her voice to sound light and lyrical, as if she were talking about a walk in the park. "And of course you're right. I simply checked into Bedlam for a leisurely holiday in hopes that your grandmother would waltz through the door and offer your hand in marriage. The torture, starvation and madness added to the novelty of my stay. How about a frigid bath, or a bit of solitary confinement, even a little bloodletting?" In a heartbeat, she allowed her temper to show. "Is that what you truly believe?"

"Don't turn this around. I want the truth so we can

end these ridiculous machinations of yours and Agatha's."

"Suppose we were hiding something. What would you do with the truth?" His answer came too slowly. "Sir, I have nothing more to say."

Briggs halted in the doorway. "Dinner is served."

Her composure gone, afraid of what she might reveal and eager to flee, Jocelyn turned to the butler. "Briggs, please have cook send my meal to my room. His lordship will be dining alone."

With a precarious grip on her temper, she faced the man she had thought charming only moments ago. "Your grace, without a doubt I'm at your mercy, a state as intolerable for me as marriage is for you. However infuriating, I find it necessary. Nonetheless, I will not subject myself to an interrogation equal to one a petty thief would suffer. Consider the information you've been given and inform me of your decision, but do not expect me to beg or lick your boot heels. That simpering behavior gained me nothing in the past." She pivoted on her heels toward the door, muttering about men, stupidity and pigs flying.

His butler aimed a look of disapproval at him, providing an outlet for his fury. "Briggs, you can wipe that look right off your face. I'm no longer a wet-eared youth to bend to your scowls. Tell cook I will eat in my study." As Briggs exited, mumbling about insolence and bad manners, Reyn called a halt. "Briggs, answer me this. This is my home, my life. I'm suddenly trapped in a marriage I didn't want, nor even knew about. Why in heaven's name am I the villain here?"

The butler, having no answer for his employer, left to deliver the various messages.

Reyn drifted awake, disturbed by a soulful melody. He sat erect in bed, all senses alert. Irritated over the fact that he had been awakened after the seemingly endless hours it took for him to reach a state of slumber, he climbed from his bed. Prepared to investigate, he wrapped himself in a black satin robe. Again he heard the sounds. Unbelievable. Some bloody fool played the pianoforte, and midnight had come and gone long since. Given his current mood, he would willingly throttle someone for such behavior.

His curiosity piqued, his temper in check, he wasn't prepared for the sight he discovered. With a single candle on the piano and soft moonlight drifting through the windows, the salon provided a stirring backdrop, a celestial stage, for the young woman who swayed rhythmically, one with the music. Gossamer shadows floated across Jocelyn's body, captivating him.

Slipping across the polished oak floor to stand directly behind Jocelyn, Reyn fought the powerful inclination to stroke the riot of yellow curls, so soft and feminine, that fell about her shoulders. Her lace wrapper clung to every curve, and his body reacted boldly even though logic warned him to withdraw. As the physical lure won the mental battle, he drew one finger lightly across the nape of her neck. Immediately, Jocelyn's hands froze above the ivory keys. She twisted toward him.

"Relax, moonshine, I have not come to cross verbal swords with you." He continued to fondle her curls, his voice whisper-soft. "So radiant, like little bits of moonlight." He gestured toward the empty space beside her on the bench. "May I?"

"Did my playing wake you?" she asked as he sat, a nervous edge to her voice.

"Yes. You do realize it's well past midnight?" He noted the shivering reaction to his purred response, a fraction from her ear.

She nodded. "I play at the oddest hours. Agatha and the staff have grown accustomed to my eccentricity."

Such innocence and his body throbbed like an eager

young pup's. Him. A man accustomed to winning marathons of endurance, in and out of the bedroom. He knew his better judgment had deserted him the moment he sat down. Hell, he'd lost his good sense long ago so far as she was concerned.

As her soft, delicate fingers rested on the keys, her breathing grew shallow and sporadic. Reyn knew the breathlessness came from fear or uncertainty. When he ran his fingers through her hair, she turned to face him. He smoothly asked, "Do you never sleep?"

Obviously befuddled, gaping at him, she gulped. "The nights are long, the darkness suffocating. I find the light of day more calming."

He dismissed the odd remark. She was staring at his lips and averted her eyes toward his chest. Giving a little squeak, she turned her face back toward the pianoforte.

Reyn decided she was definitely a fledgling at this game of seduction, and innocents such as she, their emotional expectations too high, caused trouble. Understanding the risks involved, he always preferred liaisons with experienced women. Yet tonight, regardless of the unusual relationship, he wanted her as he had never wanted another. He grasped her hand and brought it to his lips. "Play for me."

Without a word, she withdrew her hand from his. Playing haltingly at first, her fingers soon danced across the keys, the soulful notes filling the salon like the yellow butterflies dancing in the meadow of wildflowers painted on the ceiling. As she played, she seemed to merge with the music, consumed by the passion of the rhythmic notes.

She drifted back to reality, exhaled deeply and pivoted on the bench to face Reyn. The blaring signals for restraint vanished. Slowly, he raised her wrist to his lips and placed a kiss on the tender skin. Lightly stroking her palm with his thumb, he continued to hold her hand. "Thank you. That was magnificent."

"You're welcome," she managed to mumble.

"Where did you learn to play?"

"My mother."

Eyes, dark with fascination and uncertainty, gazed at him. "Is she really dead?"

Jocelyn nodded her head. "Yes."

She sat, frozen in time, large doe-like eyes fastened on his mouth. He knew he was going to kiss her. One simple kiss to satisfy his curiosity. "Close your eyes, moonshine."

He brushed his lips across her quivering mouth, then withdrew to witness her reaction. Pleased with the awestruck look in her eyes, he dipped his head to take her mouth again. More thoroughly. His tongue lightly traced her lips until she parted them to yield access.

Reyn accepted the gift, pulled her body flush with his and unleashed the passion he had harbored since the previous night. Encouraged by Jocelyn's soft mewl of surprise and then pleasure, he plundered her mouth with a deep, sensuous kiss. As his tongue darted in and out, he allowed one hand to drift to her breast. When he felt the tiny bud of her nipple in his hands, he knew he had to stop or break every rule he had ever established. Reluctantly, he removed Jocelyn's hands from his chest and pulled away. When he didn't speak, Jocelyn gave him a look of confusion and shock.

"Blessed Saint Agnes, what have I done?" she said. She abruptly stood, rocking the bench.

Knowing she had misinterpreted his sudden withdrawal, Reyn grabbed her arm. "Wait."

"I'm sorry. I shouldn't have."

"Jocelyn."

She jerked free and ran from the room.

Reyn sat, stunned by the passionate response she had freely given, but more important, he was disgusted by his own lack of control. He was furious with himself, not her. And now, he would be the one to suffer. His manhood, eager to finish what he had so foolishly started, throbbed with need.

"Bloody hell." So much for keeping my distance, he cursed. To remain at Blackburn Manor would definitely be more difficult than he thought, so he considered the obvious solution. He would travel to London and visit Celeste, for surely his mistress could satisfy his rampant lust. He would also initiate a very thorough, very private investigation into the past of one certain mysterious woman.

He left before dawn.

Chapter Six

"What the devil do you mean, she's an angel? How on earth do you know my wife?" Reyn paced about his dining room at Black House, stopping before the window to peer down at the tree-lined park that bordered his London residence. Walter Hathaway sat at the long, polished rosewood table, enthusiastically consuming breakfast.

"Surely you're joking, Reyn. The minute Agatha acquired the special license, the entire *ton*, probably all of England, knew. Don't you remember that night at Boodle's? The gossip mill ran wild even before your ship left the Thames for the open sea. And for weeks thereafter. In your absence, in case anyone missed the news, Agatha sported the girl like a new ermine cape."

Reyn groaned, attempting to gather his wits over that revelation. Walter continued to spoon eggs into his grinning mouth, irritating Reyn all the more. "How can you eat at a time like this?"

"I'm starved. As I was saying. While you were gone,

Agatha flaunted your wife with more ostentation than Lord Waytelove displays his horses at Brighton. Made quite an impression actually, with the surprise and all. Everyone adores Jocelyn."

Indignant over his friend's good humor, his surly mood clearly worn on his sleeve, Reyn said, "Bloody good for them, but I denied the rumor before I left town."

"Well." Walter laughed, obviously amused by their misunderstanding and his friend's sour disposition. "I must admit my confusion. When Agatha brought Jocelyn out, I decided you were playing a grand jest on me."

How convenient, Reyn thought, that Agatha neglected to reveal this bit of news. Considering the additional complications caused by Agatha's parading Jocelyn about town, Reyn circled the massive table and stalked the corners of the dining room, feeling much too much like a trapped animal.

Walter continued to eat. "Good heavens, Reyn, sit down before you wear a path in the rug."

Grudgingly, Reyn sat down across the table to pointedly stare at his guest.

Walter said, "I have very good ears for listening, and it appears you need desperately to talk to someone. You look awful."

As he poured himself a cup of coffee, Reyn debated what he should tell his friend. It was not a question of discretion, for they shared many confidences. The difficulty came with defining exactly what he felt. He knew he didn't want to be married. He considered the entire institution a farce, if not a lifelong prison sentence. The thought of making a love match was so preposterous, it didn't even bear consideration.

Reyn added a touch of cream to his cup. As for Agatha and her gentle heart, he had already forgiven her. In her own misguided way, she meant well.

That left Jocelyn, a beautiful, fiery . . . what? There lay the dilemma.

Walter interrupted Reyn's thoughts. "You are married?"

"More or less."

"To Jocelyn?"

Wondering about Walter's reaction when all the facts were presented, Reyn nodded absently.

"I find it difficult to believe that marriage to that divine creature would be a hardship."

"Perhaps the problem is not with the lady herself, but rather the baggage that comes with her." Reyn knew his cryptic statement clarified nothing in his friend's mind, and proceeded to tell Walter the entire story.

Walter sat for a moment, chewing a bit of toast. "Have you bedded her yet?"

As Reyn's arm jerked in response to Walter's question, his coffee sloshed from his cup to the table. "Good heavens. What a question. I've been back in England for less than forty-eight hours. You expected me to bed a woman I've known for even less time than that?"

A gurgle, sounding suspiciously like a smothered laugh, escaped Walter's mouth. Instantly, a scowl meant to render most people blathering idiots came over Reyn's handsome face, transforming him from dashing gentleman to menacing savage.

"Amazing," Walter said. "For years, I've tried to achieve that precise glare, to no avail. I shall have to practice more. Relax, Reyn. My question is justified and you know it. I've known you to meet, woo, bed and thank a woman in less time than it takes most men to wrest an introduction. I also know your penchant for the fairer sex, and Jocelyn happens to be one of the fairest I've seen in a very long time. And don't even bother to tell me you find her long in the tooth, or lacking in some way. I'd be forced to call you a liar. However, I was considering the complications of a divorce versus an annulment."

The sweet, passionate moment with Jocelyn, and his undisciplined reaction, came foremost to Reyn's mind. The fact that Walter tripped so closely to the truth rattled his nerves. "You know as well as I do that an annulment would be far simpler."

"Simpler perhaps, but no less damaging to your reputation. On what grounds?"

"Agatha suggested Jocelyn admit deceit in regard to her ability to bear an heir. Therefore, my reputation and the sainted family name would remain untarnished."

Walter shook his head. "Agatha's cunning is frightening sometimes. Do you believe Jocelyn lost her memory?"

Thinking long and hard, evaluating their few encounters, Reyn said, "No."

"Do you think Agatha knows the amnesia is a ruse?"

"In all likelihood, my grandmother masterminded the entire scheme."

"Really? How interesting. Why the pretense?"

"I don't know. Agatha explained little, except to say she has her reasons and to trust her. For years, Agatha has focused on my marriage, or lack thereof. Perhaps this is her attempt at matchmaking."

"Have you any other ideas?"

"I believe treachery on someone's part started this mess because no one would willingly submit to incarceration at Bedlam. Jocelyn certainly isn't addle-brained, but she is hiding something."

"Why?"

"Maybe to protect someone. Protect herself. The devil of it is, I'm as baffled as you. I accused her of a great many things. In retrospect, none of them ring true. I intend to discover her every secret down to her first rag doll before any true harm can be caused."

"If you believe deceit is in the air, why not cry false and throw her to the streets?"

Reyn seriously considered the question. Any number of disasters could befall her. The vision of Jocelyn begging in the streets surged along with the powerful instinct to shelter and protect. It didn't make sense, and he knew his answer would seem trite. "Damn and blast, it doesn't seem the honorable thing." Noting his friend's knowing smile, he snapped, "Besides, Agatha adores this girl and has made Jocelyn her personal mission. You know Agatha's determination. I would rather face a pack of hungry wolves."

"Then, since you just returned from an extended trip, where is your charming wife? Why are you back in London?"

Reyn twirled his fork several times, then looked directly at Walter. "I need to see Celeste." When his friend guffawed loudly, Reyn said, "If you so much as show another tooth, I will shove that sausage down your throat."

Pushing his plate to the side, Walter cleared his throat. "Excuse my poor manners and my obvious stupidity. If you're married to that incredible vision I met, why do you need to see Celeste?"

Knowing Walter felt no true remorse at all, Reyn belligerently chose to ignore his friend.

"You were saying?" Walter prodded.

Finally, Reyn relented. "I thought we could discuss dress patterns. Don't be obtuse. It's annoying. Why do you think I need to see her? I already told you I plan to stay away from Jocelyn's bed, so you know full well I intend to plant myself between Celeste's lovely thighs."

"If your current mood is any indication of your need, then by all means call on Celeste. This afternoon. Perhaps then you may be fit for civilized company."

"That is precisely my plan, and given my current frame of mind, I just might stay there the entire week."

Sighing deeply, Walter said, "Celeste will hoist her colors once again when she thinks she has you back under her spell. She wasn't pleased to discover you married. I believe she expected that boon for herself."

Reyn shuddered at the thought. "Not bloody likely."

"My thoughts exactly. Celeste might be a delight in your bedroom, but she'd be a disaster in your parlor."

"For over a year, ours has been a mutual arrangement with honesty as the basis of our relationship. If Celeste anticipated a permanent union, she has only herself to blame. She knew I had no intention of marrying."

After dabbing at his mouth, Walter laid his napkin on the table, crossed his legs and grinned. "Yet, it seems you have done just that."

Reyn tried to remain detached from his friend's teasing. It proved worthless. "Did you wake this morning with the sole intent to ruin my day?"

"Give over, Reyn. If you expect me to believe that nonsense about allowing your title and all your worldly goods to fall into the hands of some removed cousin, you're more foolish than my brother Winston. Someday, when you least expect it, you will find someone willing to tolerate your surly disposition. You will marry and probably sire fourteen children."

The small wooden chair became too restrictive for Reyn. He pushed from the table and took to pacing again. "You forget, my friend, that I witnessed the self-destructive path my parents chose every day of my childhood. Love matches are seldom successful, and my parents' was no exception. Instead of the usual acceptance, their marriage became a battleground, growing more destructive every year. And I lived amongst the ashes. When they weren't fighting, my mother vanished for weeks. Father remained indifferent, consumed by alcohol and self-induced solitary confinement."

"Granted, you went through hell, but not all marriages are like that."

"Humpf! The combination of love and hate and marriage will only destroy a man. I saw that firsthand."

"Reyn, you don't really know what happened with your father."

Forcing the ghosts from his past back to their resting place, Reyn stopped before the window with his hands locked firmly behind his back. "I know my father drank because of grief, guilt and melancholy over another woman. I know that he chose to kill himself on my fourteenth birthday rather than live with that. And I know that when my mother died five days later at the hands of a jealous lover, I rejoiced. I will never allow a woman to hold such power over me." Reyn whirled to look at his friend. "Heavens, Walter, look at your own family."

"In their own way, my parents do love one another." With a pensive expression on his face, Walter shrugged his shoulders. "It's me they can't abide."

Regretting his outburst, Reyn rubbed his hand across his chin. Walter's childhood had been as unpleasant as Reyn's, but for different reasons. "Their loss, you know."

"Perhaps." Walter crossed to stand beside Reyn. Both men watched the traffic below. Walter spoke first. "One last thing. I had the opportunity to spend time with Jocelyn. She is a remarkable young woman who I believe means you no harm. Once you discover her purpose, you might also discover that you've made an ideal match."

"You sound like Agatha. Why is everyone so determined to marry me off?"

"Your grandmother wants a tiny cherub to bounce on her knees while I, my friend, want the women who now fall at your feet to fall at mine."

As his mood lightened, Reyn chuckled. "You are a libertine."

With an unrepentant grin on his face, Walter said, "I

know." He placed a firm hand on Reyn's shoulder. "Well, now that I've succeeded in rousing us from our maudlin jaunt down memory lane, I must leave. How long will you stay in London?"

"A few days. I can't very well hide from everyone until I have the answers I need. There's another reason I came to London. I intend to set Maddox on Jocelyn's past and see what he discovers."

"Splendid. Find Celeste. Make her a happy woman and yourself a sated man. I'll see you tomorrow."

Before an ebbing fire, a brandy snifter balanced in his hand, Reyn silently applauded himself for handling everyone's best wishes with strained civility. After one week of questions and whispers, discreet glances and pointed stares, his tolerance was gone. And that restless, caged feeling still followed him.

Admittedly, his visit to Celeste had been a mistake. He'd spent a wasted afternoon in her company, valiantly trying to muster the urge to take her to bed. He had not seen her again, refusing to relegate his lack of desire to the blond-haired, dark-eyed enchantress who plagued his dreams.

In frustration, he cursed, most vividly, then reread the missive from Maddox, a bulldog of a Bow Street runner. *It appears that clues are a bit thin on the road. Will continue to make inquiries.* Blast! His man had failed to discover one whit of information. That left one obvious solution. He would return to Blackburn Hall, use whatever means necessary and ferret out the information himself.

Reyn slept peacefully through the night.

Leaning against a large elm, Reyn watched Jocelyn scurry through the lush gardens of Blackburn Manor. Her bare toes peeked out below the ruffles of her dress, and her skin glowed a rosy pink. With wild curls billowing about her head, she darted from bush to bush. Her most accommodating cat followed dutifully behind. In total abandonment, she collapsed on the woolen blanket. Caesar immediately draped himself across her chest to rub contentedly against her chin. Stretching her arms outward to pay homage to the morning sun, she openly ignored propriety as her dress hitched past her knees to reveal nicely shaped legs free of any covering.

The unguarded innocence of the scene, the smile of sheer pleasure on her lightly flushed face, left Reyn dumbstruck. Too easily did he remember the delightful taste of her rosy lips, and he found himself pondering the other delicacies hidden beneath her clothes. Jolted out of his daydream by his half-aroused state, he crossed the lawn in silence. He had a mission: to uncover secrets, not body parts.

"I must admit I envy the cat more with each encounter," he said, referring to the languid position of the cat atop her chest.

Bolting upward, attempting to right herself, Jocelyn dumped a disgruntled Caesar on the grass. She brushed her wayward curls from her eyes and pulled her naked toes beneath her dress. "That is a most annoying habit, sir."

He tried to look innocent. "What?"

"Your sneaking up on people. It makes one wonder if one is being spied upon."

"It's my estate—I can spy if I want to." His lips twitched slightly as he sat down beside her.

Open-mouthed, she stared at him. "You're teasing me."

Reyn smiled fully and leaned down on his elbow. "Am I?"

"Yes, I believe you are. No true gentleman would intentionally perpetrate such distasteful behavior toward a lady."

"I thought our previous encounters have already established my true nature." His fingers tested the soft texture of her dress, vividly aware of their close proximity, her fresh lavender scent, the blush on her cheeks, the pulse beating rapidly at the base of her throat.

Reyn said nothing. Neither did Jocelyn. He knew she probably had question after question running through her mind. Either she would ask about his unexpected return now, or she'd wait until she talked with Agatha. The silence stretched between them.

Jocelyn shifted to her knees. "Excuse me, sir. I have things to attend to."

So, he thought, she wished to talk with Agatha first. "Please, hold," Reyn said. "I believe we have some unfinished business." He watched her settle again on the blanket with both hands laced together on top of her knees, her back straighter than the iron hitching posts at the stable. She looked more prepared to receive a stern lecture. Amused by her stalwart position, he tucked his chin to his chest to conceal his grin.

He said, "While in London, I considered this situation more thoroughly. I realized I hadn't been completely fair to you and Agatha. It's in my best interest to assist, rather than hinder you. The sooner your memory returns, the sooner I have my freedom back." He reached for an apple in a nearby basket. Polishing the fruit to a bright glossy red, he leaned on his elbows to watch Jocelyn's reaction. "Correct?"

"Yes."

"I have returned to do just that."

"Do what?"

"Why, help you." As he took a bite of the apple, Jocelyn nibbled her upper lip. The poor girl, he thought. One swift glance at the creamy flesh rising above the scooped neckline of her dress and he corrected himself. Not a girl, but a woman. A very beautiful woman. A woman who had stolen his bachelorhood. "I intend to help you regain your memory."

"If the doctors discovered nothing and since I continue to have no insights, what do you propose to do?" she cautiously asked.

"I'm quite exceptional at gathering information and deciphering the salient points so that the best and most appropriate action can be taken."

Jocelyn stared at him.

Reyn continued. "In other words, I'm very good at solving puzzles. I shall extend those talents to this memory business of yours, and in no time at all we will have you reunited with those who matter in your life."

She pursed her lips into a tight line, one side slightly higher than the other. "You can surely understand if I question your sudden willingness to accept my memory loss and this marriage?"

He noted the skepticism in her voice. She was right to be nervous. "Only a temporary state."

"True."

While she contemplated his sudden change of heart, Reyn watched her face reveal every reaction. Disbelief, panic, even a hint of admiration. Or was it amusement? He couldn't say for sure, but he knew one thing. She didn't believe him for one minute. Neither did she know his strategy. He would keep her off balance, do the unexpected, become her friend. Then, when her guard was down, he would discover her secrets, help her whether she liked it or not, and take back his freedom.

Jocelyn continued to stare at her toes. Reyn continued to stare at her. He concluded it would be no great hardship to execute his plan. Her lightly bronzed skin, no doubt caused by frequenting the outdoors, served to enhance her high cheekbones, pert nose, and full mouth. Regretfully, he sighed. Perhaps he had been too hasty in declaring his celibacy. This was something new he would have to consider. Technically, she was his wife, and using Agatha's suggested grounds, he could still obtain an annulment. Direct confrontation had proven unsuccessful. Charm and seduction could very well be the tools to use. An easy task when he considered his body's eager response.

Finally, he asked. "Agreed?" With her reluctant nod, he continued. "Splendid. Now, I have an idea to help us discover your true identity. We shall try a new name every day until you find the one that fits like a silk stocking. Hmmm—" he paused. "Perhaps we should follow the letters of the alphabet. We shall begin with Antoinette. After dear, departed Marie. Found guilty of treason, yes, but otherwise a complex woman with many sides and otherwise grievously misunderstood."

He looked at Jocelyn, judged her reaction, and admitted to himself that he was enjoying this little game. He took a final bite of the apple and threw the core to a nearby tree. "Or perhaps Allegra. Latin for cheerful, sprightly. A musical name with a touch of the exotic." When she continued to stare, an astonished look on her face, he said, "No? All right. We shall try for a touch of royalty. Yes, I like that. Does Anne ring any bells, bring any special thoughts to mind?"

She continued to sit, saying nothing. For the first time in days, he felt as though the tide had turned in his favor. Yes, he quite liked this game. He took her hand in his and patted it like a reassuring parent. "You are overcome with joy at my generous offer. I can tell." As an afterthought, he asked, "Oh, by the way, will I require a food taster, or may I assume it will be safe to eat my meals without worry?"

Unable to resist his teasing, Jocelyn submitted to her urge to laugh. "I believe you are a candidate for Bedlam yourself, my lord, or completely without scruples. I made that threat in anger. You will be safe from my skills as long as my temper is not pushed to its limits as it was the other night."

He stood, signaling the end of their conversation. "In that case, I shall tread carefully."

Extending a firm hand, he easily pulled her to her feet, flush against his torso. By the slight quickening of her breathing, he knew she was not immune to their closeness. He smiled. Obviously, she remembered their moonlight rendezvous as well as he. Yes, seduction could definitely be the key to unlocking her mysteries, for he, being a man of experience, would enthrall this female to do his bidding in no time.

From behind his back he produced a pair of pink satin slippers. "I believe these are yours."

Reluctantly, she placed her hand on his arm for support and took the shoes, standing on one foot to put one on the other. She lost her balance, almost tumbling to the ground save for his quick hands, which grasped her firmly about the waist. She addressed his pleated shirt-front. "Please release me, Lord Wilcott."

"Surely you already know my given name is Reynolds. You may refer to me as Lord Wilcott, after my dukedom, or my lord or your grace, but all my friends call me Reyn. I believe, for an intimate love match such as ours, you should as well."

The heat from their closeness quickly spread to his loins. His mouth, eager to demonstrate his statement, hovered above hers. But Caesar demanded equal due. The cat leaped to Reyn's shoulders, sharpened claws penetrating the woolen jacket. Reyn straightened abruptly. "Good God. Is he always this demonstrative in his attentions?"

Jocelyn laughed, a light, lilting sound that filled the sunlit morning. "Perhaps he preferred Antoinette." She enticed the cat into her arms. "He must like you, for he doesn't perch himself on too many people."

"Thank heavens. I can only imagine what the *ton* would say if they discovered I changed the name of my wife daily, watched for odd tastes in my food and possessed a cat that attacked my guests." His ridiculous jesting continued as the trio returned to the house, Reyn silently congratulating himself on his wisdom and intelligence.

Jocelyn veered toward the library, cautious but also curious to discover what Reyn needed. Since their afternoon encounter, she'd questioned the sincerity of his offer several times and had come to one conclusion. The man was up to something.

Peering around the door, she saw Reyn sitting in a winged chair beside the fire, reading from a small leather-bound book. He looked slightly disheveled and wonderfully handsome. He'd replaced his boots with a pair of slippers and wore grey trousers and a loose-fitting cream shirt. The top three buttons were open, exposing enough flesh to spark Jocelyn's memory of their first kiss, the way his muscles had responded to her touch, the texture of the hair on his chest.

"Good evening," Reyn said.

She tore her eyes from his chest to his face. He hadn't even twitched, yet he knew she was there. Staring. Since he was smiling, he obviously found her silent appraisal humorous. She said, a bit more brusquely than intended, "Briggs mentioned you wanted to see me?"

Reyn stood, setting the book on a nearby table. "I missed you at supper, Jocelyn. Or shall I call you *Anne*?"

"Whichever suits, my lord."

"Reyn," he corrected.

"Reyn. I dined in my room."

As he crossed to her side, he clucked like a disapproving parent. "Jocelyn . . . Anne, how on earth can we sort this matter through if you hide from me?"

78

She forced herself to remain calm. Bristling over the matter solved nothing, at least not until she knew the purpose of his summons. "I wasn't hiding."

"I'm glad to hear it." Grasping her hand, he pulled her into the room. "Come. We can talk."

"As in you ask me questions and I answer them?"

"What good would that do? You've lost your memory, remember?" Stopping abruptly, he inspected her face. "Oh dear, have you forgotten that as well?"

Unsure of whether to laugh or clobber the man with the brandy decanter, she simply said, "If you're eager to match wits tonight, I shall have to decline. I'm not in the mood."

He laughed, a deep, rich sound. "Come sit down, Jocelyn. I'll teach you a game and we shall converse like two normal adults. We did quite well in the garden today. Neither of us raised our voice through the entire conversation. Have you played cards before?"

She settled herself in a chair at the small square table. "Your grandmother taught me cribbage."

He grimaced. "A bit subdued for my tastes." He pulled a deck of red-backed cards from a drawer in a nearby desk. Taking the chair opposite Jocelyn, he began to shuffle, his deft hands easily manipulating the cards into a tidy stack. "Now what to play? We have no box for faro, poker is rather complicated, and whist requires four people." He stopped to look at Jocelyn. "Jump right in if any of these games ring a bell."

"Be assured I will."

"I know. We shall play vingt-et-un, a simple yet exciting French game. Can you count to twenty-one?"

"Yes."

He slapped the table, pointed a finger at Jocelyn and proudly announced, "See there. A clue already. You're an educated woman."

As he advised Jocelyn of the basic rules, she couldn't decide if he had chosen a simple game because it wouldn't tax her mind, or so he could question her without a strain on his. They played several hands while Reyn explained basic strategies of when to take another card and when to decline.

After thirty minutes of play, Reyn said, "Shall we up the stakes?"

She didn't answer, but lifted her brow and awaited his explanation.

"Whoever wins the hand can ask the other person a question. What better way for us to become better acquainted?"

So, the man wanted to play games after all. He certainly lacked subtlety. Realizing she wanted to know more about Reyn, she decided this could work in her favor as long as she guarded her own answers. "All right."

He dealt her a ten and an eight and himself a perfect twenty-one. Grinning, he rubbed his hands together. "I win. Where were you born?"

Since he took no time to think, she decided he already knew the questions he wanted answered. Well, her turn would come. "I remember a place that ends with 'shire.' Does that help?"

"Of course not. Half the English towns end with 'shire.' "

She won the next hand. "My turn. Why did you leave for London so suddenly the other night?"

"I remembered I had unfinished business."

Neither won the next hand, then Reyn let Jocelyn deal. She gave herself two tens while Reyn held a total score of nineteen. Jocelyn asked, "Why were you in Spain?"

"I purchased a sleek new ship from an American friend of mine."

"In Spain?"

"Only one question at a time, my dear."

When she won the next hand as well, he frowned. She grinned. "Why Spain?"

"My friend had other business there as well."

And so the game continued for another half hour, with Jocelyn claiming more victories than Reyn. Finally, Reyn leaned back in his chair, rubbing the back of his neck. His grim smile revealed just how disappointed he felt about the outcome of the night's meeting. He said, "You played well."

He wasn't talking about the game and she knew it. "As did you."

"However, our time together is just beginning. I did learn that you were born and raised in a 'shire,' knew a nameless red-haired girlfriend who giggled, had a maid named Molly, owned a pet rabbit named Hippity and went to school somewhere in England."

"And you, sir, have a penchant for horse racing, love your grandmother to distraction and owned a salamander named Sally. You're twenty-eight, sailed in the Royal Navy for four years and recently bought a new ship. Your favorite color is black, which doesn't qualify as a real color, and you love lamb. Oh yes, you like to play games and you also hate to lose."

"I don't remember telling you that."

"You didn't have to. Should I go on?"

"Rather proud of yourself, aren't you? We shall try this again. With another card game. One at which I can cheat."

"You're incapable of cheating. You hate liars and cheats."

"I'm not sure how I feel about liars right now."

Admit it, she said to herself, *you walked right into that one.* She stood. "Thank you for interesting evening."

"Wait. Do I not receive a good-night kiss?"

Backing away toward the door, she said, "I'm not sure that is a very good idea."

"Are you afraid of one small kiss?" He closed the gap between them. Grasping her chin with his hand, he dropped his lips to hers.

The gentle kiss set Jocelyn at a slow burn. Sweet, soft, intoxicating. And not near enough. When Reyn withdrew, Jocelyn fought the inclination to lean closer.

"Jocelyn, remember that when I want something, I'm a very patient man. Good night."

The challenge was clearly evident. She'd never backed away from one before and certainly wouldn't now. The smug inflection in his voice irritated her, but not enough to erase the pleasure of his kiss or the evening she had enjoyed. She said nothing, her eyes focused on the floral pattern of the rug as she turned to leave.

Chapter Seven

He was a bloody fool. And if this charade continued much longer, he'd be a mindless idiot. One week, seven long days and nights, passed, and nothing. He had learned absolutely nothing about Jocelyn. Actually, Reyn conceded, he had learned a great many things about this stranger living in his house, none of which provided a link to her identity.

He had discovered something about himself, though. The physical attraction he felt for her had not lessened, but had increased to almost painful proportions. Why just last night, while playing a simple game of euchre, he'd nearly lost control, his body tormented by the lust churning wildly in his groin. No wonder he'd nearly lost the game. His mind had been tortured by her lips, her delicate tongue, her graceful fingers as she ravished a handful of candied almonds. He vacillated between self-contempt for the licentious thoughts he kept having, and pride for his ability to keep his hands to himself. The good-night kiss he allowed himself every evening wasn't helping matters. It always left him wanting more, wanting all. As he sat on the leather footstool in his bedroom, he wondered how long he would be able to manage his restraint.

Spitting out a string of words better said while alone, he tugged a boot onto his left foot and reached for the other. *Where the devil was his valet?*

The door to his room slowly slid open. He said, "No need to bother now, Dither. I've already seen to the task of dressing myself." Reyn looked up from his right foot. "Oh, it's you."

Caesar casually strolled to Reyn's side. With a twitch of his ear, a tilt of his head and a slight arch of his back, the cat watched expectantly.

"Come to attack me again? Well, you're too late. As you can see, I've already left my bed, and I can gladly say my toes are all intact. You'll have to stalk the halls for a chance at my trouser legs instead. Better yet, go find Rebel. You've already ruined him for me." Reyn studied the cat for a moment. "Perhaps you can tell me your mistress's full name? Give me a clue to her past?" Reyn crossed his arms and frowned. "No? Well, today's a new day. I shall persevere. She will slip up sooner or later."

As Reyn stood, the cat sat, suddenly more concerned with washing his tail. Reyn looped his cravat into a loose knot. "I can see I've bored you already. You've obviously had your breakfast, so I shall go have mine."

When Reyn gained the dining room, it was empty. The porridge on the sideboard was cold, as was the toast, tea and coffee. No warm, succulent meats, no sweet breads, not a small slice of cheese awaited him. Even his morning paper was absent.

Prepared to right the wrong, Reyn veered toward the kitchens and shoved open the door.

A sudden burst of laughter stopped him cold. It seemed the entire household was gathered in this one room. Flowers lay everywhere. Daffodils, hyacinth, primroses, foxglove, bluebells. Yellows, pinks, whites, purples. Some in baskets, some in vases, many still bundled on the table and any flat space available. In the middle of the chaos, surrounded by the explosion of color, sat Jocelyn.

"Did someone die?" Reyn asked, placing enough sarcasm in his voice to indicate his annoyance.

The room seemed to exhale with a collective gasp.

"Good heavens, no."

"Grandmother? Is that you?"

Agatha waved a bit of pink lace from behind a huge bouquet of green and yellow wood spurge and gold prickly gorse. Rebel hid behind her chair. "Yes, darling. Isn't it wonderful?"

"Wonderful doesn't adequately express how I'm feeling right now. Is that grandfather's prized soup tureen? I can't imagine what he'd say if he knew you used it to feed the dog."

"He would be thrilled that this monstrosity finally served some purpose. It is crude. The king had very bad taste, if you ask me. Imagine, awarding a wedding gift covered with drunken peasants involved in various states of, shall we say, merrymaking. Besides, Rebel deserved a reward. The poor dear finally came back into the house." She waved her arms in the air. "What do you think? Jocelyn decided to bring a bit of spring indoors to celebrate my return to the living."

Turning to Jocelyn to judge her reaction to his arrival, he sucked in his breath. God, she was beautiful. Her hair, in shades of red and gold and slightly curled, fell to her shoulders. A vibrant, daring red rose lay behind her left ear. Within moments he found himself thinking about the things he could do with a single red rose and one particular, very naked woman.

Vanquishing that image from his mind, he forced himself to remember his poorly attended breakfast. "Agatha,

I'm thrilled you managed to leave your room for break-fast. Jocelyn, I assume there is at least one flower left in the garden for Martin to prune. And I sincerely hope that someone in this room can find me a simple cup of hot coffee."

A little squeak escaped the cook's mouth when she realized the gravity of the situation. They'd forgotten the duke altogether.

Jocelyn interrupted. "I apologize, my lord."

"Reyn," he said, correcting her.

"Reyn. After Agatha and I ate, I personally comman-deered the staff into helping me this morning. If you wish to retire to the dining room, I will see you served directly. Agatha and I will join you."

"Are you finished in here?" he asked.

She gazed about the kitchen at the work yet to be done. "No, but I shall see to it later."

"Do you find the task enjoyable?"

"Yes."

"Very well. Keep on with it. I can never, in all my life, remember eating in the kitchen. I shall break my fast here." A copper pot fell to the floor with a resound-ing bang. "That is, if Cook doesn't fall into hysterics."

With the quick efficiency he expected, the servants snapped into action. Reyn nodded his approval and crossed to stand beside Jocelyn.

She asked, "Are you angry?"

"Actually, no. Now that I understand the circum-stances and know I will be fed. I am a most considerate man. Don't you agree?" He winked. As he continued to stare, Jocelyn fidgeted and lifted her arm to remove the flower from her hair. "Leave it," he said as his hand drifted across her cheek to her jaw, tipping up her chin. Ignoring their audience, he allowed himself the luxury of an early morning kiss. "Lovely."

The husky timbre in her voice revealed the effect of his touch. "The garden is filled with such specimens."

His thumb continued to stroke her cheek. It pleased him when she turned into the caress. "I spoke of you. The color matches your lips." Her face flushed a delicate shade of pink. Yes, Reyn thought confidently, today just might be the day he discovered something of import. When Jocelyn expected a fit of temper, he offered kindness and understanding, leaving her off balance. As he sat, he leaned down to whisper, "The letter for the day is G. I thought we might try a Scandinavian name. What do you think, Gerta or Gunda? Perhaps there is a muscle-bound, hedonistic husband who resembles Thor in search of you."

She thought for a moment, even though they both knew the morning ritual was no more than a game. He chose names of vast origin, and she willingly played along, always giving the names the proper consideration, sometimes testing the names out loud. The entire ploy seemed foolish, ridiculous and childish, and gave him some sort of perverse pleasure.

"That, my lord, is a difficult choice. Shall we try Gunda?"

"Excellent." He took a swallow of coffee. Remembering Agatha's presence, he lifted the flower arrangement off to the side. His grandmother regally sat at the head of the table, sipping her tea. A sprig of bluebells sewn along the collar accented her violet dress, while a small cluster of primroses decorated her hair. "Grandmother, you look delightful."

"Thank you. I feel delightful as well. I adore my suite, but I must admit, even I was beginning to despise those pastel walls."

"I expect you to exercise caution with your activities. Otherwise the happy little cherubs dancing on your walls will welcome you back."

"You sound just like the doctor." Agatha waved a pink napkin in the air. "Briggs, please serve him immediately. With a potato in his mouth, he won't be able to rail at me." Agatha, obviously pleased that food was being placed on the table before him, grinned at his scowl.

"Humpf. I can see all of you have conspired against me." He looked at the plate of steaming food now placed before him, then at Jocelyn. "Once again."

"I see no conspiracy here."

Jocelyn had much too much innocence in her voice to suit him. "Neither did Macbeth," said Reyn, "and look what happened to that poor fellow."

"I believe Macbeth fell prey to his own arrogance."

His wife's familiarity with Shakespeare's works offered a possible clue too great to ignore. Between bites of cheese and ham, Reyn studied Jocelyn. "Have you ever seen an actual production of the play? In London, perhaps?"

Jocelyn shook her head.

"A country performance? A group of wandering minstrels at a country fair?"

"No, I don't believe so."

"So your interest in Shakespeare stems from your education. How very fortunate for you. Most women learn to embroider and serve tea. Who taught you about our esteemed playwright?"

Toying with a yellow buttercup, she said, "I can see an old woman with greying temples, dark eyes and a rather large, hawk-like nose, reading to me."

"Is there a name with that image? An initial? A maidenly grandmother?" He added as an afterthought, "Although I find it difficult to imagine any relative of yours with a hawk-like nose."

Jocelyn heaved her shoulders in resignation. "Alas, no."

"A pity," he murmured. Forcing a smile on his face, he resumed eating.

"Reyn, stop pestering the poor girl."

He tried to look offended. "Agatha, there is no need

to tread upon my toes. To pester would mean I w
tempting to badger, harass or harangue. I was mere
conversing with Jocelyn about her keen intelligence
and whence it came." He turned to Jocelyn. "You understand the difference, don't you, Jocelyn?"

"Be assured, my lord, I understand a great many
things. Especially about you."

While Agatha swallowed her laugh along with a sip
of tea, Reyn wiped his mouth with his napkin. The rat-
tle of pots and pans reminded him they weren't alone.
Being a great tactician, he knew when to advance and
when to retreat. "In that case, you know that I am a busy
man. Briggs, I will retire to my study. Please have more
coffee served there." Reyn turned his attention back to
the woman as he started to leave the cozy setting.
"Thank you for this interesting departure from our routine. I look forward to this evening. Perhaps we can discuss another play by Shakespeare. His characters and
plots are so intriguing, with all the twists and turns to
ponder." As he left, not waiting for their responses, he
had already cataloged the various story lines that might
aid his cause.

April welcomed spring with warm days and gentle afternoon showers. Every afternoon during her walks, Jocelyn discovered a flower, a bush, a tree, each with a
new bloom to herald the change of seasons. This time
of rebirth was a favorite of Jocelyn's. But today, as she
sat with Agatha beneath a towering maple, she felt only
frustration. She ripped a petal from a yellow daisy.
"Why can't he simply leave me alone?"

Agatha cleared her throat. "Patience, my dear. Remember, he had no choice in all this."

"Every day he tries some new tactic to wriggle the
truth from me. Now it's Shakespeare. He behaves politely, sometimes to the point of being boring. He hasn't
bellowed or lost his temper since his return, and that def-

ne suspicious. I wish he would simply end
probing, whether deliberate or discreet, into

ardless of the fact that I threw the two of you to-
, I know he considers it his responsibility to keep
safe."

"My plan will keep us safe if he would leave well
enough alone."

Agatha smiled one of her smiles that seemed to say
she understood things that Jocelyn didn't. She patted
Jocelyn's hand. "A man like Reyn is not accustomed to
leaving unresolved matters in the hands of others. Besides all that, how are the two of you getting on?"

"Remarkably well," Jocelyn said. Considering his
subtle attacks and intimate innuendoes, her short temper and waning patience, she marveled that peace had
reigned at Blackburn Manor for this long. The fact that
she liked the man more each day exasperated her the
most. Reyn exuded confidence, possessed a sharp wit,
and virtually oozed masculine charm that set her toes to
tingling. She enjoyed his company and anticipated his
occasional caress. Every night before they retired, he
bestowed on her a kiss that spoke to her soul and left
her body craving something she didn't understand.

When she remembered the past week, she frowned
and annihilated another delicate petal. The day-to-day
routine remained the same. She breakfasted with Reyn
and Agatha, after which he would closet himself within
his study, or ride about the estate as he resumed the ad-
ministration of his holdings. She spent her time visiting
with Agatha, reading, practicing her music and savoring
the manicured estate gardens and surrounding woods.
The evenings varied depending on Reyn's whims, but
most often Jocelyn and he dined together, sometimes
playing chess or cards after the meal.

Thinking about the hours ahead of her, she crumpled

the yellow flower into a tiny ball. "I must return to the house. Will you join me?"

"I believe I shall remain outdoors a bit longer."

Jocelyn stood, took a calming breath and left the cool shade of the tree. It was time to tuck her past into the recesses of her mind. Time to bury those unsettling emotions swirling in the pit of her stomach and sharpen her wit. It was time for tea. Reyn expected her.

Waltzing through the front door, she stopped when she noticed the hat and coat draped on the maple hall tree in the foyer. She peeked around the doorway of the drawing room and easily recognized the short, bald man who sat in the tall, winged leather chair. A whispered plea escaped her mouth. She had forgotten all about Mr. Nobb. The peaceful existence at Blackburn Manor was about to come to an abrupt end.

She marched toward the odious little man, who bore a distinct resemblance to a well-dressed toad, and greeted him coldly. "Good day, Mr. Nobb. Shouldn't you be at the mill?"

Neglecting all proper decorum, he remained seated. "I heard Lord Wilcott returned. I told you before. I intend to speak with him myself."

"That is quite impossible." The nasty little man had the audacity to snort, yet in order to expedite his departure, she had no time to provide a lecture on proper manners. "Lord Wilcott is extremely ill."

Scratching the exposed top of his head, he ran his tongue across his teeth as if searching for leftovers from lunch. "The butler said nothing."

"I imagine he thought it best if I brought you the news. If you will excuse me, I do have things to attend to." *Like finding a way to tell Reyn about my interference before you do.* She smiled serenely, gesturing toward the door. Nobb remained motionless.

"How long will he be indisposed?" Nobb asked.

"I cannot say."

Nobb's arms rested above the bulging abdomen that pressed against his waistcoat. "If I don't see him today, you can be sure I'll return every day until I do. I intend to hear directly from him that he wants those changes you made kept in place."

"If you refer to the improved working conditions at the mill, I assure you, he stands behind them one hundred percent."

"We shall see, shan't we."

Quickly losing her patience, Jocelyn reverted to a haughty, authoritative voice. "This is utter nonsense. His lordship fully condones all the improvements I have made. In fact, last night over a medicinal tonic, he remarked about the long-term benefits of the changes. He applauded my concern and my actions."

Nobb snippily asked, "Exactly what has Lord Wilcott under the covers?"

She knew Nobb believed nothing she said, yet the first plausible disease came to mind and flew from her mouth. "Malaria. He contracted it during his travels and periodically he experiences these dreadful relapses." The nasty fellow still showed no signs of leaving. "My husband will be most upset to discover you are questioning my authority, Mr. Nobb."

"Precisely, my sweet."

Spinning like a lopsided whirligig, Jocelyn watched Reyn casually saunter to her side and place a lingering kiss on her hand, which he then kept captive. Her eyes sought his in an attempt to discover his mood and what he might have heard.

"With what is Mr. Nobb having difficulty?"

When the overseer stood beside the chair, eager to speak, she wanted nothing more than to slap the smug smile off his fat little face. No doubt he would relish any retributions Reyn directed toward her. "It seems—"

"Good to see you, your grace. Glad you're feeling better, sir."

Reyn frowned at Nobb before he smiled back at Jocelyn. "Yes. Malaria is such nasty business. Isn't it, my dear?"

Her stomach lurched. Sweet mercy, he had heard everything. "Are you sure you should be up, my lord?" she asked with overenthusiastic concern.

"A miraculous recovery," he said while he adjusted the starched cravat at his neck.

"Excuse me then. I shall attend to refreshments and leave the two of you alone to discuss business." She tugged her hand, trying to escape before the entire story unfolded.

"Unthinkable, since you were instrumental in implementing the changes. Shall we?" Reyn directed her toward the settee, where they both sat down.

Groaning, unsure what he had heard and unable to find a plausible excuse to escape, she prepared to act the devoted wife.

"Mr. Nobb, I believe you said you had some questions?"

The steely edge to Reyn's voice softened Mr. Nobb's voice, but only momentarily. "Well, your grace, while you were gone, your wife made adjustments at the mill that were enough to make a cat laugh." Chuckling at his own humor, clearing his throat when no one else joined him, Nobb continued, "I was thinking that maybe you might be having second thoughts."

Closely watching Jocelyn, Reyn nodded. "Yes, the changes. In reviewing my ledgers today, I discovered how vast they were. I must say it is amazing."

The overseer openly leered. "I tried to tell her that. Cost you some blunt, I'd say, but women don't always understand these things. Best place for them is in the bedroom, if you get my meaning."

"We are not here to discuss the roles of men and women. Pray continue."

Nobb rambled on with the flair of an overblown braggart. "Well, first off, I'd make all those women come back to the mill instead of weaving in their homes. If they'd rather stay at home and see to their wee ones, then so be it. As for the older kids attending school, we all know that's a bit of nonsense. Educating them does little good, and they can handle the work day as well as anyone. I don't think the shorter work hours a good idea, neither. I'm not convinced that those fancy rotary cutters are better than a good hand tool for shearing the nap." He paused, as if he expected a signal from the duke.

Reyn listened, his stony expression unreadable.

Jocelyn sat, her nerves stretched to their very ends. The finger-light circles Reyn drew in the palm of her hand increased her agitation. Aware of the awakening heat in the pit of her stomach, partly from fear, partly from the stimulating caress, she squirmed uncomfortably. If only she knew Reyn's thoughts.

When nothing more was said, the overseer prepared to gather his belongings. "Well, if it's fine with you, I'll set things to rights."

"Not so fast," Reyn said. "Please explain what it is you specifically wish to correct?"

"If you saw the numbers yourself, then you know less time working with the same wages makes no sense, and I don't believe this nonsense about the weaving being better, regardless of her ladyship's judgment. I think we best go back to the way things were."

Unsure of Reyn's intentions and stewing over the accusations from Mr. Nobb, Jocelyn could hold silent no longer. "How dare you, you miserable little frog! You would allow a boy of six to work from dawn to dusk, and take a mother from her home, leaving the babes to suffer. You pinch pennies on heat and light and even utilize faulty equipment. Your management destroys the very basis of the family and, given their exhaustion and lack of will, they will continue to produce an inferior product. These people are human beings. They may not be educated, they may not be peers of the realm, but they deserve decent working conditions and fair pay. You prefer to run the mill like the miserable sweat houses that occupy much of our cities. My husband has the power to better their lives, and if you are so blind as to what a bit of kindness and understanding can do for increasing one's loyalty and desire to work, then you're as stupid as you appear."

Regretfully, she wished back her words as soon as they were out of her mouth. Jocelyn bit her lower lip, peeked at her husband and was startled to witness Reyn's winsome smile.

He peered at her from behind half-closed eyelids and asked, "Are you finished?"

Baffled by his nonchalance, she sat like a deflated balloon. He whispered in her ear, "Are you sure, Millicent?"

She could only stare at her husband.

"As you can see, Mr. Nobb, Lady Wilcott feels quite strongly about these changes. Perhaps, my dear, it would make Mr. Nobb less concerned if he knew where you had gained your expertise. Feel free to tell him of your education."

Her smile held no warmth. "I am sure he has no desire to hear such a boring recitation."

"As you choose." Reyn turned back to Nobb. "As you can see, she sees me as a social reformer of sorts. I have no choice but to allow her to see the project through."

Like a white-faced cheviot sheep, Nobb bleated, "But your lordship—she's a woman!"

"A fact I thank God for every day."

The little man flushed a dark red, furious that his directives were being overruled. He stood to leave. "As you wish, sir, as long as you understand it is against my better judgment."

"So noted. Now, I have something to say. Due to your years of service, I will allow you to stay at the mill. If I hear of any mistreatment toward a worker, or one whisper of degenerating conditions, you will be dismissed on the spot. Do I make myself clear?" The man could barely nod his head. "And Mr. Nobb, do not question Lady Wilcott or gainsay me again. Ever." Like the midshipman's warning bell, his ominous message suggested to the man that he leave quietly and promptly.

Hoping for immediate escape, Jocelyn offered to see their guest to the door. Reyn forestalled her efforts as he called for Briggs, who arrived to escort Nobb from the house. With a charmed smile pinned on his face, Reyn whispered for her ears only. "Do not, for one moment, consider leaving this room."

She knew the end had come. He would order her departure today. Out on the lawn she would be. No revenge. No money. Oh lord, where would she go? Her mind, a maelstrom of the worst possible scenarios, simultaneously struggled to create answers to the questions she knew she would be expected to answer. No matter what he did or said, she would not grovel. Chin lifted high, eyes directed on Reyn, she awaited his explosive reaction.

"A drink, my dear Millicent?"

"What?" she managed to croak, knocked from her trance by his courteous manner.

"By the way, how does today's name fit so far? Any fond memories tripping about in that pretty little head of yours?" Reyn lifted one brow. "No? Well, then, I think a drink would be just the thing. Mayhap it would help my malaria."

Suspicions confirmed, although his voice gave no indication of his mood, Jocelyn knew, as surely as the sun set, that he wasn't pleased with her interference. "I can explain."

He leaned one arm against the mantel, a rapacious gleam to his eyes, "By all means. I look forward to this tale."

Unsure of where to begin, she decided that only the absolute truth would serve. "During your absence, mostly out of boredom and also hoping to contribute something for your generosity, I assumed the task of running your holdings."

"You assumed a great deal more than that."

She ignored his sharp barb and detailed her intervention, beginning with her first trip to the mill. Her shock and anger had been a volatile thing. After experiencing Bedlam, then encountering the deplorable working conditions in the mill, as well as Mr. Nobb and his disgusting demeanor, she vowed to make amends. "I was sure you were ignorant of the situation. Even you wouldn't allow your people to work without heat, suffer through their work with little food, poor light, endless hours and the abominable treatment from that poor excuse of a man. I had to do something."

Continuing to say very little, interjecting a question or two, Reyn allowed her to explain her efforts. "I did not make a frivolous decision. In the end, I calculated the workers' pay, the reduced hours and the additional costs to maintain a cleaner, more comfortable work space against the returns on the improved products to be sold. Utilizing the new rotary cutters, the nap shearing process is neater and more effective as well as faster. With the addition of weaving shawls, I determined the mill could be profitable, if not immediately, then within the next twelve months."

"A very clever plan. And risky with my money."

She shrugged her shoulders. Her revelations did not seem to ease his mind. "Besides believing that you might care, I thought it necessary."

"Don't fret so. I'm not an ogre set on abusing those who work for me. I plead ignorance. That is not a proper excuse, but the only one I have. How I ever found a single redeeming quality in Nobb is beyond me, but I will give him a second chance. I will visit the mill immediately to ensure things are as they should be." As if puzzled, he scratched his chin, "Your abilities are quite staggering."

"It wasn't so difficult."

"I assume the people are pleased?"

"Yes." In order to convince him of the rightness of her actions, she continued with greater enthusiasm. "Especially the women. I split the jobs so that some do the spinning and weaving while others dye the cloth and hang it in the fields to dry. The colors are richer, more dramatic, and the detail in the patterns is exquisite. I believe we will be able to charge a higher coin and receive the price. If you truly reviewed the books, you should be able to see the possibilities."

"Where did you learn to read and cipher?"

The question, asked so nonchalantly, caught her off guard. "Every girl had to learn. The nuns—" Jocelyn abruptly closed her mouth.

Reyn ignored the accusation in her black eyes. He raised his chin in question. "You were saying?"

"I cannot remember."

"The nuns?"

Lifting her lips into a tight smile, eliminating all traces of meekness, she spoke in clipped tones. "Like a fleeting breeze on a summer night, the thought has come and gone."

"Like hell it has." Furiously, he crossed to where she sat, jerked her from the settee and pulled her close.

"Let me go," she said through clenched teeth as she fought his hold.

"I am tired of this game you play."

"You play the game, sir. Laying traps with kind

words and false pretenses, hoping I shall reveal some master plan." Her frustration shot skyward. However could she convince this man to leave her alone? "I have no plan, as I have no memory."

"I have been patient long enough. Who are you? What is your real name? What are you hiding?"

"Is there any particular order in which you would like those questions answered?"

"No."

"Then I don't know, I don't know, and I don't know." By the time she finished, she realized she was shouting as loudly as he was. That would accomplish nothing.

"You run a household with quiet efficiency, understand the teachings of Plato and adore Shakespeare. You read Latin and French, speak both fluently and play the pianoforte with great skill. You facilitate changes in a thriving business, and I discover it will most likely be profitable, yet you can't remember whence that knowledge came? By God, do not come the innocent with me. You're a liar. Your memory is as sharp as mine."

She acknowledged the truth in his accusation, but the arrogant set of his jaw as well as his words made her resolve to see her task through. "And you are a manipulative, detestable—Jack Nasty. Let me solve my own problems." Jocelyn turned to flee.

His arm, shaking quickly about her waist, brought her flush against him, toe to toe, chest to chest, eye to eye. Hard lips fell upon hers. The kiss, sensual and demanding, allowed no escape.

Fighting the erotic sensations erupting throughout her body, she struggled to leave his embrace. His power over her grew each moment their lips touched. She felt his tongue trace a line across her mouth. Wanting to fight, but needing more, she allowed access.

The onslaught to her senses swelled as, relentless in his quest, he ravished her mouth. When she quieted, the kiss adopted a life of its own, changing, softening, seducing. She knew she should stop him, even as her arms crept up his chest to rest at the nape of his neck. Tightening his hold, thrusting his tongue into her mouth, he pulled her against the bold proof of his arousal, his hand caressing the softness of her breast, bringing her nipple to immediate life. She gasped. He moaned.

A fierce longing to remain in his arms battled everything the nuns had taught her. Behaving like a wanton, allowing him such liberties, screamed against her very being. Why did his touch excite her so? Why did she yearn for something more? Why couldn't she pull away? Admittedly, she wanted this.

Coughing. No, a throat clearing. The sudden realization that they were no longer alone diminished the flames to smoldering embers.

"Thank goodness. I thought I might have to find a bucket of water or, at the very least, a bed for the two of you." The warm masculine voice filled with laughter extinguished the embers to ashes.

Reyn snarled beneath his breath. "Great bloody hell."

Jocelyn, extracting herself from her husband's arms, flew across the room into the arms of the visitor, her excitement bubbling over. "Tam!"

Chapter Eight

The overwhelming urge to do physical harm engulfed Reyn as the two people embraced like long-lost lovers. "I do hope I'm not interrupting anything?" Reyn crossed to the arched doorway that framed the entwined couple. "I assume this heartwarming display means you two know each other?"

Jocelyn pulled away from the man she hugged. "Forgive my manners. It surprised me so to see a friendly face."

"Meaning what?" Reyn asked. "That my presence is not preferable?"

After gaping open-mouthed over the sudden accusation, she turned to Briggs, who hovered near the doorway. "Please bring refreshments. Plum cake, if possible." She whispered to Reyn, "Do calm down. You are behaving like an ill-mannered, pernicious ankle-biter."

"I'd say more like a jealous husband," Tam interjected, then extended his hand. "How are you, my friend?"

Grasping the hand of Tameron Innes, noting the silly grin on the face of his longtime friend and business partner, Reyn responded dryly, "Innes, I have always said you have a scatty sense of humor."

"And impeccable timing," Tam added as he winked at Jocelyn.

Reyn noticed the scarlet color that highlighted Jocelyn's cheek as she obviously remembered the intimate display Tam had witnessed. Good. It served as a reminder of to whom she belonged. Realizing the context of his thoughts, he scowled ferociously.

"What dreary thought just crossed your mind?" Tam asked. "You look as though you lost a shilling and found a sixpence."

Ignoring the question, Reyn continued to glower at Tam. "Sit down. You can explain the purpose of your visit."

"Do I need a reason, now that you have a wife?"

"Of course not," Jocelyn quickly inserted. "Look, here is our refreshment."

Tam beamed with open adoration at the tray before him, eagerly helping himself to a slice of the dark cake and tea. "Plum cake, my favorite. How kind of you to remember, Jocelyn."

Reyn, on the other hand, experiencing another surge of raw emotion, yanked a loose thread free from the edge of the settee. This woman never bothered to consider his preferences. At that moment he hated plum cake. In fact, he wanted nothing more than to ram the entire cake down his best friend's throat, drag Jocelyn, the true cause of his frustration, upstairs and ram himself into her. Repeatedly.

Ignorant of Reyn's simmering state of mind, she laughed and directed her next comment to him. "After Tam and I met, he visited often. One day on a picnic I happened to discover his penchant for sweets. He consumed an entire plum cake in one afternoon."

"How nice," Reyn responded decorously while his thoughts look on a darker edge. *Sweets, indeed.* "Exactly how did the two of you meet?"

Tam seemed more than willing to tell the story. "Early one morning, when riding the border between our properties, I heard the oddest sound beckoning me from the churning waters above Black Hare's Falls. Lo and behold, I spotted a flurry of yellow silk and white stockings clinging tenuously to a twisted limb trapped beside a huge boulder."

"I wasn't clinging," Jocelyn clarified. "I was crawling."

"Hah!" Tam snickered. "Anyway, Reyn, here crawled Jocelyn, deep into her rescue efforts of one enormous, agitated, thoroughly drenched black feline. I judged she needed a bit of assistance. Being my gallant self, I jumped from Nobility into the freezing water, ruined my newest, most favorite riding trousers, soaked my boots, all to aid the enchanting damsel in distress. Only afterward did I discover she was the newly married wife of my best friend."

"I see." Reyn glanced speculatively at Jocelyn. "I assume I have Tam to thank for the annoying presence of that black devil who now terrorizes my halls?"

She nodded, then giggled like a nervous schoolgirl. "Caesar likes you."

"You would find the various attacks on my person by that overgrown beast humorous."

"The cat attacks you?" Tam asked.

"He prefers the toes, but trouser legs or dangling fingers will do. Just my being seems to incite the cat to violence. Poor Rebel practically swoons when the cat comes near him. So you can see, my friend, I'm not sure I should thank you for that bit of kindness."

"I also rescued your wife."

Reyn snorted, then took a sip of tea, already planning his next line of questioning.

"And have you continued your lessons?" Tam asked Jocelyn as he continued to consume the cake with zeal.

"What do you think?"

Locking his hands behind his head, Tam pretended to scold her. "I think, the moment you escaped my clutches, you abandoned them."

"And you are absolutely correct," Jocelyn admitted cheerfully.

The pair laughed as if sharing a secret joke, unaware of Reyn's wandering thoughts. While he waited like a forgotten schoolboy for someone to clarify the current topic, he watched his wife banter with Tam and realized that she seemed completely at ease. It was as though entertaining his friend came as naturally to her as waking in the morning.

Reyn found himself inspecting his friend of many years more closely. Equal in height, but more muscled than he, Tam owned a jovial manner. His bright green eyes, red-gold mane and handsome features captured the attentions of many a lady. Tam had been close at hand while he had been at sea for several months. Perhaps their relationship had become more intimate. Reyn shook his head at the absurd notion. Tameron Innes was one of his best friends. Jocelyn was simply being cordial. Reyn gritted his teeth. She never reacted like that with him.

Weary of being neglected, Reyn said, "What lessons?"

Tam explained. "When I discovered Jocelyn couldn't properly sit a horse, I took it upon myself to offer her my expertise." He commented to Jocelyn, "Perhaps we can schedule a lesson for today."

Jocelyn laughed. "I think not. My backside finally recovered, and I have no desire to be black and blue again."

"Coward," Tam said.

Excluded from the conversation yet again, Reyn sat as if he'd been banished to the corner. The uncertainty of Tam and Jocelyn's relationship grew by the moment. To that end, Reyn lashed out in exasperation. "Jocelyn, do you not have things to which you must attend?"

Although her eyes darkened over the blatant dismissal, she obeyed. "As a matter of fact, I shall go and exercise my feet and leave the two of you to your business. Dinner will be served at eight." She stopped at the large doorway, turned and smiled sweetly at Reyn. "By the way, my lord, tonight might be a perfect time to solicit the services of a food taster. Good day."

Tam looked perplexed. "Whatever did she mean?"

Reyn glared at the empty doorway. "I believe she just threatened to poison me."

"What?"

"Never mind." Reyn pivoted toward Tam. "What other lessons did you take upon yourself to teach her in my absence?"

Eyeing Reyn curiously, Tam said, "Would you care?"

"Don't bait me, my friend. I find I am not in the mood."

"Why do you suppose that is?"

Standing statue-like, feet braced apart, Reyn tried to gain control of his erratic behavior. He felt like a boar with a noseful of porcupine quills, and eagerly blamed Tam for his foul mood. Reyn deepened his scowl.

Crossing the sunlit room, Tam helped himself to a brandy. "All right, shall we talk about London instead?"

"Fine."

Undaunted by Reyn's surly attitude, Tam maintained his lighthearted mood. "I spent an enlightening evening with Woody."

Reyn's boot heels clicked on the oak floor as he advanced toward Tam and took the crystal decanter into his own hands. "I can only hope Walter will someday take a saber to you for fostering that ridiculous nickname."

"Perhaps, but let's not shift topics. Interesting talk in London these days. What do you think the odds are that a certain marriage is scalding the tips of the wagging tongues of the *ton?*"

Normally, Reyn enjoyed witty repartee, but today's chosen topic held little appeal. Eager to end the discussion before it began, he stated, "I am sure my marriage provides a great deal of twittering for all of London. Certainly, you have not fallen prey to the ennui endemic to ingenues and old women, and have more substantial news for me than idle gossip."

Tam kept silent for a moment only to retort, "Shock, disbelief, outrage, revulsion, delight. Everyone's initial reaction proved most interesting."

Reyn, succumbing to his curiosity, found himself asking, "And you. What did you think?"

"Ah. I had an advantage, you see. I met your wife before anyone else. I must admit, surprise can't adequately describe my feelings the day I discovered Jocelyn in that river, especially since you supposedly met while up north, under my very nose. By my calculations, you met, fell madly in love and married within four short hours. Then you sailed off to Spain. Peculiar start for a marriage, don't you think?"

Reyn groaned in dismay. Tam, a remarkable man with uncanny insight and a devil-may-care attitude, could be a royal pain in the ass. Lacking the benefit of a title never deterred him, for his tenacious spirit made him what he was today, one of the richest men in England. Knowing Tam would not relent until he had his say, Reyn said dryly, "I surmise you talked with Walter and already know the true nature of my marriage. Do you wish to offer your opinion?"

Shaking his head from side to side, Tam sighed. "I hoped Woody misinterpreted the situation."

Reyn easily detected the chastisement in his

friend's voice. "Highly unlikely, given Walter's apt-
ness for details."

Tam crossed to a nearby chair and sat. "Do you remember the first day my father became gamekeeper on
your estate?"

"What does that have to do with anything?"

"Humor me. My parents ignored propriety, welcomed you into our home and allowed us to become
friends. Later, I asked my mother why she dared defy
your father and she said you needed a loving family
more than we needed the position. She offered you a
happy refuge from your dim existence."

The alcove by the window suddenly felt too restrictive. Reyn began to pace about the room, absently ex-
amining a collection of oil paintings on the far wall. He
stopped beside the celestial globe mounted on a mahogany stand.

Tam continued. "The more your parents fought, the
more you escaped to our house, and the more my
mother and father tried to show you that love could and
did exist. Do you remember the time my father and you
built that tree house?"

Reyn tried to focus on the constellations dotting the
small globe, but his mind saw only himself as a small
boy, desperate for some small token of affection. He had
adored Tam's father, Liam. As they built a special fort,
Liam had prodded, pushed, and picked until Reyn
snapped. Reyn had called Liam every name in the book.
Even threw a shovel at him. Reyn broke into tears. Liam
pulled Reyn into his arms, offering fatherly words of
wisdom. Reyn needed to know one could behave hor-
ridly and still be loved. That people fought, but still
loved. Mortified that he had allowed his emotions to run
wild, Reyn had immediately assumed his ducal air. He
thanked Liam for the lesson and explained that he understood life quite well.

"Well, do you remember?" asked Tam.

Abruptly spinning the painted sphere, Reyn said, "Hell no. I was thirteen years old."

"Odd how you remember your age, but not the event itself."

"Is there a point to all this?"

"You have been given an incredible gift, yet you refuse to open the package."

"I can only assume that this insight into my past has something to do with my wife."

A wolfish grin curled Tam's lips. "So you finally said the word."

In his mind, up until moments ago, Jocelyn had been referred to as she, her, that woman, and many other epithets too scathing to mention. Already afraid of the implication, Reyn grunted. "Wife is perhaps the wrong choice of word."

"Pity. I've known you for fifteen years, and if you are as intelligent as I know you are, you will rectify that situation. Today."

"An interesting recommendation coming from a man who has forsworn marriage for the rest of his days."

Tam stared into space for a moment before answering. "A man could make an exception for a charming woman like Jocelyn."

Irked by that offhanded comment, Reyn raised his eyebrows, analyzing his friend's true intent and whether it made a difference. "I can't believe that after life with Lisette, you would trust so blindly, knowing that Jocelyn is playing us all false."

"My wife was a cunning, beautiful bitch. Greed and malice directed her actions. Jocelyn is kind, gentle and caring. Her actions are guided by fear. She needs help and someone to trust. You could be that someone. Unlike you, I believe two people, the *right* two people, can find happiness together."

Reyn snorted at the absurdity of the suggestion.

"Good Lord, Reyn, you deserve some happiness in your life. Forget the past. You aren't your father. Jocelyn isn't your mother, nor is she some mystery woman bent on your destruction. As my mother would say, a ray of sunshine has landed on your window sill. Don't be foolish enough to close the curtains."

Damn Tam's Scottish insight. It frightened Reyn. He wanted to lash out at someone. "You wax poetic, Tam, like the finest of lords. Do you possibly have any other bits of wisdom to share?"

"No. I know when you have closed your mind to anything I might say. I'm not in the mood to beat some sense into that thick skull of yours. If you're determined to play the fool, so be it. I am here if you need me." Tam pulled an envelope from his jacket. "Maddox sent this missive."

"Why didn't you say so sooner?" Grabbing the note, Reyn tore the seal. He cursed as he read.

"Bad news?"

"Not really. Damn frustrating, though. The only girl of any nobility turned up missing is a Mary Garnett." Although Reyn couldn't imagine Jocelyn as a Mary, he knew he would mention the name just to watch her reaction. He scratched his chin. "No one seems to know the girl. Presumably, she ran away with her lover and her uncle is searching the Caribbean for her." Staring absently out to the woods, he bluntly asked, "Tell me this, Tam. If Jocelyn is the lady she claims and you believe, then why is there no hint of her disappearance? The rumor mill of London would be twittering with such a tidbit of news."

"She admits her parents are dead. Perhaps the title died with them, and she purposely chose to avoid society. Maybe someone locked her away somewhere even before Bedlam. For your sake, I wish I had the answer."

Reyn cast Tam a sideways glance, but said nothing.

"I do have one last question," asked Tam. "When all is said and done, will you keep her or send her away?"

"I don't believe that's any of your bloody business."

Crossing his arms across his chest, Tam asked, "And if I choose to make it mine?"

Reyn answered with iron ferocity. "Stay out of it, Tam."

Placing a firm hand on Reyn's shoulder, Tam said, "No need to cob on, my friend. I'm on your side, simply viewing it from a different perspective. But know this. That young woman in your arms today is an innocent, of that I'm sure. You, obviously, want her in your bed and she, obviously, isn't repelled by the idea. If you're leaning toward that direction, I encourage you to consider well what you are about. I think she has experienced enough pain. She doesn't deserve to be hurt. I don't wish to make myself her champion, but she needs someone who cares. I will remain a simple bystander. For now. If you will excuse me, I believe I shall visit with Agatha and leave you to your thoughts."

Thoughts, hah! More like razor-sharp knives whittling away at his good sense. The moment he witnessed the amiable display of affection between Tam and Jocelyn, Reyn had felt these aggravating spurts of jealousy and he didn't like it. Not one little bit. And Tam's continued badgering only opened the door to greater speculation.

From the onset of this marriage, after the initial anger and shock, Reyn's goal had centered on unveiling the truth in order to send Jocelyn on her way and revert to his previous unencumbered existence. That plan now displeased him.

If he met the situation honestly, he would admit that over the weeks they spent together, he had developed a certain susceptibility toward Jocelyn. She was witty, intelligent, strong of heart and spirit, not to mention extremely attractive. The servants adored her, and why not—she was overly generous with her praise and demanded little. Agatha doted on Jocelyn, and even though the words had not been spoken, he knew that his grandmother hoped this marriage would withstand the current strife and flourish.

He once believed he would willingly allow his estates, his titles, his worth, to follow him to the grave. Agatha had always shot him one of her knowing looks and claimed this attitude to be pure and simple denial. His feelings toward marriage and heirs would change when a woman of substance and merit entered his life.

Taking that train of thought a bit further, he reflected on the responsibilities of a wife: She would bear, nurture and raise his children, manage his household in a suitable manner, and play the hostess for the social necessities of a duke. Undying love was not a prerequisite, merely compatibility, and if his body's reaction was any indication, Jocelyn and he would be extremely compatible. Therefore, if Jocelyn fulfilled those expectations, perhaps he should consider keeping her as his wife.

The matter of her lies and "amnesia" remained, but after dissecting the information presented him, one fact screamed truth. Someone had abandoned her to Bedlam. She knew the person responsible. That was whom she feared. She believed the amnesia protected her. The little fool. She didn't yet understand that he would keep her from harm's way. With or without her help.

To the astonishment of his staff, eagerly anticipating tonight's meal, Reyn whistled as he walked to his study, feeling better than he had in weeks.

Chapter Nine

Jocelyn restlessly shifted against the vase-shaped slat in the high-backed chair. In spite of Tameron's light-hearted spirit and Agatha's commanding presence, she thought dinner had begun with an oppressive atmosphere that resembled a mournful obligation for the dead. Even the crystal chandelier couldn't lighten her somber mood. Agatha sat to one side, appreciating the mirthful antics of Tam, while Reyn sat distantly at the opposite end of the dining table.

His eyes, highlighted by his cerulean-blue waistcoat, continued to find hers frequently, seemingly penetrating her deepest secrets. In fact, since the inception of dinner, thus far through five courses, he had been courteous, attentive, and well-mannered, the epitome of gentlemanly behavior. There had been no sudden topic changes, no direct questions about her past. However, her defenses had armed the moment he entered the dining room, greeted her warmly and addressed her as *wife*. His behavior bordered on suspicious, but two

112

could play the game. He would reveal his hidden motive soon enough. He always did.

"And your thoughts, Jocelyn?"

Shaken from her reverie by Agatha's question, she caught a glimpse of the lazy grin on Reyn's face. He looked like a sly fox who had just eaten, one by one, the farmer's chickens. Jocelyn felt as though she were meant to be the next meal. She purposely let the sentence hang so someone could provide her with the current topic. "My thoughts on—"

Tam restated the question. "Wilcott Keep. What did you think of that particular holding?"

"I must admit the Keep is my favorite. The forest and rivers are wild and beautiful. The castle itself is so majestic, it makes one wonder the glorious history those enormous rock walls could tell."

"Oh, dear, think of the possibilities," Agatha said. "Deyla's story alone would galvanize those stoic women in London."

"Deyla?" Jocelyn asked.

"Ah, yes," answered Reyn. "My great-great-great-grandmother. The witch."

"Surely you jest."

"Actually no, Jocelyn," Agatha said. "Deyla married dear Harthorn Blackburn, then barely escaped the witch's pyre. People considered her a bit odd. They claim she hid in the woods near Wilcott Keep, living with a wolf, until she saved Harthorn's life using her knowledge of plants and herbs. Nevertheless, Harthorn's son, Drake, would probably rise from the dead to stop any potential scandal about his parents or the family. He maintained that no public disdain would ever cross our coat of arms. Bit of a brute, he was."

Reyn asked Jocelyn, "Do you suppose he required the services of a taster?"

Placing her fork on the table, Jocelyn tilted her chin ever so slightly. "Never having met the man, it is difficult for me to say. Knowing his offspring, one can only speculate."

"Good heavens," Agatha exclaimed, "why would he need someone to taste his food for him?"

Tam swallowed his laughter with his glass of wine.

Reyn lifted his glass to his lips as if he saluted his wife's wit. "One never knows, Grandmother. Perhaps it was a necessity, being such a *remote, savage* estate."

"What?" Tam questioned, his curiosity piqued.

"I believe my wife once likened the inhabitants of the Keep to savages."

"No," Jocelyn politely said with her teeth gritted together. "I said it *seemed* somewhat savage. There is a difference, albeit a minor one."

Reyn burst into laughter, but thankfully, he chose not to debate semantics any further and allowed the current topic to drop.

Nearing the end of the sumptuous meal, munching on candied fruits and blackberry tarts, Agatha directed the conversation to London and the remaining half of the season. "I understand the philharmonic society is presenting several new pieces at Vauxhall Gardens, and a delightful farce is playing at the Theatre Royal."

Tam warmed to the topic. "Agatha, don't forget there are also those delightful actresses performing in the farce."

"Tameron Innes, you devil. I would prefer that you consider the balls you are missing and the company of those lovely, refined young ladies."

Chortling, he said, "You forget, madam, I am the one man, should I enter the room, who can cause the mama hens to near faint and scamper to secure their young chicks behind closed doors."

"Pish-posh. I taught you better than that. Besides, I know for a fact there are several matrons who would willingly, even eagerly, welcome your suit toward their daughters. Take Lady Wellham, Lady Alverlay, Lady

Billingsly. There is also the Duchess Milston." Then she whispered as if sharing a scintillating tidbit, "Although I sometimes believe she would actually prefer to keep you for herself."

Reyn, insinuating his mock outrage said, "Enough, Agatha. I do believe Tam is blushing, and if he isn't, I am. Besides, all of us are aware of the adventures to be had in London."

"That being the case, why are we not there? I am fully recuperated and I hate the idea of missing one bit of the fun, not to mention that you and Jocelyn should not be hidden away in the country. People will gossip."

"They already are," Tam eagerly added.

"Shush, you rascal. You are supposed to aid my cause."

Reyn grinned at Agatha's obvious act of manipulation, lifted his glass to his lips and allowed his eyes to wander over Jocelyn's shoulders. "Your point being, Agatha?"

"We should return to London. All of us."

Reclining soberly in his chair, fingers lightly stroking his chin, Reyn seemingly absorbed the suggestion as his eyes glanced downward. Agatha, content to wait for his decision, picked through the sweetened fruits, settling on a candied apricot, while Tam practically mirrored Reyn's position.

Jocelyn stared in disbelief, stunned that he would actually consider the notion. She knew, in order to initiate her plans, they would return to London at some point. She assumed they'd wait until she received news of her step-uncle's return. Why on earth would Reyn wish to travel to London? With her? As his wife? They'd be invited to any number of soirées, expected to appear as husband and wife, expected to be in love. Surely, he knew their presence together would only complicate matters. The longer the silence, the greater her distress.

Finally, Reyn looked up to smile at everyone. "I agree."

"You do?" asked Agatha, thoroughly pleased, but evidently surprised at the easy victory.

"What?" Jocelyn cried.

Directing his next comment to Jocelyn, Reyn said, "Such astonishment. I am always a reasonable man, especially if you consider that rusticating in the country has hardly provided the opportunity to stimulate your memory. So why not?"

Grinning from ear to ear, Tam simply asked, "When do we leave?"

"I daresay two days should give us enough time to prepare. Do you agree, Jocelyn?"

"Yes, but—"

"Splendid." Rising from the table, his hands behind his back, Reyn said, "Excuse us, Tam, Agatha. I wish to have a word with Jocelyn."

Jocelyn watched Reyn strut toward her as though he'd just won a high-stakes contest, his expression masking any hint to what he planned. She grasped his extended arm. "May I ask where we're going?"

"The salon. Fond memories of that room warm me to my toes. Perhaps you will play the piano for me."

"And perhaps *you* will explain this new ploy of yours."

"Ploy? I simply desire a few moments alone with my wife."

"It seems my status took an upward swing for no apparent reason. Would you care to explain?"

"You are my wife."

"In name only."

His lips teased the tender flesh on the inside of her wrist. "A minor problem easily remedied."

Ignoring the warm sensation settling in her stomach, she tugged her hand from his. "I think not."

He shrugged his shoulders, tucked her arm back in his and proceeded down the hallway into the salon. "A pity. I will content myself with conversation."

The air smelled sweet from the yellow roses recently placed on the tables, and tiny candles flickered along the left wall, casting shadows across the marble floor. The familiar piano sat in the corner, reminding Jocelyn of her first midnight encounter with Reyn. Withdrawing a safe distance from him, she crossed her arms under her breasts and forced the tender memory to the back of her mind. "All right. What trickery is this?"

His face lit with an amused grin. He moved toward the wall and began to extinguish the candles one by one. The moonlight through the windows became the only light. When he finished, he turned to Jocelyn, his hand extended. "Dance with me."

A multitude of reasons for his behavior crossed her mind, but she never expected this. His mood confused and worried her. "Dance? There's no music."

"I shall endeavor to hum a tune." She stood rooted to the floor. "Don't tell me you're afraid."

Against her better judgment, she went to him, sliding into his embrace. For several minutes, they glided across the marble floor, the scuffle of their feet and the soft notes Reyn hummed the only sounds. As never before, Jocelyn was aware of Reyn's powerful frame beneath the satin of his jacket. With every step they took, their bodies pressed closer together. She warned herself to be careful. When the suspense became too great, she asked, "I believe you said you have something to say."

Reyn slowed their movements until they swayed in one place, still in each other's arms. His face looked pensive. "I've been thinking that perhaps you and I should give consideration to making ours a real marriage."

Pulling back to further study his face, she said, "Do try to be serious."

"As frightening as it all seems, I am. I never thought to marry, but today, while talking with Tam, I decided I might have been too hasty."

She needed to distance herself from him in order to

117

think clearly. Releasing her hands from his shoulders, she backed away behind the piano. "You ask such a thing, not knowing who I am, or why I'm here?"

"You yourself constantly remind me you mean no harm."

Unprepared to open her heart to this man, she stared.

"Is that true?" he asked.

"Yes, but—"

"Hear me out. I don't know why you continue this charade, but sooner or later, you'll tell me or I'll discover your purpose myself. I need an heir, and certainly you realize I find you attractive. You already run my household as though you were my wife. Why not continue? We can end this business of yours and maintain a normal life together."

His proposal was well thought out, efficient and without emotion. He wanted a housekeeper and a brood mare. Even if she considered the idea, which she couldn't, she wanted something altogether different. Something she didn't believe he was capable of giving. "Do you love me?"

It was his turn to back away as if burned. "I beg your pardon?"

Jocelyn almost felt sorry for him, so pained was the expression on his face. "I asked if you love me."

"What does *that* have to do with anything?"

"Oh, Reyn, how sad. You can't even say the word, can you? I think *love* is a large part of marriage. I won't settle for anything less."

"I'm offering you stability and a place in society. You will want for nothing."

"How inviting. No, thank you."

"No?"

"No. I think it best if we continue as we are. When I resolve my problem, you may resume your bachelorhood. If at that time you wish to arrange a typical marriage complete with mistresses, separate bedrooms and stilted conversations, you shall be free to do so."

"And if I want you?"

"You want me in your bed. I won't become your wife simply to assuage your lust, then be discarded like last week's London *Times*."

Slowly, precisely, he advanced until he trapped her between the piano and the window. "I can make you change your mind."

Maintaining her position, she lifted her chin to his challenge. "This isn't a game."

"Jocelyn, our relationship became a game the minute you stood in my kitchen and fabricated your circumstance to my face. I realize your fear overrides your good sense. I accept all that. Still, I am willing to offer you more."

Evidently, he meant everything he said. The possible implications were too staggering. "I need to think."

"By all means. Take your time."

She tried to ignore the soft caress as his fingers traced a path down her cheek and across her lips. Certainly one kiss wouldn't hurt. Tomorrow was soon enough to worry about this new wrinkle in her plans. Sighing, she lifted her chin higher.

Rather than his usual passionate assault, Reyn seduced her with gentle flicks of his tongue. When she opened her mouth, he held back. Tentatively, she touched her tongue to his lips and allowed herself to slide her tongue into his mouth. Then and only then did he pull her tightly to him. His hands cupped her buttocks, pressing his arousal into her body. She sighed. Heavens, how she had come to enjoy these good-night kisses.

"Remember, Jocelyn, there could be many benefits to a true marriage between us."

Unable to utter a sensible response, Jocelyn merely nodded as she left the salon.

Chapter Ten

Reyn admitted the truth. Agatha was a brilliant tactician. She had badgered, cajoled and persuaded until, finally, he relented. Now he gazed at his wife from the opposite end of an elegantly appointed table that ran the length of the enormous dining room. He hated dinner parties, considering them just short of torture. They were unending affairs where bored hostesses, hoping for a scintillating evening, often sat mistresses with wives, husbands with lovers, enemies with enemies, each match testing the bounds of social civility.

His grandmother, after reviewing numerous invitations, purposely chose this particular soirée for their first public outing in London. The Earl of Damford and his wife, though a bit staid in their behavior, were good friends to Agatha. The night promised to be as pleasant as he could expect. There would be no surprises. Reyn caught a whisper of Jocelyn's laughter and frowned when he realized it would be difficult to talk to her, not to mention hours before they would be alone.

While the crème de la crème ate, Reyn listened to the soft tinkling of silverware and crystal as well as the innocuous ramblings of the lady whom he sat beside. Glancing down the length of the table, he smiled. His wife sat between two portly lords known for their grace, manners and faithful marriages. Thank God, he thought, she wasn't sitting next to his former mistress, Celeste.

Reyn continued politely to engage in various conversations, participated in the toast to Lady Damford, shared a cigar and a brandy with the men. At the first opportunity, he fled the room in search of his wife. Leaning casually against a pillar at the back of the salon, he waited for his wife's appearance amongst the throng of people who filtered into the room. He straightened when a masculine voice invaded his privacy.

"If you continue to scowl like that, no one this hemisphere will ever believe you a happily married man."

Reyn shrugged his shoulders with a cleansing breath, and turned to face the grinning facade of Tameron Innes. Reyn plastered a cheeky smile on his face and said, "Is that better?"

Tam looked aghast. "God, no, that is perfectly frightening. You look more like a pettifogger caught with his hands in the till."

Reyn reestablished his normal somber expression. "Save me from insipid old women, turtle soup and another discussion on the necessity of prunes in one's diet."

As he ignored his friend's grievances, Tameron said, "I rather enjoyed myself."

"I would certainly hope so, seated between the Countess Randall and Lady Simlett. I well imagine you have already established whose bed you shall visit later." Reyn raised a brow in speculation. "Or shall it be both tonight?"

"Me?" Tam guffawed. "Either you must be thinking

121

of Woody, or you are so sunk in gloom and self-pity that you must accuse anyone of excess and gluttony."

"And shouldn't I be? Look at her." Reyn tipped his head in the direction of his wife. "Other than during our grand entrance, she has barely acknowledged my presence."

"And you? Other than hurling a stony glare her way, what have you done to represent the constant, loving husband?"

Reyn drew his lips into a tight, compressed line. "She is completely surrounded by fops and dandies, all probably attempting to solicit her favor now that she carries the marriage title. I can't even secure a spot near her."

"Never in my days have I seen you wallow in a corner, especially if you felt your territory was being encroached. Where is Agatha? I just saw them together."

"They were." Reyn nodded to a stout man with a ruddy complexion trying to hide behind a piece of marble statuary. "Agatha abandoned her charge to pursue the purse of Lord Helm. She wants benefactors to build an orphanage on the fringe of St. Giles."

Tam winced at the image. "The poor man. He doesn't stand a chance. Thank heavens they don't allow women in the House of Lords. Can you imagine the turmoil?"

"She is relentless in her causes."

"And we both love her for it."

Pointedly, Reyn looked toward Jocelyn. "Usually."

Grinning, Tam paused before he moved on to another topic. "I daresay Celeste has sent a few beckoning glances your way tonight. Is Jocelyn aware of your arrangement?"

"I have no arrangement," Reyn said adamantly, only to face Tameron's direct scrutiny. "Fine. I concede that I spent time with her during my last visit to London. Briefly. Nothing happened. I discovered her appeal no longer holds." Eager to turn the conversation away from him, he raised a brow to his friend. "Perhaps Celeste would also enjoy a sample of your lecherous ways tonight." The twinkle in Tameron's eyes alerted Reyn of the forthcoming retaliation by his friend's burgeoning wit. "Don't even speak what is on your perverse mind."

Witholding his original retort, Tameron said, "In that case, while you rescue your wife, I shall secure us some choice seats for the glee."

Reyn, wishing he and Jocelyn were alone in their own salon, groaned as he remembered they had yet to endure the vocal concert to be performed by the host's three daughters.

Adding insult to injury, Tameron mischievously whispered before he left, "Surely your wife has received sufficient offers for the duration of her London stay."

His thoughts solely focused on one woman, Reyn managed to look indifferent as he maneuvered through the crowd, blatantly ignoring various invitations to converse. He saw only Jocelyn. Draped in layers of sheer, gauze-like muslin the color of blue twilight, she looked exceptional. Hundreds of tiny pearls covered the low-cut bodice, immediately drawing one's eyes to the opalescence of her breasts. When he remembered the bounty hidden beneath her bodice, his mouth went dry, and he realized that Tam had spoken the truth. He never lurked in the shadows when poachers threatened his property, and according to law, Jocelyn belonged to him. And he was supposed to be courting her.

With new determination to reach her side, he lengthened his stride. When she saw him approach, she forgot her bevy of admirers and graced him with a smile so warm, so dazzling, it sent tremors down to the tips of his leather boots. "Excuse me, gentlemen, but I believe I shall claim this lovely lady, *my wife*." The formalities spoken, Reyn presented his arm.

"Why, Lord Wilcott, I'm charmed," she teased merrily. "To what do I owe such congeniality?"

"Purely selfish intentions, I assure you. I wearied of watching every young fop in London dribble and drool over your breasts. Remembering their delightful bounty, I decided I wanted that enviable opportunity for myself."

Jocelyn's mouth fell open at the blatant reference to her body and his desire.

"Do close your mouth, my dear. Someone will think I said something scandalous to you."

Snapping her mouth shut, she whispered, "You did say something scandalous to me."

"Yes, but you liked it, didn't you?" He continued as if they were discussing the current price of wool. "Oh, don't deny it. I can tell by your rosy blush that you like my words, even if that saintly mind of yours refuses to admit it. Now, sit down and shush. Here are Agatha and Tam." He ushered her to their chairs, helped her sit, took her hand and placed it in his lap, his thumb rhythmically teasing her palm.

Jocelyn felt as though her entire body smoldered. One small spark and she would burst into flame. A softly spoken innuendo here, a discreet yet gentle caress there, Reyn had worked his magic well throughout the interminable recital. Relief must have shown on her face as he excused himself to enjoy a cigar with Tam, because he chuckled knowingly and gave her a wink. Thankfully, Lady Battingham and Agatha sat nearby. Jocelyn prevailed on their idle chatter to fill the void until her rattled senses calmed.

After the moment of distress had dissipated, pondering her husband's tactics and motives, she knew someone watched her. Sensing yet ignoring these feelings earlier, she now sought the source, and once discovered, she simply couldn't fathom the significance.

A beautiful woman, equal in figure to Venus and dressed in a golden gown, cast a look best described as venomous in Jocelyn's direction. Jocelyn experienced an initial spurt of fear, which she quickly transformed into disdain. She returned a provoking stare to the woman across the room and was quickly rewarded with the withdrawal of her mysterious combatant. Now, she needed to satisfy her curiosity.

Opting for discretion, she questioned the vapid woman next to her. "Lady Battingham, you seem to have a talent for remembering everyone's name and title. Would you be willing to share your secret?"

Lady Battingham twittered behind her fan. "Nonsense, dear. It simply takes time. The secret is knowing whom you should remember and whom you should forget." The older woman giggled, appreciating her own wit.

"I suppose." Jocelyn sighed. "I do want to make a good impression. Now, take that gentleman standing beside the large potted palm. I feel certain we have met, but I cannot remember his name."

Both Agatha and the matron scanned the room. Lady Battingham's eyes settled on the fellow in question first. "You mean Lord Halden?"

"Of course, how could I forget?" Nonchalantly, Jocelyn asked, "Is that his wife?"

Agatha nearly fell out of her chair, but before she could speak, Lady Battingham answered. "Dear, no. That woman is Celeste Waverly. A widow of three years. And if you do not mind my saying so, she enjoys her freedom a bit excessively."

Abruptly standing, Agatha interrupted. "Mildred, my dear, I do believe Harry is looking for you."

Oblivious to the strain in Agatha's voice, Lady Battingham rambled on, more interested in idle gossip than discretion. "Inherited a lofty sum and blatantly disregards propriety, flitting from one man's bed to another. However, for the last year, I understand her lover has been—" The sentence ended with an audible gasp.

"Mildred," Agatha said. A warning seemed to accompany that single word.

"Has been—?" Jocelyn asked.

An odd croak, part whimper, part groan, escaped the matron's mouth. "Who?"

"The lover?" Jocelyn prodded, all the while wondering why Lady Battingham suddenly stammered like a mockingbird. And why did Agatha have that strangled look on her face?

"Her lover?" Lady Battingham repeated.

Agatha firmly shut her eyes. "Sweet mercy."

It was impossible for Jocelyn to believe, but the fan in Mildred's hand flew even more furiously. "Madam, are you feeling well?"

"No, not at all. Please excuse me. I feel the need for a breath of air."

"It's about time," muttered Agatha.

The exasperating matron rushed to her husband's side, leaving Jocelyn alone with Agatha. "For a moment, I thought she might swoon. What do you suppose had her behaving so oddly?"

"One never knows with Mildred. I assure you, whatever she meant to say is better left forgotten."

Jocelyn stared across the room. "Agatha, that woman, Celeste Waverly, looked as though she hated me."

"Nonsense, child. Simply too much excitement. In fact, I shall find Reyn. He can take you home."

Agatha allowed no time for Jocelyn to express an opinion, for she twisted away like a small whirlwind. Jocelyn sighed and turned covertly to study the woman across the room. Whoever she was, Lady Battingham clearly disapproved of her behavior. Other than her striking beauty, she seemed harmless enough, draped on the arm of Lord Halden. And yet, Jocelyn sensed something amiss. She watched Celeste send a blatant, sensual invitation toward someone else in the room. Discreetly, Jocelyn followed her gaze, and nearly fainted when she realized the recipient of the woman's admiration.

Reynolds Blackburn, Lord Wilcott—her husband.

Roused from her initial shock, she quietly scolded her ignorance. What a dolt. Of course the libertine had a mistress. Sharp talons tore at her heart as Jocelyn visualized the two entwined in each other's arms, sharing kisses like those he had given her.

The room seemed smaller, a hundred pairs of eyes focused directly on her. Surely everyone present knew of the lovers' relationship. The revelers probably anticipated, even hoped for, a potential scandal. The once pleasant evening evaporated, Jocelyn's only wish to escape to the solitude of Black House.

"Agatha said you were eager to leave." Reyn searched Jocelyn's face for signs of fatigue as he joined her side. Although she appeared well, she kept her eyes directed at the far wall. Her spine looked as though it might snap if she stood any taller.

"Yes," she said.

Reyn lifted one brow at her abrupt response. "I've already called for our carriage and said our good-byes." When he presented his arm, she purposely stepped forward. Once in the carriage, she practically smashed herself against the side panel. He remained silent for the first few minutes, then asked, "Is something wrong?"

"No."

"Did you enjoy yourself?"

"Yes."

"Did anyone badger you to death with questions?"

"No."

He leaned back in his seat and pondered her sudden change of mood. By his estimation, until he'd elected to visit with a few of his cronies, events had proceeded nicely. At the moment, a great northerner blowing on the Atlantic would have exuded more warmth than Jocelyn did. "I won't apologize for sharing a cigar with friends of mine."

"Nor should you. Being a man, and a duke, you may do what you wish, whenever you wish."

"What the devil does that mean?"

She turned to gaze out the window.

Fine, he thought. Silence was better than a one-syllable conversation with a woman more prickly than a currycomb. Thankfully the distance to Black House was short. He helped Jocelyn from the carriage and, following behind, watched her climb the stairs to her room. Neither bothered with the common courtesy of a good night as they slammed their respective doors.

More aware than ever that Jocelyn lay only a few feet away behind a closed door, Reyn lay upon his massive bed, hands clasped behind his head as he stared distractedly at the lingering flames in the hearth. A habit he seemed to be developing of late. "Infernal woman," he cursed.

Irritated beyond belief by her aloof behavior, furious that he cared, and frustrated by his intense physical attraction for the woman, he lay wide awake.

The mournful outcry that came from the adjoining room sent him bolting from the bed. Like a crazed man, he threw open the door to her room and, searching, turned his eyes to Jocelyn's bed. Caesar stood alert by Jocelyn's pillow, and although the room lacked any visible intruders, his wife seemed to be battling a private army.

With quick efficiency, Reyn lit the candle in the wall lamp above the bed table, lifted the cat away and clasped his wife's shoulders. She rewarded him with an immediate reaction. A keening wail escaped her lips as wildly flailing arms, intent on self-preservation, connected firmly with his jaw.

"Ouch! Damnation, Jocelyn. Wake up." His heart

wrenched at the open, searing despair revealed in her eyes as her senses returned. Tenderly, he pulled her into his arms. "Sweetheart, you're safe."

Still lost in the darkness of her nightmare, desperate for the protection offered by his strong embrace, Jocelyn collapsed as Reyn, with a gentle touch and nonsense words, stroked and soothed her ravaged emotions. Comfort gave way to tears that fell unchecked onto his bare chest as he continued to hold her, eager to provide a safe haven until her reason returned.

He kissed her temple, her brow, each eyelid, a tear-dampened cheek, finally settling on her mouth. Whether she quivered from fear or anticipation he didn't know, and his caresses, initiated in comfort, grew bolder with passion. Intimately pressed against his bare chest, her rounded breasts reminded him of her near nakedness. His resolve crumbled. Crossing the barrier of her lips, he buried his tongue deep within the warmth of her mouth, stoking the fire. Jocelyn hesitated, as if retreating, then tentatively, she touched the tip of her tongue to his. Reyn groaned and pulled her closer. Suddenly, the woman exploded in his arms, perhaps exorcising her own demons, but for him, a man accustomed to passion, nothing mattered except fulfilling his desire.

Drawing back from her lips to seek out the hammering pulse at her nape, his mouth traced a line down her neck and across her collarbone. As if seeking sustenance, he sought and found the engorged tip of her breast, reverently caressing first one, then the other, through the fabric of her nightgown.

The texture of satin on bare skin teased Reyn. In order to fulfill the driving need in his loins, he pressed her down to the mattress. Slowly, with the ease of freeing a butterfly from its cocoon, he freed Jocelyn from her gown, his eyes feasting on every inch of skin he unveiled. Her breasts, bare for his plundering, beckoned again, and he fed on them with delirious delight.

His hands swept down her belly, down to the nest of auburn curls that guarded her femininity. For a brief moment, he sensed her hesitation as she clamped her legs together. He raised his head to witness her passionate expression laced with fear and confusion. He managed to speak. "I won't hurt you, moonshine. Let me give you this." As if she acknowledged the gift he offered, she dragged his lips to hers.

Her innocent response drove Reyn into a near frenzy, and he stroked her, invoking the dew her body so willingly gave. He encouraged her legs to part further as he taught her how to feed on her own passion. Her head thrashed on the pillow and short gasps slid past her lips as her hips instinctively matched the rhythm of his hand and tongue. Lifting his lips from hers, he shuddered with need and pride when she reached her first climax with a sensual grace he never anticipated.

Her whimper sparked his sanity. Reyn cursed. What a lecher! His despicable behavior, his lack of control, had turned an act of compassion into one of seduction. Breathing deeply, stroking her lightly from shoulder to hip, he forced himself to sound calm. "Rest easy, Jocelyn, everything will be fine in a moment." Blast, he thought, it would take all night for him to regain his composure.

He knew the moment she found her wits, for she stiffened like a wet leather strap left to dry in the sun. With naked breasts, tousled hair and dark, angry eyes, she speared him when he leaned back.

"Jocelyn, I can explain."

"You cad . . . scoundrel . . . debaucher of innocents." Each verbal insult accented her movements as she jerked and tugged her nightclothes into place. As she unleashed a new litany of charges, she kicked and jabbed Reyn until he fell from the bed to the floor.

"Bloody hell."

"How dare you take such liberties?" she cried, her voice a high-pitched shriek.

"Good God, woman, you were having a nightmare."

"You baker-legged blackguard. You should be whipped, shot, or at the very least, beheaded."

Indignant over her tantrum, Reyn started to stand. "Be reasonable. It's not as if we consummated our marriage. You still hold your precious virginity tight within your body."

"*Oooh*," she screeched, hurling a pillow at his head.

As his feet caught in a discarded bedcover, he fell back to the floor. In frustration, he batted the cushion and launched his own attack. "Damn and blast, Jocelyn, I thought you needed protection."

"Is that what you call it? Mauling someone while they sleep? Protection—hah!"

As difficult as it was to maintain one's dignity while sprawled naked on the floor, he persevered. "You didn't seem to mind my mauling a moment ago."

When reminded of the recent moment of passion, as if she donned a veil of chastity, Jocelyn pulled the sheet to her chin. "No small wonder, I was half-asleep."

Reyn knew better. "Hard to believe. You were hotter than Jamaica in August. I am fair scorched from your response, not to mention the fact that I still suffer in dire need." His last words were muffled as he stood.

She gasped. "You're naked."

"How good of you to notice." He leered, glancing down at his torso.

Her gaze, full of shock and wonder, followed his and centered on his bold erection. "You . . . you are . . . it looks . . . "

Mercilessly, he taunted her. "Looks what, Jocelyn?"

She managed to turn her eyes away long enough to squeeze an answer through tightly pressed lips. "It looks . . . insistent."

131

With a grin tugging at his lips, thinking the entire scene resembled something from a poorly written farce, he agreed wholeheartedly. "So it is. And I'll wager a day's betting at Ascot that it won't receive its proper attention this night."

"Cover yourself," she commanded while she launched a second pillow at Reyn. "Then kindly remove yourself from my room. You may take your manly intentions over to Lady Waverly's, and allow her the privilege of seeing to your needs."

Lifting his brows at her outburst, he concluded the reason for her earlier black mood. She knew about Celeste. Grasping the pillow to his groin, as if he were sharing his deduction with the king of England, he said, "You're jealous."

Eager to counter his outlandish remark, she said, "You have lost your wits."

"Not so. You are unconditionally, green-eyed jealous of the fact that I have shared myself with another woman."

For lack of objects to throw, she hurled insults. "You addlebrained, manipulative reprobate. You have lost a shingle or two if you believe that nonsense."

He had endured sufficient insults. "Enough. You are in dire need of a drink."

Briefly, he left, only to return with a large snifter of brandy, silently praising his good manners, for he had donned a pair of breeches. "Here, drink this." It was an order, not a request.

Surreptitiously, she eyed him while she sipped the amber fluid. "Don't you own a robe or something?"

Her fascination with his lack of dress brought the absurdity of the situation again to his mind, coaxing a less-than-gentlemanly response. "Would you like to visit my chambers and find out firsthand?"

She started to speak, then snapped her mouth shut.

"No? Pity. Never fear, I seem to have my physical

responses under control. For now. I guarantee, should my desire run rampant again, a pair of breeches will sufficiently contain my—how did you put it? My 'manly intentions.' "

Sending a glacial stare his way, she gulped the last of the brandy only to lapse into a fit of coughing. Reyn chose the distraction to grasp both her hands in his. "Jocelyn, this isn't the end of the world. Nothing happened tonight that you should be ashamed of. If anyone is to blame, it is I. I apologize for disregarding your weakened emotional state. However, I won't apologize for giving you pleasure."

She remained stoically silent, her hands wrapped in a death grip around the white linen sheets. Gently, he suggested, "Do you want to talk about it?" When her head jerked upward, he saw the shock reflected in her expression, realized the misunderstanding and stifled the urge to laugh. "The nightmares, I mean."

She turned her pink cheeks toward her lap, but undaunted, gently grasping her chin, he plunged onward. "Do you have the nightmares often?" Considering their chance encounters, he pushed further. "The dark hours of the night, perhaps? You abandon sleep, seeking solace with the piano, reading in the library?"

When she didn't answer, he felt his frustration bubble. This was no time for anger. Calmly, he said, "Trust me, Jocelyn. Talk to me. I'm not the enemy."

"I know. It's been such a long time since anyone cared."

He tucked a wayward curl behind her ear. "Let me help you."

As if she were relinquishing a white flag, she sighed her surrender. Still lost within her own thoughts, she asked, "Do you believe in hell?"

He paused before he responded, knowing the answer mattered a great deal. If he hoped to gain any insight into his wife's past, he had to choose his words with care. "If you're asking me if I believe in a nether world for evil-doers, I honestly don't know. If you want to know if I have experienced my own personal hell, the answer is yes." Yes, he had battled the night, the oppressive darkness, until, as a man, he had learned how to cope with his own personal demons.

She seemed satisfied with the answer and rewarded his persistence. "My nightmares are manifestations of my time spent at Bedlam, enhanced by a goodly dose of fear and imagination." Once she uttered the first few words, her story flowed like a torrential downpour, filled with furious determination bent on cleansing the wounds of her mind and soul. "I'm running endlessly, fleeing down corridors that lead nowhere. Hiding. Screaming. I hope for, pray for, help, escape, even death, but no one ever hears." She dragged in a breath. "Then, the hands appear. Fleshy bare fingers, tugging, groping, hurting. There are never faces, only amber, glowing eyes, vacant and evil. Then the laughing begins. Shrill, piercing laughter, reminding me *he's* waiting. Waiting to find me and kill me." She paused. "But this time I'll be ready."

As she shuddered, Reyn pulled her into his arms with the ferocity of a doting father. Her words churned through his mind. He, whoever he was, appeared to be the threat, the impetus for her charade. And what was she ready for? This man's return, his attack? God, how he wanted to ask questions, though he knew he'd receive no answers.

Stunned by the intensity of his feelings, he cradled her within his embrace, long into the early morning hours. He fervently wished for two things: her complete trust and the presence of the man responsible, for he wanted nothing more than to beat her tormentor into a bloody pulp.

Chapter Eleven

No visible signs showed: nonetheless, the changes existed. They came from within. Changes, basic and elemental, like the sunlight that drifted through the bedroom curtains. While Jocelyn sat at the dressing table, studying her reflection in the mirror, she recognized her strong attraction for her husband for what it was. Last night, she had surrendered to her passion, but more important, in the light of day, she finally accepted the truth.

She loved Reyn.

Defining how and when Reyn had managed to wriggle his way into her heart really didn't matter. He was arrogant, manipulative and dictatorial, but she knew he could also be tender, charming, witty and honest. She harbored no foolish illusions about a permanent relationship: too many unresolved hurdles blocked the path. Nevertheless, as if drawn against her will, she found herself choosing a path she had never thought possible. She had always believed she would marry for love, and never would she commit herself to a relationship without it. Reyn didn't love her; in fact, he didn't believe in love at all. He'd said so a number of times, but evidence, especially after last night, proved that he wanted her. She was willing to grasp whatever form of happiness she could, while she could.

The brush froze in midair, for her lack of experience with men left her bewildered as to how to proceed. Did she continue to spurn his advances? What if he grew weary of the game and returned to his mistress? What if she became the aggressor? With that thought came an even greater dilemma. How did one seduce a man? Life at the convent had never prepared her for this sudden uncontrollable surge of desire. Placing the brush on her dressing table, admitting she had hidden in her room long enough, she started downstairs with a great deal to think about.

She halted in the doorway, both embarrassed and thrilled when she found her husband lounging in the salon with his grandmother. When he realized her presence, he greeted her with a lecherous grin, brimming with mischief. Instantaneously, her body remembering their shared intimacy, his fiery kisses, his gentle caresses, her stomach quivered, her cheeks flushed, her temperature rose, and drat the man, he knew it.

With his hand extended, Reyn rose, and like the moth drawn to the flame, she went to him. Lightly entwining her fingers in his, he placed one seemingly chaste kiss across her knuckles that sent her senses spiraling. Oblivious to the presence of Lady Agatha, she leaned toward him.

He whispered seductively into her ear. "Today is the letter V. I have selected Vivian after the enchantress in Arthur's legend. A rather alluring name that conjures all sorts of images. What do you think, Vivian? Can you control a man with a sigh, a look, a promise to fulfill his deepest desires?" As his seductive words floated by her ear, Jocelyn sighed and drifted closer to Reyn. "Yes, my sorceress, give me a kiss to welcome the new day, or shall you fulfill my fondest dream and take me upstairs to complete our business from last night?"

Agatha interrupted with her usual flamboyance. "Do cease fondling one another. Vivian who?"

"Never mind, Grandmother," Reyn said as Jocelyn jerked herself a safe distance from him.

"Well, come along, Reyn, we have things to do. I have come to review the final plans for your wedding ball."

Reyn muttered something under his breath.

Grasping the opportunity, Jocelyn fled to an isolated chair across the room. Holding a special soireé had been Agatha's idea. Reyn had loudly argued, Jocelyn had politely balked, but Agatha would not relent. Three days hence, the Duke and Duchess of Wilcott would be officially honored as man and wife.

Perhaps, Jocelyn thought, if she ignored Reyn completely, he would leave, forestalling further discussion about the previous night. She still needed time to decide her future. "I believe all the arrangements are in order, she said to Agatha as she seated herself. However, it would not hurt to make sure." She innocently cast a contrived smile at Reyn. "I imagine it could take hours."

The morning of the belated wedding ball arrived, and Reyn hid behind the locked doors of his study in a futile attempt to avoid the mayhem that overtook his home. At every turn, his peace of mind was thwarted by bakers, decorators, musicians and servants hustling to and fro in preparation for the night's activities. Even thoughts about his wife intruded into his mind, which caused him greater frustration. He could try to locate her, but she would simply find an excuse to avoid him. He frowned when he remembered how easily she had eluded him the last three days. It was clear she had decided not to trust him. Yet.

Assessing his options, he decided to take a long ride, then escape to Boodle's for a hand of whist. Darting between musical instruments, crossing over garlands of flowers yet to be hung, and pinching a ripe piece of fruit from a tray, he maneuvered through the hall. He froze when he heard his wife's laughter. He hadn't meant to eavesdrop, but he grew curious to know who her guest might be. He heard the one voice that could immediately send him into a frenzy. Reyn virtually attacked the salon with the single-minded logic of a mule.

"Just what the devil are you doing here?" He knew his abrupt entrance had startled Jocelyn, for she jumped from her seat, searching for the source of his ire. She didn't wait long. Reyn growled between clenched teeth. "Get out, Rodney."

The tall, gangly man unfurled his limbs and slowly rose from the settee. "Dear cousin, charming as ever, I see."

Unaware of the hatred between the two men, Jocelyn scolded, "Lord Wilcott, that is not a proper greeting for our guest."

"Guest? I think not." Reyn sneered as Rodney, stroking his bearded chin, had the audacity to laugh. Reyn pointed to the door. "You know the way out."

"Reynolds, old boy, did Agatha neglect to inform you of my visit? Tsk, tsk, a bit forgetful she is. I'm here to celebrate your marital bliss."

Reyn, ready to physically throw the flea-bitten weasel out by his over-sized ears, advanced as Jocelyn stepped between the two men. "Your cousin has been invited to stay for a day or two. I know you will make him feel welcome."

Reyn shook his head, assimilating the words he had heard. He snapped an angry retort. "I don't want him in my house, my stable, or my privy. For that matter, I don't even want him near my dog."

"We have no dog here in London."

"Fine, I don't want him near that damn cat," he stated emphatically while he pointed to Caesar, who lounged beside the fire. He decided then and there that his wife was in dire need of a reminder of her responsibilities, such as to honor and obey. "We do have a cat, don't we?" he needled. Satisfied by her barely audible response, he kept his eyes, filled with silent warning, fixed on hers. "Good. He can go."

The visitor, fingering the lace cuff at his wrist, watched the quarrel with fiendish delight. "It would seem the two of you have a few differences to resolve." Rodney continued with a nasal rasp. "I would hate to have the newlyweds harping at one another during the night's festivities." With a courtly bow and a sweep of his dusky brown hat, Sir Rodney Sithall left the room.

As Reyn turned to Jocelyn, agitation vibrated from every pore of his body. "Do not countermand my order. Ever! Do you understand?"

Clearly defiant, she crossed her arms under her breasts. "What I understand is that you are an ill-mannered cretin. How could you? That man is your cousin."

"A fact I try to forget daily." He wanted to throttle her for her ignorance, then kiss her senseless. Watching her color rise, her pouting lips pucker, he felt his body stiffen like a hundred-year-old oak. Annoyed at his undisciplined reaction, he nagged at Jocelyn. "How do you know my cousin?"

"While you were away, he introduced himself at the theater. I will have you know he has been exceedingly kind."

He reeled from her defense of the scum and closed the gap between them, nearly tripping over the black cat, who had suddenly shown an interest in their presence. Caesar wrapped himself about Reyn's legs. "Not now, you black devil." He turned to Jocelyn. "Define 'kind,' if you would."

Standing her ground, she sighed with annoyance and tapped her toe in agitation, an immediate invitation for Caesar. The cat struck out wildly for the foot dancing beneath her dress. "Caesar, stop it. We will play later."

Reyn harumphed.

Jocelyn said, "This is ridiculous."

His eyes narrowed as she divided her attention between him and the cat. "I quite agree, but humor me." He thought she puffed up like an over-stuffed guinea fowl.

"Rodney provided friendship, conversation, loyalty, trust, acceptance and companionship."

Reyn almost laughed at her sterling opinion of his cousin. What a poor judge of character. "And what have you provided in return?"

"I beg your pardon?" she asked, distracted by Caesar's efforts to gain her attention.

First, he was going to kill the cat, then he was going to beat his wife. "Cat," Reyn hissed, "you will sleep in the cellar and dine on beetles and mice for the next month if you don't leave us alone."

Rolling to his back, his golden eyes fixed on Reyn, the cat seemed to consider the threat. With a sudden twist, he landed on his feet, his tail and head held high, yawned, and lazily marched from the room.

Reyn muttered. "At least someone in this household remembers who is master." He turned back to Jocelyn. "You were saying."

"What did you ask again?"

"I asked what you gave to Rodney to win his kindness and generosity." She continued to look confused, and his words came smoothly, purring softly into her ears. "Come now, Jocelyn. Surely, Rodney indicated his purpose, expressed his desire for something. A favor, perhaps. From you?"

"No, I don't recall him asking for anything."

For a moment, Reyn relented to consider the situation. Perhaps her only crime was her naiveté. "I am telling you, that bastard never comes calling without a cause. He wants something, and he wants it badly to risk coming here after our last encounter. He knows I will not yield a farthing to him, so he must assume you will." A lurid vision struck him like a runaway carriage. "You. Of course. That lecher wants you." Another perverse thought crossed his mind. With narrowed eyes edged with accusation, he uttered his misguided assumption out loud without thinking. "Unless he has already had you."

If it was physically possible, her eyes darkened to pitch black, hot color raced up her neck, but she stood perfectly still, her hands fisted. Reyn thought her appropriately subdued until she kicked him soundly in the shin and stomped from the salon.

His mouth hung open in dumbfounded shock. Recovering rapidly, feeling her actions were unjustified, he allowed his anger to explode. He followed her into the kitchen with deadly precision. Reyn barged through the door, shooting a frigid glance at the staff, who gladly occupied themselves with tasks. They filtered from the room as Jocelyn inspected a silver tray of fruit tarts.

"That, my sweet, was a foolish thing to do."

She kept her gaze focused on the tray on the large oak table. "Go away, I have work to do."

His body, pulsing with bridled fury, held rigid, more unyielding than a well-crafted suit of armor. "I agree, one of which is to promise me you will stay away from Rodney."

Finally, she looked up from her task. "Put me in the picture, so I can understand. Give me something other than an order. Tell me why, Reyn."

He almost softened, hearing his name spoken in a

soft plea, but his need to establish authority was a volatile thing, ready to shatter if denied. With both arms on the counter, he held her prisoner to have his say. "Fine. Tell me who you are."

"One has nothing to do with the other."

"I disagree. We are talking about a matter of trust."

"This is not the time."

"Fine. I do not have the time explain my reasons to you."

"Well, I don't have to listen."

He didn't think her chin could possibly lift any higher. "The hell you say." Receiving her 'don't curse' look, he ran his hand across the back of his neck. "I am telling you that Rodney Sithall is trouble of the greatest magnitude. He is a lying, sniveling parasite."

"Surely you're exaggerating. He is young, without tact and polish, but he doesn't seem capable of any true wrongdoing."

"You are undoubtedly the most bloody-minded female I have ever had the misfortune to meet." Exasperated and weary of this discussion, he issued a final warning. "Jocelyn, I'm tired of this nonsense, so listen and listen well. Do not so much as give him the time of day, or so help me, you will live to regret it."

"Or what?" She challenged him as her finger jabbed his chest to punctuate each spoken word.

He grabbed her hand, brought her tightly against his chest, and lifted her onto her toes. "Do not press your luck. I am not in the mood. Heed my warning."

As far as he was concerned the discussion was over. If so inclined, he would offer a detailed explanation tomorrow. For now, she would obey him, for he would take no chances where she was concerned. Rodney Sithall, cousin or no, had earned his title of bastard over and over, lacking honor, loyalty and one bit of responsible behavior. He'd been kicked out of Eton. At eighteen, he'd compromised a young maid who supposedly killed herself when he refused to accept responsibility. Given a hard-earned commission in the navy, he was forced to resign six months later for cowardice and blackmail. No decent club allowed him admittance, for he cheated and ignored his bills. By the age of twenty-four, he'd squandered what little inheritance he had, his only acquaintances petty thieves, whores and smugglers. The final blow came five months before, when he was suspected of raping and murdering a young working girl from the docks. Reyn gave him a draft for five hundred pounds, informed him he could freeze in hell hereafter but he needn't bother returning to the Wilcott fold for any reason. Rodney's bitterness could lead him to extremes in retaliation, and Reyn vehemently believed that Jocelyn now held the whoreson's attention. The fact that Rodney had spent time with Jocelyn sent his shattered nerves wild with worry and anger. The little fool had no concept of the monster she dealt with.

"You are behaving like a backyard bully. You seem to forget I'm not your wife. Not really. I will do as I please."

Wrenching free, she ducked beneath his arms with no more regard for him or his words.

He followed her into the pantry and pressed her against the wooden shelving. "A minor detail that can easily be remedied. In the eyes of the law, you are my wife. You chose to make it so, and I have allowed you to remain as Lady Wilcott, although you continue to give nothing in return. Not the truth, not a name, not a glimpse into your danger. Not even the common courtesies owed to a husband. Although I thought we had established this the other night, I obviously need to remind you to whom you belong. You are mine, and you will do as I say."

Unaccustomed to giving explanations, he opted for action, pulling her into his arms. Lips, bent on mastery, descended with purpose, as if her submission to his kisses would bring about her agreement.

The moment his tongue touched hers, the urge to fight flew away on gilded wings of pleasure. Her body ached for the pleasure his caresses promised, her acquiescence complete as she pressed her arms possessively to the firm contours of his buttocks. She urged him closer, eager to cradle the rock-hard evidence of his desire between her thighs.

A growl accompanied the frenzied battle taking place as Reyn lifted Jocelyn to bring the tips of her breasts level with his mouth. Deep breaths, moist from passion, floated across her nipple as she waited for the pleasure to deepen. He held her body at bay. One nip with his teeth and she shuddered.

"Is this what you want, Jocelyn?"

Lost in her delirium of wanting, she was speechless.

"Say it. Do you want this?" he prodded, teasing the tiny bud with his tongue.

His restraint brought her desire to a fevered pitch and she supplied his answer with a cry. "Yes, oh Sweet Agnes, yes."

Thankful she wore no buttons or ties, he easily leaned her over his arm, tugged at her bodice with his teeth and bared two rose-tipped nipples eager for pleasure. The sweet torture seemed endless. The throbbing between her legs increased, almost painfully. As if sensing her need, Reyn shifted her back against the sacks of flour, ignorant of the bits of white dust that drifted over them. He raised her skirt above her waist to shift his attention to the downy nest, sweetened by her body's own moisture. As he dipped into the warmth, her hips greedily thrust against his hand, straining, climbing, to reach the summit. His tongue plundered her mouth, matching the rhythm of his hand until she conquered the peak with a shattering climax that left her breathless.

When the wild pounding of his heart began to slow, Reyn lifted his chin from the top of Jocelyn's head to find himself at eye level with a myriad of bottled jams, fruits and vegetables. He grimaced as realization struck full force. He had practically made love to his wife in the pantry of his own kitchen. But no matter how badly he wanted to unleash his anger, one look at her swollen lips, her stunned expression of satisfaction, and he simply restored her clothes to their proper place. He said, "Our relationship is far from typical, but if you have any doubts about who you are and to whom you belong tonight, remember this." With a tenderness greater than the oceans were wide, he kissed her once again.

A rainbow of colors floated past Jocelyn as the lords and ladies of the *ton* danced, laughed and consumed food and wine. Jocelyn clung tightly to her husband as he twirled her with gentle ease, joining the others in the belated wedding celebration. The few times they danced were the only private moments they shared since their encounter in the pantry. That tempest this morning had accomplished nothing, other than provide more titillating gossip for their staff, and establish Reyn's ability to reduce her to a quivering ball of wanton flesh. Although she knew Reyn considered the problem with Rodney resolved, she had never relented. Feeling bullied and ignored, she lashed out, purposely flaunting a fondness for his cousin Rodney all evening. She knew it was foolish, for she held the one man she would ever want in her arms. Her good sense had been overcome by her pride. If only Reyn would apologize or explain. The thread of their unspoken truce was near breaking.

"Enjoying yourself?" Reyn asked indifferently.

She kept her response polite, yet strained. "The evening seems to be a success."

He glanced around the ocean of silks and satins, searching for someone. "Have any long-lost relatives asked for a dance or two?"

Clenching her teeth, restraining the insult on the tip of her tongue, she smiled angelically.

He raised his eyebrows in question. "It would appear that you, duchess, are the new crown jewel. Even my dear cousin continues to dote on you."

His eyes held no malice, but neither were they warm and welcoming. Although she longed for any reason to end the bickering—a simple apology, a brief explanation—none was forthcoming. "I will not ignore the man. It would not be right."

"Jocelyn, all I ask is that you trust me and stay away from him."

"Why?"

"He is a worthless piece of garbage. That's why."

"And that should explain everything?"

"Yes! I do not feel that I am asking for the moon. My request should not matter so greatly to you unless you care more for him than you say."

Furiously, she stared at him. How could he possibly think that, especially after her uninhibited response that very morning? He asked for her trust, yet yielded nothing. If he expected the worse, so be it. "Yes," she lied, oblivious to the physical warnings of his body, the trembling of the crescent-shaped scar beneath his eye, the rigidity of his muscles. "I enjoy Rodney's company immensely. He does not question my every action, or call me silly names that mean nothing. Nor does he attempt to trick falsehoods from me. In fact, I wish I could spend more time with him."

"Be careful what you wish for, my dear."

"What are you going to do?"

"Simply what you want. Have a splendid evening, wife." He hissed his final words and abandoned Jocelyn halfway through the waltz in the middle of the dance floor.

Barely finding her footing, she smiled outwardly, as if nothing had happened. Without so much as a backward glance, her husband fled to the card room, where he remained for the balance of the evening. She saw him once more after the guests had left. With his hat in his left hand, a bottle in his right and a sneer on his face, he left the house in the company of Walter Hathaway, who could only shrug his shoulders. She hoped he meant to take care of Reyn.

When Reyn didn't return, she went to bed and drifted into a fitful sleep. In her dreams, wishing he were there with her, she smelled fetid brandy and the pungent odor of a cigar.

Reyn had returned.

As she sat up, the shadowed face leered from the foot of her bed. Instinctively, she pulled the bedclothes tightly to her chest. "You!"

Rodney's thin lips curled into a snarl of a smile, void of humor, saying nothing, speaking volumes.

She shuddered. "What do you want?"

Deliriously trapped within himself, Rodney swayed against the bedpost to mutter incoherently, "Hates me, he does. Bloody nob. So high and mighty. Tells me what to do and all. Whatever he wants, he takes, he wins. Never makes a mistake. But no more."

Although she had a fair notion, she asked, "Who, Rodney?"

"Blackburn the righteous. My bloody noble cousin." A demonic smile sent a trickle of panic down her spine. "He's still gone, you know. He made a mistake, and tonight I'll be the one doing the taking." He seemed to really notice her for the first time. "You should have been mine, Jocelyn. He doesn't love you like I do."

"You're right. He doesn't love me and I don't love him." The man teetered briefly toward Jocelyn as she attempted to calm her trembling voice. "Let me call Briggs. He can show you to your room."

With the agility of an alley cat, he swept around to the end of the bed, pinning her arms high above her head. "Oh, no, my pet. We'll have no need for anyone this night."

"Wait!" she cried as she struggled to loosen her arms from his painful grip.

"I've waited long enough. I need to be a part of you, make us one, just like him. Each and every night, when he lies beside you, he'll remember that I kissed your lips, caressed your body and gave you my seed. If only fate would intervene and make you with child. He'd hate that, you know."

Knowing what he planned, she had to do something, and sought the words that might appease him. "Reyn and I don't share a bed. We never have. He won't care, not really. Would he have left tonight if he did?" His resolve seemed to falter. Desperate to get help, she sweetly said, "I had no idea you cared for me, Rodney. You and I could go downstairs and talk."

"You've never consummated the marriage?"

"No. Let's go down—"

He started to laugh. Maliciously. "That's even better."

His rapid breaths fell closer to her face, and realizing he was beyond rational thought, she started to scream. A clammy hand descended to trap her plea for help. As she began to struggle in earnest, he continued to laugh, a thin, reedy sound that sent shivers down her spine. With his free hand, he pulled a scarf from his coat pocket to stuff into her mouth. "We wouldn't want to be interrupted, now would we?"

A paralyzing terror swept through her body. She listened to his idle ramblings, watched his trance-like moves and pleaded with her eyes. Somehow, she had to make him stop, even though she knew his mind had closeted itself within the darkness of demented reasoning.

Saint Dywn, please help me.

"You're going to like this, my sweet," he babbled as he secured her arms to the bedpost. "From the moment I first met you, I knew you wanted me, knew it would be like this." Traveling to the foot of the bed, he wrenched her legs apart only to pull two additional scarves from his coat, applying to her legs the same treatment as her arms. "You were meant for me. We were meant to be together. My cousin will regret everything he has ever done to me." The rending of fabric alerted her to impending doom as he bared her from head to toe. With dilated pupils, he assessed her body with a diabolical thoroughness.

To escape Bedlam and now this. She tried to fling herself from the bed, but the ties held fast. *Reyn, why didn't I listen to you? You warned me, and now I will pay a horrible price.*

Slowly, his hand slid up her legs, between her thighs, across her belly, to fasten onto a breast. The bile rose in her throat.

Don't let this happen.

Panting now, his mouth descended to suckle.

Reyn!

Her body buckled from the bed, but his madness was oblivious to her futile attempts to escape. She thrashed from side to side, fighting with all her strength until one hand eased from its binding. Breathing deeply, fighting a scream, she forced herself to relax and accept his vile invasion.

Lost in his own twisted self-satisfaction, Rodney moaned. "Yes, my darling. I knew you would welcome me. I cannot wait. I must have you." His hands dropped to the buttons of his breeches. "Tonight you'll be mine."

When his manhood leaped from confinement, Rodney closed his eyes with a shudder and an expansive sigh, and stroked his hands repeatedly over his own heated flesh. Filled with revulsion, Jocelyn turned away and saw the one thing that might save her. So as not to be noticed, she slowly edged her hand toward the small pair of embroidery scissors lying on her bedside table. Rodney dropped to cover her completely. She grasped the scissors firmly, raised her freed arm above her attacker, and plunged them into his back.

"You damned little bitch," he said, jerking from the bed. "Do you think this will stop me? I will still take you!" With venom in his eyes, he reached to free the small weapon from her hand. "I'll teach you to try those whore tricks on me." His hand, red with blood, descended with the power of an anvil. Pain exploded in her head. Again and again, he slammed her body with excruciating accuracy. A final thought crossed her mind as she succumbed to the pain.

Reyn. Where are you?

Chapter Twelve

Disheveled and blurry-eyed from a night of drinking, Reyn ascended the stairs. Caesar howled a high-pitched whine as he paced in a frenzied circle outside Jocelyn's bedroom door. Noting the cat's erratic behavior, Reyn suppressed the prickling sensation at the nape of his neck. "I see you have fallen from her good graces as well."

When Reyn knelt down to absently stroke the cat, Caesar wriggled between his legs. "If she had listened to me and stayed away from Sithall, all would be very different right now. I only wanted to protect her." As if confessing his sins to a priest, he continued. "I'm not am ogre. I had my reasons. She only needed to accept my better judgment and trust me." He laughed at himself. What a dunce. Trust. He had expected hers, but had yielded nothing of his own. Abandoning Jocelyn on the night of their very own marriage ball was more than stupid. Brilliant strategy, he thought, for a man bent on seducing his wife.

"Blast, I'll likely have to apologize and begin this courting business all over again." Caesar interrupted, mewling furiously. Reyn frowned at the cat. "Splendid. I have been reduced to talking to a bloody feline."

When Reyn attempted to pass by, Caesar, his black tail whipping from side to side, clawed at his trouser leg. "Have a care, cat. If she wanted you with her, you would have been admitted by the lady herself."

As if Caesar understood, he turned tail and ran back to paw the closed door. "Fine, you black devil. It is your furry backside that will suffer if you wake the sleeping princess. I will pretend complete ignorance."

Quietly opening the door a small fraction to admit the cat, Reyn hesitated when he heard a muffled sound. Curious, he widened the opening, stunned by the scene before him.

"Sweet mercy," he whispered before thundering a tortured cry for help.

He ran to the bed and yanked the gag from Jocelyn's mouth, careful of the bruises and blood covering her face. "Darling, can you hear me?"

Scanning her bare torso for additional injuries, he winced when he noticed the spattering of blood between her legs, and cursing himself for ten times a fool, he gently draped the covers over her naked body. "Dear God, forgive me."

A ragged word escaped her lips. "Rodney."

Sitting by the window in her room, leaning her forehead against the cold panes of glass, Jocelyn felt as miserable as the day promised to be. After eight days of rain, she felt the depression swell once again. Along with it came guilt and shame. What a fool she had been. So close to happiness, only to throw it away. And for what? Her stubborn pride.

The painful memory, that tortured morning, flashed before her eyes. Reyn hovered above her, and she easily recognized the undiluted revulsion etched on his handsome face when he realized the extent of her injuries. Her face, swollen from Rodney's punches, suffered a great deal of pain, as did her ribs. What alarmed her most was her naked state and the bruises on her legs. When she sat up, witnessing the blood that marred the insides of her thighs, she knew the source of Reyn's disgust. After two days and Dr. Dilby's approval, claiming her wounds mostly superficial, Reyn banished her to Wilcott Keep to recover.

With her retreat from London, Reyn had stayed behind to search for Rodney. Upon his arrival at the Keep six days later, he'd informed her that his cousin hid somewhere in the city. When found, word would be immediately sent. No other discussion about the events in London, save a perfunctory question regarding her health, ever took place.

"Good morning, madam."

Jocelyn pushed the gloomy images from her mind, and having grown accustomed to the motherly attentions Dora offered, she weakly smiled at the sound of the servant's shuffling entrance. A rotund bundle of love and joy, Dora had coddled and cooed over the new duchess for two weeks. As a member of the staff since before Reyn's birth, she also brooked no nonsense in the running of the Keep, or its residents.

"Show a leg, mum. Enough of this sulking. Go downstairs for a bite to eat. It ain't healthy to be hiding up here."

"Dora, I hate this rain. I want to go outside."

"Not today, luv. Not with this nasty bit of weather and you still on the mend."

Jocelyn knew there was little point in discussing the matter. "I feel much better. Surely, a short walk would be beneficial, even restorative."

Clucking her tongue as she often did, glancing out the window, Dora said gently, "Not with those clouds gathered over the high ridge of the Pennines. The weather can change as quickly as a cat trapping a mouse. You'll just have to be happy to catch a glimpse of the outdoors from the turrets. Off with you. Breakfast is waiting."

Dejectedly, Jocelyn stood above the great hall that still revealed a large portion of the original castle design. Over one hundred feet in length, the room boasted massive rafters twenty feet in the air with four fireplaces to provide heat to the divided sections of the room. The sitting area, separated into cozy groupings of chairs, tables, rugs and screens, occupied over half the room. Another portion hosted tall oak bookshelves and a billiard table framed by gas lamps, which left the section utilized for dining where her husband happened to be sitting.

When she descended the stairs, her hand trailing the wooden banister polished by years of use, she wished life could run as smoothly as the aged wood. She approached the long planked table. Reyn immediately stood, folded a note and placed it in his coat pocket. He delivered a courteous nod and prepared to leave. Looking splendid in a pair a fawn-colored breeches and a loose-fitting shirt, his frank rejection reminded Jocelyn of the things she would never have: his love and understanding.

"I will be gone most of the day," he said.

"Will you return for dinner?"

"I'm not sure."

"Perhaps we could play chess later."

"I doubt it."

"Reyn?"

"Yes?" he said impatiently.

Toying with the fringe on the sleeves of her dress, she sought a topic to prolong their conversation. "Dora mentioned that you received a post from London."

"Jocelyn, I must go. Tam is waiting."

Hang his annoyance. She didn't care. She matched him stare for stare. "Was it of any import?"

He dropped his eyes down to his hands, which held the back of the chair in a death grip. "Rodney is dead. It appears that in his haste to escape my wrath, he held true to form and retreated into the dangerous sanctuary of St. Giles. It seems a creditor or business partner or a common thief chose to slit his throat."

She gasped, then grabbed the edge of the table. More trouble lay at her feet. Due to her actions, Reyn's relative was dead. "I'm sorry."

"I am not inclined to discuss Rodney right now. I must go."

"But—"

"Enough. Good day." His boot heels clipped along the stone floor. The discussion was over.

Jocelyn fought the urge to call him back, to demand that he talk to her. As the front door slammed, feeling alone and desperate, she kept her eyes fixed on the tasteless food set before her. This silent conflict had to end. The few terse words were typical of their conversations. They spoke to one another only when necessary. Her fear of what Reyn might say or do if she pursued the subject always clamped her tongue as easily as a vise might. Her guilt, which fell heavily on her shoulders, increased daily. His continued withdrawal chilled her to the bone more than the bleak weather. He had to be furious with her. Why didn't he scream or rage? Anything. Instead, he tightly locked his emotions away, but she saw the occasional haunted look when he thought she wasn't looking. Like two lost shadows, they drifted without feeling, thought or substance. Although he barely acknowledged her existence, as if she might disappear if ignored long enough, Jocelyn felt his presence vibrate throughout the walls, hating her, blaming her, condemning her. Knowing he felt that way caused her more despair than she had thought possible.

And now, she bore the responsibility for the death of his cousin. Well, she thought, she felt no remorse. She was glad Rodney was dead. He deserved to die for what he'd done. And Reyn could go to the devil if he blamed her. She was through feeling sorry for herself.

Suddenly, the gray stone masonry, artfully carved ceilings, newly whitewashed walls, family portraits, the lavish surroundings that had once provided solace, converged on her from all sides. The sanctuary became her prison. Fresh air and freedom became a necessity.

Seeking escape, she grabbed a cloak from a peg in the kitchen and fled into the cold, misty day, where she aimlessly wandered, unconsciously settling on her destination. Too late did she realize her folly. She had walked a great distance from the manor, oblivious to the increasing intensity of the storm. Her clothes, now soaking wet, offered no warmth, leaving her little choice but to seek shelter and wait for the storm to break.

Welcoming any excuse to escape Wilcott Keep, hoping to purge his foul moods and Jocelyn's presence from his mind, Reyn spent a backbreaking afternoon with Tam, inspecting their coal mines. Hell would be better than facing Jocelyn every day when he knew she despised him. Had he not fallen prey to his arrogance and traipsed off with Walter, he could have protected her. Even Rodney's death did little to assuage his conscience.

Like a disobedient wolfhound drowning in water and mud, he sloshed into the Keep, shaking droplets of water from his coat. When Briggs appeared in the foyer, Reyn said, "I can't remember a spring storm this fierce."

Briggs shuffled from one foot to the other while Dora peeked from behind his back. The somber expression on both their faces, coupled with the dry cloak, gloves and boots hanging from his butler's arm raised Reyn's curiosity. "What is the matter? You both look as if you've lost the family heirlooms."

Nervously, Briggs swallowed. "It's the duchess, sir."

"Is she ill?" Reyn rapidly closed the space between him and the stairs.

"Wait, sir. She's not above. She seems to be missing."

Experiencing a sharp pain in his chest, his heart beating double time while his stomach plummeted into his boots, Reyn stopped directly in front of Dora. "Explain."

"It appears she left for a walk, and has yet to return."

"It's as dark as spades out there, not to mention that it's storming like Mercury's own mother is on the run."

"Yes, sir. I know, sir," Dora said worriedly.

"The men are looking for her," Briggs explained, "but have yet to turn a stone to her whereabouts."

Grabbing the fresh outer garment, Reyn said, "Have food and a bath waiting. If she returns, lock her in her room."

With that, he stomped from the warmth of the Keep, chilled by dire thoughts of Jocelyn suffering injury or worse. He would flay her alive, tie her to the bed—and what? That was the dilemma. He wanted her, desperately, completely, but knew she would reject his advances vehemently.

Yanking the reins of the fresh mount prancing on the cobblestone courtyard, he barked out additional commands and questions to the stable boy. As he leaped to the back of the black stallion, he racked his brain for any place Jocelyn might be. Suddenly, a memory triggered a possibility. He rode like the wind, praying she was safe.

Thankful for the tiny haven of shelter, Jocelyn huddled beneath the rock overhang, listening to the cascading water of the falls, and the uncontrolled chattering of her teeth. By this time, she imagined the household in utter turmoil over her disappearance. "Wonderful," she muttered, "another rash action that will surely cause repercussions."

She hoped that Reyn had stayed with Tam for the night. As she imagined his temper, if inconvenienced, having to tolerate her impulsiveness yet again, she heard Reyn's voice boom. Slowly, she edged into the open and answered his cry. Almost immediately, horse and rider crashed through the brush and came into view. Even beneath his heated gaze, she never saw anyone so magnificent.

"Give me your hand." From atop his horse, with the ease of a warrior, he lifted her up in front of him. A moment later, he had her cocooned within the warmth of his cloak.

She emerged long enough to sneeze. "You'll get wet."

"Rather behind the bush to think of that. I ought to turn you over my knee and spank you."

"I would not complain as long as you promised to warm me first." She shivered uncontrollably and automatically nestled closer to absorb the heat his body provided. Another unrestrained sneeze reverberated off his chest.

"If you catch pneumonia and die, I'm going to beat you every day for a month. Do you hear me?"

Smiling into his chest at the contradiction of his statement, she started to explain.

"Don't say a word. This childish behavior has persisted long enough. I'm in charge and I intend to see this ridiculousness settled tonight." He pushed her head back to his chest and closeted her from the damp night.

Upon reaching the Keep, Reyn carried Jocelyn upstairs. The household, anticipating her return, bustled with activity. Dora informed him that a fire and a steaming bath waited in Jocelyn's chambers. Tea and soup would be provided shortly.

Irritably, Jocelyn grumbled. "Put me down. I am perfectly capable of walking."

"Jocelyn, I am tired and wet to the bone. Cease your harping. You have caused sufficient trouble for one day."

"As if anyone would care." She sounded quite pitiful, she realized.

Searching her face, his eyebrows knitted in confusion, he emphatically stated, "Everyone was frantic with worry."

"Everyone except you," she whispered.

He spoke with total candor. "Especially me."

"There is no need to lie. I know what you think of me."

"Tell me then, how do I feel?" he asked as he kicked the bedroom door closed to set her down.

Shivering from the loss of body heat, she moved closer to the fire. The tears trapped behind her lids threatened to fall. "You despise me for invading your life. You blame me for my own reckless stupidity and foolishness in ignoring your warnings. I know that after Rodney's attack, my presence repulses you. And now, because of me, although I can't claim to feel pity for the man, your relative is dead."

Reyn spun her around and, with quiet efficiency, began to loosen the pearl buttons of her dress. "You know all that, do you?"

She whirled toward him, clasped the ruined bodice to her chest, and bravely challenged her husband. "I saw your eyes when you found me that morning. I know what I saw. And since that night, you have yet to say a kind word to me."

"Hmmmm." He refused to comment further. Before she knew it, her sodden garments lay in a pile at her feet, her body bathed in firelight. With quick, efficient steps, he crossed to the bedroom door. "I'll be back. I expect to find you in the tub. Then you and I can finish this discussion. And Jocelyn—you have no idea how foolish your assumptions are."

He left her alone to ponder his parting words.

After weeks of depression, self-pity and guilt, her emotions in a constant state of agitation, Jocelyn felt drained. The day had been exhausting and she still reeled from the phenomenon that she had held Reyn's full attention for more than a moment.

As the hot bath consumed the coldness permeating her body, she felt a tiny spark of hope settle in her stomach. Perhaps Reyn had forgiven her role in Rodney's death and decided to put the past behind them. But if not for Rodney's attack, then why the dark moods? She wondered if he grew weary of her continued deceit, or regretted his hasty marriage proposal. His change of heart could even be another ploy to loosen her tongue.

That depressing thought quelled any thoughts of a possible reconciliation. She scrubbed fast and furiously, wrapped in a downy wool robe, and sat by the fire to await his return. The door opened. She tightened the belt as if bracing her defenses. The time of reckoning was upon her.

"I've brought you some soup and tea, but first I want you to drink this." Handing her a warmed brandy, he sat across from her. Reclined in the high-backed chair, legs crossed at the ankles, dressed in fresh clothing, he appeared well rested but no less fierce. She feared that he was simply waiting to attack, waiting for her guard to drop. Blast him. Why did he have to look so disciplined, so incredibly handsome? "Feeling better?" he asked while rolling his own crystal snifter between his fingers.

"Yes, thank you." *Coward,* she mumbled to herself. Now that the moment had arrived, her determination for confrontation dwindled. A bite of a warm buttered roll melted in her mouth.

"Can you talk and eat at the same time?"

Offering no response, afraid that any words might betray her anxiety, she continued to eat.

"Do you consider me a shallow man?"

She nibbled on her lower lip before she answered. "No."

"Then how in God's name could you believe I despise you for the actions of a demented blighter like Rodney?" He had finally misplaced his rigid control and bellowed at her. "No, do not speak. Simply continue to place food into that delectable little mouth and listen." Standing now, he paced the length of the room. "I blame no one except myself for what transpired that night."

"You?"

"Yes, me. Rodney possessed a warped sense of right and wrong, and had balanced precariously along the edge for years. When he finally crossed the line, I think he found he liked the darker side of life. He has courted death for some time now. It was his own deeds that killed him, not you."

"I still feel responsible."

"By the saints, Jocelyn, the man deserved to die. Whoever drew the knife has my gratitude. It saved me from having to perform the task. I suspected Rodney wanted you. Whether out of revenge or lust, I do not know. Perhaps a bit of both. I didn't consider him to be so devious, though, as to attack you in my own residence. I allowed my anger and arrogance to cloud my better judgment. Something, I might add, that never happened before I met you. There are few people who blatantly disobey me as you chose to do, and I lashed out. I wanted to hurt you but I never wanted, never thought—" He stopped, unable to form the words.

Jocelyn sat motionless, contemplating what he had said. "For weeks, you have ignored me, avoided my attempts to converse, refused my apologies. Excuse me if I find it difficult to accept this grand confession."

Majestically, he stood before the hearth, one hand resting on the mantel, the other tucked neatly in his pocket. "I thought you detested me for abandoning you that night. I failed you."

"You failed *me?*" She rose from her chair like steam from a kettle. "I suspected the truth of your warnings, yet I ignored you. I openly flirted with that man. I taunted you, mocked your authority, and you tell me you failed me?"

"I agree it is rather magnanimous of me. Nevertheless, it is the duty of every husband to overcome the shortcomings of his wife, and protect her."

Although spoken in a lighthearted manner, she knew he believed what he said. He should have been there to save her from her own foolishness. Regardless of her irresponsible behavior.

"Speechless? Amazing." He grinned. She yawned. "Come, climb into bed. I can see I have exhausted you with such noble thoughts."

"How can you dismiss my actions so easily?"

"Jocelyn, I will say this one last time, then the subject of Rodney closes. You are not to blame. I should have explained my reasons that afternoon in the pantry. I didn't. I left you and Rodney to your own devices. I should have dealt directly with him, not you. His life was crashing down about his pointed ears and he knew I would not help him. He chose to betray me in the worst manner any man could. For that I will always be sorry."

As weariness seeped into her body, she fought the sensation. "Thank you."

"For what?" he asked when he held back the covers of the bed.

"Everything. It has been a very long time since someone sought to protect me."

Patiently, he pulled the satin spread to her chin, and sat beside her. "I know you are afraid of something or someone, and believe it or not I have managed to take care of myself for a very long time. If given the opportunity, I will take care of you. I want to." He clasped her chin in his hands, forcing her to look at him. "Trust me, Jocelyn. Trust me and give us a chance."

Ready to weep, she knew he risked a great deal with those few words. "I can't. Not yet." Immediately standing, he seemed to wrap himself in a wall of indifference. "Please," she beseeched. "If you truly forgive me for what transpired with Rodney, I wish this discord between us to end. Can we not return to the way we were before?"

"Exactly what was that? Enemies, acquaintances, fraudulent husband and wife? Players in a game of deceit. There is nothing to be gained by returning to the past, Jocelyn. Only the future awaits us, and as long as you refuse to let me help you, I will continue to question, to wonder, to speculate on your motives."

Rodney's betrayal was no longer the issue. She believed that and feared an even greater chasm created by her silence and her need for revenge. Yet she couldn't bring herself to tell him about her step-uncle. She knew Reyn well enough to know he would place himself directly in Horace's path in order to protect her. She couldn't allow that. She also realized the depth of Reyn's vulnerability and knew she had to make amends now, or lose the opportunity to close the gap growing between them. Scrambling to her knees, she reached for his arm to delay his departure.

"Friends. And perhaps more." Poised above her, his handsome features masked all expression. In that moment, she knew what she wanted, needed. "Make love to me."

"What?"

Growing bolder, she pressed her hands to his face. "Make love to me."

He withdrew as if scalded. "Jocelyn, you must have

straw in your head. The last few weeks have been overly stressful. You're exhausted and don't know what you ask."

"Stop treating me like a mindless dolt. If you recall, I have already lost my virginity. I have nothing left to lose, but much to gain." She could see the indecision wavering in his eyes. "Please. I would have answers to my questions."

Tentatively, almost afraid to look into the black velvet eyes that gazed warmly at him, he asked. "Such as?"

"Can you truly find pleasure with me after Rodney's attack?" She edged closer. "Will I please you like other women you've known before? Although I know little about the ways between a man and a woman, I know you want me. I was afraid at first, until I realized I wanted the same thing." She placed her fingers on his arm, watched the muscles twitch beneath his shirt. "And for all your barking and scowls, I know you to be a gentle lover."

When her eyes found his again, she saw a brooding man with a seriously disturbed expression painted on his face. Her mistake was obvious. This man felt nothing for her, least of all desire. Not anymore. *Idiot,* her mind screamed.

Feeling the need to bolt, seek a dark corner to hide and cry, she collapsed on the bed. She drew the covers to her neck, staring at the cross-stitch pattern on the quilt. *Blessed Saint Dwyn. Please forgive me. You have been more than obliging, and here I am prepared to once again take something from you. I apologize for my—*

As if he'd just run a great race, Reyn's breathing turned shallow. "Your what, Jocelyn? Your candor? Your passion? Your lust for carnal knowledge?"

"No. Yes. Oh, I don't know what it is exactly," she said defensively. "Oh bother, that's a lie." Raising her face to his, she spoke defiantly. "I do not apologize for how I feel, but rather for my foolishness in believing that you might feel something for me, a spark of—"

"Desire, Jocelyn? Blind, mind-dulling lust?" He was shouting now. "Jocelyn, my lust is so great, I'm surprised my eyes aren't permanently crossed. My fondest wish is to taste your lips until you open your mouth for me. Kiss your nipples to life. Caress every inch of your body until both of us are mindless. To bury myself so deep within your womb, you see nothing, hear nothing, feel nothing, except me. Is that what you want?"

He was so close to her, she could feel his breath upon her face, smell the strong masculine scents of heather and brandy. She could only manage reedy bits of air to escape from her mouth, her mind frantically absorbing his comments.

A gentle hand tucked an errant curl behind her ear. "Rest."

"Rest?" she squeaked. "Now?"

"Yes. I will see you later. We will finish this discussion then." A faint smile tugged at his mouth over her apparent disappointment. "I promise." He bent to place a tender kiss on her lips.

She almost laughed at the suggestion that she rest. She almost ordered him to stay. She almost cried at the intense sensation of loss. Instead, her mind drifted peacefully into oblivion and she slept, dreaming of unfulfilled promises.

Chapter Thirteen

Jocelyn felt as though she were floating like a leaf on a warm summer breeze. She yawned and slowly emerged from the sleepy fog to find herself tight within Reyn's embrace at the top of a spiral staircase she had never seen before. An ancient wooden door opened before her. When Reyn carried her across the threshold and into the cylindrical tower, she gasped. Hundreds of flickering candles perched on tiny ledges climbed the stone walls. A circle of open windows near the ceiling allowed the fragrant scents from the passing rainstorm to fill the room along with an owl's cry, an occasional cricket's song and other sounds of night. In the center of the room stood an ornately carved dais of mahogany that supported an enormous bed draped with an assortment of plush furs. Huge satin pillows in the vibrant shades of spring decorated the bed.

As she reasoned out the purpose of this nocturnal excursion, her body thrummed in anticipation. She whispered, afraid any sound would break the enchantment. "Is it real?"

"Very." Reyn's husky voice tickled her ear. "I told you I would see to you later. I always keep my promises."

"What is this place?" she asked, still in awe.

"This, my dear, is the creation of my great-grandfather. During his later years, to properly satisfy the maids in his bed, he felt he needed a bit of magic to aid his cause. A gypsy recommended he build a special chamber specific to her instructions, guaranteeing the results, of course. This is it."

"What in particular makes this room so special?"

"The dimensions from the length of the bed to the space between the candle ledges on the walls are proportional to a certain part of his anatomy."

"I don't understand."

"Ah," he said in a drawl, "my little innocent. I can only say, my relative must have been generously endowed and gifted."

"Truly?" She couldn't understand how a body part enhanced a man's lovemaking skills. She glanced around the chamber, looking for a clue to his explanation. "Did the room serve its purpose?"

"According to stories, he died a happy, sated man, a grin forever etched upon his face."

"Was the room beneficial to the ladies?"

The corner of Reyn's mouth twitched. Jocelyn thought he might laugh, though she couldn't imagine why. She tilted her head, raised her left brow and waited for an answer.

Settling Jocelyn amongst the lush furs, he tenderly kissed the frown from her brow. "The last thing I wish to do is discuss my relative's sexual prowess."

Aware of everything about her, she savored the luxurious feel of the fur on her skin, nestling deeper into its softness. Reyn's expression abruptly changed to the dark and stony lord she knew and loved.

"You little minx. Do you have any idea what you do to me?" he asked as he sank to the bed on one knee, his arms framing her shoulders. "I intend to make love to you gilded by moonbeams and candlelight."

Her entire body quivered, from the top of her head to the tips of her toes, as she remembered his sensual kisses. She cradled his cheek with the palm of her hand and said, "I feel as though I'm dreaming and will wake to be gravely disappointed."

"If you continue to watch me like that, I'm likely to forget my vow to go slowly and take you like an untried lad. Then we'll both be disappointed. Are you sure about this?"

Passion blazed in his eyes, and her breath quickened. In her heart, she knew she wanted this time with Reyn. No matter the consequences. "Very."

He dropped his forehead to hers. "Thank God. You have no idea how long I have dreamed of this." Slowly, he slipped each button of her nightgown loose. As he smoothed away the fabric, he spoke, his voice ragged. "You are so beautiful."

Reyn gazed at her breasts, saying nothing. Although she had lost her virginity, the actual mating between man and a woman was foreign to her. Dark oblivion had claimed her before Rodney's final assault. Reyn continued to stare. Her anxiety grew. At a loss what to do, she tugged the lace edges of her gown together. "Wait. I do not remember anything that happened with . . . you know." She turned her face away from his. "I don't know what to do."

With gentle ease, he clasped her chin and encouraged her to look at him. "Jocelyn, you have nothing to fear and certainly nothing to hide. I have experienced your natural taste for passion. Nothing but pleasure will come from this night. For both of us." He brought his lips to hers with the skill of a painter, brushing lightly, testing the texture of his canvas.

At first, Jocelyn lay uninvolved, weighing the sensations gathering throughout her body. As the pressure of his kiss increased, so did the hunger in the pit of her stomach. He continued to kiss her. Long, deep, drugging kisses that explored every recess of her mouth. Kisses meant to entice and conquer, that transformed hunger into a ravenous craving demanding to be fed. Masterful kisses that obliterated any shy thoughts or fears until she no longer cared or questioned the actions of the man who hovered above her.

Her skin felt flushed, and suddenly her nightgown seemed too confining. She returned his kiss with equal ardor and eagerly welcomed his hands on the remaining pearl buttons.

When he bared her breasts a second time, Reyn groaned. "I vow I will go slowly, no matter how badly I want you." With his thumbnail, he gently circled first one puckered nipple, then the other. "I cannot believe I waited this long to make love to you."

She arched her back slightly. He bestowed soft, teasing strokes down her throat, across her collar bone to her breasts, brushing the tips until she whimpered for more. He settled to suckle her right breast while his hand fondled the left. She pressed into his hands, needing his touch, thinking she'd die if he stopped. Back and forth, he alternated his attentions until he slid his hand downward, slowly dragging her nightgown lower, exposing her body. Even the night air didn't cool her desire. "Wait."

His hand on her thigh froze. His body glistened in the candlelight. "Lord, Jocelyn, please don't tell me to stop. If you've changed your mind, I'll simply have to change it back again."

Hoping her actions weren't too bold, she whispered shyly, "I only want to see you."

Reyn grinned, his relief apparent. Eagerly he shed his shirt, carelessly tossing the garment to the floor. From behind half-closed eyelids, he watched her tentatively stroke his chest. He pulled her back into his arms and buried his face in her neck. The dark, crisp matting of hair covering his chest teased her nipples. The hair at his nape felt luxuriously soft. And as her hands drifted lower, the bulging muscles of his back and tight, rounded buttocks provided interesting planes to explore. Drawn to the unknown like a conquering adventurer, eager yet uncertain of what she might find, she traced the raw power of him that pressed against his breeches.

Reyn gasped at her tender inquiry as if scalded. He stood beside the bed to quickly discard the rest of his clothing, then let her look her fill.

She gaped at the man before her. She had seen him without clothes before, felt his manhood pressed against her thigh, but confusion mixed with years of lessons in proper ladylike behavior had restrained her open appreciation of his body. Tonight, she savored every naked inch of him. He was beautiful. Hesitantly, she reached out and touched him.

"Sweet mercy, Jocelyn."

She snapped her hand back to her side. "I didn't mean to hurt you."

He dropped to his knees on the bed. Perspiration dotted his brow. He kissed her fingers. "Oh, darling, it's not really pain. More like slow torture. But enough for now, my love. I've simply wanted you for too long. It is time we advanced your lessons." He evidently saw the questions in her eyes. "Jocelyn, this is not the time for modesty. Know that everything we do is natural between a man and a woman."

"I trust you, Reyn."

He groaned, lay back down beside her and brought his mouth down to hers. Hard. Once he added her nightgown to his discarded clothes on the floor, his fingers sought and found her heated core. Matching the rhythm of his tongue, he tenderly prepared her for his invasion.

"Oh, blessed saints," she cried. She never imagined, couldn't believe men touched women like this. Although her mind fought such intimacy, her body surrendered, allowing her traitorous thighs to open. Insensible love words like a litany joined the incantations of her body while she arched shamelessly against his hand. She felt as though her entire body were on fire, ready to burst into flame. Still Reyn assaulted her, insisting she respond. When her world exploded in ripple after ripple of undiluted passion, she cried out his name.

He covered her body completely with his. "Jocelyn, look at me." His eyes bored into hers with a look she dared not defy. "Whatever happened before, nothing matters. From now on, you belong to me."

"Aye, my lord," Jocelyn said. His simple admission, electric with emotion, shot a tremor through her extremities as she felt the blunt hardness of his manhood probe her femininity. She pulled his head down for another kiss. All her senses coalesced into this single moment. She smelled the primitive scent caused by their lovemaking, saw the flickering candlelight, tasted the sweat on her upper lip, heard Reyn's harsh breathing, felt the sleek, taut heat of her body stretching, knew the shocking instant when he possessed her completely. She rejoiced in the joining.

Reyn raised himself on his elbows and looked directly at her. "My God, Jocelyn. Are you all right?"

Why did he appear so stunned? Surely, there was nothing unusual about their lovemaking. She wanted to shout to the heavens. Now she truly was his wife. Tenderly, she kissed his eyes, his nose, his lips. "Reyn, I am perfectly fine. I believe, sir, you are a sorcerer."

Dropping his chin to her forehead, he spoke. "My dear wife, it is you who have bewitched me." Gradually, he withdrew, only to sink into her depths again, watching her every response. "You sang your siren's song and captured me." Another slow, deep thrust followed his words, and she raised her hips to his in an attempt to preserve the link. "Not so fast, sweet." Retreating and advancing with the tactical skill of a major general, Reyn controlled his ardor, unwilling to yield to her growing physical demands. "I have suffered dearly and intend to extract every ounce of pleasure from both of us."

Faster. Deeper. He increased the pace as her body again began to hum with pleasure. Giving. Taking. Eagerly accepting his powerful lunges. Like a creature of the night, her cries of ecstasy blended with the sounds that filtered into their mystical domain.

After his final thrust, spilling his seed deep inside her, Reyn collapsed to the side, taking her into his arms in a tight, possessive embrace.

With her head tucked against his chest, Jocelyn slept the sleep of the dead. Reyn, on the other hand, lay wide awake, deep in thought. She'd been a virgin. A blasted virgin. Had he not been the one to breach her maidenhead, he wouldn't have believed it possible. He had seen the virgin's blood smeared across her thighs himself. A multitude of questions and assumptions trod across his mind, but the mystery would have to wait.

He cursed. Why hadn't he bothered to question her before? He knew the answer. He'd been a coward. Feeling responsible, he'd been afraid to hear the gruesome details from her lips, along with her rebuke.

For weeks, he swore he wouldn't make love to her until she told him the truth. Bent on seduction as a means to find answers to his questions, he found he had been the one to be seduced by her innocence, her sincerity, her warmth and intelligence. Not to mention the fact that he wanted her in his bed. Badly. Even then, he hadn't planned on making love to her. Not until she gave him answers. He had told himself Rodney's attack had changed that. He had wanted to erase that nightmare from her mind, to tutor her in the pleasures of the body. He scoffed at the idiotic rationalization. He would have made love to her anyway. He'd lost the silent battle tonight when she offered her tender revelations. She had sealed their fate. She was his.

Jocelyn curled into him. Like a stallion sensing a mare's need, he responded. With his randy body wishing she would wake, his mind knowing she needed to sleep, he climbed from the bed. The covers slid to the side to reveal high, firm breasts, a narrow waist, rounded hips and long, graceful legs, as well as a small mole on her left buttock. *Who are you? What is it you fear? What am I to do with you?*

Expecting no answers, he crossed to the small brazier in the corner, stirred the fire and warmed a damp rag with the heat. As he cleansed away the proof of her innocence, Jocelyn sighed, lifting herself against the cloth. Even in her sleep, she caused his blood to boil. Ready to forget his decision to let her sleep, he sighed. She needed rest. Being a patient man, he could wait. For her. And the answers to his questions. He stoked the fire one last time, then slipped back into bed.

As the faint light of dawn warmed the room, Jocelyn stirred. Reyn pulled her into his arms. When she pressed her body to his, he was stunned by the powerful urge to bury himself deep inside her. Before lust seized control, he wanted answers to his questions. He kissed her brow. "Feeling better?"

Trapped in the fading haze of sleeplessness, she yawned, then smiled. "Describe better."

He playfully tweaked her nose. "Enjoyed yourself, did you?"

His words seemed to snap her awake. Her face

flushed a lovely shade of red and she pulled the covers tightly to her body. "Thank you," she said evenly. "Since my previous experience is best forgotten, I appreciate your kindness."

"Believe me, kindness had nothing to do with tonight. Considering my body's enthusiasm, I imagine I will show you how kind I can be again. Quite soon. But first I must ask you something. I would like to know about that night. What exactly do you remember about Rodney's attack?" Reyn felt her tremble in his arms and silently cursed his stupidity. "I know I never asked before. My behavior was inexcusable, but if you feel up to talking about it, I would like you to tell me."

"Now?"

"Only if you like." She nibbled on her lower lip and twisted the edge of the satin sheet. Reyn thought she might decline. He pulled her closer to his side, providing his warmth and, he hoped, his strength. He felt her nod against his chest.

"I awoke thinking you had returned, only to find Rodney standing at the foot of my bed. He seemed strange. Agitated. I tried to calm him. He was drunk, Reyn. His mind was not right. I knew something was horribly wrong when he began to mumble this and that about revenge. He blamed you for all his troubles, said he was going to use me to get back at you."

That flea-infested mongrel.

"After gagging me, he bound my hands and feet. Then he touched me."

I would gladly castrate the bastard if only I could.

"I tried to fight. Somehow I managed to free my hand. I grabbed my sewing scissors from the table and stabbed him."

The blood.

"He was furious and he hit me. After a bit I simply blacked out. Thankfully I can't remember the rest."

Reyn's hands knotted into fists. His face contorted

with deadly rage. *Gullet him, castrate him, then kill him all over again.*

With her fingers, Jocelyn tenderly circled his brows, down to his lips. "It is over. I survived. Tonight, you obliterated an ugly, vile memory into nothingness."

He muttered, more to himself than to her, "If you only knew." He hesitated a moment. "Jocelyn, about tonight. I'm sorry—"

She interrupted. "Sorry? For what?"

"Jocelyn—"

"No! It wasn't your fault," she snapped. "I practically served myself to you on a silver platter."

"Just hold for a moment."

"Now that you know the truth about that night, you've changed your mind. I knew I should never have told you anything."

"Jocelyn, you were still intact." He felt like a bungling idiot as he struggled for the right words. "Unsullied, untouched." Blankly, she stared. "Rodney did not take you." Flustered by her puzzled look, he burst out, "You were a virgin."

"A virgin?"

"Yes."

"But how? I saw the blood. You saw it, too."

He knew exactly to what she referred. "The only plausible answer I can muster is the scissors. The wound you inflicted must have been greater than you thought. Unable to perform the deed, the bastard, knowing me all too well, planned his revenge by planting the evidence to make it appear as though he'd raped you."

Excitedly, she whooped and threw herself into his arms, planting tiny bites and kisses along his jaw, neck and shoulders.

"What the devil?" He grabbed her hands and lifted her away. "Jocelyn, didn't you hear what I said? You were a virgin. You deserved the right to know before I made love to you."

"Nonsense. From all external appearances, we made the same assumption. I refused to let the doctor examine me, so how could you have known?" Tenderly, she brushed her lips across his. "Thank you for a wonderful gift."

Disconcerted by her unconditional praise and acceptance, he opted for a more lusty comment. "I should have stripped you of your clothes and dragged you to my bed the first night we met."

"Hah! Floundering in your tub, I smelt like last week's fish. I looked pathetic," she teased. "A wisp of smoke possessed more substance than I."

He relaxed, exhaled a cleansing breath. Everything was going to be all right. "Perhaps I sensed the fire beneath the smoke. I admit I did not succumb to unrestrained lust that first night," he conceded when she stared in disbelief.

"No small wonder, being the scarecrow that I was."

Lifting her chin to gaze openly at her, he said, "You amaze me. Most women would prefer to flay my backside. I said some nasty things." He fingered the red-gold curls tumbling about her shoulders. "You must understand. I enjoyed my bachelorhood and was unprepared for marriage that day." Lecherously, he wriggled his eyebrows. "However, the first night at Blackburn Hall . . . "

"Yes, I remember." She sighed, contented to lie beside the man she loved. No tender words, no promises, had been spoken. She expected none. She would gladly take each moment as it came. What was meant to be, would be.

"Who is Phillip?"

Gasping, she had to fight for a breath of air. "Who?"

"Phillip. You called his name while you were asleep."

The question, asked so nonchalantly, stunned Jocelyn. The implications were staggering. Like a ray of sunshine before a storm, thoughts of love and possible future harmony vanished. Her defenses armed, ready for battle, she jumped from the bed. "Is this your idea of mastery? Lull me into complacence with soft words and tender embraces, then when I least expect it, attack?"

Reyn abruptly sat up in bed and grabbed her wrist. "What is the matter now?"

He sounded like a wounded animal, but now that she had her wits back, she would not fall prey to his verbal games. "Let go of my arm. I wish to return to my chamber."

He tumbled her back to the bed and trapped her beneath his body. "Jocelyn. Trust me for Heaven's sake. I only want to help."

His body instinctively reacted to their close proximity and, recognizing the subtle changes, Jocelyn began to fight. "Trust? You ask for my trust?" She laughed, a hollow, haunted sound. "I just gave you my body, something not done lightly, and all the time you thought of ways to question me. You think such underhanded conduct deserves my trust?"

"I assure you I was not hatching questions when I buried myself so deep within you that our hearts merged into one. Excuse me for being a bit curious if, after making love to my wife for the first time, she calls out another man's name in her sleep."

His words did nothing to appease her anger. She brought her knee up toward his groin. He dodged in the nick of time and launched his own assault. "You are now my wife, in every sense of the word. I think it only fair I be told the truth. Jocelyn, I want to help you."

"And perhaps I want to keep us alive."

Sitting back on his haunches, he continued to press her to the bed with his body. Both his arms folded across his chest. "What the bloody hell does that mean?"

Let him rot for all his demands. She would give the man no satisfaction by answering. She turned her head to the wall.

He sighed. "Arguing with you could turn a sane man into a loon in short order. If you recall, your last stubborn, prideful tantrum brought devastating results." He hovered close to her face again, his breath fanning her ear. "Listen and listen well. If you are in danger, I will protect you. If I am in danger, I can damn well protect myself."

Straining for freedom, she pressed her hips intimately against his aroused flesh. For a moment, she closed her eyes.

"No comments?" he prodded.

Her lips thinned into a tight line of defiance.

"I see. I shall have to find another way to persuade you to my way of thinking. I believe you need a lesson in wifely obedience." One hand held her to the blankets as the other circled her breast, drawing the nipple to a taut peak. The other obeyed as well. "Look, Jocelyn. Your body knows what it wants, what it needs, what I can give."

His hand drifted between her legs to find her body moist and welcoming. Massaging the soft flesh, he dipped into her warmth, only to withdraw and bring his fingers to his lips. "You're already wet. Your body trusts me even if your feeble woman's mind does not. Shall I take you into my mouth this time? Taste your very essence? Or shall I thrust so deeply that you forget where you end and I begin?" As he spoke he did just that, plunging hard and true to ravage her body with slow, thorough strokes until her soft pleas repeated themselves, over and over again. He brought her to the brink of satisfaction, then pulled free to place his mouth over her and, using his tongue, brought her to the towering pinnacle and forced her over the edge. With wild abandon, she bucked beneath his lips while her body exhausted itself. Hoisting himself above her, determined to pleasure her again, he entered her in search of her soul. This time his cries of ecstasy matched hers.

Chapter Fourteen

"By the toes of Moses, you're whistling like a young hobbledehoy."

Cheerfully, Reyn greeted his friend as he entered the massive hall. "Good morning to you, too, Walter."

"I haven't heard you whistle since you were a young toad experiencing your first suckle of a young lady's breast," Walter admitted, his brow knitted in confused wonder. "Did you see that, Innes?"

Sitting beside the billiard table, waiting for Walter to take his shot, Tam witnessed Reyn's jaunty approach. With a grin as wide as a door, he said, "For weeks, his gloominess has proved as prickly as a hedgehog. In fact, just yesterday, he nearly killed his horse, drove the fear of God into several miners and yelled a serving wench into a near frenzy. I doubt his change in mood has anything to do with our esteemed presence, Walter, so I can only surmise what has caused such a noticeable turnabout." He directed his question to Reyn. "Am I correct?"

"What?" Walter ranted. "Correct about what, Innes? Damn and blast, man, if you know something I don't, it is your duty to enlighten me."

Grabbing the cheroot from the nearby table, Tam watched Reyn from beneath half-closed eyelids, drew a long breath, then exhaled. "I'd wager the Rock of Gibraltar that the Duke of Wilcott, Reynolds Blackburn, spawn of the devil himself, a man abhorrent to the holy state of matrimony, spent the night in the arms of his wife. Consummating his marriage."

"I'll be damned," Walter Hathaway managed to sputter. "Is that true?" While Reyn remained annoyingly tight-lipped, Walter shouted with laughter. "No wonder you're up and about so late this morning. Well, it's about time, my friend. I was beginning to fear for your good sense. I can't imagine how you tolerated these last months as it was. Had it been me, I would have succumbed to lust ages ago, regardless of the circumstance. But then again, your willpower has always put mine to shame." Walter slapped Reyn's back. "You must be back in your boots again."

Unable to resist the infectious good humor, Reyn chuckled. He did feel wonderful, his body replete from the night spent with Jocelyn. His only regret was that he had left his wife sleeping when he discovered he had guests this morning. There was still her mysterious past to solve, but his determination had increased by yards. Today was a new beginning for them. He would earn her confidence, learn her secrets and protect her, even if she fought him every step of the way. It was ludicrous for her to believe her silence kept him safe.

"Good morning."

Jocelyn's greeting halted any other thoughts. As she waltzed into the room, Reyn thought she glowed like a shooting star.

Only a slight glimmer of apprehension hid deep in her eyes. Eager to dispel any misgivings or regrets, wishing he could greet her properly, he traversed the floor and placed a light kiss upon her lips. She blushed a lovely shade of rose. "Good morning," he said, maintaining his grip on her chin. He uttered for her ears only. "Are you well?"

Nodding, she whispered, "I didn't know we had guests. You should have wakened me."

He exhaled a regretful sigh. "That would not have been the most prudent of choices. A fact that agitates me greatly." She stared at him blankly. "After I delivered you to your bed, I was gravely disappointed when I discovered I must leave you alone to entertain these two. I craved another type of sustenance altogether. I anticipated nibbling on something other than dry toast this morning."

She graced him with a sensual pout as she toyed with a small button on his shirt. "Breakfast in bed? What an interesting idea." Glancing at his lips, she added, "I think I would like to try that sometime."

The blatant innuendo hurled his body into turmoil, his brain ringing like the parish bells on Sunday. Lurid images that would probably shock Jocelyn to her toes set his pulse to pounding. Had it not been for the harsh cough that reminded him of their guests, he would have carried her back upstairs and gladly fed on her delicious little body for another week or so. "Blast," he muttered under his breath, spinning rapidly toward his friends. "Were you two leaving?"

"Reyn," she gasped in mortification.

"Trust me. You needn't worry about their tender sensibilities."

Tam seemed to sense Reyn's dilemma. His voice held a tinge of laughter when he said, "Perhaps we should plan an outing for the day. All of us together."

Reyn growled a feral sound. "Not bloody likely."

Barely concealing his chuckles, Tam continued, "Down, boy." He addressed Jocelyn. "And you, my fair lady, have you plans for the day?"

"I hadn't really thought that far."

"She does," Reyn declared.

"She does?" Tam asked.

"I do?" Jocelyn asked.

"You do." Reyn said, his feet braced apart, openly challenging anyone to contradict him.

"What exactly do I have planned?" she asked.

Reyn crossed his arms and boasted a warning scowl as dark as his favorite boots. "A picnic." Both Tam and Walter howled with laughter, eliciting another grimace of disgust from Reyn.

Jocelyn beamed like a new copper penny. "I think a picnic sounds delightful." Another bout of jocularity from the two visitors prompted a churlish retort from her. "And what do you find so humorous that you must behave like a brace of looned mudlarks?"

Tam raised his hands in defense. "Have pity on us, Jocelyn. We have spent time with your husband in a variety of pastimes and settings. Seedy taverns, rowdy boxing matches, horse races, boisterous games of chance. We simply have difficulty comprehending the Duke of Wilcott on a picnic."

Walter added his opinion to Tam's. "Fresh air, sunshine, nasty buzzing cockchafers, little sandwiches and bits of food on a blanket." Lewdly, he waggled his eyebrows at Reyn. "E'gads, makes one wonder what else he plans to sample." That comment brought forth a new round of laughter, scowls and a blank stare from Jocelyn.

Eager to have his wife alone, Reyn interrupted. "Gentleman, and I use the term loosely, did you cross my doorstep to darken my day, or was there a purpose to your untimely arrival?"

Tam sobered momentarily. "Actually, we came to ask if you were leaving with us tomorrow for London."

Reyn watched his wife's shoulders slump as she toyed with the fragile Dresden vase, her eyes cast downward in an attempt to conceal her reaction. "I thought I would wait a day or two to make sure Jocelyn felt up to the trip."

Meeting his gaze alone, her eyes sparkled like a child's given her first stick of peppermint. Knowing his announcement pleased her, he swelled with a contentment he hadn't experienced in years. The startling sensation almost sent him running for the door until he forced himself to remember that she was his wife, his property. Of course she would accompany him to London. If that pleased her, then so much the better.

"Will you sail or come by coach?" Walter asked.

Trapped in his thoughts, Reyn continued to study Jocelyn.

"Well, blow me down with a breeze." Walter smiled impishly. "Excuse me, Reyn, but the Prince Regent has just arrived, naked, a diamond the size of Buckinghamshire tucked neatly in his navel."

"Navel? Whose navel?"

Tam's baritone laughter filled the large hall, gaining the couple's full attention. "Never mind. Woody wanted to know if you intend to sail or take a coach?"

Shaking his head, Reyn knew he was acting like a besotted piece of milktoast, yet he could not remove his gaze from his wife. He answered the question with annoyed brevity. "We will sail with one of the coal shipments."

Tam grabbed his hat and cloak, nudged Walter from his dumbfounded stupor with his elbow and launched one last barb. "It would appear 'tis you and me alone, Walter. We have been easily forgotten and shall receive no other meaningful conversation until Boodle's or White's."

As the afternoon sun peeked between the leaves of the willow bordering the lake, Jocelyn sat on a thick woolen blanket, on the planks of a shallow boat, discreetly appreciating her husband's virility. He lay opposite her, his hands clasped behind his head. His hair, catching bits of light like sun-dried wheat, contrasted his dark lashes, which enhanced the tawny color of his skin. His body, lean and muscular, appeared rigid and immovable. She knew better. After last night, she knew the touch would be warm, even hot.

Her heart thudded rapidly in her chest. When she remembered how generous he had been, she was almost able to believe he cared for her in some small way. They had made love for hours, each time his gentle patience taking her to a higher level of sensuality and passion. This morning, when she rose and found herself alone in bed, she had felt an intense sense of loss. She couldn't imagine life without him, yet she knew she would have to leave him someday. She clenched her hands into tight fists. She could not change the future, but if they could forget her past for now, perhaps they could enjoy their time together.

Leftover bits of food lay on top of the wicker basket. A slight breeze scattered bread crumbs toward Reyn's trousers. It also swept a lock of hair across his forehead. Succumbing to the powerful urge to touch him, she leaned forward to brush the curl back into place. Reyn's robin's-egg-colored eyes banked with mischief and met her frank appraisal. His full mouth rose to a mutinous smirk.

"Have you decided which part you shall begin with?" he said.

"Begin what?" she asked suspiciously.

"Your meal." The sides of his mouth curved upward. "You looked as though you wanted to devour every inch of me."

She tossed a slice of bread at his head while snorting

in a most unladylike fashion. "You know nothing then."
In order to guard her secret reflections, she eyed a pair
of merlins nestled in the heather that skirted the water's
edge. "I was thinking of how ingenious you are. Who
else would hold a picnic in a boat on a lake?" As an afterthought, she added, "Besides, you were the one with
breakfast on your mind earlier."

"Hah!" He didn't believe her for a minute. "I wouldn't
mind, you know. I've had similar thoughts ever since
Tam and Walter left." He edged closer to her end of the
skiff. "I've never made love in a boat."

"And you shan't today." His hands, resting on her
knee, inched toward her now-throbbing center. They
couldn't possibly make love. Not in a boat. Not in broad
daylight. As her mind conjured the tantalizing image,
her pulse raced and her skin grew warm. "Reyn,
please—"

"Oh, darling, I assure you, there is no need to beg. I
am more than willing to comply." His hands reached the
apex of her thighs, gently cradling her sex. "Already
your body prepares itself. Doesn't it, Jocelyn?"

Speechless, she lay perfectly still. Resistance existed
only in her mind. Yes. She would eagerly welcome him.

He lifted himself to press his lips to hers. The kiss
burst into a war of passion, tongues plunging and retreating, simulating the lovemaking to come.

Her clothes seemed to melt away under the sun, delicate linen of pink and white gingham pooling about her
body. She had become shameless, she realized. Willingly, in the middle of the day, she sat naked in a small
boat concealed only by the weeping limbs of a willow.
Sister Mary Kathleen would have banished her to the
chapel floor for eternity if she'd witnessed this display
of earthy abandonment. It didn't matter. She was beyond thinking, concerned only with feeling.

Shivering in anticipation while balanced on her
knees, she began to slip the buttons, one by one, from

Reyn's shirt to place wet kisses on the golden skin. Last night, he had tended to her endlessly. Today, his pleasure became hers. When she uncovered a bronzed nipple hidden beneath the pelt of dark fur, her tongue traced gentle circles, wringing a groan of delight from Reyn. Her delicate fingers found the bold shape that strained against his breeches, and he seemed to extend higher and harder against her palm. It was heaven on earth to know someone so intimately, to share oneself so completely. The power of her touch became intoxicating. She captured his mouth again, teasing him with her tongue as he had taught her.

"Now, Jocelyn, now."

His voice sounded harsh and raspy to her ears, and she willingly complied, loosening the few buttons to take the hardened flesh into her hands, openly marveling at the strength and texture of his body.

Like a man possessed, he shoved his pants below his hips, collapsed to the bottom of the boat, pulled Jocelyn on top of him and thrust inside her. Beneath a clear blue sky, he taught Jocelyn the beauty of power and control as he held her hips firmly in his hands and established a blinding pace until they were both transported into blessed oblivion.

In the aftermath, moist from exertion, Jocelyn burrowed against Reyn's shoulder. Her sighs of contentment, mixed with her deep breathing, sent wisps of hair dancing across his chest. The turbulent emotions calmed, and she noticed the satisfied grin on Reyn's face.

Arrogantly, he said, "Do you think we left any water in the lake?"

Tensing, prepared to flee his hold and find her discarded clothing, she felt his arms tighten around her waist. He lifted her chin, forcing her downcast face toward his.

"Don't turn all missish on me. I am greatly pleased.

Passion becomes you. You looked like a wild fairy creature riding my rod."

If possible, she knew her entire body blushed three shades of red. How ridiculous, she thought. One moment she screamed like a banshee and the next hid like a rabbity spinster. If honest with herself, she doubted she would have stopped their lovemaking short of an army invasion.

She leaned on her elbows, her hair draped like a golden curtain around them. "Are you my mythical satyr, his lot in life to seduce young maids into unrestrained debauchery?"

He pulled her face toward his and reverently kissed her lips. "Yes, I believe it was my fate to seduce you."

Jocelyn shivered when a light breeze cooled her body. While leaning against the back of the boat, Reyn nestled her against his chest and draped a blanket across them. His hand drifted outside the boat, drawing lazy circles in the water.

"Do you believe in fate?" she asked.

"Such as puppets on a string with preordained lives?"

She thought he sounded as if the concept were contagious, like the pox. "Not puppets and not preordained. But suppose people are brought into our lives to teach us lessons and present us with choices. We select the different paths and depending on what we choose and how we act, our life unfolds before our eyes. More like divine serendipity. A little guidance, a little luck." She turned to see his reaction. "What do you think?"

"I think I shall make love to you again."

She batted him on the shoulder.

"I concede. I'll play your little game. If, in fact, there is this great scheme to life—"

"Divine serendipity."

"Whatever. What is your role in my life?"

"Perhaps I was sent to help you find joy in your life."

He tried to look offended. "Are you telling me that I

have a less than congenial manner? That my moods are not as jubilant as they should be? Do you not see before you a changed man?"

Although his voice was laced with amusement, she pretended to consider the question seriously. "I will concede a small improvement."

With his gaze wandering over her body, he lifted his hand from the water and sent tiny drops of water cascading down her breasts. When he smiled at her, she felt like a piece of succulent fruit.

"And is this grand plan beneficial to both parties?" he asked.

"Of course."

Like a harem sultan, noble and arrogant, he locked his arms behind his head. "Then I have completed my instruction. For surely it was my duty to turn you into a slave to my lovemaking."

She giggled like a five-year-old. "I don't think so." Sobering, she added without thinking, "Perhaps you have been chosen to teach me to trust men again." That certainly caught his attention, for he snapped his response.

"Personally, I don't give a tinker's toy if you ever trust any man except me." He pulled the blanket back to her chin, all amorous ideas temporarily displaced. Hesitantly, he asked, "Are there any men you trust, Jocelyn?"

Instinctively, she knew he wasn't setting a trap. She wondered what she should tell him. What she could tell him. Considering her options, she decided to share some of her pain and ease some of his worry.

"Two years ago, I would have said yes. Today, I'm not sure." One look at his dark expression, and she knew her glib answer only aggravated him. In resignation, she lifted her shoulders, then exhaled a cleansing breath. Settling herself against the back of the boat as Reyn did, she locked the blanket to her chest with her elbows. "When I was very young, I loved my parents a

188

great deal. There was laughter and the joy of feeling cherished. As I grew older, I realized most of the warmth came from my mother. She worked very hard to provide a happy, loving home. One night I found her crying. I was so confused and terribly worried that I demanded she tell me who hurt her. She never did. After my continual prodding and prying, she did explain the ways of men and women and marriage, her most fervent plea that I never marry for any reason other than love. After that, she still cried from time to time, but always behind a locked door. I came to realize that she never really loved my father, but she was always a perfect wife, hostess, mother. I began to blame him for her unhappiness.

"Then one day, my father told me he and mother were going away. I begged to go with them. I thought Mother needed me. Nothing I said could change his mind, so they left, promising to return in three days. They never did. The adult in me knows it wasn't their choice, but the child still feels betrayed. All I knew was they died, and things changed."

"Such as?"

"Life as I knew it ceased to exist. I was eleven."

Perplexed, he said, "Was there no one to care for you?"

She realized she had scrunched the blanket into knots and tried to relax. "A male relative saw to my needs. Men always seemed to be in charge, and they quite changed my attitude toward that half of the species."

He quirked his brow at the odd statement.

"Past experience taught me to have little use for men, and virtually no trust of their actions." Considering that she lay, naked, next to a man, she realized her life had indeed changed. She had taken a step in trusting someone the night she allowed Reyn to make love to her. It was a beginning.

Placing his hand in hers, he brought it to his lips. "I would have kept you safe."

A forlorn expression shadowed her features. "Yes, I believe you would have."

"Jocelyn."

She knew the subject he wished to broach and grabbed her chemise buried beneath them. "Please, don't spoil this." His steely glare did not soften her position. "I think we should change the direction of this conversation. It's your turn."

"My turn?"

"I just bared part of my soul, now you must bare yours."

With his lips curled in a lecherous grin, he threw the blanket to the side. "Can't I bare something less painful, like my—"

She threw his trousers at his naked torso. "No. Tell me about your parents."

He froze before he began jerking on his breeches, his movements a mirror to his emotions. "My father was a fool."

Stunned by the animosity in his voice, she stopped dressing.

"Don't misunderstand me. I loved him and he loved me as well. As the story goes, he loved a young girl deeply. The betrothal contracts completed, he sailed off for a quick business trip to Paris, bad luck prevailing, for he met Margaret Ridgeley, my mother. After a well-planned seduction on her part, my father, the bastion of honor, married her and sentenced himself to a life in purgatory. Contrary to your family, my lady mother, bless her cold-blooded heart, didn't relish motherhood or marriage. Once she produced an heir, fulfilling her responsibility to the dukedom, I rarely saw her. When she did grace us with her visits, she occupied herself with myriad activities, most of which excluded her husband and son. The duchess spent most of her time flat on her back in some other man's bed, or she adorned the salons of the good people of London. She was a beautiful, cunning bitch."

His speech, rapid and terse, continued as he pulled and tugged his clothes into place. "My poor, misguided father confined himself to Wilcott Keep, suffering a broken heart. His fiancée, the girl he'd abandoned, his true love, eventually married, but died prematurely. The duke, however misguided, blamed himself for his lack of honor, her death, his pitiful life. I believe he mourned his loss of love until he killed himself with alcohol. The day he died, we fought. A young man's battered hopes and his lack of control are a lethal combination. I said horrible things to him. Things I will never have the chance to apologize for. He died on my fourteenth birthday. Even then he carried a locket bearing the face of the woman he loved."

Jocelyn shuddered as the harsh cadence in his voice washed over her, the bitterness so strong, it seemed a tangible thing.

Jumping from the boat, grasping her arms, he lifted her to the spongy soil. She placed his hands to her heart, tears pooling in her eyes. "I'm sorry. You deserved better."

All expression ran from his face. "Perhaps." Distancing himself, he withdrew his hands and placed them at his sides. She felt that cold wall resurrect itself, stone by stone, and regretted her choice of topics. "We are a sorry pair. You obviously have no reason to believe in love or marriage. I have no reason to believe in men yet long for a loving marriage. What are we going to do?"

"About?"

"Us."

Although the detachment remained, some of the tenderness returned. "What do you want to happen, Jocelyn?"

"I know you want to help me. Part of me believes and

even trusts you, otherwise I would never have allowed you into my bed. The part of me born from years of experience fights me at every turn. I will not allow myself to be used or hurt again. Give me a bit more time. Let us to continue to be friends until I resolve my problems; then we can see where we go from there."

"And how long shall that be?" he demanded.

"I'm not sure." Placing a hand on his arm, she felt his hidden anger. "Reyn, if I could, if I thought it best, I would tell you everything. Trust me to make the right decision."

A winging curlew's lonely cry pierced the stark silence before Reyn answered. "For now, Jocelyn. But I believe there will come a time when half measures will no longer be enough. For either of us."

Chapter Fifteen

When the prick of the dressmaker's pin stole her thought, Jocelyn turned from her image in the three-paneled cheval glass to face Agatha, who sat in a beige brocade chair beside the blue curtain of the dressing room. The dowager sipped on a cup of tea and smiled.

"My dear, the gown is absolutely stunning."

"Truly, Agatha, I have no need for another dress."

"Pish-posh. I realize that my grandson has expanded your wardrobe most nobly since your return to London, but he wants something special for the Montgomery ball next month."

"What about the peach velvet?"

"You wore that last Wednesday to the opera." Placing her teacup on the silver tray sitting on the nearby table, Agatha said, "By the way, I applaud you for encouraging my grandson to attend. The transformation in Reyn is remarkable and I have you to thank. He has attended both those interminable balls and dinner parties. Quite amazing. Lord Dalton nearly crooked up his toes when you accepted his invitation last week. But getting back to the dress, the rose silk will do nicely. I think I will discreetly murmur the color of the dress to Reyn. He might find his way to purchase a matching bauble."

Jocelyn tilted her head to the side and pursed her lips in warning. "Don't you dare. He has spent enough already."

"Nonsense." Agatha waved her hand with the accustomed air of authority. "Reyn can well afford another ruby or two. Besides, it is his duty. Do you not agree, Chloe?"

"*Oui,*" agreed the petite dressmaker. "A woman must possess new gowns so her husband has reason to purchase matching trinkets of gems and gold. To refuse is to insult their manhood. *Comprendez-vous*, Madame Wilcott?"

Yes, Jocelyn understood exactly. Both women believed such drivel. Knowing there was no reason to argue her point, Jocelyn simply shook her head from side to side and peered, once again, at her reflection. The gown would be spectacular. She smiled, already anticipating her husband's reaction. When he witnessed the daring décolletage, he would throw a loud, masculine tantrum and order her to change. She would refuse, of course. Then, if she hoped to reach the Montgomery ball in a presentable state, she would make sure Lady Agatha accompanied them in their carriage. As she remembered the passionate lesson Reyn had already taught her while in their carriage on the way to the theater, Jocelyn flushed a shade of pink she thought might match the silk dress.

Chloe winked as she adjusted the final drape of the gown across Jocelyn's shoulders. "Ah, I see you understand the other purpose of a new gown. Your husband shall have a difficult time, *oui?*"

If possible, Jocelyn knew she flushed an even darker color.

Beaming, Madame Chloe unraveled her from the dress. "I will have the gown ready for a final fitting in three weeks."

Thinking of the precious moments spent above the stairs in their bedchamber—Reyn, the ever-patient teacher, her, the ever-adoring student—Jocelyn grew eager to return home.

She stepped from behind the privacy screen only to encounter Reyn's former mistress. The woman wore a stunning burgundy-and-black gown that displayed her charms quite nicely. With her lips curled, Celeste appeared absolutely thrilled to see Jocelyn. Jocelyn squared her shoulders and lifted her chin, trying to hide the sudden wariness clawing at her stomach.

Celeste strutted forward. "My, my. What do we have here? The new Duchess Wilcott."

The taunt in the woman's voice was evident, but Jocelyn refused to acknowledge who the woman was or what her relationship with Reyn might have been. Jocelyn innocently asked, "Excuse me. Have we met?"

"Not directly. I happen to be a friend of your husband's. Lady Waverly. Celeste Waverly. Perhaps he mentioned me?"

Jocelyn spoke casually as she attempted to pass. "No, I don't believe so."

Obviously determined to make a scene, Celeste blocked the exit. "Are you enjoying married life, Lady Wilcott?"

"Enormously. Good day."

Ignoring the dismissal, Celeste continued. "The benefits must be staggering." The woman eyed Jocelyn's simple blue muslin gown with distaste. "Especially for a country girl like yourself." She flexed her hand to emphasize an exquisite emerald ring that decorated her finger. "Reyn is always so generous with his favors when pleased, if you understand my meaning."

The emotions churning through her body, concealed

until now, began to boil inside her like water in a tea kettle. If she remained, Jocelyn would make a scene she would surely regret later. Wanting to jam the glittering bauble down the woman's throat, but choosing to ignore its significance and reveal her true feelings, Jocelyn calmly said, "My husband is always a gentleman."

Celeste chortled with amusement. "Oh, you poor thing, I hope not. By the way, how is Reyn this afternoon? Last night, he seemed a bit under the weather."

Tired of the malicious innuendoes, Jocelyn armed for a direct attack of her own. "Last night, my husband seemed fine. Downright vigorous, if you understand my meaning. In fact, when I left him this very morning," she said, flashing her own, recent acquisition from Reyn, a huge diamond surrounded by sapphires, "he was quite exhausted." She watched Celeste's face turn white, her features pinched with anger.

The dressmaker, silent till now, crossed to Celeste with a vibrant sapphire gown draped across her arm. "Welcome, Madame Waverly. Your gown is ready to try."

"In a moment, Chloe," Celeste snapped. She flicked a piece of lint from her dark broadcloth pelisse, and pressed her assault on Jocelyn. "Reyn always appreciated Chloe's talents. As is his norm, I see he recommended her services. He always enjoyed seeing his women dressed in the very best."

"Enough of this," Jocelyn muttered. The woman was purposely trying to start an argument. She wouldn't oblige, but neither would she remain here and act like a timid little lapdog. Somehow she needed to disarm the annoying female. "I see you use the word 'women.' I am not ignorant of my husband's activities, but luckily I count you among the numbers in his past. If you recall, I am now his wife, and we love one another quite dearly."

"Are you really that naive?" Celeste sneered. "Wife

equates to brood mare, but means little else when it comes to a man's needs." Tossing her head back, flaunting her lush figure, she added, "And a man like Reyn needs a great deal. Furthermore, if you believe he loves you, you are more foolish than I thought. Reyn is incapable of love. I always understood that."

No longer content to remain stoically quiet, Agatha grabbed Jocelyn's cloak. "Celeste, trap your tongue behind your teeth. I see you once again elect to display your lack of tact and manners. For reasons that escape me, you once occupied my grandson's bed. You were not the first, but you will be the last. He is happily married. Remember, you prowl the halls of the finer families in London out of the good grace of these so-called brood mares with whom I regularly communicate. I suggest you take your mewling elsewhere." She turned to Jocelyn. "Come, my dear. Reyn is waiting."

For a moment, Celeste stood dumbstruck, her mouth gaping wide, her hands fisted at her sides. She laughed a harsh, condescending sound as Agatha took Jocelyn's arm and ushered her to the door. "Are you so sure he is at home, Lady Wilcott? By all means, hurry home to your faithful husband."

Desperately wanting to hurl the glass lamp at the noxious she-cat, Jocelyn launched a parting insult instead. " 'Tis a blessed thing, Agatha, the numerous congratulations and warm wishes Reyn and I have received." She glared directly at Celeste. "Especially from the older, more seasoned women of the *ton*."

Her departure was majestic, her mood volatile. By the time they reached Black House, Jocelyn had convinced herself that Reyn had renewed his relationship with his mistress. Agatha sputtered and placated, before she eagerly departed to her own residence.

Jocelyn vaulted from the carriage, charged the house in search of her libertine husband and invaded his study like Napoleon advancing on Russia. Reyn reclined against his desk, dressed in black leather breeches with a flowing white shirt open halfway down his chest. A foil lay on the floor next to a discarded face mask, and his body glistened with sweat from a recent bout of fencing. At the moment, he studied a set of papers. Caesar, the traitor, lounged beside Reyn.

Slamming the door with enough ferocity to shift the pictures on the wall, Jocelyn grabbed and hurled a three-armed candelabra toward Reyn's head. Caesar leaped out of harm's way to the nearby chair. "Sorry, Caesar," she muttered, then faced Reyn again. "You ruddy bowdykite."

Other than casting a downward glance at the now-twisted piece of silver resting at his feet, he displayed no outward reaction. "I take it your fitting did not go well?" He turned toward the windows overlooking the street. "What do you think, Tam?"

In a crazed flash, her dress flaring, Jocelyn whirled around and gasped. Intent on fury, she had missed the lazy stance of Tameron Innes, who leaned beside the window. "Oh, blast." She turned her rage back to her husband. "You wretched thimble-rigger. You have the audacity to humiliate me? Mock me? Use me? You are lower than a piece of moss-covered rock."

Watching her speculatively through narrowed eyelids, he said to Tam, "Her insults need a bit of improvement, don't you think?"

Reyn's clenching teeth and flashing eyes should have stifled Jocelyn's bravado, but the detached dismissal as he addressed his friend incensed her to launch a well-aimed porcelain dish. It bounced off his chest.

Finally he snarled, "Jocelyn."

Tam edged toward the door, tamping down a grin. "In hopes of escaping unscathed, I think Caesar and I shall leave the two of you to settle this matter. Alone."

"No need to fear, Tam," she said as sweetly as honeyed bread. "Caesar knows I won't hurt him, and I have no argument with you other than your misplaced loyalty. I am sure you already know of my husband's peccadilloes. Why not stay and hear his gallant attempt at lies and deceit? You may learn something, or at the very least have yourself a fine chuckle over my naiveté."

"Oh, for God's sake," Reyn said irritably. "Cease behaving like an infant and tell me what bedevils you."

"You sanctimonious hypocrite." She continued to mutter insults while she searched for a new weapon.

"Jocelyn, I suggest you curb your tongue and your behavior, or I will be forced to take action. You will see just how 'gallant' I can be."

Deep down, she kept hoping for some reasonable explanation. Her reaction was unreasonable, but her temper now had a will of its own. Like a costermonger hawking her wares, she screeched, "My behavior?"

He took a threatening step forward. "And I promise Tam's presence will not thwart my purpose."

Grabbing the nearby foil, she clutched a pillow to her breast and assumed an offensive position. Caesar chose that particular moment to leave the safety of the chair and curl around Jocelyn's ankles.

Tam's laughter reverberated off the walls. Each heated participant rewarded him with a fierce scowl, forcing him back to the window as the silent observer.

"Put down the sword before you hurt yourself or that cat, and explain yourself," Reyn said as he watched Caesar from the corner of his eye.

Recklessly, Jocelyn advanced on her husband, waving the foil along with her insults. "Explain a certain diamond-and-emerald ring, or where you were last night." He looked dumbfounded, but needing to hear his complete denial, she baited him mercilessly. "How about Madame Chloe? Do you send all your wives to the same modiste? The same modiste you patronize for your mistresses' finery?"

"You are the only wife I have ever had."

"Do not ignore the issue, you insufferable adulterer. I have just one word to say to you." She raised her chin defiantly, ready to deliver her trump card. "Celeste."

"And?"

Exercising little skill and even less control, she waved the sword dangerously close to his nose. "You lecher, can you not think of anything else to say?"

"Enough!" he roared, his composed veneer finally slipping. "Put down the sword."

In a final act of defiance, she thrust forward when with lightning speed he grabbed the other foil, only to knock hers across the room and trap her within his arms. "Tam, witness this example of true marital bliss; but I forget, you once experienced this holy state yourself. I believe I have a greater understanding as to why you no longer hold a wife." Jocelyn struggled, trying to kick his shins. He quickly transferred her to his shoulders like a bag of oats, his foil dangling from his wrist. "If you will excuse us, Tam, I believe my wife and I have something to discuss. Will we see you tonight at the theater?"

"I'm not sure," Tam replied.

"Well, until later."

"Oh!" Jocelyn screeched. She heard the slight laughter in Tam's voice and the arrogance in her husband's. "How dare the two of you discuss the theater at this time."

Reyn slapped Jocelyn on her derriere while Caesar grappled with a loose ribbon on Jocelyn's slipper. Reyn spoke between gritted teeth. "Jocelyn, shut up. Caesar, get out of my way." Enough was enough. He needed to get this woman alone and discover the reason for her sudden attack. With that, Reyn marched from the study, climbed the stairs two at a time, all the while ignoring the flapping, screaming burden he carried as well as the gaping mouths of an astonished staff, who peered from doors and closets along the hallway. When he reached their bedroom, he slammed the door and dumped Jocelyn unceremoniously to the floor, her dress billowing about her knees.

"Oh!" she screamed, "this is unconscionable."

Leaning against the door, his hands crossed before his chest, he said, "My sentiments exactly. I presume you have a reason for providing yet another savory tidbit to be bantered about by our servants."

Briskly, she stood, mirrored his position and blurted her question. "Are you having an affair?"

Reyn could only stare, dumbfounded. Since she left his bed that morning, her mood had changed as dramatically as a spring day on the moors. Insulted by her accusations, he casually offered his instructions. "Mistresses are not the customary topic of discussion between husband and wife."

"Need I ask twice? Are you having an affair?"

How dare she. Hadn't their time together meant a thing? With an exasperated fling of his arm, Reyn's foil sailed across the room, landing with a thud in the center of a plaster rosebud on the wall. "Good God, what would you have me say?"

Snorting indignantly, she remained stubbornly silent.

"Fine. I never claimed to be a monk. Many women have shared my bed. Does that satisfy your curiosity, or would you prefer the specifics?"

"Where were you last night?"

"I told you. I met a friend."

"What was his name?"

"I see no relevance between then and now."

"How convenient."

"What the devil does that mean?" In frustration, he threw his arms in the air. "Jocelyn, I'm warning you. I grow tired of these childish, temperamental innuendoes. What is wrong?"

"Could it be you met your mistress last night? Celeste Waverly?" With a dramatic flourish of her arm, she said, "No need to answer. I saw Celeste today. She provided a fount of information."

"What did she say?" he snarled.

She held a defiant stance, her skin flushed pink with anger, her chest rising in a rapid rhythm. She was magnificent.

"It really doesn't matter. Have you seen her?"

Unbelievable. Unthinkable. After all his kindness, his continued support, she had the audacity to question his actions. She deserved a lesson or two. He said, "I admit it. Since our return to London, I have seen Celeste several times."

Jocelyn turned to the window, but not before he witnessed the moisture in her eyes. Her shoulders quivered ever so slightly. He immediately regretted his words. A lesson was one thing. To deliberately hurt her was something else altogether. Quietly, he stepped behind her to lightly kiss the tender spot behind her ear.

"Look at me," he said, gently coaxing her to turn around. "Yes, I have seen Celeste, but not in the manner you think. I am sorry I made you think otherwise. Your temper, along with the false accusation, made me very angry. There are many issues you and I must yet resolve, but do you honestly believe I would willingly spend time in her bed when I have you in mine? As long as you remain constant, I will not leave our bed for another woman's."

With hope in her eyes, she met his gaze. Her answer was barely audible. "That woman sounded so confident. You left on an errand last night, and when you returned, you behaved quite mysteriously. She suggested . . . and I . . . well, I'm sorry."

He remembered the bauble in his shirt pocket, an exquisite bit of jewelry he had bought the night before. He lifted her chin, using his thumb to wipe away a single tear. "As to Celeste, I imagine she is not very pleased with you or me. When rejected, she can be lethal. In all likelihood, she hoped to cause this very reaction." Pausing briefly, he reached into his pocket and withdrew a small black velvet box. "As to my whereabouts last night, I thought to give you this before the Montgomery ball. You have convinced me to do otherwise."

When she opened the gift, she stared at it with eyes wide. She tentatively grasped the golden chain and lifted the heart-shaped ruby from the box. Tiny diamonds, surrounding the red gem, glittered in the sunlight. "Oh my goodness. Reyn, you shouldn't have. I don't deserve—"

"I wanted to."

Burying her face against his chest, she said, "I feel like a fool. How will I ever explain to Tam? I behaved like a complete spoony. I promise I will never let my temper run amuck. Never. Do you forgive me?"

"With all my heart."

"Reyn, I . . ."

Her unguarded gaze, filled with vulnerability, met his. What he saw there terrified him. He quickly sought a shift in topics. "I rather like this jealous streak of yours."

"I was not—"

His finger touched her lips. "Shhh. I win so few battles with you, let me enjoy this minor skirmish. I missed you this morning, and considering your outburst downstairs, I think today's name should be Kate. You did Shakespeare proud with that little performance as a shrew. What do you think? Are you a Kate?"

She giggled.

He loved the sound of her laughter. They had already gone through the alphabet once, so every day he arbitrarily chose a name, his selections bordering on absurdity, the choices growing more outrageous each day. He knew that his name game was simply a diversion now, just as he knew her amnesia was an act. Both seemed content to play the game, neither of them wanting to risk their peaceful existence.

Toying with the button on the sleeve of his shirt, she said, "I suppose you wish to tame me, my lord."

He raised his eyebrows in speculation. "You at my beck and call. What a novel concept. Well then, Kate, how do you suppose you can make up for that dreadful scene below?"

Dropping her hand to stroke the front of his breeches, she smiled like a fox in a coop full of chickens. Gone was the open adoration from her eyes, passion in its place.

"Hmmm," he purred, feeling his feet planted firmly on the ground once again. "I think that might be just the thing."

Her lips, meant as a peace offering, met his. Pent-up anxiety created a driving need for exoneration and she threw her arms behind his head, placing her heart and soul into the kiss.

He growled his approval. With equal desperation he carried her to the bed, following her down to the satin coverlet in one fluid motion. All thoughts of Tam or anything else vanished with the waning afternoon.

Jocelyn entered the private box, openly appreciating the opulence of the Royal Palace Theatre. It throbbed with life and laughter, everyone waiting for the curtain to rise on the night's performance. She smiled at Agatha. "By the riches of Midas, I am always astounded by this place. It must have cost the earth to decorate. The fortune could feed a family of orphans for a lifetime."

Agatha slipped her wrap from her shoulders. "I suppose it takes some getting used to. I remember thinking the last Palace quite spectacular before its fiery demise. I believe they did a marvelous job with the reconstruction."

Glancing over her shoulder to see if her husband had arrived, she whispered, "Agatha, I must talk to you."

Eagerly, the dowager cocked her head.

"I realized that Reyn's birthday is next month. I have decided to hostess a surprise celebration in his honor."

The dowager appeared quite stunned. "Oh, my."

"I know Reyn has not celebrated his birthday since his father's accident. This nonsense needs to end. Surely, he has punished himself long enough for his father's death."

"My dear, I couldn't agree more. I am simply contemplating my grandson's reaction. He may have the two of us shot at dawn if we pursue this."

Jocelyn would not be deterred. "I want to give something back to him in exchange for all he has given me. This seems the perfect gift. The affair will be a small dinner party with the closest of friends. We can play parlor games, laugh, dance and remind Reyn that life should be celebrated. Tam and Walter, reluctant at first, have agreed to help. Surely you see the wisdom of the plan."

Walter and Reyn entered the box together. Jocelyn said, "We can talk more tomorrow."

"Come, ladies, do sit down," said Reyn. "You can gawk just as easily without being the open target for every eye here."

As far as Jocelyn was concerned, the best part of the evening came with watching the behavior of the social elite. Giggling as they leaned over the banister, she answered impishly, "Reyn, you make us sound like a spectacle."

"But we are, my dear. Hadn't you heard?" First, he lifted her fingers to his lips, then bent his head to press a quick kiss to her lips, lingering longer than was proper.

"Ahem." Agatha cleared her throat. "Must you maul one another before the gaze of all London?" She attempted to sound harsh, but everyone knew she approved of the growing relationship.

With the soft pad of his thumb, Reyn stroked the contour of Jocelyn's mouth. "Sorry, moonlight, you force me to forget myself."

"Hah! You have never been forced to do anything in your entire life." When he widened his eyes in mock astonishment, Jocelyn added, "Well, almost never. What did you mean about us?"

Walter offered the edifying piece of information. "You and Reyn seem to be the love match of the season."

"Surely you jest?" Jocelyn questioned.

Walter simply grinned before asking Reyn a question, leaving Jocelyn to peer about the theater. Her gaze froze on a box directly across the auditorium as the lavishly dressed woman entered. Celeste Waverly. Covertly, she assessed the woman and grudgingly acknowledged her beauty. Drat her eyes. Glancing back to the two men, she wondered whether Reyn had noticed the woman's presence. Of course he had. Only a dead man would miss Celeste's entrance.

Reminding herself that Reyn spent the better part of the afternoon demonstrating his devotion to her, she felt her confidence soar. She knew he cared for her at least a little. Although she had almost said the words herself, there were no confessions of undying love, which was best. At least, her body held his full attention.

When he settled beside her, an impish whim popped into her head. She tried to sound sufficiently bored. "She really is quite fetching."

Reyn looked around the box to see if someone else entered. Jocelyn tapped him on his knee with her fan and explained. "Lady Waverly." Sighing deeply, she added, "Even with her hair."

Reluctantly, he asked, "Her hair?"

She whispered behind her fan. "I realize that brown is en vogue this season, but 'tis a pity her hair is more the color of possum fur."

Agatha joined the discussion. "Who bought a fur?"

"No one, Grandmother," Reyn promptly answered.

Batting her eyelashes demurely at her husband's dark stare, Jocelyn added. "I suppose the feet are inconsequential, since they remain secreted beneath her gowns most of the time."

Walter, hearing the odd conversation, asked, "What is wrong with her feet?"

"For heaven's sake, Walter, do not encourage this flummery."

Jocelyn blundered along. "I hear they are quite enormous, but then, quite a bit of her is rather large."

"What?" Reyn snapped.

His reaction proved priceless. His mouth opened and shut. Twice. Discreetly, Jocelyn answered behind her fan. "Her breasts."

"Pray tell, what is wrong with her breasts?" Reyn asked incredulously.

Overhearing, Agatha set aside her spyglass. "I beg your pardon?"

"Reyn, really." Jocelyn tried to sound outraged by his inappropriate outburst, then boldly continued. "They are simply too large unless you feel like scaling the Pennines or such. Considering her choice in apparel this eve, I imagine she could balance a flute or two of champagne."

Reyn's gaze flew to the box across the theater. His laughter resonated from the box, garnering the attention of several people in the crowd, Lady Waverly included. As he reined in his behavior, Celeste raised her fan in greeting, an invitation as old as time radiating from her body.

Witnessing the blatant display, seized by wifely proprietorship, Jocelyn reacted. "Why look, Agatha. I do believe Lady Waverly is extending another warm welcome to me." Smiling broadly, Jocelyn raised her arm to execute a jaunty wave. Reyn quickly grabbed her hand and brought it to his lips.

"Behave yourself," he whispered.

Before another stir could be caused, the play began. Jocelyn settled against her husband's chest, pleased with the events of the day.

Chapter Sixteen

The days drifted by, the spring months giving way to summer. Only three weeks had passed since Jocelyn encountered Celeste Waverly. It seemed far longer when she considered her feelings for Reyn. Her love grew deeper every day. The uncertainty of her future, coupled with the late nights and busy days, had begun to wreak havoc with her body.

Chloe circled, tugging here and there as Jocelyn yawned yet again. "Madame, I can see we must make a few adjustments."

"I beg your pardon?" Jocelyn asked, a thousand miles away in her daydreaming.

"The dress, Lady Wilcott. It is much too tight, *n'est-ce pas?*"

For the first time Jocelyn looked, really looked, in the mirror, understanding the remark. She had expected the bodice to be daring, but it seemed as if her entire breast spilled over the beaded top. "Reyn will never let me leave the house."

"He will prance like a prize stallion. Le duc must be greatly pleased. Accept nature's gift. We simply need some additional fabric and if you like, a bit of lace to allow for the coming months."

The comments made no sense to Jocelyn. She waited for Chloe to elaborate.

"The baby, madame. Your husband must be very happy."

Jocelyn felt as though the earth had shifted on its axis. She reached for the back of the small chair in the fitting room and gasped in alarm. "What?"

Chloe first snapped out orders for tea and a damp rag before she discreetly asked her question. "*Mon Dieu!* Could it be, madame, that you were unaware of the child?"

Jocelyn could only nod her head as she eased herself into the chair. A baby. The words churned wildly with her imagination. She was pregnant. That explained her exhaustion, queasy stomach and tattered nerves.

She felt the damp rag caress her brow, heard the soft fluttering of voices, but remained silent with her eyes closed in order to consider all the implications. She carried Reyn's child. The Wilcott heir. Her. A wife who wasn't supposed to be a wife. A murderess. Someone who had unfinished business and, once all the truths were told, would disgust her husband.

But what if, she thought, the baby represented a new beginning? What if it was fate asserting itself, providing the fork in the road that would allow her to make a choice? *Don't be stupid,* she reprimanded herself. Wishes came true only in fairy tales.

"Lady Wilcott, are you well?"

Forcing a smile to her lips, Jocelyn said, "Chloe, I am sorry if I startled you. I confess your observations have quite stunned me."

"I hope the news is good?"

"Oh, yes, of course. You understand I wish to keep

this news a secret for now. I would like to tell my husband at the right time."

The older woman patted her hand. "Of course, *ma petite*. Now, let us unravel this dress so you may return home. I know what must be done. The dress will be delivered in two days."

Still disoriented by the news, Jocelyn walked from the dressmaker's out onto Bond street, explaining to the driver of the carriage that she wished to walk a little way. Absently strolling down the street, she stopped at a small shop filled with delicate clothing for children, mesmerized by the tiny fashions. As if hearing the news for the first time, her hand drifted protectively to her abdomen.

Warm, stale breath skimmed her cheek. Abruptly, she pivoted to stare into cold, wicked eyes.

"Well, if it ain't the li'l coo all dressed up like a dog's dinner. I see you remember ol' Jocko?" Sweeping his woolen cap from his head, the Bedlam attendant executed a bow that allowed his hand to brush the side of Jocelyn's breast.

Shocked from her paralyzing fear, she attacked. "How dare you? This is not your private hellhole in which you can freely take liberties."

As he laughed with knife-edged anger, he leaned forward to whisper in her ear. "No worries, luv. Jocko knows all about that fancy man ya married, but he ain't anywhere around. The ole crone ain't here to save you this time neither."

He emphasized his words by roughly grabbing her elbow and shoving her toward the alley. Before a scream could pass her lips, his filthy hand clamped her mouth shut. What now? Just when her mind grasped the danger of the situation, her arm was freed and the sound of pounding fists filled her ears. She whirled to witness Jocko draw a firearm from his coat pocket and aim directly at the heart of Tameron Innes.

"No!" she screamed, flinging herself onto Jocko's back, forcing the shot to deflect to the ground. In retaliation, he smacked his fist into her jaw. She sailed one way even as he hurled a gleaming dagger at Tam.

"You bloody son of a bitch," Tam growled, advancing and ducking at the same time. When Jocelyn's head connected with the brick wall of the building, her anguished cry turned Tam's attention from Jocko's retreating back. Through the ringing in her brain, she heard Jocko fling back, "I know alls about ya, ducky. One word and I'll gladly kill you. Or that fancy man o'yours. Makes no matter to me."

"Jocelyn, can you hear me?" Tam asked, kneeling beside her. He continued to search the growing crowd for any sign of the big brute responsible. Seeing no one, he lifted her into his arms, carrying her to his carriage.

By the time they arrived at the town house on Park Lane, her jaw throbbed like a beating drum, her stomach roiled anxiously and tears streamed rampantly down her cheeks. Although Tam sat beside her offering gentle words of calm, she sensed his contained frustration.

Upon their entrance to Black House, Reyn took one look at her disarray, at the ugly bruise on her face, and all hell broke loose. Reynolds Blackburn was a man possessed, a thousand questions popping from his mouth.

"Please, Reyn," Jocelyn pleaded, as he carried her upstairs. "Cease! If you rail at me one more time, I swear I will empty the contents of my stomach onto your lap." She finally had his attention. "Thank you," she added as he placed her on the bed and plumped the pillow behind her head.

He removed his hands from her body and rapidly placed them on his hips. "You will not evade me this time. Do you hear?"

"How could I not hear? If you yell one more time, I shall be deaf." She changed her tack when a fierce scowl crossed his face. "I'm fine. Really. Please, allow me a brief rest. I will gladly answer any questions later." She watched the various emotions play upon his face. When his shoulders heaved a heavy sigh, she knew she had won. "I promise I will tell you everything." She yawned. "Later?" The plea with sleep-filled words gained her a nap.

The parlor glowed with lamplight as she entered to find Tam and Reyn engaged in a game of pitch-and-toss. When Reyn noticed her, he threw his coin to the table, crossed the room, gathered her into a tight embrace and placed a soft kiss upon her temple. The dark bruise adorning her jaw attested to the fact that the encounter that afternoon had not been a nightmare, but real, living terror. She hoped Reyn would be reasonable after her explanation.

"Sit down. Tell me what happened today." He settled her beside him on the brocade settee, Tam opposite them. Reyn's hand curled tightly around his drink. "I want the truth, Jocelyn. Why did that man attack you? Tam thought you knew the fellow."

Sharply, her eyes turned to Tam.

"Only an observation, Jocelyn."

"A very astute one." Until that moment, she hadn't really decided what to say. Jocko was a link to Bedlam, the part of her past Reyn already knew. Her uncertainty of Jocko's link to her step-uncle was the most disconcerting. However, she decided to take the chance. Reyn needed to know the truth in order to protect himself. "He worked as an attendant at Bedlam."

"Good. I'll go there directly and kill the bloody wretch."

She placed her palm against his fingers. "Reyn, you can't go about London killing everyone you choose." She could almost hear Reyn's mind searching for a reasonable response. "Besides, you won't find him there."

"Why not?"

Telling this part of the story became a bit tricky. Given Reyn's agitated state and her upcoming news, he would likely storm from the house and tear London apart to find Jocko. "Do you remember how Agatha intervened when she saved me from Bedlam?"

She waited while he thought back.

"Agatha found you in some room. You were being attacked by—"

He bounded off the settee, his eyes a frosty blue, his face pinched with fury. "Do you mean to tell me the man attacking you today is the same bastard that attacked you in Bedlam? I will personally kill him."

"Now, Reyn—"

"How do you know I won't find him at the hospital?"

"Agatha had him dismissed. I'm sure he resents me a great deal. You cannot kill him for attacking me."

He paced the length of the room. "I will simply break both his hands so he can't touch another helpless female."

"Believe me, I despise him, but be reasonable. File charges, do anything you like. But please do not put yourself in harm's way because of Jocko. He's not worth it."

"Jocko? That's his name?"

"Yes. Did you hear anything I said?"

"I'm not deaf."

"No. Just stupid and stubborn and . . . " She looked to Tam for support. "Tam, talk to him. Please."

"Unfortunately, Jocelyn, I agree. That brute deserves a lesson or two in good behavior."

"Oh." She should have realized Tam's opinion. He wore the same pinched expression as Reyn.

Reyn sat back down beside Jocelyn and tenderly fingered the mark on her jaw. "You think I can sit and do nothing when he hurt you? My God, woman. He left you with bruises."

"Fine." She squared her shoulders and crossed her arms beneath her breasts. "Do what you must, but don't crawl to me when he splits your head open. He's a dangerous man."

His expression grew fiercer and darker. "Your belief in my abilities is overwhelming."

She scowled back at him just as fiercely, which seemed to have no effect at all.

"Tam and I will simply keep our wits about us. If luck prevails, we shall find that bastard. Until then, I want you restricted to the house."

"Nonsense."

"Nonsense? You could have been seriously injured today."

"Other than this ugly bruise, the man did not hurt me. I won't be confined."

Studying her for a long moment, he placed his hands behind his back, stood and paced. "Have you forgotten that someone abducted and hid you away at Bedlam?"

"Of course not."

Tam added his opinion. "It might be best, Jocelyn."

"No!"

"For heaven's sake," Reyn blasted. "You trust me with that damned cat. You trust me to provide your entertainment. You trust me to clothe and feed you. You even trust me with your body. Why won't you trust me with your life?"

Tam cleared his throat.

"Don't worry, my friend. I have said nothing you don't already know."

Drastic measures such as confinement would cause countless problems when her step-uncle returned to London. She also had plans to make for Reyn's upcoming birthday party. Yet, the tiny life growing in her womb changed everything. "I will tell you my plans daily. Certainly Davey will watch more closely. Please. I could not stand to be confined."

"You will go nowhere without me, Walter, Tam or Davey to accompany you. Do you understand?"

She stood and kissed the frown from his face. "Yes. Trust me as well. I have every reason to remain safe."

He has returned.

Those three simple words cut through her as easily as a dagger might. Jocelyn steadied herself by grasping the edge of the mantel to read the message a second time. It left little doubt. Her step-uncle had ended his business in the Caribbean. He was in London.

Intent on reaching Agatha immediately and unnoticed, she whirled with a sense of irrepressible urgency only to crash into her husband's arms.

"What's all this? You're absolutely pale," he said, his hand grasping her chin.

"Nothing." She knew she answered much too quickly. Gulping a calming breath, a smile locked on her face, she stuffed the note into her pocket. "I just realized I have an appointment with Agatha. If you'll excuse me, I am dreadfully late."

His grip held firm as she tried to slip past. "What business has you running about like a small gale wind?"

"Agatha and I planned to shop. I forgot. She sent a message to remind me."

Tenderly, Reyn caressed the inside of her wrist with his thumb. "Perhaps I should accompany you."

"No!" she snapped.

His brows lifted at her abrupt response. Cautiously, he asked, "Jocelyn, if something were wrong, you would tell me, wouldn't you?"

She could not help but notice that his statement was more a command than a question. "Of course, darling," she replied brightly. "I'm sorry to seem like such a lackwit, but Agatha is waiting."

"I see." He scrutinized her face in an attempt to ascertain the truth of her statement. She was lying. He knew it. He also knew that direct confrontation would undoubtedly prove fruitless. He decided to let her go and attack the mystery from another direction.

"Do try to calm down. I am sure Bond Street will have more than enough trinkets for you to buy. Retrieve your cloak. I will notify the groom."

Yes. He would notify Davey with detailed instructions. Ever since the altercation with Jocko, unbeknownst to his wife, he had elected to keep her safe and have her watched. He would have his answers by evening.

Repeatedly, as if the devil himself nipped at her heels, Jocelyn covered the length of Agatha's salon in anxious, clipped steps. Agatha, on the other hand, sat upon a saffron-colored settee of lush velvet, calmly answering the barrage of questions.

"I have told you twice already, Jocelyn. Your Bow Street runner was most specific with his information. One Horace Mardell arrived yesterday. He has taken up residence in your London home. There is no mistake. Your step-uncle has returned."

Jocelyn paced the floor another three times before Agatha asked, "Correct me if I am wrong, but I thought this day is the one you have eagerly anticipated."

Lost in thought, Jocelyn stopped beside the walnut escritoire, absently fingered the assortment of writing materials and accepted the truth of the message. That meant accepting all the implications as well. The plan for revenge, born and fostered over the last few months, would be initiated, possibly ending her new-found happiness.

She shook away her despondency and straightened her shoulders. She knew what had to be done. "We must see that my step-uncle receives an invitation to the Montgomery ball."

Agatha looked puzzled. "So soon?"

Jocelyn nodded. "If I wait any longer, I may lose my nerve. It shames me to admit this, but I'm terrified."

"As you should be. This is definitely a time for prudent fear. Nevertheless, I cannot see any harm in waiting a week or so."

Jocelyn considered her pregnancy, and the tenuous but passionate relationship she and Reyn had settled into. Her dreams could crumble like the ancient grey stone of Hadrian's Wall at any moment. Countless obstacles seemed to remain, and one by one they had to be overcome. Until then, neither she nor her baby had a future. Like a battle-worn soldier, she sat down woodenly. "I have four days to reclaim my composure. Can you arrange the invitation?"

"Of course. Shall I ensure Lord Halden's presence?"

"You still believe he is best suited for our purposes?"

"A more crooked, devious blighter I have never known. He will most likely prostrate himself at the emergence of a new pigeon. We simply make the introductions, and given the opportunity and the appropriate encouragement, I assure you that Lord Halden will gladly embroil Horace Mardell in every felonious scheme possible. In one week's time, perhaps two, given what you have said about your step-uncle's character, he will no doubt be up to his shirtsleeves in illegal land titles, bordellos or some form of thievery, the evidence easily manipulated to bring the man low." The dowager paused to consider something. "Are you positive he won't claim you as his niece?"

Jocelyn's curls bounced from side to side as she adamantly shook her head. "No. The moment he claims any relationship to me, my inheritance reverts to Reyn. Horace won't let that happen. I think he will take his time to ascertain the truth about my memory loss and plot my demise in a more permanent manner."

A sigh, heavy with reluctance, fell from Agatha's pursed lips. "This is a dangerous game we play."

Distractedly, before she answered, Jocelyn scanned the salon as if an alternative solution might hide amongst the tapestries or paintings on the walls. "I know."

"Fine, but hear this," Agatha said, her voice firm and commanding, making the warning clear, "I will remain silent as long as I think you are safe. If, for one minute, I fear for you, I will tell my grandson everything. Agreed?"

"Agreed."

"Now tell me. How are you and Reyn?"

Shrugging her shoulders evasively, Jocelyn asked, "What do you mean?"

Agatha spoke while she set her empty teacup on the nearby table. "You know exactly what I mean."

Knowing precisely what Agatha sought, yet not ready to bare her soul, Jocelyn asked, "Did your husband love you? I mean, really love you?"

The dowager's eyes sparkled and her smile deepened, her entire face glowing with an expression born of deep emotion. "My darling Harden was like no other. I loved him as life itself, and miracle of miracles, he felt the same."

"Is that why you never remarried?"

"When Harden died, I was desolate. Once I accustomed myself to his death, I realized we'd had more love, more cherished moments, than most people have in a lifetime. I received numerous offers, but all other men paled by comparison. I contented myself with my memories and raising Reyn." Agatha's mind seemed to leave the place where daydreams linger and said, "Child, what is this all really about?"

"My mother used to tell me that marriage without love could be constant, companionable and pleasant, in a quiet sort of way. She also said that to love someone and have the love returned was probably the greatest gift one could receive. I know my mother resigned herself to being content with my father, but I believe my grandparents' marriage was like yours. I remember the turbulence, the excitement, the joy, the love. They were devoted to one another. I want what they had. What you had."

"Don't you have that now?"

The constant matchmaker in the budding relationship, Agatha pressed Jocelyn for information whenever possible. Today, knowing the possible hurdles that lay ahead, this conversation seemed pointless to Jocelyn. Still, she found herself responding. "Everything has been wonderful. Like a dream come true."

"And . . . ?" Agatha prodded.

"I love Reyn."

"Is that so horrible?"

"I am so afraid he will despise me," she whimpered miserably. When Agatha extended her arms in comfort, Jocelyn abandoned the tight rein on her emotions, crossed the room, dropped to her knees and placed her head in Agatha's lap.

Agatha stroked the riot of curls. "Have you told Reyn?"

Her shoulders tensed. Lifting her head to stare at Agatha, Jocelyn said, "Absolutely not. I won't, either, until this business is resolved."

"Has he declared his affection for you?"

Jocelyn laughed at the ridiculousness of the question. "Reyn lusts for me, but he holds no deep feelings."

"Stubborn fools," Agatha muttered, "both of you." She wiped Jocelyn's tear-stained cheek and sighed. "He does care for you, even if he has yet to admit it. To you or himself. And if you love him, you will fight for him." As Agatha continued to stare at her granddaughter-in-law, she asked, "My dear, is there something else? You seem so forlorn."

Jocelyn's heart cried out to reveal the truth about Phillip Bains, his death and her role in the incident. The fear of rejection by Agatha, the possible alienation, firmly sealed Jocelyn's lips. She stood, wiped away a wayward tear, then placed a delicate kiss on the older woman's cheek. "No, but thank you. I will never be able to repay you for all your kindness."

"Pish posh. There is no need to become maudlin." Pulling a handkerchief from her sleeve to offer it to Jocelyn, Agatha continued. "We have one more item to discuss. What of Reyn's surprise birthday celebration? Do we move forward? With your step-uncle's return, are you sure you want to add another wrinkle to the linens?"

"Everything is ready. I will not cancel the party simply because Horace decided to show his scurrilous face in London. I am through hiding from the man. Anyway, if things don't go as planned, we shall change it to a farewell party for me." For that impertinent comment, she received a light tap on her hand from Agatha.

"Does Reyn suspect?"

Crossing to the chair beside Agatha, Jocelyn plopped down as if her entire body had exhaled a huge breath of air. "I am sure he suspects a great many things, Agatha, but not this. After the altercation with Jocko, he threatened to have me followed. I dissuaded him from that idea. In order to finish the preparations, I will feign a few afternoon calls and shopping excursions. He will be completely surprised."

"And what of that scoundrel? Have they found him?"

"No. Jocko has disappeared like the sewer rat he is."

Agatha poured more tea into both their cups. "I believe the next few weeks shall prove quite the challenge."

Chapter Seventeen

Having adopted a position of masked observation, Reyn surveyed the Montgomery ballroom. The small orchestra played a tedious tune as couples danced and conversed. People milled about the alcoves and pillars surrounding the room as he watched his wife, noting every nuance, every movement, every sigh. He knew tonight was the night. But for what? As he sipped from his crystal glass, he considered what Davey, his groom, had uncovered from Agatha's chamber maid. It seemed utter nonsense. Davey had rambled on about a man recently returned to London. Somehow the Montgomery Ball factored into the equation, but Reyn had no idea how or why. And of course, there was Agatha and her obvious involvement. That bit of news came as no surprise. He had always known that his grandmother knew more than she was willing to tell.

During the past week, he had dropped hints, providing Jocelyn every opportunity to confide in him. She had remained stubbornly silent. The little fool. Somewhere in her mind, she still believed the misguided notion that her silence protected him. Fine. He was a patient man. When the time was right, when she trusted him, she would come to him. "Damn," he muttered irritably. He wanted this whole business finished. Jocelyn refused to address their future together until she resolved her past.

His thoughts drifted back to the matter at hand, and he discreetly scanned the lavish surroundings, thinking about this mystery man once again. Was the man expected to attend? Did he know something of his wife's past? Was he a threat to Jocelyn? Reyn simply didn't know, but based on his wife's erratic behavior, the tiny shreds of information he had gathered, and his instincts, he stood alert. He had also solicited Walter and Tam's aid. He frowned, wondering where they were. Walter Hathaway's deep voice drew his attention.

"I tell you, Tam, I can see by his cheery expression that the evening promises to be a delightful diversion."

Reyn threw a scowl backward over his shoulder at Walter's facetious remark.

Tam added his jibe to Walter's. "You look like a ruffled cock-grouse protecting his prized territory."

Ignoring their taunts, chiding their tardy arrival, Reyn scolded, "So good of you to arrive. Prompt, on time."

When Tam surveyed the gay surroundings, he said, "I see no signs of disaster. Has something happened?"

"No," Reyn said with disgust. He tipped his head across the crowded ballroom. "Agatha and Jocelyn have been huddled together like a pair of thugs, both of them behaving under the rose."

Folding his arms across his white satin waistcoat, Walter asked, "Exactly what are we waiting for?"

"A man."

"That explains it," Walter quipped.

Reyn's mood, already volatile at best, had little use

for Hathaway's flippant response. "Blast it, Walter, this is serious."

Tam braced a hand on Reyn's shoulders. "Relax, man. We will see that no harm comes to Jocelyn."

Irritably, Reyn clamped down the urge to throttle his friend. He knew frustration threatened his control. The anger was better aimed at the stunning ball of fluff responsible. "It's not only that. I believe this *man* is the answer to the riddle I currently live with."

"What do you want us to do?" asked Tam.

Recognizing their unconditional support, Reyn knew his friends would do whatever he requested. "We wait and watch and pray I sustain my patience not to cross the floor and choke the truth from my dear wife."

Brandies in hand, the three men began their guarded reconnaissance of the two Blackburn women.

While concentrating on the ballroom's elegant foyer of gold and white, listening with only half an ear, Jocelyn strained to portray polite interest in the conversation about her. She knew her nerves would be a bundle of frayed ends by now if not for Agatha's presence. Like a beacon in the night, she provided direction and hope.

Jocelyn glanced across the room, singled out her husband, noted Tam and Walter's arrival and smiled. Without a doubt, the three men together presented a force to be reckoned with. Very different men with a friendship held together by similar values. Briefly, she envied their close relationship. Yes, they would always be able to count on one another. Perhaps, she hoped, his friends would distract her husband tonight. Reyn suspected something; of that she was sure.

She turned back to the ballroom entrance and froze. Every turbulent emotion possible attacked her senses. Through a crippling fog, she felt herself tugged toward a corner of the room. She heard Agatha's innocuous greetings as they passed various lords and ladies.

Agatha's soft words, a thread of comfort, permeated the haze.

"Steady, my dear. We are almost there."

It seemed as though her entire body was frozen, pregnant with panic. Her feet shuffled awkwardly while her pulse raced and her breathing turned ragged. She felt the perspiration slick on her palms.

"Jocelyn, by great-grandfather's bones, pull yourself together or I shall retrieve Reyn this very moment."

The sharp command captured her full attention. Jocelyn willed her composure to return.

"That's it, child. You are perfectly safe here. No one will hurt you. Seek out your anger, not your fear."

By now, they had crossed to an isolated, empty alcove. Agatha guided Jocelyn to sit, all the while making it seem that Jocelyn provided support to the older woman.

Flipping the gilded fan into action, Agatha spoke with obvious interest. "I take it the man dressed in the scarlet waistcoat is your long-lost relative?"

Jocelyn nodded as she kept her eyes focused on the patterned floor of grey-and-white marble. One last cleansing breath, she thought. Then she could look up and face the enemy. She closed her eyes, exhaled, and lifted her head majestically, a smile of pride and courage plastered on her face.

The dowager squeezed her hand. "Well done, my girl."

"When I first saw him, I thought I might faint. I am fine now." Jocelyn gazed around the room. "Where is he?"

"To the left of the entrance, beside the large potted palm. He is talking to a man who dares to wear trousers a ghastly shade of puce."

Only Agatha could examine a man's wardrobe moments before impending disaster. The dowager's spirit fortified the courage Jocelyn needed to seek out her adversary. She grinned.

There he stood, elegantly poised amongst a group of men. She recognized the broad shoulders squared in confidence, the amiable demeanor, the false sincerity. Horace presented himself as every bit the gentleman. She knew the true nature of the man and would see to it that all of London saw what she did. Soon.

"The time has come, Agatha, to garner the man's attention. I believe I shall invite my husband to dance."

With that, she floated across the crowded room, intentionally placing herself in close proximity to her step-uncle. Each step took her closer to Reyn. She marveled at the strength, the power, the ferocity of the emotions she felt for him. Dressed all in black, save the small, starched cravat of white, Reyn was the most handsome man there. He was also the most formidable. And she loved him. Dear God, she prayed, let all go well. Give me a chance. Give us a chance.

Reaching her husband's side, she executed a gracious curtsy, then addressed her husband's companions. "Would it be possible for a wife to claim one dance with her husband?"

Playfully, Walter looked aghast. "What? And interrupt our critical discussion on the influence of our horses' dietary needs on their ability to win unconditionally at every post?"

Tam clasped her hand in his and brought it to his lips. "Perhaps you should dance with someone known for his ability to keep his feet on the floor and off his partner's toes?"

Oh, how she would miss these new friends.

She took Reyn's hand in hers. "I think my husband's arms will provide everything I need."

They waltzed into the crowd, her body pressed more closely to his than was proper. Reyn's eyes took on the color of grey-blue thunderclouds and his brows lifted. He grinned seductively. "I thought I saw to your needs earlier this evening. Did I leave you too soon?"

Remembering her wild abandon in the bath prior to dressing for the ball, how quickly her body had responded to his expert caresses and kisses, she blushed. "I will not answer. If I do, conceit will rule you."

A mischievous glint to his eye, he teased the outer rim of her ear as he whispered, "I thought you well loved when you screamed my name for all of London to hear."

"Oh, for heaven's sake, you know all you need do is touch me and I am reduced to mush with no control over my actions."

Nestling close to Reyn's body, feeling the reassuring beat of his heart, she danced with her head held high, dismissing her step-uncle's presence. She needed this secure space of time before she continued her plans for the evening. Save for a speculative glance at her every now and then, Reyn remained silent, his suspicions, if any, concealed. He, too, seemed content to savor the moment.

When the dance ended, he guided her to Agatha's side, positioning himself as if he meant to stay. The dowager quickly intervened. "Reyn, be a dear and fetch me a glass of punch."

He pursed his lips as if he meant to say something, then changed his mind.

Jocelyn watched his retreating back and fought the urge to flee, the urge to turn and accuse her tormentor, the urge to call Reyn back. She faced Agatha instead. "Did Horace notice?"

"Your step-uncle looked rather apoplectic," Agatha crooned. "You would have appreciated his reaction."

"And now?"

Discreetly peeking over her fan, Agatha answered, "As we speak, your relative circles the room like a reptilian predator. I never expected him to be such a handsome man."

"Do not let his looks deceive you. His heart is black and made of stone." Hate edged her every word.

"Prepare yourself. He ventures this way." Agatha fussed with the lace on her sleeves, portraying the typical matron with no more on her mind than her appearance. No one would ever suspect she was about to face a man capable of the lowest treachery. She issued her final instructions. "Remember, you must reveal nothing in your face. Restrain all recognition and emotion until he departs. I will lay the trap. Simply follow my lead."

Jocelyn nodded that she understood as she mentally prepared herself for the confrontation. Tapping her pink satin-covered toes helped, since the action provided an outlet for her anxiety. She fought to keep her hands still at her sides.

I am perfectly safe. No harm will come to me tonight. She repeated the litany in her mind over and over again. After all, Reyn was here as well as Tam and Walter. Hundreds of people also stood about. No matter how powerful her prayer, the moment she felt his presence, past terrors and anger wrestled for release. She froze.

"Good evening, Mary," he said boldly to her back.

He will do nothing. He will not harm me. Slowly turning toward Horace, she lifted her brow in puzzlement. "I beg your pardon?"

For a moment, staring intently, he said nothing. His lips formed a smile that looked more like a sneer. "I did not expect to see you here."

With what she hoped was a blank expression on her face, she answered, "Have we met? I apologize. My husband always teases me about my inability to remember names."

His cold eyes narrowed sharply, making him look very much like the weasel he was. He glanced at Agatha, who smiled serenely, then back to Jocelyn. "Your husband? What game is this?"

"Excuse me. I'm not sure what you ask me."

"Surely you jest. I have no need to meet this *husband* of yours."

Glancing over her step-uncle's shoulder, she watched Reyn fast approaching, a tight-lipped expression on his face. She smiled sweetly at Horace seconds before Reyn thrust the glass of punch into Agatha's hand.

Reyn spoke, his words crisp with arrogance. "Have you need of something?"

Horace bowed politely before answering. "Mr. Horace Mardell, at your service. I have just returned to London and felt compelled to make this lovely lady's acquaintance."

How genteel. How smooth. What a fool Horace was. For a brief moment, with an even darker scowl, Reyn's entire body tensed. Jocelyn thought he might challenge Horace to a duel then and there. Agatha held back, evidently content to watch the show.

Reyn displayed an uncommon proprietorship by pulling Jocelyn close to his side. "This lady happens to be my wife, Lady Blackburn, Duchess of Wilcott."

Horace's steel-grey eyes registered shock, then abruptly cleared to reveal nothing. Her step-uncle easily recovered from his temporary befuddlement. "I meant no insult. I thought I might know her." He paused to look directly at Jocelyn. "She resembles someone I once knew. I must be wrong."

His answer came as no surprise to Jocelyn. She wanted to shout, Liar. Murderer. Thief.

"How extraordinary," bubbled Agatha. "I find it extremely fascinating how people often look alike. You must tell all. By the way, I am Lady Blackburn, dowager Duchess of Wilcott. Reyn, darling, introduce yourself."

"Reynolds Blackburn, Duke of Wilcott." He purposely kept his voice devoid of warmth, hoping the man would grasp the situation and leave.

"Reyn, the dear man is obviously a stranger. We must make him feel welcome."

Welcome? Hell, he'd seen the way Mardell had touched Jocelyn's shoulder. Reyn wanted to throttle the man, and if he couldn't have that luxury, then he certainly didn't want to talk to him.

"May I say, your grace, that luck blessed you with a lovely prize."

With her fan waving in the air, Agatha interrupted. "It was fate or such that brought them together, not luck. Isn't that so, Reyn?"

"More or less." Reyn noted the peculiar expression smeared on Jocelyn's face when she tittered like a featherbrained debutante over Agatha's silly comment. Something was wrong.

"Have you been married long?" asked Horace.

Jocelyn enlightened Horace. "Five months. We met in northern England, fell madly in love and married immediately." Horace kept his face glued on Jocelyn's, watching closely. She leaned closer to Reyn.

"Mardell?" Reyn continued to muddle the name over in his mind. He felt Jocelyn tense like a well-armed bow, then tremble. If she pressed any closer, she would become part of his cravat. "I don't recollect the name."

"I traveled extensively until my stepbrother passed away. Then I spent most of my time in the country." He observed Jocelyn closely. "I spent the last few months searching the Caribbean for a relative of mine. While there, I purchased a cane plantation."

Agatha clapped her hands in delight as Lady Battingham often did. "Sugarcane, how delightful. Investing in properties is crucial to one's future, don't you think? I myself enjoy dabbling in various this-and-thats. Luckily, I have been very fortunate. Wool, shipping, corn, a bit of the spice trade, but never sugarcane. Perhaps we could trade business insights."

Growing more annoyed, Reyn cast a startled glance toward his grandmother. What the hell was she babbling about? He handled the family investments. It struck him like a thunderbolt.

The man had returned.

Judging from Jocelyn's strained behavior and Agatha's odd remarks, he knew this had to be the person in question. Whatever game his wife and grandmother played, the cards were being dealt as they spoke. Well, he had a little surprise for all those involved.

"I have recently considered investing in the islands myself," Reyn stated exuberantly. "It might be interesting to hear your opinions on the matter." Both women stood transfixed, their mouths wide open. "Come, ladies, do not look so surprised."

By now, Tam and Walter had managed to join the circle. Eagerly, Reyn introduced them to his newfound friend. As the conversation continued, Reyn, Tam, Walter and Agatha grew more animated while Jocelyn fell into a stupor. She pleaded exhaustion. Reyn knew he needed to free her of this place, and soon, or the purpose of tonight's charade would be lost.

"Excuse us, but we must say good night. As you can see, my wife is about to fall asleep on her feet. Shall you join us, Agatha?"

Calmly fanning herself, the dowager answered, "I believe I shall stay and acquaint myself further with Mr. Mardell. Besides, Tam or Walter will see me home safely."

Reyn extended his hand. "I am sure we will meet again, Mr. Mardell. Soon." The hidden challenge, barely noticeable but present nonetheless, hung in the air.

"Most definitely," said Mardell. "Good night, Lady Wilcott."

"Good night." Surprisingly, Jocelyn's voice sounded calm while her legs fought to run from the room. She bade good night to Tam and Walter, then allowed Reyn to slowly escort her to their carriage. Once inside, Jocelyn threw herself into Reyn's arms, heedless of the welcome she might receive. What a fool she had been, thinking she could maintain this cool facade. She no longer cared. She wanted, needed, to absorb Reyn's strength into her body and obliterate the last hour from her mind, her step-uncle's face, his laughter.

Frantically possessing her husband's lips, demanding a response, she could feel the tug-of-war taking place between his body and his mind. Her determination overruled any timidity as her hands traveled downward.

Jerking away as though scalded, Reyn exploded. "By the saints, Jocelyn. Do you think this will alter the course for this night?"

"No. Please. Hold me. Make love to me." Her impassioned plea, along with the tiny, nibbling kisses she placed on his chin, neck and shoulders removed all other protests from his mind.

"This is not finished," he said, nose to nose before his lips joined with hers in a desperate passion.

Reyn seemed content to languish over her, skillfully removing the dress from her shoulders to sample the delicate peaks of her breasts. Jocelyn burned with need and wanted no gentle coupling. She slid down the length of his body to the buttons of his breeches. Releasing him from confinement, determined to drive him to the same frenzied state, she let her lips descend.

"Bloody hell, woman," Reyn moaned painfully as his hand burrowed deep into her falling curls.

Relentless with her mouth and tongue, she worked her magic until Reyn lifted her from the floor of the carriage, tossed up her skirts, tore the sheer linen pantalets and buried himself deep within her warmth.

Their lovemaking matched the ageless struggle between man and woman—each stroke a thrust toward power, each withdrawal a reminder of their need to be one. No quarter was given, nor was any desired as Reyn pounded into his wife's lush body, her hips wildly greeting his. No gentle courting. No tender caresses. Simply primal needs that demanded satisfaction. Jocelyn screamed her pleasure into the night, Reyn's cries joining hers.

Collapsed within her husband's arms, each clop of the horses' hooves leaving the Montgomery ball and her step-uncle far behind, she felt herself calm, thinking clearly once again. She knew she wouldn't feel completely safe until she locked herself behind her bedroom door. One furtive look at Reyn's stony expression and she wondered whether she would need protection from him as well.

Chapter Eighteen

Nudged by her dreams, Jocelyn stirred to find herself undressed, tucked beneath the cozy covers of her bed. When she realized she must have fallen asleep in the carriage, she anxiously searched the dark chamber to find Reyn. He stood beside the large bay window, at one with the night. Dark, desolate, menacing.

She knew half-measures would no longer be acceptable. Shifting upright on the pillows, she offered her confession to her husband's back. "My name is Mary Jocelyn Garnett. Horace Mardell is my step-uncle, the man responsible for the deaths of my parents, guilty of stealing my inheritance and consigning me to Bedlam."

Slowly, Reyn's body, choked with tension, turned toward her. His face remained in the shadows. If she could see him, she knew his eyes would be devoid of warmth, his lips thinned to a tight line of resolution.

"Reyn . . . " Her words faltered.

Like a hard frost on the frozen moor, his voice rang cold and brittle. "I am waiting."

"Before I continue, I must ask you something." Reyn lifted his head. One look at his face, the twitching of the tiny crescent scar, the total withdrawal in his eyes, the rigid set to his jaw, and she almost crawled back beneath the covers. Only her determination and convictions steeled her to move forward. "I intend to finish what I started tonight. Do you promise not to interfere unless I ask?" That certainly garnered his attention, for he flew from the dark like a menacing specter.

"How dare you!" he accused her with raw fury. "The only thing I promise is not to beat you black and blue regardless of my inclination to do so."

"I understand you are irritated, but—"

"Irritated!" He savagely spit his words. "You little fool."

"I know exactly what I am doing."

"Is that supposed to reassure me? Your step-uncle, by your own admission, is a self-confessed murderer. He abandoned you in hell's own den and has done God knows what else. Tonight you acted as though the man were less bothersome than a beetle. What the devil were you thinking?"

She wanted his agreement, needed it. Desperate to explain, she tried to placate his temper. "If you would kindly sit down, I will start from the beginning."

He stomped to the nearby Pembroke table, gathered a shot of whiskey and dropped into the high-backed chair at the foot of the bed. Waves of contained anger emanated from his muscled form.

As he continued to stare in glacial silence, she assumed he meant for her to begin. "When I was twelve, my parents took a short holiday. I remained home."

"I remember."

"When their bodies were discovered, everyone believed them to be the victims of a robbery. Unbeknownst to me, the family estates and fortune were left as my inheritance through a special dispensation from the king. I could not gain control until I married or turned nineteen. My parents had seen to the financial details, but neglected to see to me. Horace Mardell arrived at Bellford Hall, a letter from my father in hand, naming him as my legal guardian. Suddenly, I found myself under his guardianship. I didn't know it at the time, but Horace had been disowned by the family and chose to use this opportunity as his means to regain his wealth. The letter was forged. To shorten an otherwise long and dreary story, he sent me to the most remote place he could find, a Catholic nunnery, and basically forgot I existed until I turned eighteen. He brought me home where he was living quite comfortably. Horace seemed genuinely pleased to see me. Having no other living relative, wanting someone to care about me, I naively believed everything he said, including his desire to see me properly introduced to London society, his goal to find me a proper husband."

She paused for a moment. Did she dare tell Reyn about Phillip? One look at his incensed expression and she wished she could ignore this part of her past. But that was impossible. If Reyn was going to despise her, it was better to find out now. Even though it would be her word against her step-uncle's, the truth would come out, and in the eyes of the law, murder was murder.

"Don't stop now, my dear. I'm savoring every word."

"Must you make this more difficult than it already is?"

"Excuse me for not serving tea and scones, but I find I am not in an accommodating mood right now."

Ignoring the caustic tone in his voice, she continued. "While at Bellford Hall, a gentleman visited my step-uncle. We became good friends. Within a few weeks, he asked for my hand in marriage. Horace gladly consented."

"A fiancé. How nice. This tale grows more interesting by the moment." His eyes narrowed to a steely glint.

"Does this fellow have a name?"

"Phillip Bains."

"Ah. The mysterious Phillip. And where is your dear fiancé now?"

The words remained lodged in her throat, her lips and tongue unable to form a sound with her mouth as dry as a three-month-old biscuit from the cargo hold of a sea vessel.

"Jocelyn?" he prompted.

Unable to bear his expression, his contempt, she addressed her fingertips. "He's dead." Don't wait, she thought. Tell it all. Quickly. "I killed him."

He must have flown across the floor, for now he towered above her, threatening and intimidating.

"What did you say?"

Something wild burst deep inside. "I killed him. With my own two hands. I'm a murderess. Does that make you happy? Are you glad to finally know the truth about your wife? Will you start to sleep with a pistol by your bed? Watch your back? Have me arrested? Return me to Bedlam?"

His strong hands gripped her shoulders to shake her. "Stop it."

"Why? Is the truth so difficult to hear?"

"Your so-called truth is utter nonsense," he said sarcastically. "You could no more kill anyone than Agatha could keep her nose from other people's business."

"I'd reserve that judgment until you've heard the entire story." As the angry fog began to clear, she pulled herself from his grasp. Her expression hardened to match his. "I'm fine. Really. Let me finish." The black look on his face revealed his skepticism. With reluctance, he retreated to the shadows of the room.

She began once again, her voice edged with self-recrimination. "Late one night, when the staff was abed and Horace was out, Phillip and I were alone in the library. He wanted to elope. I wanted to wait. He persisted and prodded until his advances became belligerent, almost desperate. The longer I refused, the more irate he became. My own temper took hold. I told him I would never marry him if I was witnessing the true man. He lunged for me. I panicked and struck him with a brass candlestick. Poor Phillip crumpled to the floor like a lead ball. He lay motionless with blood oozing from his forehead, and I stood there doing nothing, watching the life drain from his body. When my stepuncle found me, I was hovering over Phillip, blood smeared on my hands and clothes. Horace informed me that Phillip was dead. In order to protect me from scandal or possible retribution, he sent me to my room, told me to burn my garments, and that he would handle everything. By the time my good sense returned, Horace had left with Phillip's body."

"Jocelyn, you are no murderess."

"How can you say that after—"

He held up his hands to freeze the words in her mouth. "If my guess is correct, you are guilty of ignorance, self-preservation, and blind faith. Not murder."

If only his assurances were true. "But . . . "

"You said Phillip seemed desperate. Why?"

What did Phillip's mood matter? She was the one who killed him. "How should I know?"

"Think, Jocelyn. Use the brain I know you have. What did Phillip say?"

Her mind traveled back to the night months ago when her life began to spin out of control. "Phillip said he had to marry me. Immediately. Before my step-uncle returned."

"Keep going. Try to remember every detail."

Phillip's image flashed before her: the wild look in his eyes, his rapid breathing and erratic movements, the ferocity of his grip. "I already told you. He wanted to elope that night. I refused. He practically begged, claiming it was a matter of life or death. Still I refused. Still he pressed his suit. I threatened to tell my step-uncle and"—she paused—"Phillip laughed."

"Keep going and concentrate. Exactly what did he say about your step-uncle?"

"He said Horace wouldn't come to my rescue in the manner I expected, but I would have a husband one way or another. Phillip felt he was the preferred choice." As the idea gained clarity in her mind, she sought Reyn in the shadows. "You think Horace was forcing Phillip to marry me."

"The thought occurred to me. I've also considered that your step-uncle might have finished off poor Phillip himself."

His words, meant to comfort, give absolution of some sort, were still difficult to accept. "Out of anger and fear, I struck him. Then I stood there, doing nothing. I let my step-uncle protect me."

"Permit yourself to be human. You were frightened and in all likelihood in shock. Does Agatha know about this?"

"No. I've told no one."

"Good. I will begin a discreet investigation tomorrow." When she started to object, he raised his hand to silence her. "Did you love him?"

Why had he asked her that? How could she answer? Phillip offered friendship. Like an abandoned puppy, she had relished every smile, wink, secret joke and compliment thrown her way. He made her laugh, and up until that last night had shown her only kindness. "What does it matter?"

"Just answer the bloody question."

"I'm not sure!"

He practically snarled. "Go on. I would like to hear the rest of this confession."

She wanted to run, to scream, to have Reyn take her into his arms and offer comfort, but his voice had become cool and distant once again. Pulling the covers to her chin, she wrapped her arms around her knees forming a tight cocoon, as if the position would restrain her frayed emotions.

"We set off for London the next day. Prior to our departure, my step-uncle did propose marriage himself. After my emphatic refusal, he seemed content to take me to the city, but not as I anticipated. We reached the outskirts of London, where we encountered a band of ruffians. He bragged about the attack, his own grand scheme, then raged about the inheritance, claiming it should have been his. I still didn't even know I had an inheritance. That was when he confessed to my parents' deaths. By killing them, he thought the title, the estates, the monies, would fall to him. As far as I know, everything was left to me. Except the title, of course. That died with my father. He told me I should have married Phillip when I'd had the chance."

"Why?"

Shrugging her shoulders, she answered. "I don't know."

"What happened next?"

"I thought he would kill me on the spot, but he said he wanted me mollified, broken, biddable. That's when he delivered me to Bedlam. I think he planned to come back and claim me for his wife."

Reyn rubbed his palm across the stubble on his jaw. "I assume he wanted absolute control over your money and the estates. Perhaps he feared questions would be asked."

"He also said he wanted me in his bed." Hearing his obscene commentary, she realized she should have kept that fact to herself. She muttered, "I believe you know the rest."

"Hardly." He began pacing the room in a rapid, erratic pattern. "Why didn't you contact the authorities?"

"I had no proof. You think they would have believed

an escapee from Bedlam? I also feared the mishap with Phillip. I had no idea how my step-uncle would use that information."

"Why didn't you contact your father's solicitor? Surely, he would have helped you."

"For half my adult life, I lived with nuns and other young girls in similar situations to mine. I spent little time in the company of men. I believed my father had abandoned me. I trusted Phillip. He deceived me. You know what my step-uncle did. I met the family solicitor only once. I didn't know whom to trust any longer. As far as I knew, he was helping Horace. Agatha came along, promised what seemed to be the moon, and I believed her."

Clearly dissatisfied, he resumed his interrogation. "Why the memory loss?"

"Horace swore he would kill anyone who stood in his way. I hoped to protect those who helped me."

"Good God, you insult me. We have been around this bend before. I am capable of protecting myself."

She defended her decision. "I couldn't take the risk. I know this man. If he thinks I have lost my mental faculties, he will believe he is safe. For the moment. I will have the time to implement my revenge, gain a confession or some evidence to punish the man. Agatha and I have everything planned."

"Ah yes, your plan. I became suspicious the moment Agatha began to spout nonsense about investments and such. That was all a little game you and Agatha played tonight, wasn't it?" He advanced on the bed from across the room to hover menacingly above her, a feral gleam to his eyes. "Tell me about this plan, Jocelyn."

"Promise you won't interfere?" When she watched his clouded expression darken, she realized the chance of gaining any promise from him was unlikely. She resigned herself. "Agatha will introduce Horace to Lord Halden, intimating that she heard about some speculative investments. She believes that Lord Halden will eagerly embrace her interest. Hopefully, Horace will follow suit. Of course, after Horace has entangled himself, Agatha will withdraw at the last minute. Then we wait for the projects to fall apart as they often do. We also hope that Horace involves himself in the less respectable investments of Lord Halden, which we will willingly expose."

"What if Horace refuses the bait or suspects trickery? What if he kills Halden? What if he kills you?"

Her tightly leashed control vanished. She yelled her response. "Don't you think I have thought of that?"

Reyn slammed a fist into the towering rail of the four-poster bed, his voice equally loud and unyielding. "Then for heaven's sake, why don't you simply tell the authorities and have the man arrested?"

"I can't," she cried irrationally while launching herself from the bed in near hysteria. "I won't. It is still my word against his. Besides, I will have my revenge. Power, status and money are everything to him. I will allow him to think those things are within his grasp, then relish every moment he suffers as his dreams and good name turn to dust before his very eyes. I want him to feel as exploited, as forsaken, as shattered as I did when he, the last person I allowed myself to trust, abandoned me to hell."

"Enough, Jocelyn."

"I will do this no matter how angry you are or become."

Within a heartbeat, Reyn closed the space between them. "Don't you understand I am worried about you?" He savagely wrapped her in a possessive embrace. "Since the beginning, set on this course of yours, you have repeatedly lied. I have lived with that deceit, accepted your private reasons and hoped to earn your trust. I will help you. After tonight, though, no more secrets. Is there anything else I need to know?"

She could feel his gaze on the top of her head. It was

almost as if he cared. Truly cared. Yet, this was not the time to tell him about the baby. That news could wait for a happier moment. "No," she whimpered as tears rolled freely down her cheeks.

"I hope to God you are telling the truth."

She thought his whispered words were more for himself than for her.

Reyn considered everything his wife, now asleep beside him, had revealed. Her confession tonight easily explained her actions, her fears, over the last few months. He would grant her the vengeance, for he understood the need. He felt a need to throttle Mardell himself. Grudgingly, he acknowledged the soundness of her plan, though he'd be damned before she placed herself in jeopardy. The minute her step-uncle suspected larceny or trickery, she could be killed and that was unthinkable. From now on, she would be closely guarded whenever she left the house. If he allowed her to leave at all.

By the end of the Montgomery ball, Agatha should have introduced Lord Halden to Mardell, a marriage made in heaven—or more appropriately, hell. The bastards deserved one another, the difference being only that Lord Halden was a leech on society, Mardell a murderer.

If his own scene went according to plan, Tam and Walter would have befriended Mardell as well. It would be interesting to see what information and insight they gained.

An image of Jocelyn wrapped in the arms of another man sent Reyn's blood boiling. Jealousy was a new emotion for him. He didn't like it. Phillip Bains had not deserved to die, but Reyn could not quite bring himself to feel any remorse for a man he never knew, especially if it meant Jocelyn now belonged to him. Had she loved her dead fiancé? And did it matter? By defending herself, had she killed him? Or had Mardell finished the job? Those were questions Reyn intended to find answers for over the next few days.

Jocelyn stirred, nestling deeper in his warmth. Along with the overwhelming instinct to protect her came a burst of self-contempt at the sudden realization that he had given this one woman the one thing he swore he never would. After all his vows, his promises, he had fallen in love with her. When he considered the fact that he still harbored a fierce sense of betrayal, he found the revelation very unsettling. And why did he feel that she kept another secret?

Massaging his pounding temples, he hoped his instincts were wrong.

While he tore a buttered biscuit in half, a long, slow whistle slid between Tam's teeth as he absorbed the story Reyn relayed. Walter's fingers drummed absently on the arm of the mahogany Queen Anne chair. Reyn understood their need for a moment to absorb the information before he began his own interrogation.

But he quickly lost his patience. "Now you understand the necessity for urgency. How did it go last night?"

"Horace Mardell is as crooked as a coiled rope," said Tam. "Not to mention cold, calculating and a cunning card player."

Walter added, "The man has a way with the ladies, loves to gamble, enjoys his drink, but he's a sly one. I don't think he's foolish enough to allow his diversions or liquor to cloud his thinking. Power and prestige seem to be high on his list of needs. He wants them badly, but we're going to have to be very clever with this one."

"That's basically what Jocelyn said. Evidently, the family title died with Mardell's stepbrother, so he has remained on the fringe of society. What did he have to say about my wife?"

Crossing to the sideboard for another biscuit, Tam gladly answered this question. "You could tell he was biding his time, eager to gain information from us. I think his patience was wearing a hole in his seat for his waiting. Of course, Agatha gladly enlightened him on the memory loss of your poor wife. You must remember you found her wandering aimlessly across the moors, provided her with shelter and your love, which brought her back to the world of the living. Unfortunately, her poor mind suffered mightily and may never recover."

Cunningly, Reyn smiled. "Did he believe that mountain of rubbish?"

"Absolutely," Tam added brightly.

"Splendid," Reyn said while he rolled his coffee cup between his hands in contemplation. "Jocelyn and Agatha were on the right track, but I want more control and less left to chance. I believe we have just become his three best friends. Our ability to open a great many doors to society should be enough of an enticement. He should also buy into our canal project in Herefordshire. I imagine he will need a line of credit, which we shall eagerly find for him. We raise the price of shares, allow him to make a substantial purchase, then spread our own rumors of bad luck. The shares drop. A few words here and there, a bit of pressure and the bank calls his note. Simultaneously, we allude to a few nasty tidbits regarding the character of the man. Near the end, before the authorities intervene, I will allow Jocelyn her satisfaction."

"Do you think he will go for the bait?" Tam asked.

Reyn answered with absolute certainty. "Like a big-mouthed bass with his jowls wide open."

Tam said what everyone silently thought. "You do realize, when he discovers what has happened, he will be more dangerous than a hundred vipers beneath your blanket."

"Yes, I know." Reyn rubbed his jaw thoughtfully. "We will have to be extremely cautious. You have a meeting planned?"

Walter beamed like a proud parent. "We mentioned that you would bid on a rare piece of horseflesh at Tattersall's auction today. I guarantee Mardell will attend."

"Excellent. We simply need the cooperation of Agatha and Jocelyn."

"Our cooperation for what?" Agatha asked as she entered the breakfast room.

Reyn stood to place a crisp kiss on her cheek before he glared directly into her eyes to witness her reaction. "For the downfall of Horace Mardell."

Exhaling a sigh of relief, she sat in the nearest chair. "Sweet delight, she finally told you the truth."

In vexation, Reyn threw his hands in the air. "That's it? That's all you have to say for yourself?"

"Please, Reyn, do not start pontificating. The girl needed my help. I provided it and would do the same again in a moment's breath." The glacial tone of her voice signaled the end of the discussion.

As grandmother and grandson stared at one another, open challenge in their expressions, Tam and Walter remained silent. Years of experience had taught them that now was not the time to interject their opinions.

"Agatha, you have encountered countless acts of cruelty, witnessed numerous wretched souls in need, acknowledging you could not save them all. I asked before. Now I demand you satisfy my curiosity. Why her? Why Jocelyn? Why make yourself her guardian angel?"

Obviously considering her answer carefully, Agatha cast a glance downward, tapping her fingertips together. When she gazed at Reyn, her eyes seemed to weigh the character of the man before her.

"Do you remember the woman in the locket your father held the night he died?"

Puzzled, Reyn nodded.

"That woman was Jocelyn's mother."

"My mother?" The strangled response drew everyone's attention to the doorway. Jocelyn advanced on Agatha. "Why didn't you tell me?"

Reyn cursed. "Why didn't you tell all of us?"

Ignoring Reyn, Agatha touched an amber gloved hand to Jocelyn's flushed cheek. "Please forgive me, child. And an old woman's fantasy. I thought I had been given a second chance to correct the past."

"I don't understand," Jocelyn whispered.

"It begins with your grandmother. Gwendolyn Garnett was my dearest friend. After her husband died, we spent a great deal of time together. It was only natural that my son and her daughter would meet. They fell madly in love and wanted to marry immediately. Of course, we were thrilled so we agreed to the union. However, Gwen thought Madelyn was still too young. Everyone agreed to wait two years."

Thus far, everyone seemed awestruck by Agatha's admission, Reyn included. He watched Jocelyn to gauge her reaction to the news. She seemed to be taking it in stride.

Agatha looked to the ceiling as if Gwen were there to help tell the balance of the story. "During that time, Reyn's father traveled to France, where he met Reyn's mother. They were caught in a compromising position, after which he felt honor bound to marry her, leaving Madelyn alone and heartbroken. Gwen did as she thought best and found Madelyn a husband as soon as possible. Gwen and I regretted the decision to make the couple wait to marry, but there was no changing the outcome. Your mother learned to live with and accept her fate. And I think she was happy. Reyn's father was miserable. He paid dearly for his indiscretion. I have often wondered what life would have been like if they had married immediately." She shrugged her shoulders and smiled tenderly at Jocelyn and then Reyn. "But then neither you nor Reyn would have been born." The dowager sent a tender glance back to Jocelyn. "When I discovered you at Bedlam, I knew I couldn't abandon you. I felt I had been given a second chance. I even deluded myself into thinking that Gwen had sent me there that day. I hoped you and Reyn would find comfort with one another. Find the love they lost."

"I always sensed a sadness deep inside my mother. Now I know why. Thank you for telling me."

"I planned to tell you after all this other nastiness was settled." Agatha turned to witness Reyn's stunned expression. "I assume by the gathering here that you have accepted the responsibility of dealing with Mr. Mardell?"

Apparently, Agatha had no intention of letting him brood on the matter. Briskly, he nodded.

"I am available if you need me," she said as she stood. "Jocelyn, come by later and ask your questions." She marched to the door, speaking over her shoulder. "Tameron and Walter, kindly escort me to my coach."

"Interfering old woman," Reyn muttered. His grandmother had said all she meant to on the subject, so he addressed his two friends. "Go ahead. I will meet you at the auction shortly."

Privately brooding, rubbing his jaw, he waited for his friends to make their departure. He watched Jocelyn behind half-closed lids. She behaved like a skittish spinster in a roomful of bachelors. No small wonder. He knew he should say something. She needed reassurance. That last bit of news, on top of everything else, had jolted his mind into a state of turmoil incapable of coherent thought.

"You must hate me," she said in a whisper.

Reyn threw a wrinkled napkin to the table. "No, Jocelyn, I do not hate you."

"But . . . "

Reyn looked up to see a trail of tears falling silently down Jocelyn's cheeks. He couldn't deal with tears. Not right now. "Good heavens! When I was twelve years old, I witnessed my mother launch what I mistook as a mere trinket at my father. He became furious. They quarreled about adultery, obsession and all sorts of sordid tidbits. Later, after my father fell into a drunken stupor, I sneaked into his study to peek at the source of their argument. The woman in the locket was magnificent. And I hated her. As far as I was concerned, she was the cause of my parents' troubles. The reason my mother hated me. The reason my father drank and ignored me. I have hated her for the last sixteen years of my life. So pardon me if I require time to reconcile my feelings."

His unintentional sharpness, accompanied by a stony glare, sent Jocelyn scuttling for the arched mahogany doorway.

Impatiently, he yelled, his voice like thunder, "Jocelyn—Good heavens, wait!" He whisked by the ever-stoic Briggs. It was too late. His wife had already disappeared into her suite. "Well done, you fool." His voice cracked like a whip. "Briggs, fetch my cloak."

Waiting for the warm outer garment, he chastised himself for lacking the courage to walk upstairs and comfort his wife. Better later. She probably needed time to think, to clear her own mind. He certainly did.

"And I'm the king of England."

"Begging your pardon, sir?"

"Nothing, Briggs. Tell Jocelyn"—he paused—"tell my wife that I've gone out."

Chapter Nineteen

Jocelyn's silver needle pierced the delicate white linen recklessly as she formed the ruby-red wing of a cardinal. Remembering Briggs's message from Reyn for her to remain at home, she studied her handiwork. Only passing fair. She hated embroidery, but the tedium of the task kept her hands busy. Caesar kept her company, but neither could keep the mental wolves at bay.

Ever since Agatha's revelation that morning, she had felt an odd sense of bereavement. Reyn, her love, her happiness, seemed to be slipping through her fingers. She was at a loss about what to do. With more concentration on her problems than her stitching, she jabbed her thumb. Her hand flew to her mouth. When she looked up, she noticed Briggs standing in the doorway, a frown on his face.

"Yes, Briggs?" She laid the fabric to the side. Caesar seized the opportunity to drape himself across her lap.

"A gentleman downstairs claims to have an appointment with his grace. I explained that his grace was absent from the house. The visitor asked to see you."

The cat stretched under the tender strokes Jocelyn offered. "Did he present his card?" she asked.

"No. He named himself as one Horace Mardell."

Suppressing the initial wave of alarm, Jocelyn tried to calmly assess the situation. Reyn had specifically told her to stay away from Horace. Did she dare admit him? It wasn't as though she had gone to borrow trouble. Trouble had found her. And she didn't really believe her step-uncle had arrived on her doorstep prepared to do physical harm. If she didn't let him up, he might think she was afraid, planting the suspicion that her amnesia was a ruse. In fact, she could use this opportunity to confuse the scoundrel. Yes, she decided, her step-uncle could have a few guarded moments of her time.

"Briggs, I think I shall see what Mr. Mardell wants, but I need a favor. When I give a signal, I want you to interrupt us."

"A signal?"

"Yes. When I tire of the discussion, I want you to interrupt and tell me I have an appointment."

Briggs seemed to stand three inches taller. "But my lady, you have no appointment. You are to stay home until his lordship's return."

"I know that, and you know that, but our visitor doesn't know that."

"You want to play a trick on the fellow?"

While she warmed to the idea, Briggs looked as though he'd been asked to walk the cat to the butcher's for a snack. "Not really. I don't wish him to overstay his welcome. Therefore, we must have a signal."

"Perhaps madam could ask for something," Briggs suggested warily.

Jocelyn thought for a moment when inspiration hit.

"Of course. I shall ask for raspberry tea cakes. When I eat them, I become horribly sick."

"But, madam, why eat something if you know it will make you ill?"

"I will not eat them. Nor are you to bring them. You need only interrupt me when I make the request. Understand?" His thick white eyebrows furrowed together in consternation, obviously contemplating the reason for this flummery. She knew Briggs would prefer she simply tell the visitor to leave. "Do not fret so, Briggs. No one will know of your chicanery."

Mumbling as he turned to show the visitor into the salon, Briggs sent one last, fleeting glimpse toward his mistress. Jocelyn waved cheerfully as he went out. There was no need for him to sense her alarm. Her heart beat as though it contained a small minstrel band, and she pulled several deep breaths of air into her chest. Her sweaty palms gripped the edge of the settee. With a short prayer, she forced the tension from her shoulders and grabbed the embroidery, rousing Caesar long enough for him to bat at the dangling threads. Even as she scratched the favorite spot behind his right ear, she warned him, "This is not the time to play. I will need all my wits about me."

Briggs stood like a statue beside the door. He announced, "Mr. Mardell."

Briggs's sedate introduction diverted her attention from the cat to the tall man standing in the doorway. With his handsome face, his perfectly groomed mustache and hair etched with grey, his distinguished clothing, his easy smile, her step-uncle appeared as a well-bred, innocuous peer of the realm. Only she knew the depth of his wickedness.

Horace crossed the room in slow, deliberate steps, his eyes assessing the room, the furnishings, the butler and most of all, her. He stopped at the edge of the ice-blue silk gown that covered her tapping toes. Her eyes remained fixed on his.

Horace exercised proper decorum by standing until given leave to sit. "Lady Wilcott. Thank you for taking the time to see me. I seem to have crossed messages with your husband. I understood we were to meet here this afternoon."

"Dear me. What a coil," she answered, all innocence and false sincerity. She would bet her ruby necklace that the blackguard knew exactly where her husband had gone, and if he thought he could frighten, trick or bully her, he would be gravely disappointed. Instead, she would lead the man on a merry chase of falsehoods. "I believe my husband has gone to Tattersall's. Please, sit down."

"Excuse me, your grace." Briggs, who had come to stand unobtrusively beside the settee, interrupted. "I don't believe the gentleman will be staying long. Remember your appointment?"

Jocelyn curiously eyed her butler. She hadn't given the signal yet. "I haven't forgotten, Briggs." She glanced back to Horace. "Do sit down."

When Horace began to lower himself, he peered at Briggs as though he'd just claimed some small victory. "Tattersall's?" he asked.

"Ahem," Briggs interrupted again. "Perhaps, sir, you would be more comfortable in the leather chair by the fireplace. It would be most inhospitable were you to land on one of her ladyship's needles. Don't you agree, madam?"

"Definitely." Obviously, her butler intended to act as chaperone, for which she was grateful. When her step-uncle crossed to the chair a good six feet from her, she barely suppressed her sigh of relief. "As I was saying, Mr. Mardell. My husband hopes to acquire a new mare for me."

"You ride?"

The surprise was evident in his voice. "Of course," she lied easily.

"I know a great many ladies who fear horses, or have never taken the time to be properly trained."

"I feel as though I were born in the saddle. Of course, I prefer a jaunt in our phaeton, but to ride a well-trained horse is always a pleasure." Caesar, the lazy slug, as if he knew she was lying, stretched and kneaded his sharp talons in the fabric of her gown. Restlessly, Jocelyn stroked him from head to tail, glad to have an outlet for her anxiety. "Would you care for a cup of tea?"

"If it weren't a great imposition," Horace said.

"Not at all." A serene smile locked on her face, Jocelyn nodded her approval. Briggs paused, scowled at Horace, then simply shouted down the hall. Disregarding the open-mouthed stare of his mistress, he crossed back to the settee with his usual practiced formality, where he took the position of guard, chaperone or co-conspirator. Jocelyn wasn't quite sure which. She didn't care. She only knew he seemed to be taking his assignment quite seriously.

"Quite a noble fellow you have there," Horace said while his gaze followed the movements of her hand on the large black cat. "Owned him long?"

"A few months. We found each other on the moor."

"Ah, yes." His eyes lit with anticipation. "Your grandmother-in-law mentioned your unusual situation."

Jocelyn gasped slightly and bowed her head as if embarrassed. At least, she hoped she looked embarrassed. It was a good thing her step-uncle couldn't see the anger in her eyes.

"Forgive me. I spoke out of turn. I can't imagine waking one day to have no past, no future."

"It was quite frightening. Agatha, bless her soul, is such a romantic, though. She has no qualms about my memory loss. Given my circumstances—no dowry, no lineage—most dowagers would have fought the marriage. She has been my greatest champion. As for my husband"—she sighed deeply—"words cannot express my gratitude. I'm a very lucky woman."

A seductive smile formed on his lips. "I would say that he is a very lucky man."

The eyes she once thought kind and loving watched her with deadly intent. She beamed like a young woman blinded by love. "Indeed."

"And you have no idea how you came to be on the moor in the first place?"

"It's quite a mystery."

"No memories at all," he pressed. "A favorite food, a family friend? When you look in the mirror, do you see a mother with long blond hair and dark eyes looking back?"

Yes, she wanted to scream. *I see myself in the mirror and remember my mother. Then I remember every detail about my parents' deaths as you described. I remember each lie your treacherous lips told. Every miserable day I spent in hell because of you.*

"Oh, dear," Horace murmured. "You look pale, Lady Wilcott. I see I've upset you. I will not mention the subject again."

Yes, he would. She knew it. Maybe not today, but another time, another place, if he ever managed to find her alone again. "I'm fine," she said. "Each day I wake and hope that something or someone will trigger a memory, a flicker of insight. For now, I am content."

The maid ushered in a tea cart filled with delicate cups and saucers, lace napkins, an array of buttered croissants and raisin scones. Glad for the brief respite, Jocelyn used the task of serving tea to occupy her hands. Her mind contemplated her step-uncle's next ploy.

Briggs handed the teacup to Horace, continuing to hover nearby.

Horace reached inside his jacket and withdrew a small package. "By the way, Lady Wilcott, I hope you don't think me overly forward, but I took the liberty of bringing a gift. As I mentioned last night, you greatly resemble my niece. I indulged my melancholy by bringing a little something as a belated wedding present."

Briggs took the small package wrapped in gold-colored tissue and shook it before he handed it to Jocelyn. Horace appeared suitably annoyed, which seemed to please Briggs immensely, while Jocelyn forced her trembling hands to hold the parcel steady in her lap. "How very thoughtful. Hardly necessary, but I must say I always enjoy a surprise." The babbling continued, for she seemed incapable of stopping it, just as she seemed unable to stop herself from opening the present.

With a gentle tug, the tiny blue ribbon slipped away, followed by the thin paper. Cautiously, her slender fingers lifted the lid on the small tin box she uncovered. Forcing herself to squelch the rising pain, she let a second pass, then two, then three. She wanted to rant and rage. She wanted to throw the box in her step-uncle's face. She wanted to run. She knew if she glanced up, Horace, smug and cunning, would be watching her every move, her every reaction. This was the ultimate test the wretch had planned all along.

With trembling insides but steady hands, she pulled the delicate silver rose from the box. The inlaid rubies and emeralds winked back at her in greeting. How well she remembered the flower, a family heirloom passed from mother to daughter, generation to generation. The beautifully crafted piece of jewelry had been her favorite and would have become hers the day she married. It was also the pin her mother wore the day she was murdered. The same rose supposedly stolen by bandits.

The expected words of gratitude, captured by the memories swirling in her mind, lay trapped behind the smile frozen on her face. Bent on survival, the instinctive part of her brain nudged her away from the pain, the blazing fury, toward the surface. Fighting for survival, seeking a diversion, she intentionally pricked her sore finger with the pin. "Ouch." Her hand flew to her mouth.

The sudden movement brought Caesar to his feet, his stance now one of a predator searching the cause of the disruption. His golden eyes passed from Briggs to Jocelyn, back to Briggs, finally settling on Horace, who had crossed to Jocelyn's side. The hair on the cat's neck rose in warning before he hissed and lashed out at the man who came to Jocelyn's aid.

"What the devil?" Horace blurted as the claws struck his thigh. His first reaction was to raise his arm, prepared to send the cat flying into the fireplace. Before he lost complete control, he remembered where he was. Calmly, he stated, "Excuse my outburst. It would seem the cat is your protector."

Jocelyn could only nod, puzzled by the cat's animosity and shaken by the flash of violence she witnessed in Horace's eyes.

Thankfully, Briggs saved the day. "I will see to Lady Wilcott," he said as he securely wrapped a napkin around her injured finger. "I believe, sir, it is time for you to go.

Hold on, she silently prayed. *Just a few more moments and Horace will be gone.* "Yes, Briggs, I do have that appointment with Agatha." Turning to the serpent who infested her home, she smiled. "Thank you, Mr. Mardell, for the generous present. I will inform my husband of your misunderstanding. If it helps, I assume he will be at White's or Boodle's this evening."

"Thank you, Lady Wilcott. I look forward to seeing you again."

A formal nod, a slight bow and the man was being escorted from the room by Briggs. As her combined rage, fear and relief battled for release, Jocelyn surged to her feet. She found herself drawn to the curtains. It was as if she needed to verify that her step-uncle had truly left. She didn't hear Briggs return, nor did she hear him move to stand directly behind her. She did hear his gentle reassurances.

Everything burst in a torrential flood of tears. Before she realized what she was about, Jocelyn had poured her heart and emotions into Briggs's pleated shirt. Valiantly, he stood and accepted her intrusion while tenderly wrapping her in an embrace reminiscent of her father's. She cried harder. For her parents, her unborn baby. For Reyn and what she was afraid she'd lost. She cried for the loss of innocence, her belief in all things that were good. Clearly, the blame lay at her step-uncle's feet.

"Oh, Briggs." She managed to hiccup a few words of explanation as she continued to weep. "The brooch belonged to my mother. He hoped I would react. I didn't. I showed him."

"Yes, you did. Quite nicely, too," he said while patting her back.

"The man has no scruples."

"None."

"He should be shot."

"At the very least."

"I'm glad Caesar attacked him."

"Hail, Caesar."

Briggs's somber tone when he praised the cat she knew he barely tolerated brought her mind into focus. A laugh, not a timid giggle or a chuckle, but a full-blown, gut-wrenching laugh, erupted. She'd done it. She made it through the conversation and managed to keep the facade tightly in place. And now she was crying all over her very staid, very proper butler. She was laughing so hard she didn't feel Briggs stiffen. Nor did she hear her husband and Tam enter.

"Briggs, I assume there is a logical explanation for the fact that my wife is clinging to the front of your shirt." He couldn't believe his eyes. Stoic, pristine Briggs allowing a woman to hang on his finely tailored livery? It was simply too much. Jocelyn's head snapped up. The minute it did, Reyn took one look at her face, her swollen, red eyes, her tear-streaked cheeks, and fired questions like a drill sergeant. "What the devil is going on?"

Briggs seemed reluctant to withdraw his physical support. "Do you mind, Briggs? if my wife wishes to weep . . . " He turned to Jocelyn. "Are you laughing or weeping?"

"A bit of both, I think."

"Well, you can very well weep on me." Reyn pulled Jocelyn into his arms.

Tam crossed to the liquor cabinet to fetch the brandy, which in his opinion was something everyone was going to need. He knew he did.

Tenderly, Briggs smiled at Jocelyn, then scowled at the duke. "Harumph," he said as he straightened his clothing. "It is about time you returned." Having spoken his mind, he stomped from the room.

Were it possible, Reyn thought his jaw fell to the floor before it snapped shut. "This had better be good or I just might fire the pompous . . . " He couldn't finish the sentence. He was still too stunned.

Tam said, "Don't issue idle threats, my friend. You and I know we'd both serve the old man crumpets in bed if he wished it." He handed a drink to Reyn. "I'm as shocked as you are. Can you imagine the reaction of the staff if they were to get wind of his momentary lapse of propriety? He'll give himself a dressing-down that will last for days."

"For weeks," Reyn corrected.

"Oh, be quiet," Jocelyn blurted. "He's a paragon. A veritable champion. He deserves a bonus. And while you're at it, Caesar earned kidney pie for the next two weeks." Under normal circumstances, the expressions on Tam's and Reyn's faces would have sent Jocelyn into another fit of laughter. Right now she felt anything but normal. "Say something."

"Perhaps," said Reyn hesitantly, "you should explain what transpired in our absence?"

Within Reyn's embrace, she detailed the visit from her step-uncle.

Tam spoke first. "Now we know why the blighter didn't show at Tattersall's. I'm sorry, Reyn. I really thought he'd be there."

"It's not your fault. Evidently, Mardell thinks he's more cunning than we. The fool. His own arrogance provided us the evidence we need to hang him."

Jocelyn couldn't follow her husband's insinuations. "How?"

Grinning, he said, "The pin. It proves he had a hand in the death of your parents."

"Why do you suppose he took such a risk?" asked Tam.

"It had to be a test for Jocelyn. If he discovered she did not have amnesia, I imagine he would finish the game in short order. For all of us. But if he accepts her act as truth, then he probably believes the pin is irrelevant at this time."

"He's quite dangerous," Jocelyn whispered.

"I agree," said Reyn. "However, if he made one mistake, he'll make another. And we'll be waiting."

Debauchery. That one word came to mind every time Horace crossed the London Bridge to Southwark. Actresses and actors, pretty-boys and pederasts, singing and dancing girls, whores and pimps, thieves and idiots, all found sanctuary here. A few well-placed coins provided one with whatever one wished. Taverns, brothels and inns provided a place to spend the night if a weary gamester so desired. It was also the playground for many of the upper crust of London society.

Pity, Horace thought as he gazed about the street. He didn't have time to indulge.

When the carriage approached the Paris Garden, an establishment known for its cruel and vicious dog and cock fights, Horace tapped on the roof. If luck prevailed, he'd quickly find the party he sought. That would certainly improve his mood.

His impromptu visit with Jocelyn had left him frustrated. And consumed with lust. In his absence, the dear girl had blossomed into a true beauty. God, how he wanted her. He imagined himself between her thighs, riding her hard. Almost as suddenly, he remembered her husband.

Horace fisted his hands into knots. He despised Wilcott and all he stood for. Reynolds Blackburn. The Duke of Wilcott. Arrogant. Filthy rich. Accepted into every parlor in London simply because of his birth. Jocelyn and Wilcott would rue the day they married.

All in good time, Horace reminded himself. First, he needed to determine whether the chit had truly lost her memory. Thus far, she'd executed her role to perfection. When he had first seen her at the Montgomery ball, he couldn't believe his eyes. Thank God he controlled his reaction before he revealed anything. Until he knew exactly where the truth lay, he would gladly play the fop, eager to befriend a duke. Then he would dispose of him like a worthless mongrel. That was something to look forward to.

The thought left him smiling as he entered the dimly lit theater. The stench of stale cigars, whiskey and soiled clothing assaulted his nostrils. Afternoon gamesters, eager to turn a profit on the lives of the caged beasts, crowded around a roped area. At the moment, it looked as though a huge hound was winning the battle over some sort of shepherd mix. A sudden lunge from the shepherd knocked the hound to the floor, eliciting a large groan from the jeering group of men. The money was obviously on the hound.

Turning away from the dogs, Horace scanned the rest of the hall. A few people sat at wooden tables, drinking only God knew what. A barmaid sat on a chap's lap, hoping to earn an extra favor or two for her efforts. A loud cheer filled the room. The hound must have found his footing. Horace didn't care. He'd found his man.

Crossing around the bar to the back of the fighting dogs, he stopped beside a wall lined with cages. Horace said, "Well, well, I can't decide if your level of employment has taken a turn for the better or the worse."

The burly man turned, a startled looked on his face. Jocko grinned. "Well gov'ner, I wondered if you'd ever return."

"Since I stand before you, it's obvious I did. What happened, Jocko? How did my niece escape the hospital?"

Jocko, his smile erased, was trapped between a large crate and Horace. He shifted his weight from leg to leg, his hands twisting the stick he held. "I didn't help 'er, if that's what you be thinkin'."

Jocko felt guilty about something. It would be interesting to discover what and decide how to use it. "Don't panic, my friend. I come for some answers, not your head. Tell me. What do you know about my charge?"

Nervously looking from side to side, Jocko said, "I can't talk long. This job pays me well."

"Not a problem. This will only take a moment."

"Well, sir, the girl kept talkin' to people, you know. So I decided to hide her 'til you returned. This ol' battle-ax ruined me plan. Had me fired too. I followed them. Somehow, your niece got herself married to a duke."

"I'm aware of that."

"Well, one day I thought to nab her, but another bloke jumped me. I've been hiding in Southwark since."

Wondering who might have intervened, Horace inspected his fingernails. He needed a manicure before the Kenricks ball tonight. He smiled. Since he'd located Jocko so quickly, he'd even have time for a whore. "Very wise. Lord Wilcott seems to have a rather nasty possessive streak toward my niece."

Jocko cleared his throat. "Gov'ner, I could use some extra blunt."

"And what do I receive in return?"

"Well, while I was following the girl around, I noticed another bloke."

"Another man?" Frowning, Horace considered the possibilities. "What did he look like?"

"Skinny fellow with a round face. About twenty-four or the likes. Kinda reddish hair."

Impossible. "What else?" asked Horace.

Jocko rubbed the whiskers on his chin, thinking. His eyes brightened. "He had a red birth mark on the side of his cheek."

Unbelievable. If what he suspected were true, Horace required Jocko's services after all. Horace withdrew a few bills from his pocket and pressed them into Jocko's greedy hand. "Excellent, Jocko. Here's what I need you to do."

Chapter Twenty

Standing in the small glass shop on Bond Street, Jocelyn watched the tiny grains of sand drift through the hourglass. Like her days with Reyn, time was running out. Her intuition told her so. She had sensed his withdrawal on the night of her grand confession, and ever since then his cool detachment had seemed to grow. At night, he made love to her with a ferocity that left her limp. As soon as as the sun rose, a door closed between them. She attributed his withdrawal to the fact that he had a great deal on his mind.

Agatha's startling revelation had opened a wound that had been festering for years. Only time would tell whether Reyn's wound, along with their relationship, would heal.

Every day, Horace fell further into Reyn's neatly laid trap. They seemed to have become the best of chums, their business dealings occupying a good part of her husband's days and nights.

Reyn had become obsessed with her safety. It was a

small miracle she had been allowed out of the house today, but Reyn had taken Horace to Herefordshire to see the canals for himself. Davey agreed to drive her about for a bit of last-minute shopping for Reyn's upcoming birthday celebration.

Then there was still the matter of Phillip's death. True to his word, Reyn sent a Bow Street runner to investigate. Any news would be welcome compared to uncertainty.

All she could do was take one day at a time, one problem at a time. Therefore the final plans for Reyn's party moved forward. And she needed to find the perfect gift.

As she turned, her gaze settled on an intricate crystal glass figurine, a majestic knight decked in shining armor resting imperiously atop his powerful war horse. It was perfect.

Eager to make her purchase, she whirled and upset a stand of baskets. Directly before her, almost eye to eye, a smug grin plastered on his round face, stood her supposedly dead fiancé.

"Phillip?"

"Jocelyn, my love. We meet again."

"You're alive." With the realization came the ramifications. She was furious. "You worm. Do you realize the worry your death caused me?"

He patted her hand, draped it across his arm as any gentleman would and directed her toward the door of the shop. "I understand completely. You must have been miserable without me, dear heart."

"Don't patronize me, you idiot." Unwilling to draw attention to herself, she scanned the small shop and lowered her voice. Where in heaven's name was Davey? "I did not mourn you."

Unbelievably, Phillip looked devastated. Exasperated, she sighed. "Not that way. I thought I killed you."

"Yes, but . . ."

Necessity allowed no quarter. "Why didn't you contact me before today?"

Like a petulant schoolboy, he whined, "I can explain."

"Of course you can. We can also visit my husband right now and vastly improve one part of my life."

She tried to free her arm, but his grip restrained her action. "Calm down. I have no intention of going anywhere except to have a private conversation with you. We will take a brief ride in my carriage and discuss our business."

She would go nowhere with this man. Determined to make her point, she countered as majestically as Agatha. "I think not. Besides, my husband's groom will not allow it."

"Do you mean the young fellow driving your carriage?"

Instinctively, knowing Davey was no longer available to help, she asked, "What have you done to him?"

"Don't worry. I haven't hurt the boy. I sent him on a false errand. That is all."

"Have you forgotten our last encounter?"

"Yes. You were overwrought and irrational."

"Irrational?" She managed a sputter before she hissed through her teeth. "You swine. I attacked you because you were trying to compromise me. Your last attempt, I might add, at gaining my inheritance before I broke our betrothal." His mouth dropped open in confusion. "Yes, Phillip, before my dear step-uncle locked me away, he explained your duplicity in his grand scheme to steal my money."

"I thought you and I could deal with one another in a civilized manner. It seems you still maintain that nasty rebellious streak. I will make life quite difficult for you if I have to. Now, come along."

Something in his eyes, a gleam of hostility, a hint of desperation, suggested she do as he say. She didn't believe he would physically harm her, and answers to her

questions could prove helpful later. Anyway, she ratio-
nalized, what better opportunity to convince him to
come forward and support her story? After one last
glance about for Davey, she said, "You have fifteen
minutes."

They crossed to a plain black carriage. Phillip settled
himself opposite Jocelyn, then clasped his hands in hers
to begin his quest in earnest. "Jocelyn, I want you to
come away with me."

Dumbfounded, she stared until a single giggle escaped, cresting into a wave of laughter.

He tried to sit taller as he indignantly brushed lint
from his burgundy-colored trousers. Out of habit, he
rubbed the birthmark on his left cheek. "I was hoping
you would be reasonable. I care for you."

Wiping her eyes, she managed to find her voice.
"Phillip, you wanted my money to save yourself from
scandal, debtor's prison and my step-uncle's wrath.
Now you claim to want me without my inheritance."
She snorted her disbelief in a rather unladylike fashion.
"You can't expect me to believe you. Besides, I'm hap-
pily married."

For the first time, she noticed the dark circles under
his eyes and the tension around his mouth. The hair,
grown longer than normal, the dirt under his nails, the
worn elbows of his coat, were inconsistent with the
young man she had befriended. The past few months
had been difficult for him. "What did Horace promise
you?"

"My life. Freedom from all my debts. And a comfortable monthly stipend that would have provided well
for us."

Like a stern taskmaster offering a silent reprimand,
she crossed her arms and shook her head.

"God's bones, Jocelyn, he was going to kill me if I
didn't help him. I agreed. Do you remember the night in
your study? Just that morning, he had informed me he

no longer required my services. I was frantic when I attacked you. I apologize. You did bloody my head, you know. It ached for days."

"I see you are sufficiently recovered to once again wreak havoc with my life."

He waggled a finger before her mocking eyes. "Tsk, tsk, Jocelyn. Pettiness does not suit you. Anyway, your dear relative returned and tried to finish what you started. Luckily, when he threw me over the cliff, I fell a fair distance down. He actually tried to throw a boulder on my already bruised head. When I didn't move, he must have considered the deed done."

Angrily, she tugged at the delicate beads lining the fingers of her gloves. "Horace claimed you were dead. I was so gullible. I wanted to go to the authorities. He said he'd already hidden your body and that no one would ever believe me. He is an evil, hideous man."

"On that we agree, and he is back in London."

"What does that have to do with me?"

"I need funds to leave the country."

"You expect me to give you money?" she asked in astonishment.

Like an abandoned pup, his whining grew in intensity. "Mardell will kill me if he finds me. There is also the matter of a few recent unpaid debts. I must have funds to start anew."

How could she have ever considered marriage to this man? "Your wits have turned to straw."

"Only a few thousand pounds."

"By the staff of Moses, you are serious."

The fractious schoolboy resurfaced in full force. "Jocelyn, I will do whatever I must."

Like a captain struggling with his ship through a hurricane, she felt the control slipping through her hands. "Such as?"

"I considered killing Lord Wilcott and marrying you myself, but that would be so very messy. I would still have to deal with your step-uncle. I know you have a fondness for the dowager. She is such a kind woman. I hate to think of her in harm's way. I could buy my freedom by telling Mardell that your amnesia is all a ruse, but I really have no desire to see you harmed, or since Wilcott is known to be the possessive type with a nasty temper, I could tell your husband we are lovers. What do you think? Do any of those ideas have merit?"

They all did and she hated being manipulated. To confide in Reyn about Phillip, this meeting, his treachery, would be a great risk. Flinching when she felt Phillip's hand on her sleeve, she watched him with empty eyes while he pressed his case further.

"Jocelyn, I will do whatever I must. Do you understand? All I need is a few thousand pounds." His voice sounded almost pleasant.

"How do you expect me to obtain that kind of money?"

"Surely, your husband keeps bills at home, or I could convert some of your jewels to banknotes."

"Phillip, come home with me. I promise Reyn will protect you. If I ever meant anything to you, you'll do this for me."

He studied her for a moment. "I will consider it. Until then you will do as I say."

Cursing her stupidity for ever experiencing one particle of feeling for this man, she exhaled in resignation. Too bitter for words, she gave a curt nod.

"Splendid. Meet me at the Two Sisters Inn, near the docks, in three days. Ask anyone, they will tell you the way."

She reached for the door. She had to escape or be sick. Phillip grabbed her wrist, lightly kissed her cheek, then reminded her through the carriage window, "Three days, darling. I'll be waiting."

She needed to go home, find the peace she knew she'd find in her husband's arms. Staring blankly ahead, ignorant of the three pairs of eyes that watched her depart, she forced one foot in front of the other.

The most distressful bit of business that littered Reyn's massive desk was the note from Maddox, the man hired to follow Jocelyn. The daily report clearly stated that Jocelyn met a man in a shop on Bond Street, someone she seemed to know. They left together in a closed carriage and drove a short distance, at which point his wife left the vehicle. Alone. When he read that his wife and the man had appeared to be "more than good friends," Reyn's glare nearly scorched the paper.

Hearing Jocelyn's voice drift upstairs from the entrance of the house, he promptly tucked the note inside a drawer. When she entered his study, he played the wealthy aristocrat, leaning lazily against the corner of his desk, a brandy in one hand, a cigar in the other, a bland expression on his face.

"Where have you been?" His question sounded more like a demand. So much for tact and patience.

"I went shopping for a few things, then I visited with Agatha."

He took a long drag on the cigar, watched her pull the pink gloves from her slender fingers with her teeth and felt the physical tug on his groin.

"Is there something wrong?" she asked as she crossed the threshold and closed the door.

"I was going to ask you the same thing," he countered, thinking she seemed composed, almost serene, for someone just returned from an afternoon rendezvous.

"As you can see, I'm hale and hearty. I went by to discuss my mother with Agatha. I'm willing to discuss my mother with you if it would help."

"If you don't mind, I'd rather forget that for now. There will be time to settle those differences after this other business is finished. At least I understand Agatha's motives."

Eagerly, she agreed. "Did Horace meet you today?"

"Yes. Your step-uncle is everything you said. He is chomping at the bit to invest in our project. I rushed the papers so the transaction should be completed by tomorrow. He also inquired about Lord Halden. If he wishes to invest in both directions, so much the better." Reyn decided to offer his wife every opportunity to explain her actions. "I imagine the shops were busy today. Did you see any of our acquaintances?"

"No. Have you scheduled another appointment with Horace?"

"I meet him tomorrow at the bank. He definitely likes the idea of having a duke as a friend." She plucked the bit of white straw and pink feathers from her head, placing the hat on the nearby chair. His mouth turned to straw as the fabric of her jacket pulled tight across her breasts. "Did you find what you sought today?"

Seductively, she smiled. "Yes, I did. Did my step-uncle ask about me?"

"Very casually and very carefully. He still believes me to be a jealous husband prone to overreaction. I made it perfectly clear that no man spends time alone with my wife. I'm not convinced that he believes this entire amnesia business, but he's definitely curious and considering the possibilities. Neither is he foolish enough to ask too many questions." Watching her remove her pink jacket, he considered the feasibility that Maddox had misinterpreted what he had seen. "And what trinkets did you purchase today?"

"That is a surprise." Crossing the room in slow, provocative steps, she lifted both hands to his cheeks. "I missed you." She pressed her lips to his in a searing kiss filled with promise.

All the other questions he meant to ask quickly slipped his mind, as did his discipline. Impatiently, he pulled her against his eager body, sealing his lips to hers. Normally, he avoided his wife during the day.

Today, he could not deny himself the pleasure of losing himself in her delectable body. There was plenty of time to meet with Maddox. Later.

"As usual, darling, you look magnificent." Like a trained courtesan, Celeste Waverly reclined suggestively against the red leather of her sleek phaeton.

"Your note sounded urgent. What do you need?"

"I need a great many things," she purred as she drew a light caress across the stitching on the leather glove that grasped the side of her carriage. When the hands abruptly withdrew, she scolded, "Good heavens, Reyn, I have no intention of accosting you here in Hyde Park. Be a dear and help me down."

With great annoyance, Reyn did as she requested and lifted Celeste to the ground. This was the last place he wanted to be, yet after receiving her note, his curiosity had forced him to leave his wife buried beneath the covers of their bed. He also needed to locate Maddox and meet Mardell, Tameron and Walter.

"Out of deference to our past relationship, I agreed to this meeting. I do, however, have important things to do."

"I don't doubt they include your little wife?" she said, ignoring his churlish attitude.

He glanced from the dirt track to the sapphire velvet back that retreated to a copse of maple trees. His stride matched hers. "What the hell is that supposed to mean?"

Placing her lace-covered hands over his, she nestled closer to his side. "I do not wish to see you hurt."

"Stop the theatrics, Celeste. Say what you must."

Her chest heaved as she exhaled in vexation. "Did you know that your wife had a fiancé?" Reflexively, his hands tightened on a low branch of a nearby tree. "Did you know this man is here in London and your wife has been with him?"

Dark, swirling storm clouds gathered within him. The coincidence of this information with that from Maddox was too much. Somehow he managed to keep all emotion away from his face. "How did you come by this tidbit of news?"

"I will not reveal my sources, but I will share what I know. Supposedly, they were madly in love and planned to be married until catastrophe struck and Jocelyn disappeared. This mere lad, heavily in debt, claims his luck is about to change. Expecting a windfall in the next few days, he will gather his lady love and flee to Paris. What do you suppose he means by that?"

Having been Celeste's lover, he knew her temperament well. Ambitious, she was not above using charm, cruelty or blackmail. She was also intelligent. She knew nothing would be gained by a pack of lies.

"What do you hope to gain by offering me this information?" Reyn asked.

She grazed the outline of his upper lip with a fingernail. "I have missed you."

"Celeste . . ."

"Shhh." She pursed her lips together. "Let me finish. Your wife will meet this man on Friday." She handed him a neatly folded square of paper. "I have written the address for you. If you find I speak the truth, perhaps you will, once again, feel generous with your time." Emboldened by his silence, she traced his jaw with the tip of her tongue. "We were very good together."

He withdrew as though scalded and fled to the path where he left his horse. Without looking back, he said, "Not a word. To anyone."

The ground seemed to fly beneath his feet as he strode toward the black stallion, untied the lead and jumped onto his back. Rage born of betrayal gnawed at his stomach as he thundered down the dirt track as if the hounds of hell were nipping at his heels.

* * *

Jocelyn stood outside the Two Sisters Inn, feeling that time dragged at a snail's pace, yet knowing events were happening far too quickly.

During the last three days, the entire Wilcott household, secretly whispering and plotting, had executed the final touches on Reyn's birthday party. Everything for tomorrow night's celebration was ready.

As easily as Walter had predicted, her step-uncle now owned shares in their canal project, financially leveraged beyond his limit.

"Give the man enough rope to hang himself," Reyn had said, "then we wait, watch and tighten the noose. Slowly." The waiting game had begun.

Under strict orders from Reyn, she had not seen her step-uncle again. Unexpectedly, Mardell stopped by Black House once again and Jocelyn, quite happily, pleaded a headache. Reyn promised her the final satisfaction before the lecher was carted off to prison.

The waiting seemed to be a strain on everyone. Even Reyn. He came home every night, said very little except to apprise her of the progress of her step-uncle. He ate dinner, then retreated to the privacy of his study and eventually his own bedroom. He had not touched Jocelyn since her first encounter with Phillip, their odd conversation in the study and their fiery lovemaking on the plush rug of that same room.

Her body warmed remembering the delicious pleasure he had bestowed upon her as she had wantonly stood naked before him, his face nestled between her thighs. Generous in his giving, savage in his demands, he had sent her soaring amongst the stars. Repeatedly. They had moved from the study to their bedchamber, where Reyn had continued his plundering. She had submitted to his mastery, and had almost blurted a confession about Phillip.

Deep-seated fear quelled that impulse. She had no

choice but to succumb to Phillip's blackmail. The loss of the jewels meant nothing to her except an act of betrayal.

The weight of her purse reminded her of where she was and of her purpose. She entered the small inn, eager to put this business behind her. Other than two doddering sailors collapsed at a corner table and the weary-looking barkeep, the taproom was vacant. Thankfully, most of the customers occupied themselves elsewhere at this time of day.

She clutched the small reticule, held back the unshed tears and climbed the stairs. A silent warning rang in her head. She knocked anyway.

Phillip appeared in the doorway, a toothy grin on his face. "Jocie, my love, so good of you to come."

Like the lamb near the lion, she backed away when he extended his hand. "If you recall, I had little choice."

"You disappoint me. Do come in." Rubbing his hands together, he asked, "And what have you brought me, my dear Jocie?"

The door closed behind her. She spat irritably. "Stop calling me that."

"Tsk, tsk. You used to love that nickname."

"That was a long time ago. Now it simply reminds me of a foolish young girl I no longer recognize."

He stroked his thumb across her cheek. "Such passion. A pity we could never share that."

Anxious to finish their business and leave, she thrust the bag at Phillip. "Take the jewels. Leave England. I swear, if you contact me again, regardless of the consequences, I will tell Reyn everything."

"This is not the time for a temper tantrum. Remember what we meant to each other."

"The only thing I wish to remember is the sight of your backside boarding a ship."

His belly laugh grated on her already tender nerves as his fingers toyed with the lace decorating the dainty hat she wore. "Oh, Jocelyn, how you delight me. Are you sure you do not wish to accompany me?"

She shrank away. "I would rather take my chances with my husband."

"So be it." Dumping the contents of her bag on the narrow cot, his eyes ogled the bounty before him. "Very good. Very good indeed."

He caressed the jewels as if he held the world in his hands. A chill coiled down her spine. Suddenly she realized the extent of his desperation, acknowledging its power to drive him to do any number of things. It was time to leave.

She edged toward the door, pulled it open and stepped onto the wooden balcony. Her breathing came easier. "I assume you are satisfied. Therefore, I will take my leave."

"Wait," he called.

"Yes?" She spoke casually, feigning a calm she did not feel.

Grabbing her beneath her arms, lifting her high into the air, he whirled about the landing.

"Put me down, Phillip."

He slid her down the length of his body and pressed a deep kiss to her mouth. Oddly enough, all she felt was pity.

"Come with me. I promise to take care of you."

"It would never work. I have done all I can for you. Leave me be to enjoy the happiness I have found." His mind seemed to clear before her eyes.

"Very well."

She thought he had already forgotten her as he fingered the bounty in his pockets. She bounded down the stairs, desperate to be free of her surroundings.

He called after her. "I do love you, Jocie."

With her face flushed, her hat askew, a loose tendril over her brow, she nodded and stepped into the sunlight. At that moment, she knew she must tell Reyn the truth.

Chapter Twenty-one

Something was terribly wrong. Try as she might, Jocelyn could find no excuse for Reyn's absence. She blamed her nervousness on her afternoon encounter with Phillip, but deep down she feared it was something else.

She glanced out the bedroom window for what seemed the hundredth time that night, and once again wondered where her husband was. She needed to tell him so many things. She had realized her stupidity the moment she left Phillip.

Reyn deserved the truth. All of it. Phillip's return. His blackmail. The baby. That she loved him. Then and only then, could he make a choice about their future. Prepared to tell him everything, she waited. When he failed to arrive for dinner, she nervously paced and fretted the evening away. At midnight, she withdrew to her chamber, succumbing to a restless sleep that lasted an hour or so. Now she attempted, most pitifully, to read.

A sound disturbed the night. Hoping it was Reyn, she grabbed her robe and slippers and crept down the stairs to find the lower rooms cloaked in darkness. No small wonder. It was well after three in the morning. "Reyn?" she called.

A dull thud pierced the night. Warily, biting her lower lip, she turned toward the darkened salon. She halted at the door. "Reyn?"

"No need to linger in the doorway, my dear. Come in. Your timely arrival saves me a trip upstairs."

The dispassionate welcome almost sent her back to her room. Crossing the room on trembling legs, following the voice and the burning glow of the cigar, she found the back of the closest chair. She heard the sound of a match striking flint, then a candle caught flame to cast the room into haunting shadows. Reyn sat beside the fireplace, now cold and lifeless. One look at his fierce expression confirmed her fears. Brandy, strong and pungent, flared her nostrils. "You've been drinking."

"Well, give the girl a bloody blue ribbon. Sit down."

"I will talk to you when you're sober."

He stood, his voice filled with contempt, his body rigid. Three strides brought him to her side. "I said sit down."

Whatever had he discovered? She sat in the nearby chair.

"How long were you going to wait before you told me?" he said.

"I beg your pardon?"

"The truth, Jocelyn? How long were you going to wait before you revealed all your nasty, hypocritical, precious lies and secrets?"

Had he discovered her pregnancy? Yes. That had to be it. He'd discovered her pregnancy and felt trapped. Once again. He didn't want this child after all. She closed her eyes. Please, let me wake. Let this be a nightmare.

"Well?" he said, towering above her.

This was no simple dream, but her husband in the flesh. And he was furious. "Secrets?" she asked, afraid to say the words.

He reduced his cigar to shredded tobacco with his fist. "God's bones, stop acting the injured pigeon."

While panic tore at her grip on logic, her mind whirled, her stomach roiled. As if denial would grant her clemency, she feigned innocence. "I don't understand."

"You once threw a name at me. I have one for you." He leaned within an inch of her face. "Phillip Bains. Your fiancé."

"Phillip?" she muttered, now thoroughly confused. Unless Reyn—No, she dismissed the idea as quickly as it came. Only two sailors had occupied the inn today. "I told you about Phillip."

"Apparently, you neglected to tell me a great many things about your friend."

He knew. Somehow he knew. But how? "I don't understand," she managed to whisper.

"You mean he's not alive? Or that you haven't seen him here in London? You are not lovers and are not running away with him?" With the cunning determination of a hunter, he watched her and laid his trap. He threw a handful of glittering gems in her lap. Observing the tremor, disgusted by her reaction and the searing pain he felt, he jerked away.

"I suppose you intend to tell me these jewels, the ones I myself bestowed upon you, were lost. Perhaps stolen." He laughed with no warmth, only malice. "Maybe you simply can't remember. Maybe you're wondering how I found them in the possession of a pimply-faced clod like Bains." He circled behind her chair and leaned forward to breathe a warning in her left ear. "And before you attempt to lie again, you should know that today I spent a few hours in a tavern. The Two Sisters. An unobtrusive little place affordable to seamen. Perhaps you've heard of it."

"It's not what it seems." She forced herself to stay calm as her mind recreated everything Reyn might have seen or heard. Her hand felt as cold and lifeless as the gems resting in her palms. "Let me explain."

"No. Not one word. I have listened to the last of your lying, fanciful tales. I simply want to know one thing before I leave."

"Leave? For where?"

Ignoring her pleas, he swung back around to trap her in the chair. "Was it the money or the title, Jocelyn? Did you simply need someone to deal with your step-uncle before you could run away with that little roach?" He drew his hands through his hair in barely contained fury. "Lord, how you must have enjoyed yourself as this idiotic farce played itself out." He dropped into the opposite chair as his angry fever began to cool. "Was there anything between us that smacked of the truth?"

"Reyn, listen to me." She had to make him understand. Dropping to her knees before him, she begged. "Everything I told you about my step-uncle and Phillip is true. Horace was blackmailing Phillip. They had an agreement. I didn't understand it all until the other day. Phillip and I would marry, and we would receive a small stipend while the rest of my inheritance went to Horace. Phillip was willing to marry me, but only to save himself. I never loved him. I truly thought I murdered him."

He continued to stare blankly at the far wall, showing less regard for her presence than a flea on a mange-ridden dog. She cried in earnest. "Phillip blackmailed me. I didn't tell you about Phillip because he—he threatened to kill you or Agatha or tell Horace the truth about my amnesia."

Watching her closely, recognizing the possible truth, he forced himself to remember Phillip and Jocelyn embracing, to hear the tender words spoken again, to feel the seething anger he had felt. He had asked for trust. She had offered betrayal.

He leaned forward and traced the tears that fell unchecked down her cheeks, his voice more chilling and detached than ever. "How clever you are. Magnificent, in fact. Like a fine piece of cut crystal. And just as cold and dangerous. Unfortunately, I would no more believe you than I would believe England will ever rule France again."

"I never planned on leaving with Phillip. Never. He lied to protect himself."

"You should suit one another quite well. You have much in common."

"You idiot!" she cried. "I love *you*."

"My, my, you are desperate." He swilled a large dose of brandy directly from the bottle, wishing for the foggy bliss that would ease his bitterness. His state of mind grew more explosive every moment he lingered there with her, with each word she said, with each look of practiced anguish he saw on her face. "Well, that's just too damned bad."

She grabbed his hands. "You must listen to me."

He wrenched away from her, launched the bottle of aged brandy against the fireplace, stood and shouted, "No!"

"Where are you going?" she asked as he stumbled toward the door.

Bracing himself against her soft plea, he taunted, "I don't think you want to know. It's not at all proper to discuss certain things with one's wife." Turning a deaf ear to her sobs, he left the house, slamming the door behind him.

Dressed in a stunning sapphire gown, small yellow roses sewn upon the hem and shoulders, Jocelyn stood beside the fireplace in the salon. Restlessly, she fingered the silver-wrapped package, Reyn's present, that lay on the mantel. In readiness for the party, she waited.

The house sparkled like a newly minted gold sovereign while the musicians warmed their instruments in the ballroom. Tantalizing scents of spice and wine floated from the kitchen.

With her head held high, she ignored the whispers of the staff. Like her, they wondered if Lord Wilcott would even bother to make his presence known tonight. Already the guests had begun to arrive and still one irate, belligerent husband seemed to be missing.

Agatha threatened to track down her scoundrel grandson, pummel him with her brass-handled cane and drag him to the party. Vehemently, Jocelyn rejected the idea. Instead, Walter and Tam assumed the duty of finding her husband. They would calmly explain about the party and bring him home. He would come because he recognized the truth, loved her, forgave her. Otherwise there was no point in his returning at all.

She touched the soft swell of her abdomen, glad for the life that grew within her. But when she thought that Reyn might never support her pregnancy, never help her select a name, never hold their baby in his arms, she felt a new urge to cry.

No, she told herself. Regardless of what happened tonight, she would maintain her dignity.

Tam interrupted her gloomy thoughts. "Jocelyn, may I say you look absolutely stunning?"

She whirled, eager to see her husband beside his friend. "He is not coming," she stated flatly.

With unspoken regret clearly etched in his eyes, he nodded. "I'm sorry."

Entering on Tam's coattails to hear her assumption, Agatha peevishly threatened, "I shall string the fool up by his toenails."

"I can think of a different part of his anatomy I would gladly tie in knots," said Walter, offering his fierce opinion.

Jocelyn looked to Tameron. "Where is he?"

"Jocelyn."

She recognized the pity and silent warning. Closing her eyes, gaining control of the tears she had held at bay all day, she said to Tam, "Take me to him."

Agatha sputtered this and that as Tam and Walter openly argued this decision.

"All of this is entirely my fault. I want him to have tonight, so much so that I am willing to beg. If I must, I will find him myself. I would prefer an escort."

Agatha shushed all concerned. Reluctantly, she said, "Best go with her, Tam. She means what she says. Walter and I will see to the guests until you return."

Thankfully, Tam kept his thoughts to himself as the carriage ambled through the bustling evening traffic. He had explained nothing about where they went, or whom they would encounter. She suspected her husband was with Celeste.

The coach halted in front of a three-story brick mansion where a large party seemed to be under way. Tam jumped from the vehicle and turned to lift her down. "Are you sure, Jocelyn?"

In order to spare her any pain, he offered one last chance of retreat. He didn't realize how deep the agony already dipped, that her body functioned on sheer determination to see this through. "Do not look so forlorn. I will be fine." She extended her arm with a gentle grace. "Shall we?"

Mustering every ounce of courage, every particle of pride, she majestically entered the infamous lion's den in search of her husband. She didn't wait long. The two couples encountered one another at the door.

Tightly pressed to Reyn's side, Celeste gave a smug

smile of satisfaction while Reyn raised his eyebrows in a mocking salute. He ignored his wife and addressed Tam. "I thought you had grand plans for the evening?"

Undaunted, Jocelyn answered anyway. "He does. We have a very special evening planned. We hoped to convince you to join us."

Deadly sparks flew from Reyn's eyes. "Not on your treacherous little life."

With his hands fisted at his sides, Tam said, "Why, you bloody fool. I ought to—"

"Tam." Regardless of how she felt, Jocelyn kept her voice calm and reasonable.

Reyn's face contorted with disgust. "If this isn't touching. Have you bedded her yet? She really is quite good. I would prefer you wait until our annulment goes through; then you may have her as often as you like. You aren't titled, but all that money should have her on her knees declaring undying love in no time."

Tam pulled his arm back, ready to drive a punch through Reyn's stormy face. "Go to hell."

Reyn sneered. "You forget. I've already been there."

Jocelyn placed a hand on Tam's sleeve while looking directly into Reyn's eyes. "I know you hate me right now, but tonight is for you. I promise, if you come home with us, everything will be self-explanatory. Please. We have a wonderful surprise planned. After that, perhaps we can talk?"

Reyn jerked their wraps from the attentive doorman. "I've had more than enough surprises lately. I thought I made myself perfectly clear last night. I want nothing more to do with you. I will finish this business with your step-uncle. Then I want you gone. Until that time, stay away from me. I will gladly do the same." He stormed from the house, ushering Celeste before him.

"Smile, Tam." Jocelyn fussed with a tassel on her cape. "We seem to be attracting a crowd. I won't tarnish my husband's reputation. He deserves that much."

"I swear, I will break the blighter's neck."

"Dear Tam, thank you for your friendship. However, your loyalty should remain with my husband. I never meant to hurt him, but that is exactly what I did. For that, I will never forgive myself."

"Give him time, Jocelyn. He'll see his way clear after he has time to think things through."

She cleared her throat. "We shall see. If you don't mind, I would prefer everyone thought you and I, that we—Oh, goodness, this is more difficult than I expected. Would you do me the honor of pretending we care for one another? If everyone believes you and I to be involved, then Reyn and Celeste's relationship will seem more acceptable."

Tam understood exactly what she wanted. Tilting her chin toward his, he placed a tender kiss on her cheek before presenting his arm to return to Black House. Empty-handed.

Reyn felt as though he'd been knifed and gutted. The physical pain might have been easier to accept than the haunting vision of Jocelyn. She had looked so beautiful tonight. He reminded himself that beauty provided a cold substitute for honesty and truth and love. Yet, her image, so proud and loving, her eyes, sad and broken, filled his mind. Along with her startling declaration of love. God, how he wanted to believe her. In fact, that was the only reason he found himself on the doorstep of his own home, willing to give her a chance to explain one last time. The cynical man laughed at his foolishness. The lonely youth hoped.

A bright streamer caught the tip of his boot, snagging his attention. Odd, it looked as though someone had given a party. He saw the large banner decorating the foyer entrance. Not just a party, his mind corrected, a birthday party. His birthday party.

"So, the prodigal husband returns."

Startled, Reyn's face lifted to find Tameron Innes balanced against the dark balcony rail.

"You're drunk." Reyn charged the stairs, more confused than ever.

"Not really, although I'm giving it one hell of a try."

Reyn came eye-to-eye with his friend. "What the devil is going on?"

"You seemed to have missed your party. You remember, the party? Walter and I tried to tell you about it. The same party your wife practically begged you to attend." Tam crossed the hall to the study to pour himself another whiskey.

Like a whipped dog, Reyn obediently followed, his mind in shambles as he attempted to sort through this information. "Where is Jocelyn?"

Tam appeared to be in no hurry to provide any explanations. "Until tonight, I never realized how incredibly lucky you were. I also decided you're the biggest fool I know. Your wife waltzed back to this house filled with revelry and your well-wishers, proudly explained that you had made other plans, and told them to have a grand time. Hopefully you would end your business before the night was over. Blamed herself, she did. Told me she didn't want anyone thinking the worst of you. Can you imagine? That beautiful young woman chose to protect you. And what were you doing? Breaking her heart. You really are a cold-hearted fool."

Finally, Tam fell into silence. He settled himself beside the fire, eyes closed, a half-empty crystal glass in hand.

Reyn felt as though he had kissed the gunner's daughter, tied to the breech of a cannon and whipped. "Where is she now?" he managed to rasp.

Peering through one heavy eyelid, Tam said, "In her room, I imagine. Never said another word about you. Never shed a tear. She managed to last for hours before she thanked us all for our kindness and excused herself with a headache."

Reyn didn't bother to explain. A deep, searing need for exoneration drove him to bolt up another level of stairs to storm her bedroom, where total darkness greeted him. After lighting a lamp, pure terror filled him. The room was empty. Prepared to search the house, he noticed a glittering package balanced on top of her dressing table. With his palms sweating and his pulse beating rapidly, he reached for the white note perched beside it.

Dearest Reyn, it began. *Tonight, I realized I have relied upon your strength, your infinite charity and tenderness, far longer than I ever should have. I took my burdens and made them yours, ignoring the possible consequences. That will happen no longer. I will take back what is mine and return your life to you. I can never apologize enough for hurting you. That was never my intention. When all is said and done, I hope you can remember me with a bit of kindness. I do love you, you know. By the way, I left Caesar in your care. I believe he has grown fond of his surroundings.*

Yours, forever. Jocelyn.

His anguished wail reverberated off the walls. Jocelyn had left, but the most frightening thought was the instinctive knowledge that she had gone to confront Horace.

He stumbled down the stairs and collided with Tameron, roused from his stupor by Reyn's cry.

"What happened?" Tam asked.

"Jocelyn's gone. I believe she has gone after Horace."

"Holy Mother," exclaimed Tameron.

"My sentiments exactly." Reyn turned to a stupefied Tam from the bottom of the stairs. "Are you coming or not?"

Chapter Twenty-two

She huddled in the dark, numb with defeat, the pistol in her trembling hands. Cold, empty, alone. That was all she felt. Only her resolve guided her to Horace's house. Now Jocelyn awaited his return, calculating everything she would say, everything she would do. She would wait for hours, if need be.

She would not cry, nor would she fail. She might not have Reyn, but she did have his baby. Nothing or no one would keep her from vengeance or her inheritance. Not anymore.

With senses honed like a predator's, she jerked her shoulders at the scraping of metal against metal followed by the sound of a door opening. Was he alone? Please, let it be so.

She choked back her fear, stepped from behind the curtain to encounter the enemy, and found the courage needed to raise the gun toward her step-uncle. "Put down the lamp and sit down."

Horace reeled about to find a pistol pointed at his

chest. Narrowing his eyes for the space of a second, a wicked smile on his face, he said, "Well, well, well. If it isn't my beloved niece." He set the lamp on the nearby table. Lifelike shadows danced on the walls as he reached inside his jacket.

"Don't move," Jocelyn snapped, "or, by heaven, I will shoot you." Slowly, she maneuvered toward the door from which he had entered, gesturing for him to sit in the chair near the curtains she had vacated.

"Nothing more sinister than a cigar hides in my coat pocket, my dear. Do you mind?" He didn't bother to wait for a response and withdrew a small metal canister, pulled out a cigar and reached across the table for a match. "So, the ruse has ended. I admit you played well. I even believed you for a time, until I located a former attendant from Bedlam. Someone you might know. Jocko? Yes, I can see by your expression that you do remember him. He told his version of events. Then poor Phillip managed to surface long enough to waggle his tongue."

He watched her over the tip of the cigar, paused long enough to light it, then nonchalantly asked, "Where is your husband? Surely, he should be here for the closure of this little drama. Or doesn't he know the entire story, Jocelyn?"

His blasé attitude sent tremors through her upper body, yet she managed to hold the pistol steady. She tried to speak evenly. "I decided this business demanded my attention, not my husband's." She nodded toward the table. "I prepared a statement, a full confession, for you to sign. Afterward, I will present it to the authorities. You will be arrested. You can spend your life in Newgate for all you have done."

When he burst into laughter—deep, chortling, malicious laughter—she nearly dropped the gun. "Stop it."

"Oh, my dear. You are simply too delightful." He dabbed at the tears in his eyes before exhaling a restraining breath. "I am sorry. I can't do that."

"I will shoot you."

"I think not. At least, not until you have some answers. Don't you want to know why, Jocelyn?" He sat down in the tall leather chair, crossed his legs and took a long drag of his cigar.

She kept her back to the study door, her eyes fixed directly on her step-uncle's face. "I already know why. You are a greedy, evil parasite."

"Some might think so." He watched the glow of his cigar before he continued. "I think I am a clever opportunist who made the best of whatever came my way. You see, Jocelyn, I had little choice. Your father, my dear stepbrother, was such a paragon, he made my life a living hell. Nothing I did pleased my father after he married your grandmother. Your father delighted in pointing out my minor indiscretions until my father gave me the choice: disinheritance or prison. I vowed, then and there, I would have my day. Luckily for me, my father kept his mouth shut, so no one knew of my dilemma."

"Am I supposed to feel sorry for you? After all you did to me and my family?"

"Not in the least. I am simply explaining who I am and how I came to be that way. When the earl died, I returned home to plead with your father, my dear stepbrother. I told him I had changed. Do you know what he did? He laughed. That's when I made up my mind. I deserved my inheritance. He had no right to deny me, so I used my skills, shall we say, to maneuver my way into the money. I was very upset when I thought I would be denied the title."

"Why did you have me placed in Bedlam?"

"When you accepted Phillip's suit, I was quite pleased. Then I discovered that the title was not lost to me after all. I disposed of Phillip, but you refused my attentions. I simply had to marry you. Besides, I didn't quite have the heart to kill you. I intended to bring you home, hoping your mental state had degenerated enough to accept our marriage. You'd be insane; I'd be an earl as well as your rich, faithful husband. And Jocelyn, I've wanted you in my bed for the longest time."

"You make me sick. Sign the confession."

"I simply can't do that." He gave a slight nod of his head, and suddenly Jocelyn felt a muscled arm around her waist, the gun plastered to her side. Like the fox suddenly trapped in a snare, all she cared about was escape, kicking and flailing, only to be pulled closer to a hard chest, her breath blowing in wheezing huffs.

"Easy, Jocko," said Horace. "I don't want the chit flat on her back." Openly leering, Horace closed the distance between them, loosened the pistol from her fingers and pressed a kiss to her pursed lips. "Not right now, at least."

All rational thought vanished. She spat in his face.

"Let her go." Horace wiped away the spittle from his eyes. "Now that, my dear, will cost you."

His brutal blow toppled her to the floor. While she crouched on her knees, tasting her own blood and real fear, painfully aware of her danger, she frantically sought some means of escape.

"Help her," said Horace.

Jocko leered. "With pleasure."

When his meaty hands wrenched her up and propelled her to the chair, she noticed a pair of worn boots beside the door. She winced when she recognized the bloodied body of Phillip Bains. "Is he dead?" she asked Horace.

"Phillip? Not yet. I have not decided whether he has lived out his usefulness." Horace raised a brow in speculation. "I'm surprised you care. After all, he did attempt to blackmail you. Don't look so shocked, my dear. The poor lad has little tolerance for pain. With a little encouragement, he confessed all, willingly corroborating what I thought. Your amnesia was all an act.

"You do realize I shall have to kill your husband?" Horace shook his head. "You really shouldn't have married the man. I will have that inheritance. And you. One way or another. Consider Phillip's beating a gift for all his misdeeds toward your person. It will be your wedding gift for our marriage."

"I will never marry you."

Horace toyed with the fallen curls that rested above her breast. "I can see your temperament remains as prickly as ever." Swiftly, the soft caress turned savage, his hand yanking her hair by the roots, dragging her obstinate face toward his. "I will kill Wilcott. I will marry you. I will gain the inheritance. And I will decide whether you live or die. Believe me, I look forward to removing your thorns, Jocelyn. One by one."

His bald statement of expectation chilled her. She shuddered at the image of Mardell touching her, knowing there would be no tenderness, only dominance and pain. She would rather die.

Promptly, she amended her thoughts. If suffering his caresses meant a possible chance for the life she carried, she would tolerate what she must.

"Does your husband know you are here?" Horace smoothly asked.

She refused to answer and stubbornly glanced across the room to the ornately patterned wall clock.

Again, a discreet tilt of the head from her step-uncle and Jocko took action. The solid *wumpf* of a boot and a tortured moan drew her eyes from the wall to the man huddled in a ball on the floor.

"Leave him alone. Haven't you done enough harm?"

"You always did have a soft spot for injured creatures. I believed Phillip has a purpose after all. There are several foggy details that yet need clarification. Since you deem to display your impertinence right now, we shall play a little game. I ask a question. You answer. For every insolent act or remark, Phillip receives a kick, a punch, a slap. The choice is yours. Of course, I will understand if you choose not to answer. He is a dead man either way, but then I shall be forced to turn my attentions to you."

She knew he would do exactly as he said. "You animal."

A look of sensual pleasure grazed his features, drawing forth a new wave of shudders from her. He fondled the inner ridge of her ear with his fingertip, allowing his hand to drift to her breast. "I look forward to proving you right. Now I shall have answers to my questions."

Like a banshee, Phillip rose from the floor, an unearthly scream torn from his lips. Throwing himself at Horace, he froze before Jocelyn, his eyes wide with shock. "I'm sorry," he gurgled before he dropped in a heap.

When she saw the knife in his back, the wound oozing red with blood, Jocelyn screamed at the top of her lungs. Jocko simply carried the body from the room.

Precariously balanced on the rickety wooden box, Reyn cursed himself for a fool. He should never have agreed to Tam's plan. The two had chosen stealth rather than direct confrontation until they located Jocelyn, so here he stood, attached to a battered trellis, peeking through a curtained window, trying to catch a glimpse of his wife. He hoped Tam would draw attention long enough for him to slip through the open window behind the curtain, discover her whereabouts and take her home. Briefly, he wondered if this was the means she had used to gain entrance to the house.

As the box tilted slightly to the right, he grabbed the brick wall and nearly missed Tam's entrance into Horace's library. Settling back to gaze through the crack in the curtains, he saw the broad mahogany doors burst open and Tam fell to the floor in their wake.

With his hair tumbling before his eyes, his shirt

hanging from his trousers, one pant leg tucked inside his boot, Tam looked and smelled like a man who had reveled in every sin imaginable. He rolled to his back to grin at the angry face peering down at him. "Good evening. I seem to have fallen."

Reyn heard Tam struggle to an upright position, huffing and puffing like a stuffed pig, and took the opportunity to ease himself onto the window ledge, into the house and behind the heavy brocade drape. He waited and listened. Where was Jocelyn?

"Horace, old chap," Tam said, his voice slurred, "give a man a hand, will you?"

From his hiding place, Reyn watched Horace help Tam to his feet. If this method provided no information about Jocelyn, he could easily slip back outside. If need be, he was here to give aid to his friend.

Horace pursed his lips together, closely watching Tam. "I must say, Mr. Innes, I am surprised to see you here at this time of night."

Swaying from side to side, Tam managed to sputter. "A fellow needs a friendly chum to drink with now and then, don't he? By the way, what does a gent have to do to earn a drink here?"

Horace forced a smile on his face and poured the drink. "Where are your good friends, Hathaway and Wilcott?"

"Bloody gentry, high-boned nobs. Stuffed, tucked and pleated shirtfronts, that's what they are. No sense of adventure. I prefer the company of real men and"— Tam grinned—"real women." As if remembering something important, he frowned. "Where is my brandy, man?"

Reyn saw Horace clench his hands at his sides. Undoubtedly, he would rather have planted a fist in Tam's nose, but luckily, Horace seemed more interested in gaining information.

Tam nodded to one of the chairs. "Do you mind?"

Horace handed the drink to Innes. "By all means. Sit." Guiding Tam toward a chair, Horace tapped his fingers together under his chin.

Tam reacted immediately. "Well, now, if it isn't my special lady herself." He continued in an overly loud, drunken slur. "Jocelyn, have you finally come to your senses and left that whoreson husband of yours?"

"Are you all right?" she asked. She sucked in her breath when Tam winked. Taken aback by his erratic behavior, she looked closer, but he seemed to stare past her until he scratched his ear and smirked like a cockeyed sailor making the most of one day's shore leave. Didn't the fool realize the danger he was in? She knew if she said anything, it meant both their lives. And where was Jocko? He hadn't returned since he'd left to dispose of Phillip's body.

Horace crossed to take Jocelyn's hand in his. "Trouble in paradise, my dear?"

"If you value your life at all, you will remove yourself from *my wife*."

Horace straightened. Otherwise he didn't move, forcing Jocelyn to peer around his body to witness the rigid stance of her husband, who was wearing a thunderous expression and aiming a gun at her step-uncle's chest.

"Did he harm you, Jocelyn?" Reyn asked.

Dumbstruck by the fact that he had come to her rescue, she managed to shake her head.

"And that mark on your cheek?"

She had forgotten about the blow. His voice sounded calm enough, but she knew better. He was bloody furious. "It stings a bit, that is all."

Reyn's eyes darkened to black. He spoke to his friend. "And you?"

Tam adjusted his position, combed his hair from his brow and winked again at Jocelyn. "Told you my plan would work. Nary a scratch."

Turning his full attention back to Horace, Reyn gave his order in a hoarse whisper. "Turn around."

Immediately, Reyn's fist connected with flesh and bone, the grisly sounds indicating that his punches found their marks. "Get up, you miserable excuse for a man. You're very lucky. Had you harmed my wife further, I would have had to shoot you on sight. I'm not sure which I would prefer, you dead at my feet or your neck dangling from a rope."

Horace wiped the blood from his cracked lips with a white, starched handkerchief he pulled from his pocket. "Personally, I prefer neither. Now, Jocko!" As he yelled, Horace reached for Jocelyn. A shot ripped through the air, winging by Reyn's ear as he dodged to the left.

By the time Reyn regained his footing, Horace held Jocelyn, his arm wrapped around her neck, while Tam, a knife at his throat, insolently glared at Jocko.

"Drop your gun or I will snap her neck," said Horace.

"Really?" Reyn knew the odds had shifted dramatically, but he also understood that no one inside this room would leave alive if he relinquished his firearm. Bluffing was the only alternative. Leveling the gun at Horace's head, he spoke with all the disdain he could muster. "Be my guest."

Satisfied when Horace appeared stunned, Reyn fought harder than ever to maintain the cold facade of indifference after glancing at Jocelyn. She looked as though someone had knocked her in the solar plexus. Why couldn't she have a bit of faith? He knew his lies would shock her. He had no choice right now. Her pained sensibilities would have to be soothed later. After they reached the safety of their home.

Horace recovered quickly enough and laughed. "Do you expect me to believe that nonsense?"

Although Reyn's eyes glittered ominously, his shoulders shrugged noncommittally. "You will be dead and I will have my bachelorhood back as well as her inheritance, all the blame placed on your ignominious shoulders."

Still disbelieving, Horace scrunched his brows together before speaking. "If she means so little to you, then why bother with the heroics tonight?"

"Actually, there are two reasons. First, masculine pride. Tonight my wife chose to leave me. She couldn't quite understand a man's need for a wife *and* a mistress. Second, I protect my property. In fact, it's a bit of an obsession for me. It is one thing if I decide to discard something, but no one, I repeat, no one leaves me. Neither does anyone take what belongs to me. Once a possession, always a possession."

Oddly, the arrogance of that statement seemed to make sense to Horace, for he started to evaluate his options. "And your friend? Jocko would gladly slit his throat."

"Just like our times at Oxford," Reyn said as he eyed Tam speculatively, hoping his friend would understand. "Innes will simply have to take his chances."

Tam hissed between clamped teeth, "You cold-hearted bastard."

Reyn snickered. "I've never pretended otherwise, my friend."

"Reyn," said Jocelyn as everything fell apart before her eyes. "You can't mean it."

He merely shrugged his shoulders. She couldn't believe it. Reyn cared nothing for her. Because of her idyllic fantasies of love and her hateful need for revenge, Tam might die and so would her child. In fury and determination, she sank her teeth into Horace's hand.

Seizing the opportunity, Reyn lunged, throwing all three of them to the floor, toppling the chair and table, shattering the lamp. Instantly, flames began to lick their way across the woolen rug to the curtains and fabric-draped walls. Dazed by the fall, Jocelyn lay on the floor as she gasped for air, surrounded by wild destruction.

Reyn delivered a solid punch to Horace's abdomen. With a roll and a kick, Tam quickly dispensed with Jocko. Reyn yelled to Tam, "Get her out of here!"

When Tam heaved Jocelyn to her feet, she began to scream. He threw her over his shoulders to forcibly remove her from the burning house.

"Please, Tam, don't let Reyn die." She continued to plead after he set her down on the street outside. "He doesn't deserve to die because of me."

"He won't die," Tam stated vigorously.

"Please, help him. I will be fine."

Studying her face, he reluctantly agreed. "Don't move," he said, waving a finger at her. "Do you understand?"

Consumed with emptiness, she nodded. Reyn had saved her, but for what? To salvage his pride. To gain her inheritance. Everything had been a farce. Slowly, she edged behind the gathering crowd, immersing herself in the throng of people watching the house dissolve into flames. She waited long enough to see two men stumble to safety. She held her breath when they took the steps two at a time to escape the falling debris. She watched until she recognized Tam and Reyn, then turned and walked into the foggy mist, her ears and heart closed to the haunted voice that called her name.

"I will see your uncle now, Jonathan, or I swear I will break your ruddy neck." Reyn threatened the younger man while he lifted him to his toes by his ruffled cravat.

As he leaned against the six-foot tall mahogany case clock that decorated the dim foyer, Tam added his glib opinion. "I do believe he means it this time. What do you think, Walter?"

"Now that you mention it, he does look a bit piqued. I haven't seen him in such a state since the night he threw that one-armed sailor out the third-story window of St. Ives for lifting his purse. That was only money. This matter regards his wife."

Nervously, the young man's eyes flitted back and forth between the three visitors, nearly popping from their sockets at the last statement. Jonathan cleared his throat in an attempt to gain their attention. Reyn loosened his grip enough to allow him to speak.

"I don't believe," Jonathan coughed, "you will harm me. I told you, my uncle is already abed. He is aware of your request. He will see you in the morning."

Growling, Reyn dropped his hand, leaving the man to lean heavily against the wall, his pale hand at his throat. "Fine," Reyn brusquely said before he bellowed up the stairs. "Dievers! I suggest you drag your arse from your warm bed, or I shall happily trudge up these stairs and do so myself."

The younger Dievers stared, appalled by the duke's behavior. Walter and Tam grinned like two happy puppies. Reyn tapped his toes, counting to ten, his eyes set on the stairs like a hawk.

"You are a madman," the young man snapped.

"Are you just realizing that?" Tam taunted Jonathan further. "I would have thought you grasped that much after our last visit."

"You must remember, my young pup," Walter clarified with relish, "before you stands a haunted man, a man without substance or joy. Truly, madman is inappropriate. Obsessed, despondent and nauseatingly struck blind with love is what he is. He simply wants his wife. Is that so hard to understand?"

"Walter."

Tam laughed fully now. "Give over, Reyn. You know that everything Walter says is the absolute truth. Admit it."

Turning his head upward, Reyn noticed the startled

appearance of a spectacled man, draped in a velvet dressing gown of deep russet.

"What in Aunt Martha's name is happening down there?" Samuel Dievers, as round as his nephew was thin, waddled down the stairs. "Well, Jonathan? What is the meaning of this?"

"Uncle, this rabble-rouser, Lord Wilcott, insisted he see you. I told him—"

Moving back, allowing Dievers space to maneuver himself onto the foyer floor, Reyn interrupted. "I apologize, sir, for disturbing your rest, but this young pup neglected to realize the import of my needs. I have waited months for your return to London." At that point, Reyn's composure evaporated. "I will not wait another minute. Where the hell is my wife?"

Clearly unruffled by Wilcott's display of temper the solicitor belted his robe. He signaled that they move the tiny gathering to the study. As the older man levered himself into a large leather chair, his nephew took a support position at his uncle's right shoulder. Reyn elected to remain standing, pacing the room in long, frustrated strides while Tam and Walter lounged at the study entrance.

Dievers didn't wait long to offer his disapproval. "According to my nephew, you are a brute, a nuisance and a general pain in the ass. Tell me, why is it so important you locate Jocelyn?"

"Yes, why?" With his chin tilting to the ceiling, Jonathan mimicked his uncle.

Briefly, Reyn glowered at the young assistant, then addressed the older man. "We have unfinished business."

"I thought her settlement most generous. Overly so, actually."

"I do not want a farthing of her money, her titles or property."

"Hah!" blasted the nephew, clearly disbelieving

Reyn's denial.

The other men scowled at the interruption. Dievers asked again, "Then what could you possibly need from Jocelyn?"

"She is my wife."

"Not good enough," Dievers stated matter-of-factly.

"Precisely." Jonathan spat out each syllable.

Four men cursed in unison.

Jonathan began to protest when his uncle glared at him. "For goodness sake, Jonathan, go find cook and bring me something to eat." While Jonathan left, his feet dragging ever so slowly, Dievers removed his glasses and rubbed the contours of his face. "Excuse my nephew's exuberance. He takes his position as my assistant very seriously."

"And he called *me* a pain in the ass," Reyn muttered.

Dievers laughed. "You should meet his brother."

"Sweet mercy, there are two of them?" Walter exclaimed with disgust.

"Tenacious in their responsibilities, loyal to a fault," Dievers sighed, "and my nephews." Leaning back in the chair, his hands folded comfortably across his belly, Dievers delivered his bald observation to Reyn. "I think you are an arrogant young stallion, but I find myself curious, and hopeful, as to why you are so desperate to find Jocelyn. I will ask you one last time, why have you harassed this household to locate your wife?"

"That is between my wife and myself."

"Not any longer. As the family solicitor, I served her father for twenty years. I shirked my duties to that young girl once by allowing that scoundrel Mardell to outsmart me. He had the audacity to whisk her away from her home, hide her away in Bedlam—and where was I? In bloody Scotland, settling a dispute between two stubborn lords. I'll be damned if I will allow her to be harmed again. I'll tell you, duke or no, you won't bully me. You'd best sit down and tell me what's on your mind."

A muffled laugh escaped Walter's compressed lips, and Reyn frowned at him like a dark cloud settling over the Pennines.

Walter grinned unrepentantly. "Stow your scowl, Reyn. You have met your match. I admit it does me good to see you squirm a bit."

In weary submission, Reyn sat in the nearest chair. From the moment he'd stumbled from the blaze, discovering Jocelyn had vanished, his life had become a living nightmare. He'd turned London upside down, frantic with worry, when he received the first missive. She was safe, having left of her own free will. She thanked him, once again, for his kindness and her life, but knew he relished his freedom. It was now his.

Bitterness and hurt ruled him day and night, as did uncontrollable gambling and drinking. No one could reason with him. Not Walter. Not Tam. Not even Agatha. Jocelyn's name, as well as her belongings, were banished from his house. Even Caesar resided at Agatha's. His wife had never loved him, not really. If there had been an ounce of truth in what she had said, she would have had faith in him. She would have stayed long enough to hear his explanation.

Two weeks passed when he received the legal documents that itemized the extent of her inheritance that, by law, now belonged to him. Her solicitor, Samuel Dievers, specifically noted that Jocelyn requested two things. One full year before he initiated divorce proceedings and a reasonable annual stipend for herself. She left no forwarding address and apparently had no intention of doing so. Any future transactions or correspondence would be handled through her solicitor.

With rather explicit suggestions as to what Mr. Dievers could do with the papers and Jocelyn's inheritance, Reyn returned them to the solicitor. In order to escape the past, the torment, he fled to Wilcott Keep, where the violent storms, cascading rivers and placid lakes always provided sanctuary. Now everything reminded him of her. Finally, sitting desolate in the cylindrical tower that sang with sensual promises and memories, he admitted he still loved her. It was amazing how one small admission could change a man's perspective, his focus. Unfortunately, by the time Reyn returned to London, Dievers had quit the country, leaving his nephew in charge.

Reyn implemented a plan of attack that would have put Napoleon to shame. He nagged and harassed and threatened and pleaded with the younger Dievers to tell him where Jocelyn hid herself. The young man swore, time and again, that only his uncle knew her whereabouts.

Reyn hired five Bow Street runners to track her down, repeatedly grilled Agatha for any information that might provide the answer, yet his wife seemed to have vanished from the face of the earth. Reyn was a lost man.

Now, three months later, sitting before this portly man who had no title and less money than Reyn's annual stable bills, Reyn acknowledged that this same man controlled his future. Dievers knew where his wife was. He would do anything for that one bit of information.

Chapter Twenty-three

Sister Mary Agnes welcomed Jocelyn with an open ear, a loving heart and a warm embrace, providing a small cottage outside the convent walls and the encouragement to search her heart for the answers she sought. As life renewed itself, summer came to St. Mary's on the Isles of Scilly, the cold days giving way to warm afternoons, blossoming flowers the colors of the rainbow and the lusty songs of migrating birds.

Jocelyn kept her days busy as she assisted the nuns with the children in the village. Her nights remained lonely. The weeks came and went, and even though her mind knew Reyn didn't want her, her heart expected him to come. Learning to accept the truth, the pain eased, but not a day passed when she didn't think of the man she had loved, betrayed and lost.

The sour notes forced her attention back to the processional she had been attempting to play on the organ for the last half hour. Finally, she submitted to her anger and frustration and pounded the same chord over and over and over.

"I do not believe I recognize that particular hymn."

Jocelyn edged to the end of the bench to stare around the side of the large chamber organ tucked away in the corner of the chapel. "Sister Mary Agnes, I didn't hear you come in."

"No small surprise." The older nun waved her arm. "Remain where you are. No need to rise, my child. Were you banishing the demons back to Satan?"

"The notes escaped me today."

Settling herself in the front pew behind the oak railing that separated the sanctuary from the remainder of the chapel, the spry little woman, who seemingly knew more than humanly possible, watched Jocelyn with a gentle face netted with wrinkles. "I have allowed you time to search your heart, Jocelyn, but I find I must ask you something."

Obediently, Jocelyn placed her hands in her lap. "Of course."

"This man, Lord Wilcott—do you still love him?"

"I do not see what difference it makes." Jocelyn knew she spoke too quickly and too defensively.

"When we received the first missive, I did as you requested and denied all knowledge of your whereabouts. The second, I did the same, thinking the man simply tenacious. This third message has caused me to question my judgment. I find myself wondering if I did the right thing. Help reassure me. Do you still love this man?"

Jocelyn shifted uncomfortably.

"I take that to be a yes?"

"Sister, whether I love the man or not changes nothing. He is a lifetime away in London. He doesn't love me. In fact, he can barely tolerate my existence."

Reverently clasping her silver crucifix in her fingers,

Sister Mary Agnes thought for a moment. "A man does not send three messengers to find his wife unless he has good reason. Would you, please explain what he wants, if not you?"

"Is there a problem? Does Mother Superior want me to leave?"

"We all want you to be happy, Jocelyn. If you wish to remain here the rest of your days, you may do so. But I fear you may be choosing to stay here for the wrong reasons. Now, tell me why you think he doesn't love you."

Sister Mary Agnes wielded her influence with quiet authority. Jocelyn knew she expected an answer. "When in Bedlam, I sought only revenge without thinking through the possible consequences. I fell in love with a man incapable of such affections. I'm also afraid I hurt him. I left at the first opportunity."

"Excuse the addled mind of an old woman, but did you allow him to say good-bye? Did you tell him you were leaving?"

"Why?"

"Why indeed."

It was as though the older nun probed her most private thoughts. Jocelyn fidgeted under the intense scrutiny.

Sister Mary Agnes continued. "If given a choice, would you remain here?"

"I have no other choice," she stated. "Since my parents died, I always considered this my home. I have no place else to go. At least until the baby is born."

"Do you honestly believe you can hide from your troubles? Keep this man away from his child? Keep your love secreted away on this lonely island? The truth, Jocelyn."

"I can try." The words burst from her mouth.

A smile lighting her face, the nun stood to go. "Thank you, my dear, that was enlightening. Before I go, I want you to remember something I thought I taught you long ago. In order to find happiness, you must first be honest with yourself. Many things said under duress mean nothing. Humanity can be painfully cruel to one another sometimes. I thank God he gave us the ability to forgive. I dearly love my life here and can think of nothing that would give me greater pleasure. I chose to devote my life to the church and quiet solitude. Not everyone is meant to choose the same path."

Confused by the abrupt end of the conversation, Jocelyn could only stare at Sister Mary Agnes's retreating back. Although she had revealed almost everything upon her return, she had answered only a few questions. Now, she wondered at the timing of this visit, the choice of topics.

From the rear of the church, standing before the weathered wooden doors, Sister Mary Agnes turned. "Trust your heart, Jocelyn. The answers lie there."

The shaft of bright light surrounded the small woman as she left the dim chapel. Then the doorway filled with a larger, broader form. Other than wrapping her arms protectively around her abdomen, Jocelyn didn't move. She couldn't move. She blinked. Had she imagined the shadowed image? No. The footsteps clicking upon the cobblestone floor as the apparition approached affirmed the truth.

"Reyn?"

"I must say, Jocelyn, when you elect to disappear, you do a thorough job of it. Do you realize, in order to find you, it took a small army of runners, an enormous amount of capital, a special audience with the king, a midnight assault on your solicitor and a verbal blistering such as I have never had from a nun too old to be alive?"

Slowly, knowing her face must be the color of the whitewashed chapel walls, Jocelyn faced the man she had thought to see only in her dreams. Dressed in a dark, dusty riding habit, tousled and blown, with dark circles under his eyes and at least two days' whisker growth on his chin, Reyn looked more handsome than Jocelyn had ever thought possible.

"You were searching for me?" she asked.

As his eyes adjusted to the dark interior of the chapel, his weary expression settled on her guarded one. "Search seems a rather paltry description. Obsessed, bewitched, plagued, haunted. Take your pick. Any mood will suit."

"Why? Mr. Dievers delivered my proposal. Was it not acceptable?"

He now stood near the front row of pews. Vehemently, he said, "As a matter of fact, it was not."

Her staccato chatter sputtered this and that before she could form the appropriate answer. "I cannot believe you are here to quibble over the inheritance. There were more than sufficient funds to reimburse everything spent on my clothing and jewels. I kept one insignificant piece of property, took no more money than I felt would be necessary for myself. Everything else went to you."

"Jocelyn, I did not travel over half of England to discuss your inheritance."

Sadly, she realized the truth. He had more money than he could spend in a lifetime, so of course her measly estates and holdings meant little to him. His freedom was an altogether different matter.

"I understand. The one year. It must seem odd to you, but it is important. I will be happy to move the date forward by a few months if necessary. As for a divorce rather than an annulment, well, we did—I mean, we did consummate our marriage. Besides, I don't believe a divorce will tarnish your reputation. I know they are difficult to obtain, but I am sure you will manage. You will be free to remarry within no time at all."

As she brushed the swirling patterns engraved in the mahogany of the organ, she rambled on, attempting to cover her dismay. "Have you selected your bride-to-be?"

"Jocelyn." The last thing Reyn wanted to do was discuss future brides. Only she tormented his dreams. Surrounded by colored light from the chapel windows, she looked so beautiful with her flashing eyes and her hair skimming across her breasts that all his patience and good intentions were evaporating. His practiced words ebbed like the receding tide.

Lifting his leg onto a wooden pew, he anchored his elbow on his knee, his chin in his hand. "Thank you very much. The last thing I need is another wife."

"I'm not surprised. You haven't seen many benefits to wedded life."

"I did not come here to discuss a divorce or an annulment either."

"You didn't? Then why are you here? I know how troublesome it can be to reach this little island. Surely, you didn't travel all this way to wish me a good afternoon."

"No, I didn't, Jocelyn, and this place is the very devil to reach. It took me one full day to find someone willing to make a small fortune just to cross the channel, which was not the calmest I ever sailed. And in a puny skiff I thought would surely capsize with the first large swell. A lesser man would have turned tail and returned to London."

His unexpected visit made no sense at all unless he had somehow discovered her pregnancy. Had he come to claim his heir? Not without a fight, she promised herself.

Glad she wore the modest blue empire dress that revealed little, she inched back on the bench, hoping to obstruct his view of her body. Now suspicious, she asked, "Then why are you here?"

"Why did you leave?"

"I asked first."

"I want you to return with me to London."

"Why?"

His patience snapped. "Blast it, Jocelyn, you weren't supposed to leave."

"I wasn't?"

"No!"

"It took you three months to decide that?" she exclaimed in disbelief.

"No!" Five minutes with her and he was already bellowing. He stamped his foot. "I knew I wanted you to stay before you ever left. It took me three months, four days and eighteen hours to find you. Your solicitor left the country and only returned two days ago."

"But you told me to leave," Jocelyn said, feeling more unsettled than before.

"Momentary insanity."

"You thought I loved Phillip."

"A minor misunderstanding."

"At my step-uncle's, you called me a possession. You said you wanted my money."

"I wanted us to escape alive. I needed an edge. God's bones, why is it you can remember every bloody thing I said except the important things?"

"Such as?"

He yelled to the carved beams overhead. "Such as, I love you."

"What?" she countered just as loudly. "You never said that."

"Well, I thought it."

"How was I to know that?" She glared back at him, thankful that the wooden banister stood between them. She needed the space to clear her rattled senses. "Exactly when did you realize you had fallen in love with me?"

"Perhaps when you disregarded my order to stay home, and went out to meet that sniveler Bains?" he

310

said irritably before he added, "Truly, Jocelyn, I cannot give you an exact moment. It crept up on me like a bad toothache."

She scowled. "Why do you love me?"

"After all the trouble you have caused me, I have asked myself that question a hundred times."

"If this is your attempt to regale me with your charm and wit, then you can turn around and return to London. By yourself."

"Not without you," he stated flatly.

She realized that beneath his abject misery and single-minded determination, he was enjoying himself. The cad. "You are a sick, misguided, stubborn man, Reynolds Blackburn."

"Me?" he cried in exasperation. "Jocelyn, I love you and you love me. If you allow me to come closer, I will be more than happy to prove I speak the truth."

Holding up her hand to stay his movement, she warned, "That is close enough."

"Are you afraid of me?" he asked, appalled by the possibility.

"Of course not. I think more clearly with you over there."

That admission, he thought, proved something. Watching her fingers absently caress the instrument, remembering those same slender hands on his body, he barely contained the urge to leap over the wooden barrier, pull her into his arms and kiss her senseless. But the time was not yet right. He sat down in the pew closest to the organ, discarding the speech he had rehearsed for months. He spoke from the heart. "May I tell you a story?"

"I would rather you tell me why you are here," she grumbled.

"Humor me."

She sighed.

He smiled. "Once upon a time, there was a man. A

very ill-tempered man, who unfortunately didn't realize how lonely he was until a beautiful, vibrant, brave young woman came into his life. This knave, so jaded, so cynical, ignored the emotions he felt, afraid he would be hurt. He treated this rare treasure callously with little regard for her feelings, and too late, after she disappeared, did he realize he had lost his heart, his soul, his reason for living."

She started to say something. He held up his hand. "Wait. My moods are so volatile, they banned me from Boodle's and White's. Agatha threatens to personally recruit new members to my household staff. Tam and Walter refuse to talk to me. Caesar torments me day and night. And women have begun to hound me for the position as my mistress. Jocelyn, you must return to save me from myself."

When he finished his impassioned plea, hot tears were streaming down her cheeks. Her whisper was barely audible. "You said you love me?"

"With all my heart."

"I lied to you repeatedly. I know now I was wrong. I never meant to hurt you."

"As punishment, you may spend the remainder of your life proving yourself. May I hold you now?"

Jocelyn froze, knowing Reyn might yet despise her for her final revelation. Before she could answer, he jumped the barrier between them, and pulled her torso flush with his, eye to eye, lips to lips, chest to chest.

He drew back to stare at the rounded protrusion in front of him. Both his hands gently caressed her belly. "Either you have been eating enormous quantities of food or you seem to be carrying my heir."

She threw her arms around his neck and she wept with joy. "I love you."

"Oh sweetheart, when I couldn't find you, I thought I would never be able to hold you again." He pressed his body into hers, kissing her deeply. "I will spend the rest of my days showing you precisely how much I love you." Their tongues met again to battle as his hands acquainted themselves with the added bounty of his wife's breasts. Reyn forced himself to pull away. "Jocelyn, if we don't stop, I believe we will be struck by lightning. Right now, my thoughts are far from chaste."

Jocelyn continued to place nibbling kisses along his chin and neck, bringing her hands down to rest on the bulge that fought the restraint of his breeches. "I see what you mean, my husband."

"Sweet mercy." He groaned as he lifted her into his arms. "Please tell me you live nearby. That you have a bed. A large bed. Never mind, it does not matter. I don't believe we shall make it past your front door."

He had reached the chapel door when his expression became frantic. "Jocelyn, you are healthy? There are no complications? It will be acceptable for you and I . . . for us . . . ?"

Persuasively, using the tip of her tongue, she convinced him that lovemaking would not only be acceptable, but demanded.

"Jocelyn, I'm warning you. I intend to make love to you until dawn. Of course, if we need be creative, then I will be happy to oblige you. I have three months of lurid fantasies I wish to fulfill. Which way?"

Overlooking three startled novices, she pointed down the hill to her stone cottage. Reyn kicked the door open with his boot and set Jocelyn down long enough to close the door, tear the front of her gown from chin to toe and bury his head between her breasts. Unabashedly, she offered herself to him.

"Heaven help me." Gasping, he stepped back a foot to enjoy the naked vision before him. Her breasts, ripe from pregnancy, were thrust high, her nipples a shade darker than he remembered. As his eyes drifted downward, she crossed her arms in front of her distended abdomen.

"No, Jocelyn, let me look my fill. You are beautiful."

With callused fingertips, he traced a circle around each swollen nipple, wringing forth a whimper from her open lips. His hands joined to slide over her belly to the warmth that awaited him. He nearly spilled his seed then and there. Dropping to his knees, fully dressed, he loved her endlessly until she writhed against his mouth, seeking her release.

She tugged on his hair, frantic, and begged, "Reyn, come to me."

Ready to burst, more than willing to comply, he carried her to the small, unadorned bed to place her amongst the white embroidered pillows. Like a sailor returned from six months at sea, Reyn shed his clothing in little time under the appreciative eyes of his wife. His wife. He smiled. How that pleased him.

Jocelyn spoke genuinely and clearly as he knelt beside her. "Thank you for my life, your trust and your love. I love you."

"Jocelyn, you are my life, my heart. With luck, I will endeavor to make you happy until the day my final breath leaves my body."

"Then, husband, would you mind loving me? It has been entirely too long."

"Greedy wench, aren't you." He grinned, but happily obliged her.

Heedless of the call for evening vespers or the sounds of dusk, they lay entwined, content with the peace found only in one another's arms.

CONQUER THE MIST

Susan Kearney

Promised in marriage to Britain's foremost Norman knight, Irish Princess Dara O'Dwyre vows that neither the power of his sword nor the lure of his body will sway her proud spirit and her untamed heart. But as enemy troops draw close, Dara realizes that only when she learns to trust this handsome outsider can they save her homeland and unite in rapturous bliss.

___4437-4 $5.50 US/$6.50 CAN

Dorchester Publishing Co., Inc.
P.O. Box 6640
Wayne, PA 19087-8640

Please add $1.75 for shipping and handling for the first book and $.50 for each book thereafter. NY, NYC, and PA residents, please add appropriate sales tax. No cash, stamps, or C.O.D.s. All orders shipped within 6 weeks via postal service book rate. Canadian orders require $2.00 extra postage and must be paid in U.S. dollars through a U.S. banking facility.

Name_____
Address_____
City_____State_____Zip_____
I have enclosed $_____ in payment for the checked book(s).
Payment <u>must</u> accompany all orders. ❑ Please send a free catalog.
CHECK OUT OUR WEBSITE! www.dorchesterpub.com

Flames of Rapture

LARK EDEN

"Great reading!"—*Romantic Times*

When Lyric Solei flees the bustling city for her summer retreat in Salem, Massachusetts, it is a chance for the lovely young psychic to escape the pain so often associated with her special sight. Investigating a mysterious seaside house whose ancient secrets have long beckoned to her, Lyric stumbles upon David Langston, the house's virile new owner, whose strong arms offer her an irresistible temptation. And it is there that Lyric discovers a dusty red coat, which from the time she first lays her gifted hands on it unravels to her its tragic history—and lets her relive the timeless passion that brought it into being.

_52078-8 $4.99 US/$6.99 CAN

Dorchester Publishing Co., Inc.
P.O. Box 6640
Wayne, PA 19087-8640

Please add $1.75 for shipping and handling for the first book and $.50 for each book thereafter. NY, NYC, and PA residents, please add appropriate sales tax. No cash, stamps, or C.O.D.s. All orders shipped within 6 weeks via postal service book rate. Canadian orders require $2.00 extra postage and must be paid in U.S. dollars through a U.S. banking facility.

Name_____
Address_____
City_____ State_____ Zip_____
I have enclosed $_____ in payment for the checked book(s).
Payment <u>must</u> accompany all orders. ❏ Please send a free catalog.

BELIEVE

Victoria Alexander

Tessa thinks as little of love as she does of the Arthurian legend—it is just a myth. But when an enchanted tome falls into the lovely teacher's hands, she learns that the legend is nothing like she remembers. Galahad the Chaste is everything but—the powerful knight is an expert lover—and not only wizards can weave powerful spells. Still, even in Galahad's muscled embrace, she feels unsure of this man who seemed a myth. But soon the beautiful skeptic is on a quest as real as her heart, and the grail—and Galahad's love—is within reach. All she has to do is believe.

___52267-5 $5.99 US/$6.99 CAN

Dorchester Publishing Co., Inc.
P.O. Box 6640
Wayne, PA 19087-8640

Please add $1.75 for shipping and handling for the first book and $.50 for each book thereafter. NY, NYC, and PA residents, please add appropriate sales tax. No cash, stamps, or C.O.D.s. All orders shipped within 6 weeks via postal service book rate. Canadian orders require $2.00 extra postage and must be paid in U.S. dollars through a U.S. banking facility.

Name_____
Address_____
City_____State_____Zip_____
I have enclosed $_____ in payment for the checked book(s).
Payment <u>must</u> accompany all orders. ☐ Please send a free catalog.
CHECK OUT OUR WEBSITE! www.dorchesterpub.com

Pure Temptation

Connie Mason

"Each new Connie Mason book is a prize!"
—Heather Graham

Spirits can be so bloody unpredictable, and the specter of Lady Amelia is the worst of all. Just when one of her ne'er-do-well descendents thought he could go astray in peace, the phantom lady always appears to change his wicked ways.

A rogue without peer, Jackson Graystoke wants to make gaming and carousing in London society his life's work. And the penniless baronet would gladly curse himself with wine and women—if Lady Amelia would give him a ghost of a chance.

Fresh off the boat from Ireland, Moira O'Toole isn't fool enough to believe in legends or naive enough to trust a rake. Yet after an accident lands her in Graystoke Manor, she finds herself haunted, harried, and hopelessly charmed by Black Jack Graystoke and his exquisite promise of pure temptation.

_4041-7 $5.99 US/$6.99 CAN